# THE GODDESS EYE

CASSIDY CLARKE

THE GODDESS EYE
Copyright © 2023 by Cassidy Clarke

All rights reserved. Printed in the United States of America. No part of this book may be used or reproduced in any manner whatsoever without written permission except in the case of brief quotations em- bodied in critical articles or reviews.

This book is a work of fiction. Names, characters, businesses, organiza- tions, places, events and incidents either are the product of the author's imagination or are used fictitiously. Any resemblance to actual persons, living or dead, events, or locales is entirely coincidental.

Website : cassidyclarkewriting.com
Cover Designed by: Hillary Bardin (@reebardin)
ISBN: 978-1-957993-01-0
First Edition: August 2023


10 9 8 7 6 5 4 3 2 1

~Dedication~

*To Nay, who refused to let me hole up in my apartment and let the world forget I ever*

*tried to be a storyteller.*

*Thank you for not letting me lose my endings.*

## <u>Content Warnings</u>

The Goddess Eye contains content involving death, amnesia, blood/gore, religious terminology/rituals, grief, kidnapping, possession, illness, food descriptions, mild language, violence, physical and emotional abuse, non-domesticated animal hunting and death, hallucinations, manipulation, and panic attacks.
Please read safely. <3

# CHAPTER 1

# RAQUEL

"*Just a little farther, Stormcloud.*"

Static crackled at the nape of Raquel's neck as she pushed between two snow-laden trees deep in the north of Nyx, her breath staining the air with mist, the only heat to speak of buried beneath her fur cloak.

"*Just a little farther.*"

She ground her teeth together against the echo of a voice she'd left behind in her childhood; a voice she never wanted to hear again.

A voice she drew closer to every day she traveled north with her two insufferable companions.

Just one more mile. One more, and she'd be back at camp.

The dark clouds swelling above her called out in low, rolling growls, jagged white light forking through their bellies like arrows shot into hearts. She tasted metal on her tongue, a shiver of anticipation setting her hair on end in a way that had nothing to do with static.

She had to beat those clouds back. Hailstones and snow and miles between her and a warm fire weren't a good mix. But still, the promise of lightning and storm danced at her heels, beckoning her back. The wind sang a siren song past the shield of her hood, smelling of danger and long-dead daydreams and the promise of a coming frost.

For her, chaos had always been more comfortable than calm. When things got too quiet, her hands tended to twitch and her mind tended to wander down paths she'd rather avoid. And even though it would leave her a shivering, hypothermic mess…still, her skin ached for the kiss of something other than her woolen shirt.

She wrenched her thoughts away from that place, blowing out another ghostly breath, cleaning the craving for storms from between her teeth. Those sorts of dreams belonged in her childhood, when the idea of catching snowflakes on her tongue and hailstones in her palms had still seemed possible. When dancing in wild circles among stormclouds had been her greatest joy.

She had not tasted the sky in years. The grief for those she'd lost kept her feet snared to the ground they were buried in.

Now wasn't the time for such thoughts. Royalty was waiting in the woods, and she couldn't let old losses bow her before them.

Her teeth gritted painfully against each other, biting down on a different craving, a different taste she'd acquired during tumultuous weeks spent in the heart of a fire-blooded mountain. A taste not for hailstones and lightning, but for fabled ocean-green eyes and a bearded mouth bent in constant worry.

The only thing she should have wanted from Kallias Atlas was the feeling of his last breath heaving beneath her hands. But the moment he'd gotten that close, when his lips had drawn so near to hers she could taste the salt ever-present on his breath…

She'd leaned in. Parted her lips to taste that salt on her tongue. And if Safi Aquila hadn't interrupted them, if she hadn't been saved from some irrevocable foolishness by that feisty weaponsmith…gods knew what would have happened.

Weakness. Old and well-acquainted, a familiar enemy that had kept her company on her very first downfall.

*From Eye of the Storm to blood-traitor. Seems a fitting progression, Stormcloud.*

Raquel squeezed her eyes shut against the voice that still cut notches of terror into her bones, snowflakes melting between her lashes.

Thunder embraced her body, its rumble murmuring into her ear: *He was nothing but bones and dust. What are you, Raquel Angelov?*

*I am the Eye of the Storm, the peace within chaos, the power within peace. He cannot touch any piece of me I do not offer.*

Weaknesses. She knew hers intimately enough by now that they shouldn't have surprised her any longer. But it seemed the girl who'd stumbled through these woods weeping blood from her empty eye socket and tears from the other, a circle of metal weighing down her finger like a shackle, hadn't finished learning all her lessons.

This was getting her nowhere. If she didn't focus, she'd lose her path.

The pine forest that surrounded her showed nothing of the spring that had started touching the other kingdoms by now; Nyx was the northernmost kingdom on the continent, and it certainly showed it. Snow weighed down every needled bough; they'd lost valuable seconds while Kallias stopped to marvel, letting the needles brush against his gloved hands like a reverent worshipper touching fingertips to a statue of their god.

Finnick, at least, knew how to stay on task. She appreciated that about him and very little else. Though something about him did remind him of Soren…and the girl Soren had learned so much of her wickedness from.

She heard those princes well before she saw them—Finnick's voice raised in complaint, as it had so often been since they crossed into colder climes, and Kallias's much lower. But tired and hoarse as it was—hoarse with thirst, she guessed, an insatiable craving for water that had driven him near-delirious on more than one night of their travels—she could still hear him, as if the wind considered itself the eldest Atlas prince's personal messenger, delivering his every word to her unwilling ear.

When he spoke, she listened. Whether she wanted to or not.

The crunch of packing snow beneath her boots brought both of their heads up as she crossed into the clearing where they'd made camp, Finnick's hair sheathed beneath a thick wool cap, Kallias's head entirely bare. The winter tones that encompassed everything else did little to mute the blazing auburn-gold of his hair, the thick waves hanging past his shoulders—his freckled, well-built, *also bare* shoulders.

"Finally!" Finnick exclaimed, throwing his hands toward the sky; his voice chattered like a shaken bag of bone-dice, terrible shivers accosting him visibly, even with his thick winter gear. His fleece-lined brown coat was buttoned all the way up to his chin, a dull rust-colored scarf tied around his throat, and his finely crafted leather gloves creaked as he splayed his fingers toward his shirtless brother. "Tell this *maniac* to put his coat back on before he turns bluer than your boots."

He'd nearly paid far too much for all that gear—the merchant caravan in Tallis seemed to know warm-blooded folk when they saw them. But she'd saved him from their greedy mark-ups, and ever since, his attitude toward the *violent Nyxian soldier* had softened up considerably.

"They're gray, not blue," she sighed, dropping down beside the sputtering fire, frowning at the weak flames. "Which of you built this?"

The brothers pointed to each other.

"Finnick," she warned.

"Fine," he groaned. "It's harder to do out here than at home, all right? You try finding any wood that isn't soaked through."

"I offered to help," Kallias muttered, rocking back as she drew her sword and began to tease the fire with its tip. The flames flared up in response, and her eye caught on a drop of moisture that rolled down his temple before he moved back another foot. "He wouldn't let me use my magic to dry it out."

"And he was right not to," she snapped. "Look at you. You're about to sit through a hailstorm wearing nothing but the skin on your back?"

His brows furrowed over stormy eyes—had they always been that dark? That blue? Hadn't they once been green, pale and fresh as new spring growth, like the mint leaves her mother used to grow in their garden?

*Focus, Angelov.*

"I was hot," he said, like that explained everything, like it was normal for a beach-dwelling prince to sweat his way through a winter storm.

Once the fire looked healthier, she rocked to her feet, crossing the camp and pressing the back of her hand against Kallias's forehead. He grimaced, but didn't pull away. Still, her fingers leapt back instinctually at the glacial bite of his skin, like she'd pressed them to a frozen metal streetpost and left a layer or two of skin behind.

Unease flooded from her gut to her throat, but she disguised it as irritation before it made it to her tongue. "You're freezing."

"I'm fine."

"Your brother's right. You need a coat."

"Thank you," Finnick mumbled into his scarf, huddling closer to the fire, water glazing his eyes as the oncoming storm beat him with its frigid wind.

"I'm *fine*," Kallias insisted, catching her hand when she tried to touch his forehead again.

Lightning lanced up her arm, and she jerked away again. But this time it was buzzing heat that lingered, a shiver of warmth that tickled at the base of her bones.

"Coat," she repeated, sharper. "*Now.*"

His scowl could've frozen his precious ocean mid-tide. But under the force of her steady glare, he eventually thawed, a softening to his gaze that pinched her in uncomfortable places. "All right. Sorry."

A grunt was the only response she offered. But even as she tromped back across the fire and sat on one of the logs they'd dragged in while she was off fetching fresh water from the nearby branch of the Vela River, that lightning lingered. She could taste iron on the back of her tongue…and the memory of salt.

"How far out are we?" Finnick's voice saved her from dawdling too long on that thought.

"Not far." She gazed into the flames, keeping Kallias in the periphery of her one eye while he ducked into his and Finnick's tent. "Another day or so of walking. Longer if we have to wait out the storm."

A huff of breath wearing white. Finnick hunched deeper in his coat. "I hate snow."

"So you've said." Uncountable times since they'd left Artem. "Do you ever stop whining?"

"Not really," he said.

"Do you ever stop talking?"

A snort. "I'd hate to divest you all of the privilege of my company."

"If you don't shut up soon, I'm going to divest you of the privilege of having a tongue."

Finnick's grin, toothless and tight, reminded her of a slit throat. "I see why Kal likes you."

Thankfully, she'd long ago learned not to bother with embarrassment. She barely blinked. "Is that a joke?"

"It'd be a pretty poor one if it was. No, Kal's always been starry-eyed for people like you. People who are…" He gestured vaguely in her direction, curling his fingers into a fist and mock-swinging at the air. "Passionate."

Her mouth quirked. "You mean angry."

"No, I meant violent, but close enough." Finnick leaned in, his eyes— brown like the Nyxian chocolate stowed away in her pack, but far more bitter— meeting hers with unexpected intensity. "Do you still plan on killing him?"

She gritted her teeth. They were starting to ache. "You'll forgive me if I keep that my business."

"That's a no, then."

Raquel mirrored his posture, leaning closer until the heat of the flames cradled her cheeks like a doting parent. "Does he know?"

"That you don't want to kill him? Doubt it. He's still uselessly attracted to you, so—"

"Not that." He wouldn't distract her with ridiculous verbal jabs. "Does he know what you are?"

Finn studied her carefully, folding his hands below his chin, brown darkening to black as he tipped his head forward into shadow. "You need to be more specific."

She held his gaze. "No, I don't."

He smiled, rueful, harmless. It didn't fool her.

"You Nyxians are cleverer than I ever gave you credit for," he finally sighed. "You and my little sister both."

Jira's cunning eyes flashed behind her own. "The two of us have seen your type before." Those who dealt in masks and shifting personas, those who could bend themselves into anything they liked to play any part. Spymasters. Tricksters. Geniuses hiding behind innocent smiles and big brown eyes. She'd sometimes wondered if Jira worshipped Occassio in secret with the way she reveled in her masterful pranks.

"Hm." The younger prince reclined, resting his ankle on his opposite knee before finally shaking his head. "No. He doesn't."

"Does anyone in your family?"

"Soleil does." *Does*, not *did*. "Jericho and Vaughn do now, I suppose. I let the fish out of the net just before I fled."

"Why keep it secret?"

He studied the fire like it might offer him an escape. "Thought you wanted me to be quiet."

"I do."

"Then perhaps stop poking your nose where it doesn't belong, hm?"

Even if she'd had an argument, it wouldn't have mattered. Because just then, the tender caress of steel against her jugular removed all thought of speech.

"Strangers lurking in the shadows," mused a familiar voice—roughened with age, but still nameable. "What brings you to our little corner of Nyx?"

Finnick, eyes wide, dropped his hand to his hip, but Raquel darted her gaze side to side, a silent warning not to try it. She kept her breathing even, though her heart tried desperately to race ahead of her, fueled by fear even older than the scars along her temple. Whips of memory struck hard enough to arch her back beneath their blows, but she braced herself against them.

*Eye of the Storm. They cannot touch any piece of me I do not offer.*

"Not a stranger, Norcina," she said lightly, minding the blade at her throat. "I see your eyesight hasn't improved since I left you all."

"Nor yours, I imagine." The jab fell flat into the snow, finding no purchase in her heart. She'd proven long ago she didn't need two eyes to be deadly—though she'd happily prove it again, if given the opportunity. But the old woman's blade only pressed in harder, a pinch of pain followed by a trickle of warmth down her neck. "What are you doing here, Raquel Angelov?"

"We seek an audience with Stormspeaker Caelum," she said. "I have an ally who seeks his counsel."

"Caelum is dead," said Norcina. "Just this past spring."

Now *that* was a true blow; no pain, but it stole her breath anyway.

Caelum was dead. And not by her hand.

"Who killed him?" It wasn't the right question, but she had to ask it anyway. Whoever had stolen that honor from her…she either wanted to punch them soundly in the gut or shake their hand. She'd decide on the way.

"Illness, of all things. A fever tore through the village, and he couldn't shake it."

Damn. She couldn't begrudge or congratulate a sickness. Perhaps she'd toss a salute to the snowclouds and call it even.

"And his…successor?" Dread. Hope. She didn't know which was stronger. Didn't know which she ought to feel.

"Stormspeaker Aeris now oversees Skyhaven." Norcina's voice ached with reverence now, halfway to prostrate with her words alone. "As he was destined to."

*Aeris.*

A flicker of brilliant blue eyes and a painfully shy grin flashed like lightning between clouded memories. Hair the color of snow. The brush of a cold hand. The hesitant press of lips against hers.

The pain in his face while she screamed for help, over and over and over again.

The pain in her heart when he turned a deaf ear to her agony.

"I see." Her fingers flexed, sticky with new sweat beneath her gloves. A flicker of movement from behind Kallias and Finnick's tent caught her eye, but she refused to follow it—Norcina might track her gaze. "And would he accept an audience?"

"With *you*?" The scorn in her voice was answer aplenty.

The rasp of a sword unsheathing rang through the clearing, and Kallias's growl broke through the air like the warning purr of thunder: "Not with her. With me."

Norcina's body tensed behind Raquel, and her blade twitched briefly before going stock-still. Though Raquel was trapped in place, she could see Kallias in her mind's eye: his sword pressed to Norcina's back, his hand braced on her shoulder, ready to run her through at the slightest provocation.

"Release her," he said, voice so low it was nearly lost to the oncoming storm, "or your next breath will be your last."

Norcina's exhale stirred the hairs on the top of Raquel's head, her breath bordered with a chill, like she was chewing on a mouthful of ice chips. "I think you'll find you don't have the advantage you think you do, Atlas fiend."

The clicking of crossbows being primed and the hiss of more blades being drawn whispered to life in the woods around them, coming from every direction.

They were surrounded.

"Release *me*," Norcina purred, "or *her* next breath will be her last."

Kallias's fury was a tangible thing, the air tautening with promised lightning. But a moment later, his blade slid back into its sheath.

"Good boy." Despite her age, Norcina had always been strong—she dragged Raquel to her feet and turned her around, sneering at her from a face lined with wrinkles and scars and weather-wear. Her gray hair was curled into a tight twist at the nape of her neck, and her fur cloak swept a layer of snow away as she turned with Raquel still pinned. Kallias was similarly held, though there were two people—a man and a woman—flanking him, the man holding a crossbow pointed at his chest, the woman holding what appeared to be an ice-tipped spear against his bobbing throat.

Even so, his eyes were locked on Raquel—and the blood carving a path down her neck. The pure fury guttering in his ever-darkening gaze sent her stomach swooping toward her feet.

"An Atlas man seeking an audience with our Stormspeaker and defending a Nyxian with his own blade and blood," said Norcina. "Unusual indeed."

"Are you through being cryptic?" Finnick's exasperated voice brought every eye to him. He too was under guard, but he looked perfectly at ease, one brow cocked as he rubbed at his arms with a dramatic shiver. "If you're going to kill us, get on with it. If you're going to take us where we need to go, I'd just as soon get walking. I'm freezing my ass off standing here listening to you ramble."

Raquel almost made the mistake of laughing, which surely would have encouraged him to go further—and probably would've gotten them killed. As it was, she restrained herself to a cough, and Norcina merely scowled in his direction. "Another Atlas boy."

"The best of them, in fact." Finnick sketched a bow, heedless of the crossbow bolts that bobbed along with his movements. "The pleasure's entirely yours, believe me. Can we start walking?"

The more time she spent with Atlas princes, the more sure she became that they were brought up to flirt ceaselessly with death.

The forest seemed to hold its breath while he and Norcina stared at each other, waiting for each other to back down. But the longer Finnick smiled, the more that smile seemed to twist until it hardly resembled a smile at all—no, he was wearing a threat across his lips, a sneer sharpened to an edge that could pierce flesh and bone if he decided it fancied him to do so.

She felt Norcina shiver. "Luckily for you," said the old woman, sounding perfectly composed in spite of her chill, "Aeris is a more welcoming man than his father was. Follow me—any funny business, we shoot first and ask questions after."

Finnick's mouth loosened into his usual cocksure smile. "Lovely. I knew you'd see reason. Shall we?" And he marched forward, leaving his guards to scramble after him, a look of disbelief in their gazes as they kept their weapons trained on him.

Somehow, he'd chosen the correct path, though he'd never stepped foot in this forest before. It wasn't the first time he'd shown proof of knowledge he couldn't possibly have possessed—he'd warned them of the burgeoning storm before even she or Kallias sensed it, before the first cloud had even begun to form in the sky. And then there were his nightmares…

But she couldn't think on that now. Because the path Norcina shoved her down was familiar to her, her feet sinking into a well-known pattern, a road she'd walked a hundred times in both memory and nightmare.

For the first time in nearly five years, Raquel Angelov was returning to Skyhaven.

She'd always pictured herself returning with revenge borne on her blade, Stormspeaker Caelum's death the only one left on her list.

Instead, she walked with blade sheathed and hands clenched against trembling…and the eyes of an Atlas prince boring a hole into the back of her head.

* * *

Skyhaven had not changed.

Not a single stone that made up the circular fountain. Not a single log in the cabins that circled the vast, snow-coated clearing. Even The Haven, the gathering house built of carefully rosined logs and a roof crafted for shedding snow, where the village ate together and played together, where they schooled their children, where they worshipped…everything was exactly as she'd left it.

Like she'd never left at all.

The Atlas brothers were an increasingly familiar wall at her back—Kallias a crackling stormfront, Finn a coil of razor wire. Kallias walked the earth like a force begging to be unleashed, a wild thing who'd only been given tastes of freedom, and Finn…

Well. Finnick Atlas was three terrors stacked inside a bundle of purple yarn and a saccharine smile.

But after these weeks of traveling, she found she no longer minded. It felt less like turning her back on her enemies and more like wearing two new weapons at her sides.

It said something that she trusted the two Atlas princes at her back over an entire village of her own people. Her old family.

There was no sign of Aeris…no sign of anyone, actually. Silence was the only spectator present to witness Raquel Angelov's return.

She tried not to be enough of a coward to be relieved by it.

Norcina led them to The Haven, ushering them through the door…but she held Raquel back as the princes moved forward, the old woman's icy gaze piercing into her.

"Get cleaned up," she ordered, "and I will inform Aeris of your arrival. One wrong move, Miss Angelov, and you will be swiftly dealt with."

Up ahead, Kallias had halted only a few paces in the doorway, his eyes still fixed on her. And that alone gave her the presence of mind to nod to Norcina; that alone gave her the ability to ignore the slap of *Miss*, the purposeful refusal to speak her title.

"Remember our rules." And with that, Norcina released her.

Oh, she remembered the rules. Her scars would never let her forget.

With a steadying breath, Raquel stepped into the heart of Skyhaven. And though a scrap of fear begged her to, she refused to look back.

Not even when the door shut behind them, trapping her inside.

# CHAPTER 2

## SOREN

In the darkness, Soren Atlas dreamed of wolves.

Pelts of frosted moonlight and ebony shadow wove through the forest ahead of her, a monochrome river leading her down a path she'd never walked. Her bare feet found purchase on the path by following the pawprints left behind, great divots in the dirt larger than her head, and with every few steps she took, a head would turn within the pack to ensure she still followed. But though its ice-blue eyes pierced into hers with feral intent, though its teeth were long as a paring knife's blade, there was no fear—only adrenaline, a building urgency that heated her veins and urged her to *run faster, Soren, faster, faster.*

The air tasted of evergreen bite, a hint of home so strong and sharp it pierced straight through her heart. But even as she breathed in the air of Nyx, even as she searched in the darkness for a trace of familiarity, she found nothing to lead her back to Andromeda.

It occurred to her then that she was very, very lost. But still she was not afraid.

She walked with wolves. What was there to fear?

*Run. Run!*

Faster and faster her feet assailed the forest floor, her soles pricked with pine needles and discarded twigs, bits of branches thrown down by disdainful trees who'd tired of waiting for them to realize their potential. Every step wavered between elation and homesickness, the familiarity of dense foliage forever at odds with her longing for the sand she'd taken her first steps across.

Nyx and Atlas, night and sun, winter and summer. Both. Atlas blood through a Nyxian heart. That fight was over.

So what was she running from?

*Not from.*

*Toward.*

Distantly, in the way dreams traveled through the mind, she knew she was not truly running. Knew that *running* was something she could only do in sleep, because wakefulness would find her bound ankle and wrist, her mind held captive by a goddess and her body held captive by two mercenary bastards who seemed determined to rappel their way up her list of most-hated enemies. And there was a list, ranked in order from least to most bastard-ish.

But still the voice shouted to her, a voice she could almost name, a voice that called brutal training sessions and aching muscles and bonfire stories into this lurid cage of her mind: *Keep up, Soren! We won't wait for you!*

"I'm coming!" The cry tore painfully from her throat, as if every word was a hook ripped from her flesh. "Wait! Don't leave me!"

A canine growl. A flash of teeth bared in anger…in disappointment. *You left us, Princess.*

In a flash like lightning, the dark forest disappeared, the only trace of the wolves a lone howl that lifted the hairs on her neck—a howl filled not with the exultation of the hunt, but with sorrow, with grief.

Her feet sank into sand now, damp and cold, every step plunging her into a slurry of saltwater. The cold lanced up her bones, a shock that warmed to an ache as she struggled to keep moving, panic taking hold as she took in the landscape around her.

Atlas. The beach—*her* beach—but barren, not a soul in sight. The palace beyond was crowned in dark clouds, charcoal with scarlet underbellies, and the sea…

The sea itself ran red, coating her feet in cold, coagulating blood.

Vomit climbed up the column of her throat, and she dug her heels into the shifting sands, working to leverage herself out of its sinking grip. But it only pulled harder, sucking at her ankles, her calves, her knees, until she'd sunk hip-deep in the carnage, panic stitching her chest tighter with every breath she gasped in.

"Elias!" His name came first, then the others: a waterfall of beloved names pouring from her mouth as desperation crawled across her skin. She scrabbled at the bloody sand, but her fingers found no purchase, sliding through the clotted grains with a horrible squelching sound. "Kallias! *Finn?*"

But there was no answer borne on the sour wind. No longer pine and sap but rot and fester, it wound itself through her hair with a scalding touch like pestilence, like a promise she wished would be broken. A gag jolted her whole body as that wind forced itself into her lungs, and it burned, gods it *burned*—

*Find it,* commanded that voice of weapons and war-bonds as the sand dragged her down to her ribs, her shoulders, her neck. *Find it. Or the kingdoms fall…we all fall.*

And with a final, awful pull that sundered something deep in her core, the sand pulled her under, drowning her in blood and dirt and abyssal darkness.

***

*Her* nightmares, at least, belonged to her and her alone.

Whenever she woke as she did now, with dread festering in the pit of her stomach and adrenaline pulsing through every vein that still answered to her, she always expected Anima to wake up screaming right along with her. But it seemed the goddess did not share custody of the horrors that came to play on Soren's side of their mind.

Unfortunately, when Anima had nightmares while Soren was awake, Soren was not offered that same mercy.

Lucky her.

"Almost time for her next dose," called one of the mercenaries across the cave—the greater evil of their two captors, a man who probably wouldn't grin so much if he knew how ugly it rendered the contours of his leering face. Not that she could see that face, with Anima's slumber keeping their eyes closed. But she could hear the smugness just fine.

If not for the drugs keeping her body docile, she would have relieved Arthur Rath of his entire mouthful of teeth by now. But no, he and his condescending brother Colin continued to slip god-doping drugs in her food and drink, so the fool got to keep his unpleasant smile intact for now. All her effort was focused on keeping herself awake even while Anima and her body slept, taking in what details she could without the help of conscious hearing or sight, focusing on what sensations her body could feel even in sleep.

Which wasn't much, especially when the nightmares came to visit. But *not much* was a good bit better than *nothing at all*, and to have gained even that much ground was a victory.

Even an inch of ground could make up a mile in this fight.

Tonight saw them camping in a mountain cave, a sight that had sent Anima spinning off into her own nightmares of hungry bears and red-eyed mountain goats as the tranquilizers took hold of her for the evening.

When Soren had thrust herself through the wall that separated them to halt the vines that had nearly crushed Finn's neck beneath their grip, her body had thrown a complete gods-damned hissy fit—and by the time she and Anima had come back to consciousness, the wall had been built back up without either of them making the effort to rebuild it. But it was thinner now than before, less brick and more gauze. More and more of Anima's thoughts leaked over to her side, but she couldn't tell how much of it was the drug and how much was damage she'd done with her reckless attack.

It brought up the question of how many of *her* thoughts were filtering through that barrier now. But there were bigger things to worry about—like the fact that Captain Condescending was making his way over to her. Colin's footsteps were always more hesitant than his brother's, patters rather than clomps, and he smelled better, too—an evergreen sharpness that brought the distant echo of dream-wolf howls with it.

*Anima,* she hissed. No response. *Anima, wake up, for gods' sake. You barely drank a sip!*

Still nothing. Her body dozed on without her permission to do so.

*Damn lightweight.* This was embarrassing. Her company would wheeze their way straight to the infirmary to see her knocked senseless by a drop of concentrated herb-juice or diluted poison or whatever these Tallisian mercenaries were using to do the job.

*What good is your magic if it can't heal you from this?*

*Unngh,* was the groaning response she finally received, a voice soft and frail as flower petals. *Let me sleep.*

*No can do, Goddess Great. We have company.*

Anima opened their eyes, blinking to reveal Colin's blue gaze far too close for either of their liking. His face was solemn as ever, all his features just slightly too big for comfort—ears, nose, eyes, and mouth all just a bit off-kilter. It would have been endearing if he wasn't holding them captive. And if he didn't like to speak to Soren like she was a frightened child rather than a pissed-off princess.

"Goddess," he greeted Anima. "Red."

*Red.* Soren had refused to let Anima hand over her name—either of them—so Colin and Arthur had chosen one for her. A little simple-minded, but she'd borne worse names on her back. They could have called her *raging bitch.*

Anima swallowed, fear a matchstick blaze that couldn't grow past the miasma of Soren's irritation. "Mr. Rath."

*Stop being respectful! He's our* kidnapper. *Call him Captain Condescending. Major Asshole. General—*

*Will you stop?* Anima snapped at her inwardly, sharp enough that Soren nearly preened with pride. Seemed she was rubbing off on the goddess, after all. *I can't focus on him and you with this rotting cloud in my head.*

*Then stop eating what he gives you,* Soren hissed, throwing a mental kick toward the wall. A sliver of satisfaction cropped up when Anima winced again.

*If we starve ourselves, we'll only get weaker.*

"We're nearing Craghaven," Colin said, unwittingly interrupting their silent argument. "This will all be over soon, I swear it."

So he said every day. And yet here they were, tied like a slain deer ready for transport, just like they'd been for the past three or four or seven days. Even though Soren remained conscious in her corner of her mind, the drugs still dulled every sense, and it was difficult to track whether it was day or night. But it felt like it had been some time.

"They're going to come for me," said Anima…as *she* said every day. But that was just as much a lie as Colin's constant reassurances seemed to be.

Elias didn't believe she was alive; of course he'd pick now to favor logic over blind faith. Finn and Kallias would prioritize Atlas over her—at least, Kallias would, and Finn likely would have no choice but to follow. Raquel had no real stake in whether she lived or died now.

They were on their own. Which meant she had to get Anima to *stop* eating and drinking this *gods-damned—*

Colin pressed the canteen to their lips without answering, though the pinch of pity in his gaze suggested he was thinking along the same lines as Soren.

The moment the sweet-tainted water touched their tongue, Soren gathered all her strength and shoved at the wall, screaming a silent command to her disobedient body: *spit it out.*

Water sprayed from their lips to coat Colin's face, and Soren took hold of her tongue long enough to rasp, "Piss off."

The last thing they saw before their muscles seized up and their eyes rolled into their head was Colin's eyes widening in pronounced shock.

# CHAPTER 3

# SOREN

So. That was a tad stupid.

Not out of character, but stupid nonetheless.

The fits were an unfortunate complication of her attempts to steal her body back. They left her with pain in every limb, a soreness that spoke of twisting muscles and bruised skin, and a fog in her head that had nothing to do with the water in Colin's canteen—though she guessed he'd managed to force some of it down her throat while she was senseless, because her tongue was coated in a numbing film that tasted of lemon juice gone bad.

But in spite of the fog, the sour taste, the exhaustion weighing down every limb like she'd put herself through a truly punishing workout…something was different. Something felt…sharper. Less like a dream than she'd grown used to.

Anima was still and silent on the other side of the gossamer wall, slumbering on dreamlessly, nothing but velvet-soft darkness smothering her thoughts. There was nothing there to fight; nothing there to try and take control back.

She focused all her energy on where she thought her eyes were and issued a quiet command: *open.*

They obeyed immediately.

For the first time since she'd closed them in a temple filled with bones and blossoms, Soren Atlas opened her own eyes.

A sob climbed the column of her throat with alarming speed, but she swallowed it down—*she* did, not Anima, not anyone else.

She curled a finger. Two. Three. They each responded in turn, if sluggishly.

She formed a fist. Flexed it outward.

Moving. She was *moving.*

Quaking sobs tried to take hold of her, but she bore down on them, forcing herself to cry in silence as she took in her surroundings. Colin and Arthur were bickering with their backs to her, facing their campfire, both bundled tightly in their thick coats and snow boots while she shivered beneath the thin excuse for a blanket one of them—likely Colin—had thrown over her. She was curled on her side, gravel gritting into her cheek, the arm stuck beneath her twice as numb as the other.

Not at all ideal for an escape, especially when her consciousness kept dipping in and out, the world warping into twos and threes as she tried to get her bearings. But she had to try.

She silently began twisting her wrists, thanking every higher power that might yet exist that Jakob had insisted on training them all how to break free of different kinds of bonds. She'd whined and groaned about it the entire time, even made a scathing comment about his *tastes* that had earned her a solid pop on the back of the head, but when she saw him again…gods, she'd kiss the paranoid bastard for having that kind of foresight. And earn herself another flick on the head when Varran got jealous.

After what seemed like hours of squirming and raking her wrists against the cave wall until her skin scraped raw, the faintest *snap* echoed through the air, freezing her in place; she watched the brothers with bated breath, her chest aching with the effort of holding it in.

But they both kept talking…or rather, Arthur kept talking at Colin, whose hitched-shoulder posture told her enough about how very little he wished to be listening to his brother's raucous laughter tonight.

She happened to be of the same mind.

Slowly, so painfully slowly, she swung her arms around, forcing down a groan as the blood rushed back into her hands, a tingling ache that tunneled straight to the core of her muscles. It was a good few minutes before she could curl her fingers closed; another few before her arms felt steady enough to brace against the ground and—

Arthur rocked to his feet in a sudden rush of movement, and adrenaline struck her so hard in the heart that she nearly choked. Whipping her half-dead arms behind her back, she crashed back to the floor so hard that skin ripped, hot blood dousing her freezing cheek with unpleasant tingling.

*Ow,* Ani grumbled drowsily.

Terror trapped Soren's tongue between her teeth, and she waited…afraid to think, afraid to breathe. Far more afraid of that slumbering goddess regaining consciousness than what the mercenary currently loping her way had planned.

Though, the two fears drew neck-and-neck when she realized Colin had risen as well, ducking out of the cave, his crunching footsteps fading even as Arthur's clapped louder against the stone.

"Evening, girlie." Arthur's rough hand scraped over her injured cheek without a care, digging into her scalp and dragging her head up by her hair, leering down at her. For once, though his tone was still packed full of condescension, there was no underpinned slur of drunkenness in his voice; he knelt in front of them with a grin, his golden hair falling over one eye. "Good news. In short order, I won't have to drag your soon-to-be carcass around any longer."

"Get out of my face." Soren's words, not Anima's—the goddess was still woozy, mostly asleep, her thoughts half-lingering in dreams. The words kicked off Soren's tongue like sparks from a flint.

If only they were accompanied by fire.

"Oh, the little bird's got bite." Arthur chuckled, reaching forward to run his fingers down their lips, fingers lined with dirt and ash and her own blood—

Rage burned away whatever was left of the haze that lingered in Soren's side of their mind, and she snapped forward like a hunting hound unleashed, her teeth sinking into Arthur's finger with a vicious abandon she normally reserved for the Loch family's molasses bread.

Hot metal flooded her mouth, bone snapped, and Arthur's scream jolted Anima fully awake, the leash of the goddess's control bringing a swift end to Soren's attack. Her jaw sprang open against her will, and Anima spat out the blood they'd drawn, gagging as if she'd swallowed poison. *What did you do?*

*I taught him a lesson.* Seething hate bubbled and blended with the satisfaction warming her chest. *I told* him to get out of my face.

*You almost bit his finger off!*

*It would've been better than* almost *if you'd let it be.*

Before Ani could scold her again, before the goddess could fully spit Arthur Rath's blood out of their mouth, something calloused and warm slapped their already-raw cheek.

There was no pain—shock numbed the impact better than any tonic or ice—but shock did nothing to numb the murderous venom that flooded Soren with acid rage.

Arthur gripped the hinge of her jaw with his uninjured hand, his nails digging in so hard that her jawbone protested as he forced her to look him in his muddy eyes. "You're going to regret that," he hissed through his teeth.

Anima had already drifted again, or perhaps she'd retreated at the sensation of being struck. But Soren wasn't sleeping…or scared.

Whatever drug they'd been feeding them, Anima couldn't fight past it—but she could.

She *would.*

Soren leaned closer, licking his blood from her lips, loosing her best feral grin. "Come this close again, and I'll aim much lower next time."

Arthur's teeth gritted, his hand rearing back for another strike. But she refused to flinch, refused to cower—

"Arthur!" Colin's voice cut through the air like a thrown knife, and he caught his brother's wrist, forcing him away from Soren. The dark-haired Rath brother's hair was dusted in powdered-sugar snow, his forest-green leather jerkin creasing beneath his now-open coat as he pinned his brother against the cave wall, his lips peeling back in a snarl when he leaned in to hiss in his ear: "The princess was *very clear.* She wants the goddess unharmed."

"Well, I want me unharmed!" Arthur snapped back.

A snort escaped her. "Maybe you should try being less of a bastard, then."

"That's enough," Colin said, though his gaze lingered on her, and she didn't know what to call the emotion lurking there—surprise? Caution? Fear? "Arthur, take a walk. Stick that finger in a snowbank."

Still swearing, still sneering, Arthur jerked away with a huff and stormed out of the cave, cursing so viciously it stung Soren's near-frostbitten ears.

"He's a delight," Soren said. She kept her arms pinned behind her back, the snapped rope bundled up within her fist—she was angry, not stupid, and she could strike blows without the satisfaction of using her hands if it made escape possible later.

"You bit his finger off."

"*Almost*." That was the key thing to remember, the *almost*. "Besides, can you blame me?"

"What is this?" The Tallisian mercenary stared at her with a furrowed brow, genuine confusion glazing those impossibly blue eyes. "Earlier, you were different. Softer. Your eyes glowed gold. You spoke with a different voice. You were not…this."

It was foolish to give up her name—offering it would give them another avenue, another ransom to ply from two different kingdom's coffers.

Or it might win her some room to bargain.

"Princess Soren Marina Atlas, at your service. Or rather, for you to serve at your pleasure," she said with a bow of her head, spitting another glob of Arthur's blood at her still-bound feet. "I'm a princess in two kingdoms, so really, I shouldn't be bowing to anyone."

"Impossible," Colin said, but the conviction had fled now, only a shaken bend to his mouth left behind. "Those taken by the gods cannot take their bodies back. Not on their own. And even if they could, I know of no Atlas royal who goes by Soren."

"You might also know me as Soleil."

"Impossible," he said again, and she only just leashed an eye roll. "Soleil Atlas is a decade dead."

"Despite the best efforts of myself and others, Mortem doesn't seem eager to make my acquaintance." Which was going to become a problem in short order if that goddess remained intent on using Elias as her own version of a godly puppet. "What does Princess Raini want with me?"

She remembered Raini, vaguely. They hadn't encountered each other much in their childhoods, but she remembered silver-blonde hair, boots and satin pants rather than dresses, and piercing gray eyes that had left Kallias cowering in terror. A formidable girl carved from river rock and mountain stone, intent on a crown even then.

"Nothing with you. The goddess. She—"

Anger bubbled up in Soren's throat, becoming words before she had the chance to stop it: "Her name is Anima."

There was no reason for her to defend Anima. None at all. But somehow, it felt wrong—or at least petty—to let him talk about Anima while she wasn't there.

And while Soren was normally perfectly happy to be petty, she'd take any chance she got to put this man in his place.

Colin scowled, an expression that convinced her in one fell swoop that he and the bumbling oaf outside were actually related. "I'm not even supposed to be talking to you," he muttered, turning away with a quick jerk of his fingers through his hair. "This is some divine mind game."

She almost laughed; the idea of Anima succeeding at anything involving trickery or cleverness was well beyond her imagination. "You've got the wrong goddess, sweetheart."

To that, the mercenary only unclipped the canteen from his belt, shoving its mouth against her lips. "Drink," he ordered…though he sounded unsteady, somehow, as though she'd shaken his sturdy footing.

So she did—taking the tainted water into her mouth and mock-swallowing, holding it deep within her mouth until he seemed satisfied, turning away and capping the canteen.

He didn't ask her to open her mouth and prove she'd swallowed. A beginner mistake—he might have been dedicated to his mission, but he clearly wasn't suited to this sort of task. Even Finn wouldn't have let that trick slide.

An absurd urge to laugh bubbled up in her throat, but she choked it down. What kind of life was she leading, that she now could rank her kidnappers from least to most meticulous? And that her *brother* was somehow below a bounty hunter on that list?

She let the drugged water dribble silently from her mouth to the ground, then settled back on her side with an awkward shuffle. She shifted her hip to hide the evidence of her trickery, then pinned her hands against the stony cave wall, ignoring the torturous burn of her raw skin pressed to abrasive rock.

Soon. The brothers would have to sleep eventually, and when they did…

When they did, she'd see just how far her half-numb legs could get her.

***

Only when both men were curled tightly in their bedrolls—and Arthur's snores guttered through the cave, threatening to rupture her eardrums—did Soren ease herself into a sitting position, making quick work of the knots keeping her ankles bound.

Every movement held the risk of sending a pebble clattering, of changing the air in the cave just enough that one of the two men woke; but luckily, armed with Soleil's memories of sneaking out of the palace before sunrise to surf, she was well-versed in walking through the world without leaving a trace.

Every movement took an eternity. Every thunderous heartbeat promised to give her away. The roaring in her ears drowned out all thought, all reason, as she rose to her weak and wobbly legs and made her way toward the cave mouth.

She could practically hear Elias's chuckle. *You look like a foal that just dropped. Shut your mouth, jackass.* Spectral and imaginary though that mouth might be.

Outside the cave, as the firelight faded behind her and shadows wrapped her in a protective embrace, all was quiet. It might have been eerie if she wasn't so used to it from home—from Nyx. In Atlas, the sea never stopped its roaring deluge of noise, but snow muffled everything beneath its heavy blanket.

*Crunch. Crunch. Crunch.*

Except for footsteps, gods damn her to the depths.

The moment she crossed the cave's threshold and set her too-thin boots to the snow, the very air seemed to freeze in its tracks. No wind through the trees, no creaking of branches; only a bitter, bone-deep cold that stirred a fierce ache in her ears and reminded her quite harshly that she'd fallen out of practice when it came to cold weather.

She gritted her teeth. Bound her coat more tightly around herself. Took a deep, forceful breath that chilled her down to the pits of her stomach.

*You are Nyx-raised, for crying out loud. Start acting like it.*

"I eat icicles for breakfast," she mouthed to herself as she shuffled through the snow, calling back the memory of hunts and patrols taken through the woods. Back then they'd had the advantage of boots crafted for traipsing silently through the snow, but Tallisian border merchants couldn't be expected to stock *everything.* "I've slept in a snowdrift. I have skinny-dipped in the gods-damned *fountain* in the middle of a *blizzard.*"

Given, she'd been considerably less sober at the time and had been soundly dared by Raquel and Lily, but still. Her teeth shouldn't have been chattering this loudly; she nearly broke her neck twisting to search for undead bones coming at her, but no, it was just her own skeleton deciding it was time to rebel.

The pine forest loomed above her, the silvering of the moon and snow rendering anything darker into a shade of impenetrable ebony. Though she knew the pines to be green and vibrant, their branches laden with pinecones and nesting birds, tonight they stood over her as silent soldiers rendered in black, a landscape drawn in charcoal. And every step she took beneath them, trying to pick out any gap in the trunks that might have indicated a path, her heart climbed one rung higher up her throat.

This was foolhardy, even for her. Wandering through the forest weak and alone, Anima slumbering on with no healing magic to do its job, and without the proper equipment…it wasn't likely she'd make it till morning.

But at least she would die trying.

Fatigue pulled at her muscles, an exorable weight that tugged on her eyelids and took away her sight in slices at a time, her legs doing their best to fold beneath her. But she forced another step. Another. Another.

She would crawl if she had to. She would not close her eyes for the last time without knowing she'd done every gods-damned thing she could do to get back to her family…to Elias.

Even if he believed she was already gone.

*Crunch.*

Soren froze, one hand braced against a tree trunk, blinking away the dizziness trying to knock her legs out from under her. She dug her fingertips into the prickly evergreen bark, holding her breath, listening.

*Crunch. Crunch.*

Those were not her footsteps.

A curse tried to fling itself off her tongue, but she leashed it sharply, pushing herself off the trunk. Arthur and Colin couldn't have woken *already*, she'd been so careful, she wasn't—

Another crunch. A slow, quiet breath. Too close. *Too close.*

She broke into a run.

Pain crashed through her legs as she forced herself to move, but she had endured worse; would likely endure worse at the hands of these mercenaries, too. Stab after stab of agony cracked through her bones as she ran, a sobbing cry of frustration breaking through her teeth as her body betrayed her, as her knees gave out and sent her crashing to the ground—

Arms wrapped around her, snatching her up before she could fall. One soiled hand clamped over her mouth while another *grabbed* her, digging so deeply into her haunch that she cried out against the palm muffling her voice.

"Good try, girlie," said Arthur's voice in her ear—Soren arched her neck, desperately seeking some sign of the gentler brother, but Colin was nowhere to be seen.

*Soren?*

"Ani," she gasped.

As if called forth by Soren's panicked acknowledgement of her, Ani's influence swelled and stretched, spread and spread…

Until, with a curse that only half made it off of her tongue, Soren was pushed back into the void where her body could no longer hear her commands.

***

*Anima*

Ani hadn't meant to shove Soren out.

In fact, she hadn't even realized Soren had been *in* until the princess started cursing, desperately pounding at the other side of the wall. *Anima! Gods damn it, let me out, let me—*

*What's happening?*

She'd drifted to sleep in the cave, abandoning the taste of blood on her tongue and the familiar sting of palm against cheek, blood swelling beneath the thin sheath of her skin, staining the flesh purple with pain…

And now there was no cave, no blood, no light. Snow and stars had replaced stone and smoke, her ropes replaced by hands…

No less trapped, but somehow worse, somehow strangling, because—

Because ropes did not seek to humiliate and violate. Not like this.

Arthur crushed her in his arms, his gloved hand covering her mouth, snow melting against her bruised chin, silencing her with barely any effort.

Her heart halted under that vicious, mocking touch.

His breath, hot and heavy with imbibed liquor, brushed against the shell of her ear as he breathed, "Maybe I oughta get a better grip—"

He didn't get to finish that sentence.

He barely even got to *start* it, because the sensation of someone else's hand on her body…a hand she didn't trust, a hand she hadn't invited…

Instinct replaced thought, and her magic speared outward, seeking whatever it could find to manipulate into a weapon.

Her necromancy answered first…it found bone, still infused with life, still willing to bend to her commands.

She meant to break his hand…she meant to force him to let go of her.

But when the *crack* of crumbling bone reached her ears, it was twice as loud as it should have been…twice as loud and twice as high, echoing above her head rather than beneath her clavicles.

*Wait!* shrieked Soren, her voice shredding through the wall like it had been built up from smoke, not adamant. But the command came too late.

The sound of shearing bone grabbed hold of something deep in her gut—some piece of memory that lived in Soren, not her. Still, a ghostly shiver of horror chilled her skin, and Soren shrank back from the wall keeping them apart in their head.

But there was no further protest, no snarky comment, no questions. Only silence that stank of something Ani didn't want to know about.

Weight crashed into her from behind, knocking her weakened body into the snow, driving the last of her breath from her lungs as she impacted with a choking cry. She scrabbled out from beneath it, her nails digging into the frozen ground, and she flipped around to find Arthur, to see how close he was to grabbing her again—

And her scream caught in her throat.

His leering brown eyes were strangely dim, his mouth twisted into a permanent sneer. His gloved hand was bent into a frozen claw, and it took a moment for her to sort out why her eyes wouldn't fully take in his body, why something seemed jilted, wrong…why her stomach flipped upside-down at the sight of him.

*Upside-down.*

That was it. His body was lying face-down…except his face wasn't down.

His neck was twisted all the way around, staring toward the sky, bone jutting unnaturally against his skin.

Anima didn't realize she was screaming until Soren's control leeched back in, her own hand clamping over her mouth to muffle the shrieks, Soren chanting reassurances and warnings to keep quiet in her head. But she couldn't hear her over the horror building inside her, keening louder and louder and louder until she heard nothing, felt nothing…

Saw nothing.

Muscle seized. Vision faded. And with one last sob, Ani let the fit whisk them away into darkness.

# CHAPTER 4

# KALLIAS

Hours after their long trek through the woods to reach the strange, silent village, Raquel's neck was still bleeding.

But that was not the only reason his vision was frosted over with silver rage. No, that anger had started some days ago, and in fact never seemed to stop—it only transferred from target to target, an ever-moving arrow intent on hunting down new prey.

Gods, he was so *thirsty*.

Nothing quenched it—not water, not fresh snowmelt, not even the wine he'd bought off a Tallisian merchant's cart in a moment of weak-willed desperation. He'd polished off the bottle under cover of night, watching Finn's sleeping face for any sign of stirring, guilt spreading mold up the sides of his stomach with every swallow. But when the last drop petered off the rounded glass lip, its cloying flavor coating his tongue, it hadn't even sated the edge of his thirst…and even more alarming than that, it hadn't done anything to dull his fearful thoughts.

No unsteadiness. No soothing warmth. No relief from the constant worries buzzing in his head like a kicked wasp's nest.

An entire bottle of wine, guzzled down in less than five minutes.

And if anything, he'd ended up more sober than when he started.

He'd buried the bottle in the woods. And ever since, he'd done his best to leave their rations of water to the others. If it wasn't going to make a difference whether he drank or not, they shouldn't waste resources on him.

He scratched at his dry, itching skin beneath his shirt, unable to tear his eyes away from Raquel's bloody neck. He'd begun to think his days of claiming Nyxian lives with his blade were behind him, and he'd never even once considered harming an old woman. But watching Raquel grimace as she bathed the wound in the washroom…he was reconsidering his stance.

"Raquel," he said once she'd dried her neck and started to bandage it, "are you safe here?"

She kept her eyes fixed on the mirror. No answer offered. But he knew where she carried her fear by now, and it wasn't hard to catch the flutter of muscle in her left arm, the narrowing of her glass eye in a half-flinch.

He stood up. "Finish up here while I find Finn. We'll leave as soon as you're taken care of."

"Don't be stupid." Raquel didn't take her gaze off her task, but the eye roll was implied in her tone, as she was so talented at. "We didn't hike all the way here for you to decide you're worried about me now."

"I've been worried the whole time."

Her fingertips paused against her bandage, her throat bobbing. Then she resumed wrapping. "You should have said something sooner, then. It's too late now."

She wasn't wrong. This argument should have been had days earlier—well before they crossed the border into Nyx. Before they left Artem, even. But at the beginning, the lingering effects of Tempest's intrusion had made even breathing a chore, and he hadn't had the strength to try and interrogate her about their destination. And after he'd recovered enough…

Festering thirst raked his throat as Raquel ducked her head and splashed her face with water, crystalline droplets plunking into the basin. If he was in possession of a pinch less composure, a *shred* less dignity, he would have drunk straight from her hand if she'd offered him a palmful.

This was worse than addiction. This was *need*, pure and simple, and there was no telling how long he'd be able to bear it.

He hated it. But he hated himself more, because he should have kept pushing for their immediate departure. Should have insisted flat-out that he wouldn't stay in this place another moment if Raquel was at risk, his own well-being be damned.

Instead he said, "Fine. Then at least tell me what I should expect."

"I had a better idea when it was Caelum in charge," Raquel admitted, turning away from him to dry her face. She tossed him the towel, gesturing for him to take his turn at the sink while she stole his perch on the edge of the bath. "He was a bastard through and through, but he was predictable. Aeris…"

She said that name with a pronounced softness she'd never offered to his. His grip on the edge of the sink tightened. "You don't know him as well?

Damn him. Even *he* could hear the halfhearted hope in his voice. What did it matter to him if she cared for this *Aeris* or not?

He'd offered her the truth of his feelings—had rambled them while delirious with a toxic fever, and was now pretending with all his might that he didn't remember saying it at all, but had offered it nonetheless—and she hadn't so much as hinted at a desire to continue the conversation. In fact, she'd found it to be so utterly mad that she'd first accused him of being drunk, quickly followed by the realization that he'd been poisoned.

Because surely the idea of him and her being anything beyond reluctant allies—if not thinly-veiled enemies—had to be the ravings of a man drunk or dying.

Because even Kallias Atlas couldn't be that much of a fool.

Even Kallias Atlas wouldn't fall in love with a woman who wished he was dead.

"I do—I did." Only when she spoke did he realize he was staring at her instead of cleaning the travel-grime from his face. He cleared his throat and splashed his own face, nearly gasping in relief as the water sank into his flaking, wind-chapped skin. Raquel's voice echoed against the water-filled basin as she continued: "When I knew him, he was charming. Eager to please. Worshipped the ground his father walked on, but he never showed the same cruel streak…at least not back then. But when I left…let's just say we parted on poor terms. I don't know what my welcome here will be. Or how it will affect yours. But he's the only person in all the kingdoms that I *know* can help you get rid of Tempest's influence over you."

Water coursed down his face to soak his neck and shirt as he raised his head to frown at her. Something about her voice, the tinge of fear that corrupted her conviction, struck him wrong. "How do you know?"

Her lips pursed, and she tilted her head away, favoring her scarred side. "Because he was there when they did it to me."

He blinked at her. She blinked back.

"Pack your things." He tossed the towel to the floor and snagged his coat from the hook, but he didn't bother putting it back on. The frigid anger coating his veins was colder than the winter that awaited him outside this place. "We're going to want to make camp before nightfall, but if we leave now—"

"I already told you, we're not going anywhere."

"Angelov, there's no gods-damned way I'm asking you to stay with a man who had a hand in—"

"Kallias, *stop.*" Gods, he hated when she used his first name. It made it so much harder to want to argue with her. She stood and blocked him from the door, halting him with a firm hand against his chest. It burned like fire, like frostbite. "You're not asking. I offered. I can handle this. Besides, this isn't just about you. We need that relic regardless. And I'd bet my life that it's in Aeris's possession."

Kallias unwound her hand from his shirt, but didn't let it go, never breaking her gaze. "I'm not a fan of betting. Least of all with lives."

*Least of all with yours.*

Her eye darkened, but she didn't snatch her hand away. "We're here. Let's not run from an enemy we haven't gotten the full measure of yet." Her words hung heavy with hidden meaning. "After all, people change, don't they?"

Before he could even begin to work his way through *that*, the door opened, Finn's head poking around it. "Are you two through yet? If I don't get a bath before the hour's up, my armpit hair's going to start growing mold."

Kallias wrinkled his nose, but Raquel actually barked out a laugh—a sound that never failed to ram him in the ribs. As she made her way back to the sink, expertly removing her false eye and pulling her own soap from a box in her bag, he scowled at his brother. "Do you stay up at night practicing terrible things to say?"

Finn's smirk crumbled immediately, his dimple vanishing, a shadow passing over his freckled face. "Just let me in."

That look forced Kallias back a step, and Finn took advantage of the gap, pushing his way into the bathing room and waiting his turn behind Raquel. He peered over her shoulder as she washed her eye. "I wish I could do that."

"You could," Raquel answered. "You just wouldn't be able to put it back after."

Finn snorted, but his mouth didn't quite finish bending into a smile.

Once Raquel was finished cleaning her eye, she made her way out of the bathing room; Kallias followed. Finn took his place at the sink and kicked the door closed behind them, leaving them standing alone in the hall.

"Whatever Occassio did to him," he muttered to Raquel, "I want her punished for it."

"And she will be." Raquel gave him a look. "If we get Tempest's relic, we stop whatever Tenebrae and the rest of them are planning."

"I don't know if Finn can last that long." Even now, in the daylight, he was haunted by waking to his little brother's screams. Screams filled not just with fear…but with something he might've named madness.

It scared him.

"I think you'll find that your brother can handle himself."

Kallias just grunted, turning away from her to take full measure of the hall they stood in. The floors were covered in artful rugs, each embroidered in navy and silver and black. The walls were rosined wood, built from logs like every other home in this village. He wouldn't have expected it to be comfortable, but it was startlingly warm.

Though, everything felt warm to him lately.

"It's so quiet here." Empty, too, eerily so—besides the scouts who'd dragged them here, he had yet to see another human being.

"It's just past dawn." Raquel thudded back against the wall, propping one foot up, her eye glazing with memory. "They'll all be at the river."

"What's at the river?"

"Water. Some rocks, if you're lucky. Maybe a duck or two."

"Ha, ha. You know what I mean, Angelov."

Coaxing out her smile when he'd become so used to her scowls was one of his new favorite victories. "It's part of our…*their* daily ritual. The Vela flows down from Tallis's mountains and through Nyx…all the way to Atlas. From the mountains, through the snow, all the way to the sea. And guided by the wind all the way." Her smile turned wistful. "Stone, water, wind."

"All of Tempest's elements." He'd retained that much from his classes on the various religions of the six kingdoms. "Not fire, though?"

"Not fire, not living things. Those fall under the domains of his sisters." Raquel sat cross-legged on the ground, gesturing for him to join her. Once he did, she held out her hand in silent command; after a long moment of waiting and watching to make sure he was reading her correctly, he finally settled his hand in hers.

Thankfully, she didn't snap at him or shrink away or stab him for his insolence. Instead she flipped his hand so the palm was facing up. Goosebumps erupted over his arm as she trailed her fingertips over the creases in his palm like she was mapping them out in her mind, her brows furrowed in concentration. "Like all the other gods, Tempest-blessed can be born with any of his three magics: elemancy, aeromancy, and aquamancy. Mastery over wind or stone, mastery over storms and weather, and…"

He flexed his hand, easily calling the power to him—it was harder *not* to coat his hands in ice these days. Hoarfrost gathered and grew in his palm, crackling up Raquel's wandering fingernails. "Mastery over water and ice," he finished softly, looking up to find her bruise-black gaze already fixed on him.

The door to the bathing room opened, and both of them released their held breath in chorus. Raquel took her hand back, dashing the frost off on her armored vest. It scattered on the floor with a series of soft plinks.

"No, please, don't stop on my account," Finn deadpanned. He dropped down to sit beside them, pinning Kallias in the middle, scrubbing moodily at his damp hair with the even damper towel. "I've decided I don't like it here."

"It's barely been an hour," said Raquel.

Finn blinked. "Has it? That's longer than I thought. I really did give it a fair shot."

Kallias snatched the towel from his brother's hand and batted him in the face with it. "I appreciate you suffering through the entire hour on my behalf."

Finn sputtered, snagging the towel and shoving it back in Kallias's face. "Stop it! Gods, you take his title away and suddenly he's a mannerless son of a—"

"Ah!" Kallias caught the towel, leaving them at a stalemate, both their fists clenched around it, water dripping to the floor as they squeezed. "Watch it. I'll tell Mama if you speak ill of her."

Finn blinked. "He's…a mannerless son of a brilliant queen with impeccable fashion and a keen sense for gullshit?"

Kallias dropped the towel, but popped Finn on the back of the head with his palm instead. "Better."

"Princes," Raquel warned, shoving herself up from the ground as footsteps made their way closer. He exchanged looks with Finn, all humor dissipating, and they both stood with haste.

Someone was walking toward them with a decisively professional gait.

And there was still a puddle of water on the floor.

Kallias kicked the towel toward Finn. Finn pinned it under his shoe, gave it a quick swirl to mop up the spilled water, then kicked it behind him, shielding it from view with his legs.

No sooner had they completed the maneuver than the man approaching finally stopped at the mouth of the hallway, offering a slight bow. "The Stormspeaker has returned. He's very eager to speak with you, Princes Atlas…and you, Raquel."

Raquel's jaw worked. "It's Officer Angelov now."

The man's smile didn't twitch. "Of course. Forgive me. It's just been so long since—"

"You said he's ready." Kallias stepped forward to join Raquel, crossing his arms over his chest. "We shouldn't keep him waiting."

Now the man's amiability faltered. The barest hint of a sneer. "Of course. Follow me."

As they made their way through glass-paned or woodworked hallways, an errant breeze tiptoed in behind them, perching on Kallias's shoulder to whisper in his ear: *You are making the wrong choice, Prince.*

He batted at the breeze until it dissipated. *I'm choosing to stay alive. It's hardly a choice.*

*Your life at the cost of your family?* A buzz of static just below his ear. *At the cost of your kingdom?*

His stomach turned, and his new friend *rage* purred beneath his skin. *Is that a threat?*

*No, Prince. I don't threaten people to achieve my ends.* No deception, no mocking. Only…apology. *You alone are not enough to save your people. They need a god on their side. They need* me. *Atlas was my kingdom first, you know. It still holds my heart. I could never leave it to ruin.*

There wasn't much he could say to that. Since he was a boy, he'd been lulled to sleep by his mother's stories of Tempest founding Atlas—how the god had coaxed the sea back from the shore until it revealed a brand-new kingdom, how he'd welcomed all who felt the insatiable hunger for the sea in their blood to make a home there, how he'd gifted them with powers that would aid them in building a life beside the untamable ocean.

Atlas might have adopted Anima as its patron goddess, growing to mistrust Tempest after decades of sunken ships and hurricanes and ruined crops, but his mother always held some small reverence for the god who'd drawn their home up from the depths. A reverence she'd passed on to him, though the chain seemed to have stopped short of Finn, who'd long been content to ignore the gods entirely.

Before he knew it, they were being escorted into a surprisingly plain room. There was no furniture, only a large navy rug stretched out before a concave pool in the center of the birchwood floor—a pool paved in white ceramic and filled to the brim with water so clear and still Kallias almost thought it was glass.

Sitting cross-legged on that rug was a man barely older than Kallias, if older at all. His hair was white-blond, cut short but coiffed to the side a bit in the front, well-trimmed sideburns framing a face like the ice sculptures he'd seen once, during a diplomatic visit to Nyx years before the war. His skin was pale as the snowfall outside, eerie and beautiful all at once, and when he opened his eyes, their piercing blue color struck a pang of homesickness deep in Kallias's heart.

But crueler than that was the *smile* that broke across his face like dawn spreading welcoming arms to greet the day—the smile he gave to Raquel, and only Raquel, not even sparing a glance to her companions.

"*Stormcloud.*" A near-giddy laugh, and the man was on his feet before Kallias could even think about intercepting him, throwing his arms around Raquel and embracing her with all the tenderness of an old friend. Or something worse.

Kallias's face burned. He ached to draw his sword. There was *absolutely no reason* to draw his sword.

"Aeris." Raquel did not look remotely comfortable. Maybe there *was* reason to draw his sword. "It's been…a long time."

"I'd say so!" Aeris pulled back, his hands fastened too tightly around Raquel's arms, his eyes wide with wonder…and something Kallias couldn't read. "Five years, Raquel. I've been worried sick. After my father banished you—"

"After *all of you* banished me," Raquel corrected softly. Pain unimaginable underlaid her words, a foundation filled with cracks that could never be filled.

Still, that assertion built a dam between them. Aeris didn't speak for a full twenty seconds.

Maybe, if they were very very lucky, he'd go longer than that. Possibly forever.

"I didn't want to," Aeris whispered, his pale lips reaching down toward the floor instead of his near-invisible, utterly useless eyebrows.

This venom wasn't necessarily fair, and he knew it. Aeris was a decisively beautiful man. But the way Raquel held herself around him, like he might strike her just as easily as kiss her, like she was *afraid*…

It didn't matter if Aeris was a gods-damned saint. Kallias wanted his hands off of her.

But Raquel could handle herself. If she asked, he was ready to step in. But not until she asked.

"I know." She didn't. Kallias could hear it in her voice, see it in her eyes. She took a step back, gesturing over her shoulder. "Actually, my friends here are the ones seeking your counsel."

Aeris looked at them for the first time, albeit reluctantly. "Yes, so I was told. Princes Kallias and Finnick, enemies of Nyx. You've wandered far from home."

That hardly covered it. "Raquel promised us you were the one to see about our…problem."

*His* problem. The blizzard roaring fierce and furious through his body, the voice muttering in his ear, the faintest memory of a god wearing his skin like a custom-tailored uniform.

Sometimes, the pain in his skin felt like anger. Felt like longing. Like his body *missed* belonging to someone else. Someone better.

Not even good enough for the body he'd been born into.

Aeris frowned, pulling back from Raquel, though one hand lingered on her shoulder. "I'm happy to help if I can. Tell me what you need."

Just as he'd said to Tempest, there was no true choice. He told Aeris everything—about his own plight, anyhow. He left out the bits about Jericho and Tenebrae and Anima. And when he was done with the story, the man regarded him not with fear, not with pity…but with something worse.

*Envy.*

"A scion," said Aeris slowly. His fingers crept up to his chest, curling around something beneath his shirt—a pendant of some kind, maybe. There was a simple leather cord around his neck that disappeared beneath his neckline. "A chosen host. That is…rare, indeed, Prince. And thought by many to be a privilege."

"Not to me." No matter how thrilling the power in his veins might feel at times. How addictive. "I just want to go home. And I can't trust myself to do that when *I* could be usurped by another's will at any moment."

"I understand." Aeris tipped his head to the side, studying Kallias for a moment before turning back to Raquel. "You know what might be required."

"Yes."

"Has he been warned?"

Raquel glanced at him out of the corner of her eye. "Yes."

"Good." Aeris blew out a breath and stepped back from them, perching his hands on his hips. "I'm sure you're all exhausted from your journey, and this ritual isn't best done on the verge of fatigue. Princes Kallias and Finnick, we'll happily provide you your own accommodations. Raquel, if you wish to reclaim your own quarters…there's still room in our old cabin. I haven't changed much of anything. It wouldn't be difficult to put it back where it was."

As innocent and kind as the offer sounded, only a fool could have missed the absolute *terror* that flashed through Raquel's eyes.

"Well, that hardly seems proper," Kallias interrupted sharply, a thought forcing itself to the forefront of his mind with barely a beckon. There was only one way he could save her from that without looking suspicious.

Aeris's smile, for the first time, darkened. "I don't gather what you mean."

Kallias crossed his arms over his chest. "What kind of husband would I be if I took kindly to another man sharing quarters with my wife?"

Oh, that was a *mistake*. The drop of Raquel's jaw and the flare in her eyes explained that fully, no words necessary. But Aeris's hand finally fell from her shoulder, incredulity scribbling a brand new look on his face. "*Wife?*"

To Kallias's left, only loud enough for him to hear, Finn mumbled a dirty, horrific curse.

But in his other ear, the wind only laughed. *Oh, you're going to need a better god than me to save you from* that, *Kallias Atlas.*

# CHAPTER 5

# FINN

"What in the pits," seethed Raquel, her sword bumping against her leg in a murderous rhythm as she paced, tearing at the roots of her blue-black hair, "were you *thinking*, Atlas? Wife? Your gods-damned *wife*?"

To his credit, Kallias *did* look properly mortified, sitting on the one bed— the very lonely, definitely singular bed—in this room he and Raquel had been given with his hands clasped in his lap and his cheeks burning redder than spilled blood. "I wasn't thinking, all right? I just—I could tell you didn't want to go with him, and—"

"And so your *first* idea was to claim that I, a Nyxian without a drop of royal blood, somehow married an Atlas prince in the middle of a *war*?"

Finn honestly couldn't care less about the whole thing, but maybe he was just used to his brother's foolhardiness—and his horrific lack of skill when it came to weaving falsehoods. He lay stretched out on the bed behind Kallias, watching the two of them bicker while the pain behind his eyes slowly grew.

And grew.

And grew.

The headaches were back. They'd vanished for a time; all the while he was in Fidget's company—no, damn him, *Occassio's* company—he hadn't felt so much as a throb in his temple. But after he'd discovered the truth of his new *friend's* identity, her magic had accosted him tenfold, leaving him in pain throughout every one of his waking hours.

Waking hours that were fewer and fewer in number lately.

Every day, it seemed as though he was awake less and less. Entire hours vanished shortly after he'd finished living them, and he only knew they'd happened at all because Kallias would occasionally get frustrated when he had to repeat information they'd apparently already discussed.

Raquel never got angry. She only watched, pensive and suspicious and seeing too much, and it took effort not to shout at her to stop judging him, stop looking at him, stop *seeing* him.

He was not going mad.

He *was* mad. Mad Prince Finnick, preacher of portents, misplacer of memories, doll of deities.

A feminine voice intruded upon his silent reflections: "Scheduler of sparklers. Robber of relics. Master of…mm, no, that's not right. Is there an *M* word for someone who's been tricked? I'm trying to do something with Mirror."

Gods, couldn't he have one damned moment of *peace?*

When he didn't answer her, Occassio sighed in the way that promised there was an eye roll behind it. It was easy as anything to imagine her pouting, sitting cross-legged on the bed beside him.

Easy, because he didn't have to imagine it. His hallucinations of her hadn't been left behind in Atlas like he'd hoped; no, she'd been beside him every second of this journey. Sitting beside him at meals, kicking the backs of his heels while they walked, chattering away in his ear all night long until exhaustion forced him to sleep. And in sleep, her annoyances turned to attacks. From bothersome voices to lurid, inescapable nightmares.

She'd chosen to appear with her hair in pigtail braids today, her curls woven tightly against her head, fastened with bejeweled ribbons near the ends. The sections of hair below the fastenings poofed out in tiny clouds of corkscrew curls, and he might have smiled at that if he wasn't busy despising her with every gods-damned bit of energy he could spare. She flashed a smirk at him over her shoulder, her ruffled eggplant-purple skirt tucked beneath her crossed legs, the hem of her matching cropped shirt brushing the top of her midriff, baring an inch of shimmering skin. The sleeves were ruffled as well, reaching from the tops of her arms to her wrists, but her collarbones and shoulders were uncovered, showing off the mirror pendant dangling from her neck.

Goddesses didn't get cold, apparently.

"You should probably intervene soon," she added, hiking a thumb at Raquel, who had started fingering the hilts of her knives. "They're about to come to blows."

He ignored her. Squeezed his eyes shut. Wished with all his might that it could be that simple to lock her out.

"It's rude to ignore someone who's talking to you," she sang in his ear.

"It's rude to torment someone with hallucinations and visions of doom," he sang back under his breath, low enough that hopefully Kallias and Raquel wouldn't hear—or would only hear a muddled hum.

"It's not my fault you're all barreling toward a future filled with bloodshed and death." Her skirt brushed against his arm as she scooted backward, walking two fingers up his shoulder and tickling behind his ear. "I don't choose your path, Trickster. I only show you its consequences."

Maybe she could show him the consequences of Kallias's latest attempt to get himself killed.

"I could." Her fingernails dragged lightly down the side of his neck, each one carefully filed to a subtle point and decorated with tiny rhinestones. "But that would take all the fun out of watching."

The sensation of her creeping nails stirred an unbearable itch beneath his skin. He surged up to face her, his hand shooting out and snatching her wrist, halting her hand's path toward his collarbone. "Do. Not. Touch. Me."

There it was again, that grumpy pout; her favorite accessory. But to his surprise, she obeyed, pulling away the moment he released her wrist. Her kaleidoscope eyes twinkled, a hoard of jewels that would make any thief crazed with need. "Sorry."

"Finn?" Not Occassio this time. Kallias had his hand out in a *stop* gesture toward Raquel, his eyes riveted on Finn with sudden intensity, his shoulders cocked back like he was preparing for an attack. "What are you doing?"

Finn blinked to find Occassio gone, his fist strangling thin air.

"Charades," he said. "Thought a game might dispel the tension. One word, two syllables…what Raquel wishes she could do to you right now?"

"Finnick," Raquel warned.

"No, that's not it. Try again."

"Look," Kallias sighed, rubbing his eyes—did they look more bruised underneath with every passing second, or was that another hallucination? "I'm sorry, all right? I am *sorry*. If you want to…if I overstepped, if I was wrong, then I'll fix it. I'll explain it to him, and—"

"No. I can't—no. It's not the lie I would have picked, but…" Raquel crossed her arms over her chest. "I don't trust him, and I don't like the idea of the three of us being separated. At least this way we're all in the same building. Besides, it's not like we haven't shared a room before."

Kallias's shoulders relaxed visibly, a hint of relief tracing the lines of his posture. "I'll sleep on the floor."

Hopeless. The two of them had been dancing around each other like two seagulls attempting a mating ritual for the first time for weeks now. It was painful to watch.

"I wouldn't do that," Finn warned. "If anyone ever comes in and catches you sleeping apart, it will ruin everything. Cons require commitment."

There. Let them do with that what they would. Forced proximity could work wonders, and *gods* he hoped it did, because if he had to watch them pretend to hate each other for any longer—

"What was that?" Kallias looked at him incredulously as Raquel paced to the closet, opening it and shoving her pack inside.

He blinked. "What was what?"

"*Cons require commitment?* What do you know about cons?"

*Only that I practically invented half the methods used in Atlas today.*

"It's just an expression," he mumbled. "I read it somewhere."

Kallias narrowed his eyes. "You read adventure books."

Of course he picked *now* to be observant. "Con men can go on adventures."

"All right, enough," Raquel cut in. "We can talk out everything else later. Did you two see the cord around Aeris's neck?"

"I did," Kallias said.

Finn blinked. Schooled his features into the mask he wore to lie. "Me too."

Had…had they already met with Aeris?

No, of course they had, that made sense—they wouldn't be in a room if they hadn't. They'd just been *talking* about him, they'd…hadn't they?

He grappled for the memory, trying to drag it back, but it had already turned to vapor, slipping free from his fingers without leaving a single imprint behind.

Blankness. Nothing between walking into the bathing room earlier that day and…and *cons require commitment*. When had he gotten here? Had he fainted? No, if he'd fainted Kallias would have started his mother hen routine by now. He must have walked in here under his own power.

But how long ago?

Fear riled in his stomach, climbing his ribs to push at his lungs. He forced himself to breathe evenly.

*It's fine. We're fine. We're* fine.

By the time he walked himself back to the present after chasing so far after the past, Raquel had settled herself to his right, using him as a wall between her and Kallias. She was chewing on the inside of her cheek, circling her thumb over the hilt of one of her many knives.

"I'm sure," she said—answering a question Finn hadn't heard. Or didn't remember hearing. "I've seen that cord before. He's wearing the relic. If he's followed his father's example, he never takes it off."

*The relic.* He remembered that much. *An ice shard that never melts.*

"How are we supposed to steal it if he never takes it off?" Kallias demanded. "That's going to be impossible."

"I said *if*," Raquel said. "He might be less paranoid than Caelum was."

"Can we bargain for it?" Finn croaked. "Is there anything he wants badly enough to part with it?"

"Not a chance in the pits." Raquel shuddered—the most open gesture of fear he'd ever seen from her. She always hid it behind subtle flinches and angry scowls. "That relic is…holy. Holiness of a different nature. It's like Elias's prayer beads, but infinitely more precious. He would die before parting with it."

"Is that an option? Three against one, would we win?" Finn asked—then regretted immediately. Kallias shot him a look like a man shuffling the deck of his thoughts; shock rearranging itself into incredulity. Then something like anger. Maybe worry.

Gods, he was never this blasé with his Second Prince face. His masks were falling one by one, and he didn't even remember to try and catch them until they'd already clattered to the ground.

"No," Raquel muttered. "Here, it wouldn't be three against one. It would be three against the entire village. And everyone here is Tempest-blessed—*everyone,* even the children. At least half are twice-blessed. It's…a carefully cultivated community."

Well, that sounded…creepy. "Lovely. Why are we here, again?"

"So what do we do?" Kallias pushed. "There's no way we'll get that relic from him without him noticing, and once he realizes it's gone, we're worse than outnumbered—not just outnumbered, but out-blessed. We're hoping to have culled Tempest's interests in me by then, and Raquel, you said you don't have access to your magic. Which leaves Finn, and I don't think seeing the future is going to help us much."

Raquel leaned forward until her face took up most of his vision, her eyes demanding contact.

"What?" he rasped.

She nodded to Kallias. "Tell him."

"I don't know what you're talking about."

"Tell me what?" Kallias demanded.

Raquel held Finn's gaze without blinking. "This is a matter of life and death," she said. "For all our kingdoms."

Finn held her gaze. Held his silence.

"And for your *family*," she added through gritted teeth. "Tell. Him."

This went against *everything* he stood for—everything he'd built, everything he'd protected through lies and costumes and spilled blood. He had fought for eight years to hide this side of him from his family, swathing all his sharp edges in velvet and lazy grins while quietly building a weapon beneath.

Jericho's desperate face, sallow and scared before Tenebrae had taken over her body, flashed through his mind.

Soleil's shaking hand as she held Anima back from hurting him, giving him the chance to run.

His parents, now robbed of all their children but one—and even she wasn't truly there.

So he closed his eyes. Silently mapped out the edges of his most familiar mask, tracing corners so long-worn they'd practically fused to his skin, a façade so flawless he no longer had to remind himself that it was fake in order to hold onto it.

At least, he hadn't. Not before *her*.

Slowly, inch by inch, he peeled his final mask free from his skin.

No more games. No more bluffs. Finnick Atlas, for perhaps the first time in his life, was going all in.

"If he takes it off his neck, I can steal it," he said. "Without him even noticing it's missing. But it's going to take one massive distraction."

It took effort not to flinch when Kallias's gaze shot to him, his mouth opening in disbelief, a hundred questions teeming in his eyes…none of which made it out. Good—he didn't think he had it in him to lie proficiently at this point, anyway.

Raquel's eyes glimmered. "Trust me," she murmured, glancing at Kallias, "you'll get one."

# CHAPTER 6

## SOREN

Anima had killed Arthur.

Killed him, then vanished, burying herself so deep in their mind that Soren couldn't have coaxed her out even if she tried.

That shouldn't have worried her. It should have been a relief, the fact that she'd woken from their fit to find herself alone in her head, the fact that she'd woken soon enough that Colin had not found them lying beside his decidedly dead brother, but…

No Anima meant no medimancy. And no medimancy meant that if Soren's body finally succumbed to the frailty gifted by their latest fit, she could very well fall asleep in the snow and never wake up.

She had been walking for a full day.

Everything hurt.

And gods, she would have *killed* for a mug—or a wine glass—of piping hot cocoa right about now.

At least she'd been able to steal Arthur's coat; without it, she would've definitely died the night before. But even that could only offer so much protection from the elements.

Deeper than the chill of the elements was the chill of memory…the chill of Arthur's broken neck shifting sickeningly as she removed his coat, the reminder of her hands desperately trying to keep Elias's broken neck from doing the same as she pleaded with her sister for his life.

Arthur, at least, had earned it. It wasn't the method of death she would have picked—a little too quick, a little too familiar—but she couldn't really complain.

Literally, she couldn't complain. Her lips were too cold to form any true words.

She bit down on those ice-cold lips as she stumbled stiff-legged through the never-ending woods, gnawing at a chapped flake of skin until she drew blood. The pinprick of pain kept her mind off of the much more dangerous, much scarier numbness seeping into the rest of her body, a promise that all the tricks she'd learned in Nyx to stave off frostbite and hypothermia wouldn't work for much longer.

But she couldn't stop. Wouldn't stop.

She didn't even know where she was gods-damned *going*, but at least no one would be able to say she died easy.

Eyes burning, breath bubbling in her lungs, she fixed her gaze on her boots—the only proof she still had feet to walk on.

One more step.

One more step.

One more…

A gust of wind barreled through the trees, so bitingly cold it might as well have borne fangs, tearing so deep into her body that her bones cried out in aching pain.

"Come on," she panted voicelessly…then again, cursing as she tried and failed to lift her foot to take her next step: "Come *on*!"

But her feet would not budge. For all she knew, they might've frozen at the ankle and snapped clean off.

Cursing again, she lifted her head, even the dimming light stinging her eyes. Sunset had passed her by, golden sunlight fading into silver moonbeams…and with it, the temperature started crawling back down from *I may freeze to death* cold to *wait, I was wrong before, now I'm* definitely *going to freeze to death* cold.

Deep in her gut, in the place where her sharpest instincts were buried, a tiny voice told her she would not make it to the next shift change between the sun and the moon.

But she couldn't stop.

If her feet didn't want to move, fine.

She would gods-damned *crawl*, pride be damned, so long as she could die knowing she'd done everything she could to get back to her parents. Her brothers.

Elias.

She tugged the coat sleeves down past her knuckles to shield her black-tipped fingers, holding her breath, bracing herself to drop…

When she held her breath, the wind did the same.

And in that pocket of silence, she heard it…the faintest brush of cloth against bark.

Her stomach jumped into her throat.

*Colin.*

He'd tracked them. Gods damn him, he'd—

Another slight rasp told her there was no time for cursing and complaining…nor would crawling do the trick.

She had to run.

*Please*, she silently begged her body. *Please, just one more time.*

And it tried. To its credit, it did. When she took her first stride forward, it held, but on the second…

The ground rushed up to meet her, and she squeezed her eyes shut, waiting for the impact. Waiting for the blade in her back that would surely follow.

When arms wrapped around her once more, they were so warm she nearly forgot to fight.

Nearly.

Let go!" She kicked, she cursed, she even bit, but it was no use—she was too weak. "Let go, you bastard, you cheap-hearted greedy little—"

"Animal!" snapped a voice from above her…and her heart fell clean out of her chest.

That wasn't Colin.

She knew that voice better than she knew her own. She knew the shadow hovering above her, his arms anchored around her waist with unyielding strength, one eye dark and the other ringed in fire.

She would have thought it was a trick of the moon if she didn't know the *exact* width and breadth of that shadow; if she hadn't been saved by it once before, when it had emerged from a dark Atlas hallway and knocked Second Prince Finnick senseless with a left-handed blow to the temple.

If she hadn't once been pinned to a wall by that shadow, its mouth clumsily seeking purchase against hers, its hands awkwardly roaming over her waist in search of a somewhat-proper perch and failing miserably.

It was a dream. That was all. A cruel, useless dream that wished to see her miserable as well as dying, as well as—

The shadow leaned from the darkness into the beaming moonlight, and her heart broke every one of her ribs in its reckless attempt to get to him.

To Elias Loch, shadow made man, man made flame, his pupil rimmed in fiery gold like embers nestled against onyx stone.

He'd come for her.

"Elias." It took no strength at all to mouth his name, her lips forming it all on their own, a plea that couldn't drag her voice out with it. All sound was robbed now by the weakness she'd earned by trying to flee, but it didn't matter—he would hear it anyway. Because he was Elias, and he always heard her, and if he would just *look* at her then he would know—

He set her down, putting a finger to his lips. When he looked at her face, though his eyes flared in boiling rage, they did not gentle—and when he tugged a pair of gloves out of his pack and secured them on her hands, he did so roughly, avoiding her gaze entirely.

"Elias," she tried again. *Look at me. Look at me, I'm here, jackass.*

He shook his head at her. "Quiet."

There were so many gods-damned things she wanted to *say*, not the least of which being *don't tell me to shut up, you asshole,* and one of the foremost being *you're an idiot, you're an* idiot, *and I love you anyway because the gods cursed me to be even worse of an idiot.*

But that last attempt to run had taken the last of her strength.

Instead, a pitiful rasp was her only hello as Elias hauled her up into his arms. Her head lolled limply against his shoulder, greasy tangles of hair catching in his thin Artemisian armor, her bruised and tear-stained cheek protesting as the unforgiving steel dug into her damaged skin.

"Close your eyes, Anima," he breathed, the slightest growl underlying his words. "Don't push yourself. I'm getting you safe, gods only know why."

*Anima.*

Oh, gods damn her to the bloody, putrid *pits,* then wash her off in the cold and clammy depths, then toss her right gods-damned *back* into the pits—

He couldn't see her. Couldn't hear her.

He couldn't *see her.*

A fissure broke open in the half of her heart that still felt like hers.

*Look at me,* she pleaded silently. *I'm not her. I'm not her.*

But he kept his eyes glued ahead, only the warm constant of his hand cradling her head to his chest telling her that Finn's story might have tunneled partway into his iron-plated skull.

*I'm not her.* Gods, why couldn't she find her voice now that she *needed* it? *See me, see me, see me…*

She kept asking until her vision swam into deeper, darker waters, plunging her back into a choiceless sleep. And no matter how much she begged, her battlemate kept his eyes locked on some invisible horizon, cutting through the forest with an utter silence only a specter of death could possess.

# CHAPTER 7

# ELIAS

He had to sleep.

What base amount of sense he still had told him that much. He'd forgone true, deep rest for days of traipsing through mountain snow and biting wind, fueled by the fire constantly burning in the hearth of his heart, but the sight before him had rendered him well and truly burned to cinders.

Soren, but not. His battlemate's body bundled in the few clean blankets he'd managed to scrounge up in this empty, rarely used Nyxian outpost just past the Tallisian border. The foreboding stone structure only occasionally hosted border patrols; it had been a long time since they'd bothered directing their attention to Tallis's relatively quiet border. It was a lucky break that it was one of the places Jakob had brought them to for conditioning during their training; if not for that hellish experience, he might not have known where to go.

So now Anima rested in one of the turret chambers, her dirty hair cast akimbo across the thin pillow, her abused cheek raw and red from sleeping on gravel…and possibly from taking a blow or two from the hands of those mercenaries.

He'd wanted to track Anima's footsteps back to their camp and slit their throats for it. Only Mortem's voice in his ear had stilled his hand.

"Not yet," she'd told him when his hand had crept to one of his scythes. "Soon, perhaps, but not yet."

He'd ignored her wisdom before, and it had nearly seen him to his final grave. So he'd forced himself to abandon that hunt, even though it made his fingers ache with death ungiven.

He put those aching fingers to work, kneeling by the dust-coated stone fireplace and breathing new life into the paltry fire he'd started an hour ago, glancing over his shoulder to check that she still slept.

In spite of everything, in spite of passing through fire and letting his lesser parts turn to ash, he still possessed enough weakness to be relieved that the shivers wracking his battlemate's body were beginning to die down…and to wish desperately that she would wake and demand to know why he was sitting there gawking at her instead of joining her, his arm wrapped around her waist and his socks stolen to warm her own feet.

He couldn't remember the last time he'd held her.

Not the way he'd carried her here, only touching what skin he couldn't avoid. The way they'd used to hold each other, comfortable and casual, only rare pieces of themselves still subject to self-consciousness.

He hadn't slept in a bed since losing her. It only made waking from the nightmares worse.

His fist tapped against his knee in time with his heartbeat, his eyes fixed unseeingly on Soren's—Anima's—sleeping face.

It felt like a wake. Like watching a corpse breathe past its allotted time.

It would have been easier if she'd burned on a pyre or been buried in an Atlas grave. At least then he could be free of her tangible ghost.

The lump in his throat turned to stone, to steel, and he forced himself up in a single swift motion, tearing his eyes away from her like a seamstress ripped out sloppy stitches.

He couldn't sit here all night and stare at her. He needed to *do* something. And if sleep wasn't going to be that something, he would find another way to make himself useful.

So he started cleaning.

First, he climbed down the narrow, creaking stairwell that led from the turret room to the main floor, bunching his shoulders inward so they didn't catch on the sides of the walls.

The main chamber of the guardhouse was designed for defensibility, not comfort; there was only one true window. The rest of the light-leaking holes in the walls were actually arrowslits, and even they didn't let much of the sunset in. Still, it was enough to light his path as he crossed the beast-fur rug to the barred window and sliced a scrap of cloth from the single curtain hanging over it. Dust and mildew corrupted the stale air as he tugged it down, and he hurriedly covered his mouth with his scarf to avoid breathing it in.

And he got busy attacking the dirtied floors and dusty walls.

*Busy hands make for still thoughts,* his mother's voice reminded him as a splinter stabbed into his nailbed, a bead of blood welling for only a moment before a spark popped from his fingertip. The blood scalded immediately, its texture—and gods, the *smell*—decidedly unnerving.

Still. Better than having to deal with a clumsy, bandaged finger.

Hours smoldered to ash as he painstakingly took a rag to every dust bunny making its nest in the crevices of the guardhouse, dealing blow after merciless blow to clusters of spiderwebs and moldy bits of what once might have been food. Though the arrowslits welcomed in plenty of drafts, the building was otherwise in surprisingly good repair, and there were no signs of rats or other creatures making a home of it.

It was better than some of the inns he and Kallias had stayed in over the course of their journey. He might never shake off the memory of waking up to a mouse scrabbling through his hair, its tiny claws mistaking his scalp for a fortuitous new bed.

Kallias had screamed at a pitch so high the quality of the glass in the unbroken windows was proven beyond a doubt. His lips twitched at the memory of the prince's wild eyes, his terror palpable as he bobbled to his feet on the bed and drew his sword against a rodent no bigger than one of his fingers.

He'd never thought he would miss that Atlas bastard, but he'd take his constant talk over this too-short silence.

Wood creaked behind him, close to the stairwell—a sound that lashed across his chest and arrested his breath.

"Elias?"

Hoarse. Hesitant. Holding his name out like a peace offering.

He didn't turn from where he stood by the dilapidated sink basin of the guardhouse's small kitchen, washing dishes in snow-water he'd melted over the fire. "You should be resting."

"Elias…"

Anger, a familiar beast he'd only barely tamed, tried to rear up and throw him into a rage. He tugged its reins taut with a slow, even breath. "You should go back upstairs. I'm not in the mood."

"Will you just look at me?" Anima pleaded, but he wouldn't. Couldn't.

He kept his hand moving. Circle after circle on the dish in his hand, scrubbing away layer after layer of grime until the only thing being removed was the film of soap from the previous pass. "I'm not ready to have any kind of discussion with you, so unless you're prepared to pit biomancy against pyromancy—"

"*Look at me, jackass!*"

All the world caught its breath.

All the world, for two people who had not asked for this, who had chosen each other in the midst of tragedy that should have rent their hearts to ruin, who had walked side by side so closely that their hearts stitched together unto inseparability.

All the world for him, for her, for them. Who had survived where none other could. Who had fought for what none other would.

The world made space for the reunion of Soren Nyx and Elias Loch.

Elias turned to face her, and he was on his knees before he even saw that her eyes were green. Before he even truly heard that name from her mouth. Before he could begin to muster the echo of *smartass* that would let her know he heard her.

But his eyes sought her anyhow, and somehow—*somehow*—there she was.

Green, glorious eyes. Curls doing their best to escape from the torn ribbon Anima had tried to tame them with. A quivering lower lip. Constellations scattered across her face like speckles of sienna paint, their patterns long ago memorized by eye and by touch. Her beautiful, crooked, *beautiful* nose.

"Look at me," Soren choked, taking a step that shook her from toe to head, a tremble that spelled terror. "I'm not her. I'm not *her*, Elias, I'm me, I'm—I can't—just see me, *please.*"

He forced himself to his feet. Took a step forward that was just as unsteady, just as afraid, every piece of sense rallying against hope. Against dreams. Because that was exactly what this was: one of his cruel and beautiful dreams, a figment of grief that lured him in with the gift of her before twisting into a nightmare of golden eyes or dying whimpers or a body without a head.

"This isn't real," he heard himself say, somewhere far from here. "This can't…you're not…you're *dead*—"

"Do I *look* dead to you, jackass? Don't answer that, actually, I don't want to know what I look like right now. Just…please, just—" An edge of desperation whet itself to razor-sharpness in Soren's eyes, and she took another step, reaching out—then stumbled.

Dream or not, real or not, he would never let her fall.

The second he caught her beneath her elbows, her wasted muscles and shaking limbs nothing he would have thought to give her in his imagination, a strangled sob jerked his chest so hard that a rib or two might have broken.

"Soren." A prayer or a plea or a praise to the gods, he wasn't sure and didn't care to be. "Soren?"

"Elias," she sobbed, and it was her, he knew it in his heart and head and his very bones—

Not a dream. *Not a dream.*

And then he held her, *gods* he held her, tugging her into his lap and clutching her against him with all his might, weeping so hard he couldn't see, couldn't breathe. She wrapped her legs around his hips and her arms around his neck, burying her face into the side of his neck, her tears hot and slick against his skin as she made an awful sound, some ugly cross between a laugh and a sob that he loved so much it nearly broke him.

"Don't leave," he rambled. He pulled back and caught her face in his hands, planting kiss after kiss along her cheekbones, her forehead, her chin, the tip of her nose. "Don't you leave me again, don't you *ever*—"

Soren laughed through her tears, her nose crinkling beneath his kiss, a quivering grin spreading across her face. "Don't tell me what to do, jackass."

A thrill of fierce joy twirled his head into the clouds, and the smile that stretched across his face dug so hard into his cheeks that it actually hurt. "Oh, I'll tell you what to do, smartass. If you think I'm not—"

"I love you, too." She gripped his face between her hands and made him lower his head so she could kiss him between his brows, then rested her forehead against his, running her thumbs along his temples. "Don't ever die again."

"I'll do my best."

Her snorting laugh made up for every nightmare he'd borne during her absence. He couldn't look away from her eyes. If she blinked wrong, if they lit up gold again…

Fire-forged or not, if this miracle only lasted long enough for him to give her a proper goodbye, there would be no fixing what that false hope broke.

"Is she gone?" he whispered.

Soren's mouth pinched, and the shake of her head plunged his heart to his feet. "No. Just sleeping. Since she killed one of the bastards that took us."

"They're dead?"

"Just one," Soren said—the impatience in her tone suggested she'd said that already, and he'd missed it in favor of other details. "The other never showed. For all I know, he's still sleeping in that wretched cave."

Not good. They'd have to watch for the other one. Still, he couldn't imagine some Tallisian mercenary could do much damage against someone blessed by Mortem in triplicate.

"I don't know if it's the shock or the poison, though," Soren added. "They gave us this vile stuff…I think it's made to suppress magic. I could stay awake even after they dosed us, but Ani can't."

"*Ani?*" Please, gods, she couldn't have possibly gotten cozy enough with the goddess who had *stolen* her body to give her a *nickname.*

She wrinkled her nose. "Don't start with that tone already, I've barely been back for two minutes—"

"I don't have a *tone*—"

"Oh yes you do. It's the *Soren's-being-an-idiot-again* tone, and I didn't appreciate it before and I certainly don't now—"

Despite his caution, his worry over how much or how little she might have been permanently altered by having her mind invaded, he let out another shaky laugh. "Do me a favor?"

She blinked, frowning, pausing mid-rant. She reached up and stroked a thumb over his beard. "What favor?"

"Keep being mean to me. It…it helps." Anima had never been anything but meek, shy. Rudeness meant the miracle was still in effect.

She barked out a laugh, tweaking his cheek with her fingertips. "Listen, jackass—you promise not to shave this beard, and I'll give you any favor you ask for."

His cheeks flooded with heat. "Okay, maybe not *that* mean, smartass."

"I'm not being mean! I like it." She pinched his cheeks and stretched them out to get a better look, and he caught her wrists with a quiet protest, though he couldn't bring himself to pull away. He might never be able to let her go again. "It makes you look all grown up."

"It itches."

"Beauty is pain, I'm afraid."

He could have gone an eternity like that. An eternity of just him and her on the dusty floor of a guardhouse that hadn't seen life in gods-knew how long, and it would have been enough.

But her next hoarse whisper stirred him to life, a hushed confession that barely made a mark on the stale air: "I don't know how long we have until she wakes up."

Fear plowed into his gut with a vicious uppercut, and he wound his fingers tighter in her hair, careful not to hurt her. "What happens then?"

"I don't know. She…she's stronger than me without this drug in us. And when we fight, it gives us these awful fits, and I don't…" A helpless shrug. "I don't know, Elias."

The confession cost her. He could see it in the slump of her shoulders, in the way she tried to avoid his gaze while she whispered it. Soren was not one used to being the weaker of any pair.

"I will find a way to get her out," he rasped. "No matter what it takes."

Her gaze flicked up to his. "It might take my death."

Promises came to life and died on the tip of his tongue as he absorbed that reminder—and the bleakness lurking behind it.

"I don't believe that," he said finally. "You've already survived well beyond what anyone thought was possible."

"Exactly. I don't…" Her voice wobbled, and she scrubbed her palms over her face, avoiding his gaze as moisture fell like a shield over her eyes. Like she was ashamed. Like she couldn't bear to look him in the eye as she admitted, "I don't know how much more impossible I have in me."

Elias tightened his hold on her. "You were ready to go to the ends of the earth to cure me," he whispered, brushing a tear from the corner of her eye before it could fall. "Let it be my turn. Let me give you a miracle."

"You're miracle enough."

"I need you to stop talking like this is our goodbye."

"But we're getting *really* good at them."

"Don't," he whispered—frayed, terrified, so far past pride that he would beg without reservation if she required it. "Don't leave me. Don't, don't, please, don't leave me—"

She reached up lightning-quick, cradling his face between her hands, pulling him down to press her brow to his. "Elias Loch. As far as it is in my power, I will *never* leave your side again."

For tonight, that was enough.

"How can I help you? What do you need?" He helped her to her feet, cursing under his breath as her legs gave way. He scooped her up before she could protest against it, the slip of her body unfamiliar to his arms. She'd lost so much of herself that she barely burdened him at all, and he hated it. Hated how Anima had allowed her to waste away. Hated how her Tallisian captors had likely made it worse.

"I need you to stop acting like a fretful hen."

"Soren."

She sighed, deflating until her head came to rest on his shoulder. "I'm starving. And I need a bath. My skin's crawling. I think some spiders might have nested in my hair."

"So what you're saying is that you've finally realized your potential to be a forest hag."

"You're being so *mean* to me."

"I missed you." Even to his own ears, he sounded pathetic. Near-broken. But that was the truth of this moment, and he'd never been a talented liar. He pressed a kiss to her brow. "Let's get you that bath."

"That's a very roundabout way of asking me to get naked," she mumbled into his shirt, and he started laughing so hard that the weeping began all over again.

# CHAPTER 8

# RAQUEL

Sleep did not come easily that evening.

Once Finn left to settle in his own quarters—after an extended silence from Kallias that left both her and the younger Atlas brother on edge, even while they chatted strategy—Kallias had ducked into the bathing room, muttering something about needing a moment.

Which left her to choose which side of the bed she wanted to claim.

Tempest was punishing her for daring to stand against him. That had to be it. In no other world would she have ended up forced to share a bed with Kallias Atlas.

The right side was closer to the door—if anyone came in to attack or otherwise, they would reach that side first.

She tossed her pack on the left side.

Once she heard the faucet in the bathing room turn on—a promise that Kallias would be busy for at least the next thirty seconds—she made quick work of undressing, digging her one pair of sleepclothes out of her pack. The soft knit pants—dove gray, cuffed at the ankles—were one of two things left in her pack that didn't smell of campfire or the mildewy scent of damp that had crept in over the weeks traveling through inclement weather.

The other was the shirt she'd borrowed from Kallias after injuring her ribs in Artem.

She hadn't quite forgiven Elias Loch for handing her one of the Atlas prince's shirts to wear instead of one of his own. He'd sworn up and down it had been a simple mistake, an absentminded slip of his hand into the wrong pack. But she knew the keen edge in his eyes when she saw it—a pinch of mischief left behind by his half-feral goblin of a battlemate.

Bastard. She would have punched him if he hadn't already been punishing himself for sins not his to bear.

She fingered the cloth, silently considering.

It was either hope that Kallias didn't notice the shirt was familiar—and two sizes too big—or wake up smelling like mold for her next meeting with Aeris.

Damn it all. She put on the shirt.

By the time he came back out wearing his own sleepclothes, the front strands of his hair a bit damp at the ends, she'd claimed her side of the bed. It took effort to smother a smirk, to keep her eyes down while she sensed him taking in the right side of the bed, stripped to sheets—and to the left side, where she'd bundled all three woolen blankets around herself.

*Your move, Atlas.*

He cleared his throat. She looked up, expecting to see the scowl he always tried to stitch together with politeness, but instead found his eyes fixed on her torso, a slight glaze to them.

"You still have that?" he asked, slowly leaning against the doorframe, the old wood creaking beneath his bicep.

She hated the way he was looking at her. It set her face aflame. "There was never a good time to give it back."

"Keep it. It suits you."

Gods, he needed to stop looking at her. "Not going to complain about the blankets?"

He shrugged lightly, using one hand to play with the ends of his hair. "I haven't been using them anyway. Better that you don't get cold."

Unbearable. That was what he was—*unbearable.* "Gods, Atlas, doesn't anything set you off?"

The corner of his mouth twitched, and she nearly shivered at the darkening of his gaze—not an unpleasant darkness. The kind that made good starwatching weather. The kind that let the light in. "I think you know the answer to that."

Her fist tightened over the blankets. "Why are you looking at me like that?"

"Like what?"

*Like you're enjoying the view.* "Just get in bed."

His smile struck outward into a grin, but he didn't say a word—and thank the gods for that. He simply crossed the room and sat down on his side of the bed, tugging out the leather binding his braid and shaking it out, his hair cascading down his back like a waterfall of copper and gold.

Three blankets was too much. She could barely breathe beneath their weight.

She tossed one blanket to Kallias, but he offered it back. So instead she bundled it up and shoved it between them.

"This is my kingdom," she said, circling her finger over her half of the bed before switching to his. "This is your kingdom. And this," she patted the rolled-up blanket for emphasis, "is the border."

Kallias's eyes narrowed in amusement. "And let me guess—no crossing the border?"

"Not unless someone wishes to lose the limb that crosses it."

The amusement fled, replaced with fear. "Understood."

Still, even with that barrier between them, even after the lamp was put out and he'd long since fallen asleep, his closeness was…distracting.

*What am I, Raquel?* The question he'd asked with barely an inch of space between them in an Artem infirmary, his thumbs brushing her hips, his breath tasting of winter and mint. Salt and summer.

*You are my enemy, my mission, the murderer of my sister. I swore an oath to end you.*

*You are a king with no kingdom. A brother with no sisters. You ran into fire to save my life. I think I dreamed about you last night.*

Despite all her dire warnings, his arm fell across the blanket as he turned over, his face slack and smooth in sleep. His hand brushed hers once. Again. Lightning striking twice.

*You're beautiful.* The last words he said before crumpling in their borrowed Artem chamber, his eyes rolling into his head, nothing but dead weight in her arms.

His chest falling still.

His heart stopping beneath her hands, halted by a poison she could not cure.

She'd thought he was dead.

*You're beautiful.*

She hadn't wanted him to be dead.

She rolled onto her back, hugging her blankets to her chest, scowling at the ceiling.

Sleep had never been a giving bedfellow for her. Tonight didn't look like it was going to be any different.

"Raquel?" The hand that had brushed against her fingers now settled on her shoulder. Kallias peeked up above the blanket wall, groggy concern etched in every frown line. Stray strands of reddish hair framed his face, catching in his beard. "Are you all right?"

"Not your business."

Not even a flinch. He only blinked at her. "You look upset."

"Then stop looking." Gods, what was with him and his need to *fix* everything?

Despite her tone—the knife-sharp hiss that usually made just about everyone tuck tail and run—his gaze never wavered. She was about to snap at him to *stop gawking at me, gods, Atlas*—but then she saw the glassiness of his gaze. The slight parting of his lips. The way his eyelids bobbed a bit, like they were fighting to close.

He wasn't awake, not truly—just enough to ask questions, it seemed.

Her rage guttered out with alarming speed. She gentled her next words— aggression might only draw him further to wakefulness, and then there'd be no getting any peace, because he'd push and push and push until something broke. He was good at that. "Go back to sleep. Everything's all right."

His eyelids sank obediently, but he fought to hold his head up, squinting at her with innocent worry pinching his mouth. "Are you sure? Do you need me?"

Her heart spasmed. "I'm sure." Taking his hand off her shoulder, she gently guided it back across the blanket barrier, settling it against his chest. "You can sleep."

His eyes finally sank shut, but his hand flexed around hers, pinning it over his heart. "Wake me if…" he mumbled, but the rest of his words were lost to the slur of sleep, quickly followed by a rattling snore.

There was nothing wrong with her that he could help. Some things couldn't be fixed. Some people had to cross kingdoms to save someone who'd wronged them. Some people had already lost everything they had to lose.

Some sisters didn't come back from the dead.

*Jira's youthful face contorted in fury, in desperation, her hands wrapped around Raquel's wrists like manacles. "You can't go back there. I won't let you go back there!"*

*She tore her hands away before her power could sizzle from her fingertips to her little sister's arms, folding them beneath her biceps. She took a step back. Another when Jira tried to close the gap. "It's my home."*

*"I'm your home. You promised me you wouldn't let them have you. What happened, Kel? What did they do to you?"*

*Raquel gritted her teeth. "They gave me a purpose. I'm not disposable to them. Unlike you all, they would never give me away."*

*She practically heard Jira's heart crack. The younger girl stepped back now, her lips pressed tight, quivering against each other. "I didn't give you away. I want you to come home."*

*Raquel turned away, closing her fists, relishing the buzz of storm-static just beneath her skin.*

*"Skyhaven is my home," she said. "Skyhaven is my family."*

Some mistakes couldn't be undone.

And this…this was another one of those mistakes.

But she fell asleep with her hand pressed against Kallias's heart, its rhythm a quiet certainty that soothed her into dreamless darkness.

# CHAPTER 9

# KALLIAS

Kallias was used to rising with the sun. It was a favorite morning ritual of his to slip out in his wetsuit before the palace truly woke up, following the path the dawn laid out for him in rays of gold, the taste of ocean spray and the chill of the morning waves a better wake-up call than any coffee could manage.

But this morning, it wasn't the sun that woke him.

It was the brush of warm breath against his chest. The weight of an arm draped over his waist. Ridges of scarred skin pressed against his shirt.

He opened his eyes to *her*.

Raquel's head was resting over his heart, her arm slung over him, every hard and angry line of her face softened in sleep. The morning sun filtered through the window of their room, the light drawing out the blue buried in the blackness of her hair. His stolen shirt had slipped off of one of her shoulders and climbed up her ribs, baring more scars that slashed across her deep brown skin and stretch marks that streaked across her muscled abdomen like bolts of lightning.

He couldn't move. Honestly, he was afraid to even breathe.

She was so beautiful it *hurt*.

This wasn't fair. It was hard enough to control his feelings when she was threatening him with a blade or scowling at him over a campfire. What in the depths was he supposed to do with her head nestled against his chest and her hand draped across the small of his back, sending pins and needles dancing up his spine?

Torture. This was worse than any injury he'd borne yet, either by blade or by speech.

Torture, to *feel* like this for someone who hated him. Who, if she had been conscious, would have likely shoved her knee into his groin and done her best to carry out the threat she'd delivered seamlessly last night: *"Not unless someone wishes to lose the limb that crosses it."*

But she was the one who'd crossed over, in the end. And as selfish as it was, as *dangerous* as it was…he wasn't ready for her to wake just yet. Wasn't ready to lose the sight of her sleeping so peacefully, not even a snore interrupting her slumber, her hair bunched up in seaweed tangles against his shoulder.

Her wearing *his* shirt.

He could not have this. Could *never* have this. He had given up his title to save his kingdom, but he still intended to go back—*needed* to go back. Atlas was his home, and Nyx was hers.

But he could pretend. Just for one more minute.

Maybe two.

The sunlight playing with her hair lured his fingers in like an angler's light drawing in prey, a strand of vivid ultramarine streaking like a stray lightning bolt across her forehead and over her eyelids. Lightly, so lightly he barely felt it, he brushed that strand out of her eyes, tucking it back into the rest of her unbound hair.

When his hand passed in front of her eyes, they opened.

Kallias flinched, waiting for the blow, the shout, the hatred that would leave behind yet another scar on his mangled, tired heart.

But none of it came.

She did pull away with haste, but she didn't leave the bed—she only bundled herself up in her own blankets, pinning her arms to her chest. She rubbed at her eyes, avoiding his gaze. "Sorry. I must've been tossing in my sleep."

"It's fine. I only just woke, anyway." A half-lie, but it might help her save face. "How did you sleep?"

"Deeply, apparently." Gods save him, was that a joke? A smile curling across her mouth? "You?"

"The same, I think." And that was even more of a surprise. It felt like an eternity since he'd slept without nightmares. "What time are we meant to meet Aeris?"

"After breakfast, he said." Raquel twisted away from him to peer at the clock on the wall. "We have some time. The villagers will be gathering to eat in about an hour."

"Does that mean we have time for you to finally explain what he'll be doing to me?"

He'd asked the question before, multiple times, and she'd deftly dodged it, claiming it was too long of a story or that she couldn't be sure the process would be the same. But if he had to guess—especially judging by how she curled inward this time, shielding herself without a threat nearby—she was actually avoiding reliving what they'd done to her.

He'd tried to respect that. And he hated to force her, but they were out of time. He needed to know.

She took a deep breath, holding it for so long that she probably could've made a great diver if she'd ever been so inclined. But finally she let it out, rolling back over to face him.

He nearly shivered at the look on her face.

"It's been a long time," she began, "and it was…a different situation with me. They took my magic away as a punishment."

His blood ran cold—well, colder—and he leaned a bit closer. "Punishment for what?"

Her smile was bitter, angry, but beneath it…guilt lurked in the shadows of her gaze. "For loving Tempest too much."

"I don't understand." This whole community worshipped Tempest. What could there have been to punish?

"Since long before I came to Skyhaven as a girl, there was a legend…a prophecy, of sorts, left to them by an Occassio-blessed seer who passed through when Stormspeaker Caelum was just a boy. The seer claimed one of Skyhaven's blessed would be chosen as Tempest's favored warrior—something similar to what Elias is to Mortem. Not a host, necessarily, but someone who bore an extra blessing. And by the time I was growing up here, everyone knew it would be Aeris. He was twice-blessed, he was the Stormspeaker's son, he was…brilliant. And I…worshipped him. I loved him." She said the word *love* like a dirty sailor's curse. "We planned to get married once the prophecy came to pass. We were the most powerful below the Stormspeaker himself…Caelum didn't play favorites publicly with anyone who wasn't his son, but privately, he treated me as a daughter. He was thrilled when Aeris shared that he'd proposed to me. A perfect union, he said, to strengthen Skyhaven. To please Tempest." Raquel laughed, a quiet thing filled to the brim with pain, with scorn. "But when the day came, we all gathered in the sanctuary at the prophesied time, and…Tempest didn't choose Aeris. He chose *me*.

"I was an aeromancer—a wielder of storm magic—and an aquamancer. When Tempest blessed me, the strength of my magic…it increased tenfold. Lightning struck the fountain. The thunder from my storm shook the world." Wistfulness clouded Raquel's natural eye, and she reached up to tap on the glass one. "And my right eye was ringed with gold around the iris. We don't have a name for it here, but in Artem they call it—"

"A goddess eye," Kallias finished softly. Awe tingled in his fingers, but unease was right beside it. He already knew the end to this story couldn't be good.

"The Stormspeaker was…furious. I thought he would be proud." Raquel's voice broke on another dark laugh. "He claimed it was a mistake, that I'd stolen what was rightfully Aeris's, and that they would force it out of me if I didn't give it up. When I told him I didn't know how, they pinned me down and…and they ripped it from me. Tempest's blessing—not just the new power, but *all* of it. They took my eye, and with it went my new blessing. They did something else…I'm still not sure what, but when I opened my eyes afterward, all my magic was gone. All of it." A flex of her fist. "They whipped me as a final punishment and tossed me into the forest to find my own way out…or to die trying. Aeris didn't hold the whip, but…he didn't stop them, either. He turned his back on me while I screamed for help."

Kallias's vision went white.

Ruthlessness was not something he engaged in. But taking in Raquel's scars with new eyes, something began to hum beneath his skin, a crackling flurry of ice and lightning that froze the marrow in his bones. Changed his leaning from mercy to murder.

Raquel Angelov, proud and angry and more likely to fall on her own sword than let go of a grudge, had faced her tormenters with her head held high, her weapons sheathed, and had asked them for *help*.

For *him*.

"Say the word," he said calmly, "and he's dead."

A barking laugh, and she rolled away from him, her tangled hair swinging downward, covering the jagged scars carved into her back. Scars he'd always assumed came from war or a training accident or an animal attack—not her own people. Not her own *family*. "That's the first thing on your mind? Not what that means for you? Just because they aren't punishing you doesn't mean—"

He grabbed her shoulder and turned her back over, catching her cheek with his hand. "Say the word," he repeated, stroking his thumb over one of the scars below her glass eye, "and he is *dead*."

She blinked at him, dark eyes wide.

He dropped his hand, a flush blooming so deeply through his cheeks that he almost felt feverish. "Sorry. I'm sorry, I shouldn't have—"

She grabbed his face with both hands, and before he could figure out if he was being attacked or not, her mouth collided with his.

The entire world shifted around him to make room for a new impossibility made truth:

Raquel Angelov was kissing him.

*Kissing* him.

Kissing *him*.

His frozen bones thawed, rage heating into something deeper, lower, *hungrier*. His body moved faster than his mind, tugging her closer and rolling onto his back, groaning softly against her mouth as she pinned him beneath her. She braced her legs on either side of him, her hands clawing into his hair with near-ferocious intent, and all thought of magic and murder fled beneath her touch.

"What—are you—doing?" he rasped between kisses, his head reeling with every brush of her lips. She smelled like rain and tasted like bitter chocolate, like…like danger and mistakes and that strange waxy lip balm she applied every morning. He didn't like its taste—or the stickiness it left behind on his skin—but he would actually, *genuinely* rather die than stop kissing this woman over something as petty as un-chapped lips. She could have tasted like seaweed for all he gods-damned cared.

"Something very foolish," she breathed against his mouth. "Do you want me to stop?"

A wild laugh. He shook his head emphatically. "Oh, *gods* no."

There were a million reasons why his answer should have been yes. His kingdom. His family. The fact that he was about to march off to be tortured. The fact that only a handful of weeks ago, she'd held a knife to his neck and promised she was the harbinger of his soon-coming death.

But the reason for saying *no* was greater than any of those:

Kallias Atlas had never made a selfish choice.

And if there was one thing in this world worth being selfish with, it might just be her.

This was just like his nightmares, trapped in the center of a storm, ice and lightning colliding as he drowned in a flood of his own making. But it didn't frighten him now—no, every spark that burned between their lips only honed his thirst, his hunger, and he couldn't kiss her deeply enough, couldn't pull her close enough, couldn't—

A sharp gasp.

Raquel jerked back from him, her features contorted in pain, and it took him two heartbeats too long to realize what had happened. He reached out for her, concern replacing craving. "Are you—"

His voice died on his tongue as he took in the sight of his own hands—hands tipped in frozen talons, crystalline ice tipped in vivid, sickening red.

Blood.

Raquel's blood.

She moved her hand to cover her shoulder, but it was too late—he'd already seen the bloody furrows clawed into her back. Over those old scars these people had dealt her.

Nausea churned his stomach into a whirlpool, and he shoved himself back, nearly tumbling off the bed before righting himself. The frozen tips of his fingers caught on the sheets, shredding the edges to strips, and he shook them off, shame and horror curdling in his veins. "I'm so sorry. I—Raquel, I swear to the gods, I didn't mean to—"

"It's all right," she said quickly. It wasn't. He knew it wasn't, because she held herself turned away from him, the heated passion in her eyes vanishing behind a wall of ice. "It happens, Kallias. Magic can be—"

He couldn't stand the look in her eyes. Couldn't stand the fact that he'd *earned* it this time.

Couldn't stand the reminder that he'd seen it before, in brown eyes instead of black, in a little boy's horrified face instead of her stoic one.

Selfishness. There was a reason he'd never allowed himself to indulge in it before.

For one moment of irrational hope, he'd forgotten that.

He would never forget it again.

"Aeris is expecting us," he choked, snatching up whatever shirt his hands touched first and tugging it on, ignoring how the ice-talons scraped against his skin. Pain for pain. It only seemed fair. "We need to go."

The pity in her voice was unbearable. His hands ached to tear his own ears, to ruin them so he could never hear it again. "Kallias—"

"Don't." Raw. Angry. Sorry. He didn't know which tone won out in the end, but all of them held equal sway in his parched throat. "I want this damned magic out of me. *Now.*"

He didn't wait for her. He walked out and shoved the door shut behind him, raking his nails down the wood until the ice finally shattered, leaving his fingertips bloody and numb, peppered with splinters. His breath came in ragged huffs, and even that felt cold, winter wind that blew in from his own lungs.

Enough of this. He'd allowed himself the luxury of pretending he could handle the burden of being chosen, special, for far too long.

Kallias Atlas was born to be forgotten—a spare heir in case true disaster stole both his sisters, a bit of currency meant to be spent on Atlas's safety, a body built to house someone greater than he could ever be.

The only thing he'd ever truly been allowed to choose was the manner of his sacrifice. And he was choosing this.

*It doesn't have to be this way.* One of those errant drafts that always seemed to lurk in this building whispered in his ear with Tempest's voice. *Ridding yourself of my blessing may doom your kingdom. I can save them.*

"I don't trust you," he muttered.

*I've never been anything less than honest with you, Prince. You know I want a body. You know I'll promise you anything to get it. But you also know that unlike my siblings, I keep my promises. Your brother is alive, isn't he?*

Alive, yes—scarred, tormented, but alive.

When he didn't answer, Tempest sighed, a sound like the wind rustling the trees. *Think on it quickly, Prince. Once you make this choice, there's very little that can reverse it.*

Kallias shook his head violently until the breeze tickling his ear vanished. And once silence was his only companion, he marched forward alone, clenching his fists at his sides.

It didn't matter what it cost him, how much it hurt, how much he regretted it afterward. The people he loved would *never* suffer by his own hand again.

Right as he passed the door of Finn's borrowed room, it opened, revealing his tired-eyed, apparently multi-talented brother.

Speaking of those who'd suffered at his hand.

They both stopped in their tracks, mouths opening and closing as they silently decided who would speak first. So instead of speaking, Kallias simply jerked his head toward the exit, a silent command: *It's time.*

Finn shut his mouth. His jaw flexed, but he only nodded in return, ducking back into his room and shutting the door. They couldn't be seen leaving at the same time, after all.

Aeris was waiting in the sitting room of the common house for him, looking as though he'd just come in from outside; though his pale skin didn't show even a hint of blood-flush, snowflakes clung to his long lashes, and he wore a cloak fashioned from pure white fur. It jutted out at the shoulders—presumably to make them look broader—and ended just shy of the floor. He turned to face Kallias the moment he exited the hall, putting on that perfect-host smile…though Kallias could've sworn the ice didn't thaw from his eyes. "Ready, Prince?"

"As I'll ever be."

Despite his clipped tone, Aeris's smile didn't drop. He just swept out one arm toward a hallway Raquel had warned them against exploring, though the haunted look she'd cast its way had been enough to sate any curiosity Kallias might have had, anyway. "Shall we?"

The cord wasn't wrapped around his neck.

Very rarely did Kallias find himself smiled upon by luck, but gods, he was grateful it had picked today to be kind to him.

The only thing left for him to do was serve as the distraction. So despite the keening of his instincts begging him to run the opposite way, Kallias followed Aeris down that hallway.

# CHAPTER 10

## SOREN

Anima was a very heavy sleeper.

Soren had never been like that. Even before the hazing in the barracks had trained her to wake at the slightest shift in the tension of a floorboard or the faintest breath exhaled from a mischief-maker's lips, she'd only ever stepped one foot into the depths of sleep. As a child, it had been because she couldn't wait to wake to surf with her family in the mornings. When she arrived in Nyx, it was because the nightmares hiding in the deeper tides of sleep were too much for her healing mind to bear. And now…

Now, sitting on a stool in the guardhouse's simple bathing room, she was more afraid to close her eyes than she'd ever been, even though the smell of lavender and the steam of hot water threatened to drag her under anyway. There was every chance she would open her eyes again to find her body no longer obeyed her commands.

"Well, it's not exactly the royal bathhouse, but it'll have to do," said Elias, sweat tracing a path down his temple as he crouched with one hand submerged in the ceramic bath, his ebony hair glued in unwashed clumps over his forehead. Now that the rush of reunion had faded, she could see the lingering signs of grief etched in sharp relief across his body…the cheekbones that had yet to fill out since his recovery from his illness, the way he kept raising his head to look at her with something like confused dread, the way his hand shook as he trailed fire-tipped fingers through the snowmelt-water to heat it.

The new tattoo branded into his chest; a braided cord that no longer hung from his hair.

He wasn't any more all right than she was. And in some strange way, though she hated it, it was also…comforting. To know she wasn't alone. To know this experience had sculpted them both into new shapes, had created new angles the other wasn't familiar with.

When she didn't speak, he looked up again, catching her gaze and holding it, anxiety thinning his lips like pressed paper. "Are you with me, smartass?"

"With you, jackass. Sorry." Even her apology didn't sound right. She'd never offered him a *sorry* packed with that much sincerity. She got up, took one step toward the bath—

And her body folded beneath her.

A cry of anguish, of *anger,* ravaged her throat as her knees jammed painfully into the splinter-laden bathing room's floor, and as punishment, she drove her fists down into the floor alongside them. Again. Again. Again—

"Soren!" Elias's knees knocked against hers as he fell down before her, catching her bleeding fists and clutching them to his bare chest. "Soren, stop, *stop.* It's—"

"It's not okay! Don't you gods-damned dare say it's *okay,* jackass, I can't—" A huff of rage convulsed into a sob of shame, and she thrust her stinging fists into his chest. "I can't even gods-damned *walk.*"

Anima had taken weeks, *months,* of her life. Had taken her agency, her strength, her *mind.* And now…now what? Her dignity, too?

"Hey." Elias released her hands to reach for her, then paused, his fingertips hovering an inch away from her face. With her nodded permission, he gently slid his hands into her hair, cradling her head between his palms, pressing his forehead to hers. He looked into her eyes as he stroked his fingers through her hair. "No one is mocking you. No one is laughing at you. This does not make you weak. You endured something no one has ever survived before. You are the strongest of us, smartass, and I'm not about to let you forget it. Understood?"

For once, she didn't make a joke or a comment soaked in sarcasm. She only nodded against his forehead, squeezing her eyes shut. A soft, pained sound escaped Elias when a tear trickled down her cheek, and he pulled her against him, pressing careful kisses across the crown of her head. A shuddering sob trembled through her shoulders.

"This," she rasped, "was not how I imagined being naked in front of you for the first time."

A laugh barked out of him. "And, she's back."

She laughed too—a smaller, shakier thing than she was used to—but she felt able to smile again, and that was enough. That was everything.

"Let me help you," Elias whispered. "You know that it never leaves this room."

She swallowed against the lump trying to block off her breath. Then, finally, she whispered, "Can you wash my hair?"

He nodded. "Absolutely."

"You could use it too, honestly." She had to take back *some* dignity here, after all. "Your hair looks like you fried it in an oil vat."

"That's a very roundabout way of asking me to get naked."

This time her grin stretched so far it actually hurt. "I know."

He chuckled, sweeping her up and lowering her into the bath. At first the water felt blistering, heat searing so deep beneath her skin that even her bones cringed, but after a moment it began to soothe rather than scald. Her aching muscles released, and she sank deeper in until the surface of the water barely lapped at the bottom of her chin.

She didn't see Elias get in—her eyelids were too heavy, coaxed to rest by the mollifying scent of whatever lavender oil Elias had dug out of the cupboard and the warmth easing the tension from her muscles—but she felt it, his legs sliding into place between and beside hers, a sort of staggered arrangement that made enough room for all four limbs. The water surged and receded, the overflow spattering to the floor as Elias awkwardly adjusted his posture to make himself comfortable while giving her as much *proper* space as he could.

When she opened her eyes, she found him with his muscular biceps propped against the ceramic sides of the bath, his limbs traced with scars and tattoos both new and old, his black eyes focused on her with such intensity that it almost shoved her breath back down into the depths of her lungs.

He'd left his undershorts on, and she would've laughed if she had any energy left. Modesty felt like a luxury from a time that had long since passed for her.

"Talk to me," he croaked. "You're so quiet."

A snort huffed out of her nostrils. "I don't think you've ever had to ask me to talk before."

"Exactly why I'm worried."

Well, it might have been easier to muster her usual flood of words if she wasn't so busy trying to ignore that ring dangling beside two bits of cloth and a blackened feather over his heart, a reminder of confessions traded on the cusp of a deathbed bargain. She wasn't even sure if he *remembered* what he'd said to her that day.

*I was going to ask you to marry me.*

"I don't know what to say," she admitted.

"I didn't think I'd ever see the day when Soren Nyx was speechless."

"Atlas."

A pause. Then: "Sorry?"

She winced. That wasn't how she'd meant to bring it up. "I…I want to be called Soren still, but…Atlas. Soren Marina Atlas. A bit of both."

He gazed at her for a long moment, and she found she couldn't breathe—not until he finally blinked, and to her surprise, a small smile played on his lips. "Kallias is going to weep when he hears."

Hearing her brother's name come so casually from Elias's mouth…that was another marvel. "Where…where is Kallias? And Finn?"

It was a question she was afraid to ask—now that she'd remembered them, remembered Soleil's love for them, their loss would not be as easy to bear as it might have been before. The mystery of their absence was a thorn she had to pluck before she could truly feel at ease again.

"Honestly, I'm not sure." Elias frowned, scrubbing a hand over his bearded face. "Raquel said she knew a place where they could spare Kal his Tempest-blessing, but she wouldn't say where. All I know is that we're supposed to meet them in Ursa—and if we miss them there, we head to Sirena."

*Sirena.* Splotches of color spattered against the canvas of her memory, painting a muddled memory of vine-wrapped trellises and plucking flowers from the lower boughs of trees while Kallias carried her through the town on his shoulders. "Why Sirena?"

"Best place to charter a private ship to Arborius."

Elias kept talking, explaining something about relics and trying to stay ahead of Tenebrae, but Soren's mind was stuck on Arborius. On hazy memories of trees taller than the Atlas palace and a gaggle of wild, bow-wielding, tree-climbing cousins.

Wolf. Sage. Brook. Sparrow. Oak. Juniper. Nutmeg. Seven princes and princesses she only barely remembered playing with during their sparse visits to Atlas, Sage most of all; her older cousin had taken great joy in showing her the "notes" he took during the meetings his parents subjected him to, notes that were actually sketches done in a special kind of ink that only appeared when it was viewed in the dark. Sage was a talented artist, but for those sketches, he always skewed things on purpose—giving particularly snotty nobles ridiculously inflated features that never failed to make her giggle until she lost all her breath. He was also the one who'd taught Finn sleight of hand, card tricks, little bits of magic that relied on fooling the eyes of others.

"They probably still think I'm dead," Soren said out loud, not realizing she'd interrupted Elias until he frowned at her, confused.

"Who?"

"My cousins. My aunt and uncle." King Cypress and Queen Genevieve, the royals she'd planned to entreat for Elias's cure—her *aunt* and *uncle*.

A chill ran down her spine that even the warmth of the bath couldn't touch. Had she succeeded in convincing Enna to let her make the trip, her true identity might still have been discovered—if they'd looked at her and seen the same features that had stopped Kallias in his killing tracks, if even one of her relatives had dared to point out her odd resemblance to the Atlas family, she would have ended up in Atlas's palace anyway

Perhaps destiny was unavoidable. Perhaps all paths would have eventually led her home.

Perhaps that resemblance was why Enna had refused her request in the first place.

Silence fell between them for a moment, and she hated that she couldn't read the expression on his face. Hated that she didn't recognize it.

Then: "Come here. Let's get your hair clean."

This wasn't the first time they'd bathed together; the barracks bathhouse wasn't exactly private, and whole companies often had to take turns bathing to make the most efficient use of the hot water. But it was the first time they'd been alone, the first time it hadn't been dim to the point of rendering every single body to the barest streaks of charcoal shadows against weak torchlight; still, Elias was ever the gentleman, and his gaze hadn't once strayed below her eyes. Hadn't once tried to snatch a peek beneath the froth of soap-clouded water.

She couldn't help but smile as she carefully twisted to let her back face him, gathering her tangled curls and tossing them over her shoulder. By the time she finished readjusting her position, her arms were shaking; even if she'd wanted to keep space between them, she couldn't have held herself up. Cursing quietly, she leaned back against his chest, squeezing her eyes shut. Maybe if she didn't look at him, he wouldn't see the shame, the anger, the—

Fingers gently snagged her chin, coaxing her head upward. "Look at me, smartass."

She swallowed. Opened her eyes to find a starless sky gazing back, one pupil outlined in a halo of golden fire.

"It's just me," he reminded her, pressing his lips between her brows, trailing his fingertips down the damp hollow of her throat. "Just you and me."

Goosebumps broke out across her skin. "I know, jackass."

"You've seen me far weaker than this."

"I *know*." But that didn't make it any easier.

"Let me take care of you," he said, and there was a rasp to his voice that guttered her shame. A hint of pleading she didn't often hear from her battlemate. "Please."

Maybe this wasn't a burden to him at all. Maybe it was a balm, to be able to help her now when he couldn't before.

So she nodded, easing back against his bare chest and letting her eyes close, a shaky sigh winding free from her throat as his fingers began to comb through her hair, loosening each tangle with the patience of a saint. And when he started vigorously scrubbing that same lavender soap into her hair, that sigh became a relieved moan that towed itself up from her very core.

Elias tensed behind her. Took one long, slow breath before he went back to his ministrations.

She bit down on a grin. "You good back there?"

"Shut up," he said.

"If I'd known it was that easy to rile you—"

"*Stop*," he pleaded, the heat of embarrassment flushing across his skin almost tangible…and another kind of heat, the kind that added a huskiness to his voice and threatened to shred apart what remained of her self-control, weakness and fatigue be damned.

"I thought you wanted me to be mean."

"Not like *that*. Not now. You need to take it easy."

*Now might be all we get,* she thought, but she didn't say it. That thought would only have set him shaking again, and she didn't want to ruin this.

It was over before she was ready. Despite her best efforts, she drifted in and out of dozing while Elias scrubbed every trace of oil and dirt and blood from her scalp, only waking in truth when he roused her to rinse and dry off. After that, he helped her dress in one of his spare shirts and settled her on the creaky bed before dressing himself, and she nestled her cheek into the pillow while she allowed herself the guilty pleasure of watching the muscles within those broad shoulders ripple as he tugged a shirt on over them.

She'd forgotten how strong he truly was without Viper venom gnawing away at his body. It wasn't an unpleasant reminder.

He turned back to her, mouth open to speak, and she watched as his entire body stuttered partway through the movement. His fingers stilled on the buttons of his shirt, and he stared at her as if struck stupid.

"What?" she demanded.

His eyes glazed over. "I've had this dream before." He shook his head, swallowing thickly, his hands dropping to twist the hem of his shirt. "If I wake up back in that tent, I think it might just kill me."

"Elias," she whispered, pushing herself up and reaching out for him, "tell me how I can help."

"I don't know. Gods, I...I don't know, smartass. This can't be real." But he came to sit beside her anyway, his expression contorted with a terror more vulnerable than any she'd seen from him before. "I can't shake it."

"I have an idea," she said. A bad one, maybe, but she'd had plenty of those, and they always seemed to work well enough.

"And what's that?"

Now or never.

She swung herself around, forcing every ounce of strength she had left into pulling herself to sit in Elias's lap, wrapping her legs around his hips and her arms around his neck, leaning close enough that she heard the hitch of his breath.

"If you don't kiss me now, jackass," she breathed, "I will never give you another chance."

# CHAPTER 11

## ELIAS

This might truly be the end of Elias Loch.

"If you don't kiss me now, jackass," Soren breathed, "I will never give you another chance."

He held her gaze, wavering between the two halves of him: the one who knew he was unworthy of her and the one who wanted her so desperately that her nearness was driving him to madness.

The one that was afraid to lose her again, and the one that loved her so much it was killing him to try and be noble about this.

"Don't say that unless you mean it, smartass." One last chance for her to change her mind. One last chance for things to go back to normal, for them to be best friends and let that be enough.

And he would. If she said the word, he step away from this and never come back to it.

He would not hold her to confessions offered to a dying man.

Soren's grin faltered. The gleam in her eyes changed, became a mirror held up to him, reflecting his own longing. Her teeth worried her bottom lip, and heat flooded his core so suddenly that if he'd been standing, he would have buckled before her.

As if that was anything new. She could bring him to his knees with a single look whenever she liked. But this...

If she cut him down now, he wasn't sure he'd ever find a way to stand again.

"Elias," she said, "*please* kiss me."

Her *please* snapped that last tether on his self-control.

He gripped her beneath her thighs and shifted with her, flipping over and pushing until her back was pressed to the headboard of the bed. He released her to brace his hands on either side of her head, slamming his palms into the headboard, and she tipped her chin up to meet him as he claimed her mouth with his.

This kiss was not resentment and whiskey and secret curiosity. This kiss was not dare-born or long-forgotten. This kiss was years late and hungry, so godsdamned *hungry*, a lost-and-found kiss, an *I'm sorry, smartass* and *you're forgiven, jackass* and *I love you, I love you, I love you.*

It wasn't until she breathed those three words back to him that he realized he'd said them first, a litany of prayers punctuating every kiss, making up for every time he hadn't said it the way he ought to, making up for every missed confession.

Between every breath, between every kiss, between every scrape of teeth and tongue and hands wandering where they'd never dared to before. *I love you, I love you, I love you.*

Soren laughed against his lips, a feral, wicked thing, and wrapped her arms around his neck, stretching upward to claim his mouth again. He dropped his hands back down, bracing her thighs as her mouth explored his lips, his jaw, his neck—

A low moan escaped his throat, and Soren's lips froze there, right over the place where his pulse thrummed. Slowly, too slowly, she lifted her head, blinking at him owlishly.

Fearing that he'd done something wrong, Elias started loosening his grip. "What?"

But she clung on tighter. That awful, beautiful grin spread across her face, the one that had taunted him his first day in the barracks and had absolutely ruined him every day since. "Elias Loch, did you just *moan?*"

Fire flashed up the column of his neck. "Shut up."

Soren threw her head back and cackled. "You did! How does Mortem feel about that, hm? Doesn't seem too holy to me—"

Elias caught her chin and tugged her head back down, giving her his very best glare. "Are you going to shut that mouth so I can go back to kissing it, or are you going to keep being a smartass?"

Soren's nose crinkled with the force of her grin. "I don't see why I can't do both, jackass."

"I will push you off this bed," he said.

"You will not."

"I will. Right on your ass."

"But then I would tug you down by your ankles, and then we'd both be on the floor, all bruised up, and somehow I think that would ruin the mood."

"I love you," he said.

"I know that," she said.

"*Soren.*" Her name came out with all the pleading reverence of a dying man's last word.

Soren laughed again, breathless, and leaned in to steal his breath for her own. "I love you too," she murmured into the kiss. "And as long as we're discussing it, perhaps we should lay some ground rules."

"Oh?" It was incredibly difficult to think in this particular position. "Like what?"

"Mmm..." she lowered her mouth to his neck again, and he held his breath to keep from embarrassing himself a second time. "Like blanket-sharing rules. And sock-borrowing rules."

Desire twined hands with annoyance, and he pinched her thigh until she yelped. "Keep your damn thieving hands off my socks."

"Hey, now! That doesn't seem fair. Relationships are about compromise. Give and take."

"Right. And I'm *giving* you one last chance to stop *taking* my things."

She laughed against his neck. "Never."

And it hit him all at once—that she was here, that she was alive, that she loved him—she *loved him*, and he didn't have to pretend, didn't have to dance around the truth anymore.

Joy thrilled through him, and he simply tightened his arms around her, burying his face against her hair.

"All right," he rasped. "All right. Whatever you want."

"I'll share my brassieres, if you need reciprocation," Soren suggested, and if he wasn't still afraid she was going to disappear if he let her go, he really would have pushed her off.

"You're unbelievable," he groaned.

Soren's grin was nothing short of wicked. She untangled herself from his hold, taking his face and pulling it down to claim his mouth in a slow, surprisingly gentle kiss. She leaned her forehead on his again, their noses brushing, her lips hovering so close to his that he could practically taste her.

"You really do need rest," he mumbled—reminding her as much as himself.

Her mouth screwed up in a knot, and he waited, trying to think past the dizzying desire in his head and the warmth of her body settled on his.

She blinked. Frowned.

Alarm drove through him, dousing the fire flickering in his gut like a bucket of ice water. "What's—"

"Shh." She pressed her finger to his lips, her gaze darting to the door— once, twice. A silent signal he understood immediately.

*We have company.*

She eased off of him, and he rolled off the bed, landing silently on his bare feet. Now that she'd drawn his attention to it, he could hear it, too—the creaking of door hinges, the thumping of booted feet.

He didn't turn when her fingers tapped on his shoulder; didn't dare, even as she leaned close to his ear and breathed, "How many?"

He paused, listening—then held up eight fingers.

Soren didn't speak again, but he could sense the unspoken curses in that silence; his ears burned anyway. Had the mercenaries snagged a Tallisian patrol for backup? If they were hunting on Princess Raini's orders...

He turned toward Soren, motioning to his discarded scythes; she swept them up and tossed them in his direction, but her strength failed them both—her aim fell short. He dove to catch the scythes, snagging the loop of the double-sheath just before they hit the floor...

But he landed too hard on his right foot.

The thud of his boot echoed in the sudden quiet below them, and he and Soren locked eyes, both of them mouthing curses—his much milder than hers.

"Hide," he mouthed to her.

She flashed him a particular finger.

"*Hide*," he hissed aloud, gesturing fiercely at the wardrobe to the left of the bed.

She flashed both hands this time, middle fingers up on each.

He gave her a meaningful once-over, eyebrow raised: *You plan on fighting with no weapon and no pants?*

She spread her fingers in a wild, fed-up shrug. *Maybe!*

He unsheathed his scythes, jerking his head so hard toward the wardrobe that his brain punched against the side of his skull. Miming like she was going to strangle him, Soren finally relented, sliding off the bed and quietly prying open the wardrobe door.

The fact that it took her a moment to climb into it—her gait unsteady, uncertain—told him all he needed to know about her ability to cover his back right now.

Luckily, he'd grown quite familiar with the sensation of fighting with no battlemate behind him.

Elias flattened his back to the wall behind the door, pressing himself flush to the stone as he listened to the footsteps making their way up the staircase to the rooms above. He palmed the hilts of his scythes, drawing in deep, steady breaths to feed the fire in his chest. Letting those flames leak from his lungs to his veins, his tattoos gradually beginning to glow, he braced himself as the door creaked open…

"Show yourself!" called a familiar voice—a voice that slammed into him with the memory of jealousy and disbelief and the sight of his battlemate tangled in another man's arms, her lips tearing away from another man's mouth to scowl at his intrusion.

It couldn't be true. It couldn't be *him*.

But Soren's sudden screech of delight as she stumbled out of the closet— as well as the sight of the man's eyes blown wide with recognition as he stepped in, his ruddy brown skin and dark hair the very reflection of Elias's, though their features were otherwise quite different—immediately confirmed the intruder's identity. His winter armor was covered in a cloak of deer hide, his recognizably Nyxian sword still extended; his face dropped in sheer shock as he took them both in.

"Rian Loch," Soren greeted his cousin with all her usual haughtiness, the exhaustion in her eyes countered by the vivid grin on her face. "Fancy meeting you here."

And he wasn't alone—disbelief melted into something that threatened to reduce even Elias to tears as familiar faces entered the room, one by one by one, each one lighting up in varying shades of joy and stunned confusion as they recognized him and Soren.

Kriss. Frigga. Varran. Samhain. Nikolai. Andrei. And bringing up the rear, cursing loudly and saying, "Mortem curse you, Rian, I keep telling you to let me take the lead, you useless…"

Soren began to cry as Jakob Petrov stepped into the room, his voice trailing off as his boots thudded to a stop, his eyes widening as he locked gazes with Elias. He, strangely, looked worse for the wear himself—there were dark spots under his eyes and healing bruises mottling his jaw, and the fact that he'd been at the back of the group rather than the front…that was strange. But when his gaze flicked from Elias to Soren, those troubled eyes softened in worry…in hope.

"Soren?" he asked, so cautiously that Elias suddenly remembered that he'd warned their captain of the goddess lurking somewhere behind her skull.

Still, his battlemate offered Jakob her broadest, most terrible grin. "Now, what are all of you and your pits-ugly faces doing oafing about all the way out here?"

The sound she made when Jakob caught her up in a lung-crushing bear hug brought Elias closer, a warning about her weakness and injury on his lips, but it seemed Jakob wasn't content to settle just for Soren—his hand shot out and gripped Elias by the coat, tugging him into the embrace with a harsh mutter of "Get in here, Pious,"—and the rest of the company followed in short order, voices raised in question or joyful shouts or accusations of scaring them half to death.

And between one heartbeat and the next, Soren and Elias were truly home.

# CHAPTER 12

# SOREN

"I'm sorry, repeat that. You were imprisoned by *who, where, for what?*"

Jakob blew out a heavy sigh, leaning back against the musty armchair he'd chosen as his seat. His pale hair was longer now than it used to be, no longer shorn to his skull—his beard was fuller, too, darker, with a hint of ginger color buried in the blond.

Once the shock of reunion had faded—and Jakob had explained that they'd been put on border duty after Enna had gotten word about the fall of Mount Igniquit, unsure if Tallis might be next—Elias had insisted they continue the conversation where Soren could rest. So while she and Jaik sat on their asses doing nothing, the others were busying themselves making the guardhouse more hospitable, Elias included. He and Samhain, Rian's green-eyed, raven-haired battlemate, were talking quietly as they built up a healthy fire, tossing amused looks toward Elias's cousin, who was helping Andrei and Nikolai prepare the rabbits they'd caught and skinned outside…and visibly struggling not to gag.

Varran was working alongside Kriss and Frigga to wash dishes and set the table in the dining area, but every time Jakob so much as shifted, he shot a warning look across the space so fiercely that even Soren felt the mental push. The order to *stay put* couldn't have been more obvious if the dark-haired, ebony-skinned man had hollered it from right beside them rather than two rooms away.

"I may have taken a matter or two into my own hands, and it may or may not have set me in the path of that pits-dwelling Second Prince," Jakob muttered, petulant and ever-scowling in Varran's direction. "A certain *den mother* has yet to forgive me for it."

Though Jakob hadn't raised his voice, Varran still shot a hand toward him in a silent but rude retort. A snort burst from Soren as she lowered herself into the chair beside Jakob, and he shifted to sit on the arm, giving her the luxury of the cushion. "I know a thing or two about that."

"Yeah, I noticed."

All was quiet between them for a moment. The venom in his voice when he spoke of Finn…it was personal, and likely earned. So she let it lie, though the hatred that flickered behind Jakob's silver gaze pinched sharply at the defensive edges of her heart. "What did he do to you?"

Jakob frowned. "The prince? Nothing by his own hand. But he certainly didn't offer much assistance when I was down in that dungeon."

Soren blinked, a memory teasing the frayed edges of the boundary between her and Anima's minds…a memory of screaming and commotion and a Nyxian man being dragged from the entrance, caught by one of the many layers of guards in place to defend Atlas's palace.

"Oh, gods," she whispered. "I was there, wasn't I?"

Jakob glanced at her. "Not *really* you, I gather. What's going on with that, by the way? A goddess in your head? That sounds pretty screwed up."

"She's…" A pause. "It's complicated."

Jakob barked out a laugh. "No, what you and Loch have going on is complicated. This is wolfshit. When Pious was here last, he told us you were dead."

That explained the silently awed—and somewhat uncomfortable—looks their company kept throwing her way. Though they were chatting with Elias as normal, she could see some of them awkwardly avoiding his gaze, or staring too closely to try and determine the origin of that strange fire in his eye.

"A lot has happened since then," she mumbled. Chaos gods, mercenary kidnappings, muscle-wrenching fits… "We're…not friends, but she was lied to. Tricked into this. I can't really tell how much of it is her fault."

No, all she knew right then was that she was a coward—justified, perhaps, in not reaching out to try and wake Anima, but a coward nonetheless. Rather than talk this out, she'd allowed the goddess to slip back into oblivion, letting her fade away just the same way Anima had done to her.

But that was not a problem to solve tonight. Not while her body was still recovering from the latest of their fits and her desperate, death-tempting trek through the woods.

"So," Jakob said, with an air of attempted innocence that didn't even come close to succeeding, "did death finally get him to do the deed, or what?"

She glanced at him out of the corner of her eye. "What do you get if I say yes?"

His teeth gleamed in the newborn firelight. "Ten silver from everyone in the company."

"Hmm. Pity I don't kiss and tell."

Jakob's face dropped. He twisted and planted his soles on the cushion so he could look her more fully in the face, an absurd urgency in the movement. "Wait. There was a kiss?"

She shut her eyes, wriggling into a more comfortable position against the back of the chair, using the wooden support buried in the upholstery to scratch an itch between her shoulder blades. "Go race a bear up a tree, Jakob."

Jakob's scrabbling attempts to leap to his feet drove his heels into her hip, and over her cursing and shoving at his back, he bellowed, "It happened! It happened!"

She balled up the blanket he'd tucked over her and lobbed it at his head; it missed by a pitifully wide margin. "Will you *shut up*?"

"Jakob, sit *down*!" Varran snapped, abandoning his work to stalk across the guardhouse and grip his battlemate by the shoulder. Despite his needled tone, he pushed at him with absolute tenderness, a hand on his shoulder and a hand on the crook of his neck. "Gods, you fool, are you trying to call the whole kingdom to us, there are still mercenaries out there—"

"It happened!" Jakob crowed again, gripping his battlemate's wrists and pressing a triumphant kiss to his cheek before spinning out of his hold, jabbing a finger at the rest of the company. "You pit-jumpers all owe me ten silvers!"

Samhain dropped the firewood she was holding, her full lips parting as she whirled on Elias. "You *kissed her*?" she demanded, at the same time Varran looked at Soren with wide eyes, mouthing, "You *kissed him*?"

Fire scorched Soren's ears, and she looked up to find Elias watching her with unreadable eyes, his teeth worrying at his lower lip.

"Of course not," she said, and everyone slumped as if she'd delivered news of some great tragedy. "You're all ridiculous."

"That's right," Elias agreed. Absurdly, her heart sank, hiding in the cage of her ribs. But before it could sink any further, Elias tossed aside his firewood and crossed the span of the living room in three strides, tugging one glove off with his teeth as he did so, that one gold-circled eye utterly blazing. "I didn't just kiss her. I let her know in no uncertain terms that I absolutely, foolishly, whole-gods-damned-heartedly *adore her*."

And with a movement so swift she couldn't have hoped to parry it if it was a blade, Elias swooped down and captured her mouth with his, a kiss so passionate and tender and *demanding* that for a moment, the world forgot it was winter. Everything was warmth and sweet and smoke as she snagged his collar and pulled him down to his knees at her side, and her smile curled into his as their company lost their gods-damned minds around them. And, after a moment, the ring of coins exchanging hands joined the tumult.

It was over before she was ready, Elias standing to his full height and throwing his hand around in an arc at their company, a glare of deadly promise shuttering his eyes. "She and I have our own discussions to have, but as far as I'm concerned, I'm in this as long as she'll have me, and I'm not going anywhere. Have I made that fact incredibly clear, *Rian*?"

Rian put his hands out defensively, mouth rounding out in denial. "Gods, Elias, we kissed one time! She was just trying to get back at you, anyway!"

"Don't say that like it wasn't the best kiss you ever had," Soren snorted, and Samhain burst into full-on belly laughter.

Elias blinked, his hands dropping to his sides as he turned back to Soren. "You *what*?"

She fluttered her eyelids at him with her best pout. "You abandoned me at that party to flirt with Sam."

Samhain only laughed harder, strands of black curls escaping her braids as she bent in half, wheezing, "Wait, was that flirting, Pious? You should have told me!"

"No!" Elias's voice rose in distress. "Soren, for the love of Mortem—"

"All right, all right!" Jakob called out, clapping to regain order, though he was still grinning broadly himself. "Everybody settle—yourselves and your debts. Andrei, don't think I don't know you haven't given up your coin. Cough it up before the night's out."

"I don't bring money on border patrols," Andrei muttered with a sullen eye roll. He and Nikolai were the youngest of the company, twins who had come up in training together, and their sharp features, auburn-tinted hair, and shadowed eyes now reminded Soren painfully of Finn. "It's just asking for a bandit raid."

"Well, you'll see to it when we get home, then, pup." Jakob rubbed his temple, and though his grin didn't fade, that gesture seemed to be enough for Varran—he looped his arm around Jakob's waist, giving him a firm tug toward the broad chaise they'd claimed for the night. "Everybody get some sleep. We'll talk more in the morning before we make for home."

"Actually," Elias said quickly, "we'll be departing in the morning. We aren't finished yet."

The whole company went quiet, and a gentle chill of warning rolled over Soren's skin.

"You're not coming home?" Jakob's brow furrowed.

"Not yet," Soren croaked. "My, um…my brothers are waiting for us in Ursa. Raquel, too."

"You don't have brothers," said Nikolai, at the same time Samhain blew out a relieved breath and croaked, "Raquel's all right?"

But Jakob was looking at her still, and his gaze was no longer soft, no longer amused. It was the face of a Captain, stoic and stern…and maybe suspicious. "You mean the Atlas princes. *Raquel* is with them? And they're not dead yet?"

Elias's mouth quirked—almost a smirk. "She's briefly released her claim on her vengeance for now. For the sake of the greater good."

"Isn't the First Prince the cowardly prick that killed Jira?" Rian muttered in an aside to Samhain…not quietly enough. Soren's hackles rose, but before she could even *begin* to formulate a retort, Elias rounded on his cousin, teeth gritted, eye flaring.

"That *prick* is the only reason I'm not ashes on a pyre," he snarled. "And you will *not* insult him again within earshot of me, am I clear?"

The hush that fell over the room was worse than surprise…there was hostility buried in it somewhere, indignance on behalf of Rian for once, each member of their company regarding them with the exact same caution they might wield to face a pack of wolves.

"What did they do to you two?" asked Samhain—a hushed growl, a threat buried in the driftwood-fire flash of her eyes, in the restless tap-tap-tap of her fingertips against the ornately forged handle of her favorite dagger. And she wasn't alone—chills tumbled down Soren's back as she took in the host of feral eyes and wolfish snarls around her, each member of her company scenting vulnerability, scenting trauma…and assigning it to the only enemy whose face they knew.

A face she now shared, even if not all of them knew it.

And could she blame them, really? If Elias had disappeared into Atlas hands *alone* and come back listing their merits over their detriments, she absolutely would have assumed torture-induced manipulation over any actual innocence on their part.

Even so, the part of her that finally remembered her home couldn't keep her mouth shut in the face of such accusations.

"Nothing," she snapped—then, at Elias's skeptical glance sideways, she added, "it's a long story. I…*we* have a lot to tell you all. Stories that…that maybe aren't best told tonight."

Because she was a coward. Because she was tired. Because she couldn't bring herself to look any of them in the eye and admit the truth of her blood, the truth of her heart. That Atlas and its princes now held equal claim to her love that they all did.

"She's right. We have a lot to discuss," Jakob said finally, "but it will keep until tomorrow. Best to sleep on it, yeah?"

Though everyone nodded and muttered agreements, the confused, irritated, and even *betrayed* looks didn't stop, each member of their company throwing one of the three toward her and Elias as they shuffled off to their respective pieces of furniture…Samhain stealing the armchair when Soren stood, Rian propping himself against the ottoman; the twins spreading out on the smaller chaise with their heads on opposite ends, already bickering over the one blanket they'd been allocated; and Kriss and Frigga simply curling up on the floor, no pillows to be seen.

She'd come to terms with the truth of herself—well before her memories had come back, even. But she hadn't considered that others might not be able to reconcile the two halves of her at all. That her Atlas blood might cost her those her Nyxian heart loved.

It wasn't a cost she was ready to pay, but it might have come due regardless.

Before she could fully comprehend that thought—or figure out how to take a step on her own in spite of her useless, exhausted legs—Elias's still-bare hand appeared before her face, pale droplet-like burn scars spattered over his palm like a spray of light.

"Come on," he said softly. "Let's get some sleep."

And because of the buried promise in those words—the promise of their first night of almost-normalcy since she'd been stolen off to Atlas—she didn't say a word. She only took his hand, letting him lead her back up to the room they'd already claimed before the company arrived, her head sinking into the steady warmth of his shoulder.

"Hold," said a soft voice behind them—Jakob. For such a bulky man, he moved like a windblown snowflake when he wanted to. "We still need to get clear on something. You said you're Ursa-bound, yeah? To meet with Kallias and that Second Prince snake?""

She grit down on her smile, forcing it to stay in place even as tension tied a knot in one shoulder. "That's the plan."

"Get a new plan," Varran said bluntly, craning his neck around Jakob— the two broad men could barely fit in the small stairwell together. "No one's allowed in or out of Ursa."

Adrenaline struck her like a whip. "Why not?"

Before Varran even opened his mouth to answer, a hundred calculations flew through Soren's head, anxiety building and building until she did the math three times and reached the same exact conclusion—no, there was no way Kallias and the others would have reached Ursa themselves by now, even if they'd left directly after she'd last seen them. Whatever had happened, it couldn't have happened to *them*.

"No one really knows," Varran admitted, leaning one shoulder against the wall. "Just that anyone who goes there comes back wrong, if they come back at all. The last two companies who went out there to bolster our border defenses like you and Prince Kallias said to do, Elias…we never heard back. The third time, only one man made it back, and he was…"

"Not right," Jakob muttered with a shudder. "Sick or something. Babbling tales of corrupted creatures stalking the forests, of illnesses that wiped out entire cities. We sent for physicians, but by the time they arrived, he'd lost all composure…his eyes turned wild, and he started ranting. Promising destruction and conquest and chaos unending, blah blah blah, a world turned dark by the smothering hands of the gods. When Queen Ravenna came to speak with him herself…he tried to kill her. Wasn't much else to do; we put him out of his misery."

Soren's blood dried to nothing in her veins.

"Chaos." The whisper barely tumbled off her tongue; it nearly stuck at the tip, disbelief trying to choke her. "You're certain that's what he said?"

"You know something?" Jakob's voice sharpened from warning to command, a captain's bearing tugging his weary back straight.

"You're sure he wasn't just mad?" Elias pressed. "The woods out there are dense. Get lost long enough, it's enough to drive anyone out of their head."

"This wasn't madness. I know what that looks like. This…this was something else. It was like…hunger, maybe. Some kind of craving for violence." Varran shrugged. "We think there might be illness in Ursa. Ravenna put out orders—no one in, no one out."

But that was just it—it was nothing so simple as an illness, nothing that could be cured by a physician or medimancer's gentle hands, nothing that could be washed away like the touch of illness left behind by a cough or drawn out like infection buried in a wound. This was not sickness, nor was it madness; the first could have been helped, the second could have been blamed on a certain other goddess, but this…

"Not illness. Chaos magic." The words fell from Soren's lips as venom dripped from the fangs of a snake, and abruptly, every eye in the stairwell its way to her. Her fingers curled into trembling fists against her hips, and she drew in a breath through her nose. "Tenebrae's begun his assault on the other kingdoms."

Jakob frowned. "Chaos magic? I've never heard of that."

"Well, it's not technically a magic of its own," Elias said—his fingers were worrying his bearded chin, eyes glazed with memory she couldn't hope to guess at. "I only ever heard one story at the temple. It's actually a type of corruption, infecting magic where it can find it and warping minds where it can't. It creates—"

"You sound like you're quoting from a book," Soren interrupted.

His brow twitched. "That's because I am, smartass, listen—it creates a hunger for destruction within its victims that can only be sated by sowing discord. Whether through violence or quieter means, those infected by chaos magic can only find relief in the midst of havoc."

Silence reigned for only a second before Soren poked him in the side and whispered, "Is that the end of the quote?"

Elias rolled his eyes, catching her fingers and pulling them away from his ribs. "I saw it in Artem…or at least, I think I did. I hoped I was wrong. But the people who started the uprising there, they wielded unnatural flames. Corrupted pyromancy. It must have been Tenebrae's influence."

"Who's Tenebrae?" Varran's brow creased.

"The creepy little shit who's taking over Atlas," Jakob reminded him. "I told you—"

Varran rolled his eyes. "You were half out of your mind on whatever tincture the physicians gave you at the time. Forgive me if I don't remember all the details."

Guilt bit down on her heart—not a careful bite, testing whether she was truly prey. A tearing of teeth into flesh, a hunter intent on devouring whatever it could.

"How badly were you hurt?" Soren whispered.

In Atlas. In her home. While she'd been lost in the back of her own head, taking a leisurely walk through her own lost memories.

Jakob shrugged one shoulder, but his head turned slightly in a half-flinch, favoring one side of his head where a new scar had yet to heal. "They're pretty brutal to Nyxian faces when they recognize them. Not that I'm surprised. Prince Kallias was lucky you were there to introduce him, Pious. He wouldn't have been half as pretty afterward."

Varran's mouth carved a divot into his cheek, a dark scowl Soren recognized from a glimpse or two of herself in the mirror after battles that left Elias in the infirmary for a night or two.

"I'm sorry." Her hand slipped from Elias's, wandering to fuss with the sleeve covering her burn scars…remainders of the wounds dealt against her by Nyx. "I should have been able to stop it."

"Hey." Jakob stepped forward, taking her shoulders in his hands and giving her a quick but soft shake, reaching up to rumple her matted curls. "Cut that out. You weren't right in the head at the time, yeah? Not like the damned Goddess of Life had any reason to stop them from beating my ugly face in."

"Honestly, it's an improvement," Elias deadpanned. "I think they actually knocked a bit of handsome *into* you."

Jakob pointed at him without looking away from Soren. "You're demoted."

"Pretty sure you can't do that."

"Pretty sure I'm going to stick my boot up your—"

"Enough," Varran sighed. "Gods help me, I forgot how much you all bicker. Who is this Tenebrae person, again—not you, Jakob, I'm asking Elias," he added when Jakob opened his bruised mouth with irritation already primed in his gaze. "Who is he, and what does this have to do with Ursa?"

So Elias gave him everything he knew, and Soren helped, offering what she'd gleaned from her time with Tenebrae in Atlas…and what she'd seen in Ani's brief spurts of memory and nightmare. In tandem, they told the story manipulation of both Nyx and Atlas's fates by the hands of Occassio, of lines drawn between the godly sides of this deific war, of hosts claimed and relics uncovered.

"Ani—er, Anima, she thinks Brae's—gods," Soren cursed, tugging as her curls, hoping it would shake the familiarity from her tongue. "She thinks Tenebrae's relic is here somewhere. I couldn't tell you why. Finn said the same. But if it is, it sounds like someone's found it…and they may be testing it on Nyxians first."

"Or," Elias added, "it might be a distraction to slow us down. He knows you're still alive, and he knows Nyx is home for you. This could be a trap to try and get Anima back in his hands."

It could have been a hundred things. Some poor idiot could have even discovered the relic by accident, used it, and died painfully directly after. But somehow, based on how everything had gone for them up to this point, she didn't think they'd get that lucky.

She turned to Elias, fiddling with her clumped curls, trying desperately to think—something her exhausted, war-weary mind could barely manage. "So what do we do?"

The logical thing to do was to stick to the plan and head to Sirena—it was what Kallias would know to do if he reached Ursa and found it blocked off.

Still…something about that didn't sit right.

Elias clearly felt the same, because he fussed with the braided cloth on his necklace for a moment before saying, "If Tenebrae has agents working within Nyx and that relic is in use, it's only a matter of time before whatever happened in Ursa starts happening elsewhere."

The dread in his eyes caught and flared in Soren's heart, and she cursed quietly. "We have to find it."

"No one is going anywhere," Jakob said sternly, "until you both get your asses home and brief the Queen on all this."

"We don't have time—" Soren began, but Jakob held up a hand in silent command.

"Make time," he said. "You have to pass Andromeda to get where you're going, anyway. Consider it a brief errand. And no offense, Soren, but I really think you should see a physician but before you go much of anywhere. You have a look about you I don't like."

"I'm fine." It was a silly lie. No point in saying it when everyone knew it was false. But it was habit, and habit was easier than truth.

"It might not be a bad idea," Elias urged quietly. "It would give me a chance to ask Priestess Kenna about your…issue."

*Issue* was a funny way of pronouncing *Anima*.

She bit down on her protest. Not that it was even fully formed yet—something about her brothers waiting and the promise Elias had made and the fact that going to Andromeda meant a whole heap of discussions she wasn't nearly ready to have. Because now that the idea of going had been voiced, it only took one glance into Elias's eyes to see the longing there. The plea.

He hadn't seen his family in months…had left them in Andromeda to come and save her, knowing he would likely die in Atlas, never to see them again.

How could she deny him that?

"We'll get moving right away in the morning," said Jakob. "We won't be able to cross the distance in a day, but we can find an inn for the night, regroup, eat a good meal…" His eyes found Soren's with composed command. "And we'll hear your story…all of us. Your sisters know, as does Enna, obviously, but I haven't told anyone else."

Varran cleared his throat. "Well…"

Jakob waved his hand impatiently toward his battlemate. "She knows I tell you everything, dear, I don't need to say it."

He didn't, but somehow it did make her feel better…that Varran knew and had not immediately pushed for her removal from their company, nor did he look at her with hostility now. Still, best to clear the air.

"Is that going to be a problem?" she asked. Beside her, she sensed Elias tense up, his fingers twitching in the way that suggested want for a weapon.

"Not with you," said Varran promptly. "Never with you."

The weight that lifted off of her shoulders…she was surprised by the breadth of it, the intensity of the relief that followed. She reached out toward Varran, hand extended, and he clasped it without hesitation.

"Thank you," she croaked. "That means more than you know."

Finally, his gaze softened a touch, and he pulled at Soren's hand until they met in the middle, bumping foreheads with her. "You didn't choose the blood in your veins. I can't say how the others will fare, but I know you…I know your love lies with us. I trust that over any blood-claim those bastards might have to you."

Soren's grip tightened—her knuckles whitened, taut against her skin. "Varran—"

"We'll talk more in the morning," Elias interrupted, slipping his arm around her waist. "We need rest…all of us."

"One of us more than others." When Varran released her, Jakob took his place, pulling her head close and pressing a kiss to the top of it. "Sleep. You look like the pits."

"You stink like them," she mumbled. He merely tossed her two middle fingers held high in the air as he turned and walked away.

"Come on, you," Elias murmured against her ear. "Let's get inside."

The second they stepped together into the room, heat prickled at Soren's eyes, and it had nothing to do with the heat and light flaring in the lantern that Elias had lit in this bedchamber hours ago. No, this had everything to do with the homey scent of pine and wool and the promise of slumber mixed with the familiar scent of Elias's shirt beneath her cheek. This had everything to do with the fact that she couldn't remember the last time she hadn't slept entirely alone, trapped behind Anima's slumbering presence and love of bare feet, longing desperately for the lullaby of her battlemate's heartbeat and the thick weave of his socks warming her toes.

She didn't realize that heat had formed something more tangible until Elias's knuckle dashed gently over her cheek, wiping away the tear that had escaped. "What's the matter?"

"Nothing." She almost choked on the word; it tasted like a lie, even though she hadn't built it that way. "Can't I cry just because I feel like it?"

"Sure you can. But that's not what your eyes are telling me."

"If my eyes are talking now, we have much bigger problems than I thought." The way his chuckle rumbled through his chest brought more tears, and she cursed thickly, wiping at her traitorous eyes. "I'm sorry. I don't...I don't know why—"

Pressure in her throat choked her voice to nothing, a lump forming no matter how hard she tried to swallow it.

He took her face in his hands, tipping her gaze upward...gently pushing until she reluctantly met his gaze.

"Never apologize to me for what you need," he said quietly. "You've more than earned a good ugly cry."

She sniffled. "I don't *ugly* cry. I pretty cry."

Elias pulled back a bit, his hands still bracing either side of her face, examining her carefully, his mouth pinched in deep thought. "Mmm...I don't know. You're getting kind of blotchy."

She meant to laugh—she really, truly did. Really, truly thought that the pressure in her chest was a guffaw waiting to happen. But when she let it go, it ripped from her chest as a tattered sob, a noise shredded to ribbons from forcing its way through her gritted teeth.

"My mother always says," Elias continued, drawing her into his embrace as she fell apart, each heaving gasp and flood of tears taking a bit more of her strength until they sat knee-to-knee on the wooden floor, his hand ever-stroking her matted hair, "that sometimes we don't realize how much we're carrying until we can finally put it down."

If that was true, she must have been carrying this very mountain on her back, because the the *ache*…the *depth* of it, the way it went on and on and on…

"I want to go home," she sobbed. "I want to go *home*."

His grip tightened; his voice roughened, a hint of smoke drifting on his whisper in her ear. "I know."

But how could he, when even she didn't?

Until her memories had come back, she hadn't thought that *home* could mean two different places—hadn't known that she could miss one so fiercely until she returned to it, only to have that longing shift just as strongly to the other.

Was this going to be her life forever? Always aching for whichever kingdom she wasn't in?

"I don't know how this ends," she whispered miserably, pressing her forehead to Elias's chest as he patiently held her, pinching a tear-soaked curl from her cheek and tucking it behind her ear. "I don't know how we *make* it end. I can't…I can't see how we make it all right again. I can't see how we win."

"We start by getting rid of Anima." Not a hint of doubt in him; nothing but unfaltering defiance. "Priestess Kenna will have some idea of what to do. And once we meet back up with Kal and the others—"

All at once, her tears halted. "*Kal?*"

She looked up just in time to catch him scrubbing a self-conscious hand through his hair, a defensive twist to his mouth. "What? Kallias is a mouthful."

"It's really not." Gods above, they were on a *nickname* basis now? "What in the depths happened while I was dead?"

Memories glazed his eyes in place of tears, and he swallowed so hard his throat bobbed. "He saved my life," he confessed. "More than once, in more than one way."

Yet another thing she had to thank her brother for. Yet another thing to get on her knees and beg forgiveness for…that he'd had to fill that role in her absence. That he'd had to fill *so many* roles in her absence.

"They're going to meet us in Ursa? Or Sirena?" This time, the ache in her chest caught on the edge of her words and stretched out, a tendril of emotion drawn inexorably from within her. She needed to see them—needed *them* to see *her*, to know that she knew them, that she had never stopped fighting to come home. "You're sure?"

That every time their names had come back to her, she'd wielded them as a battle cry against magics much stronger than her mind, fighting with all her might to make it home.

"Yes." The absolute certainty in Elias's voice was more of a balm to her fears than she cared to admit. "If I had to pick three people who would make it out of anything alive, they're the three I'd choose."

Her nose wrinkled. "Really? Kallias is on that list?"

Elias paused, and she watched his lips form a wry knot of doubt. "Well, so long as he's with Finn and Raquel, yes."

"What happened between him and Raquel, anyway?" Yes, this was good— better this, better gossip and stories than tears and homesickness. "The death-right was hers. Why didn't she take it?"

"At first, because I wouldn't let her. Then…" Elias loosed a grin, something so close to mischief she almost demanded to know what he'd done with her real battlemate. He rose to his feet and started making his way around the room, pounding the drafty window down and pulling bedclothes from a nearby trunk. "I think there were some breakfasts. A patrol or two. And Kallias, I mean, he gets useless around anyone attractive holding a sword…"

As Elias went on, telling her stories of mooning looks and lives saved and something about a burning tavern that changed things between all of them, the ache of missing slowly twisted into something…sharper. Uglier.

She'd never been jealous *of* Elias before. Jealous of certain members of their company who'd managed to hold his attention for several minutes too long at a party, yes. Jealous of the goddess who seemed determined to take him as early as she could, yes. But never jealous like this…jealous of the knowing amusement that danced in his eyes when he spoke of her brother, *her* brother, and the familiarity with which he spoke of Kallias's habits and weaknesses.

Somehow, Elias knew Kallias better than she did, even with her memories back. And that didn't sit right with her…in fact, she almost looked down to see if she'd turned some bitter shade of green.

"Do you think he hates me?"

The second the question was out, she wanted to snatch it back, curling her nails into it until it crumbled beneath her touch—it sounded so gods-damned pathetic, so *sad*, and this wasn't a time for that. She had her battlemate back, he'd *kissed* her in front of the whole damned company, they were about to spend their first night together since the godly schemes of those beyond their world had torn them apart…and she was here whimpering over the possibility of her brother holding a grudge against her? A grudge he'd more than earned?

But Elias didn't roll his eyes or scoff at her for it—not that she'd expected him to. He was always too good for that. No, instead he paused in his preparations for sleep, his fingers curling and uncurling around the edge of the quilt he'd retrieved as he stared at her.

Then, after a too-long pause: "I gave up on you, you know."

*That* was not what she'd expected to hear. "Excuse me?"

"I gave up on you." Simple, soft; shattering. "I believed you were dead. I told him that. Do you know what he said to me?"

It wasn't the kind of question one was supposed to answer, so she let it sit, trying to tamp down the betrayal that hammered at the divot in her heart.

"He told me he would never give up on you. That he had once, for ten years, and you paid the price for it. He promised he would never do it again—said he owed you that." A scoff—a dash of a knuckle across his lower lid. "He doesn't hate you, Soren. He hates himself; blames himself. And if I had to wager a guess, I'd say Finn does, too. I'm not going to pretend to understand that pits-crawler, but I know he loves you. You might be the only thing he loves in this whole gods-damned world. There's no hate there. Not for you."

It was only the barest scrap of bravery left in her that made her capable of whispering her next question: "And what about you?"

Elias stopped breathing. A harsh, near-wheezing sort of halt as tension rippled across his shoulders. As he straightened to his feet, his shirt falling back into place around his waistband, hiding those new tattoos that marked him as a full priest of Mortem.

"You know I could never."

She did. She'd had to ask anyway. "But you are angry at me."

"I…" Elias swallowed, another bob of his throat that reminded her of her father's fishing lures. "Angry's not the right word. We'll talk about that later, all right? You need to rest. You're pale as a sheet."

"My sheets are pink."

"Well, you have been crying."

She might have laughed if he hadn't so obviously dodged her question. But he was right; even now her eyelids were sinking, trying desperately to shut on what felt like the longest day she'd ever lived through.

She didn't realize they'd done exactly that until she was suddenly lifted into the air, darkness coating the entire world as Elias's lips pressed to her forehead…then her nose, then her lips, the gentlest caress that threatened to reduce her to tears once more.

"Did that very public announcement not make my feelings perfectly clear?" he murmured against her mouth, a low rumble of words that almost, *almost* coaxed her eyes back open.

"Well, it wouldn't hurt to be reminded," she mumbled, and his laughter was the last thing she heard as she drifted off to sleep, her aching heart warming with every chuckle that tumbled from her battlemate's chest.

# CHAPTER 13

# RAQUEL

She'd kissed Kallias Atlas.

Shit.

She hadn't done enough to reassure him after he'd cut her—probably because she was too busy coming to her own gods-damned senses, something she'd clearly taken leave of sometime between last night and this morning. Sometime between *Not unless someone wishes to lose the limb that crosses it* and *Say the word, and he is dead.*

Somewhere in Arcaea, her younger sister was either cursing her name or laughing her ass off.

Knowing Jira, probably both.

Raquel stormed through the common house, doing her best to walk past every condemning pair of familiar eyes as if she could still throw out chains of lightning or shake the earth with thunder beneath her heels. Like she still walked with the protection of Aeris's ring on her finger and the approval of the Stormspeaker draped over her like Artemisian chain mail.

It was a bit easier, knowing she *was* actually wearing Artemisian chain mail, a gift from Safi before they'd left Artem. It was the lightest piece of armor she'd ever worn, simple to hide beneath her ordinary clothes.

Knowing where she would venture to today, she'd needed the reassurance it brought with its subtle weight.

The common house was really just a glorified lodge, built from rosined logs and iron reinforcements and frosted glass windows, the floors covered in rugs made from the pelts of all kinds of hunted creatures—polar bears, mountain cats, even some from the giant wolves that hunted these very woods. Queen Ravenna had banned the hunting of those rare creatures, but this was Skyhaven— technically, this community was built just beyond Nyx's furthest border, tiptoeing into the unclaimed winter wastes no kingdom had been mad enough to try and survive in. Stormspeaker Caelum had always said they answered to no one but Tempest.

Once that had brought her comfort, the thrilling sense of living free of any ruler's decrees beyond her beloved god's. Now she recognized it for what it was: Caelum establishing ultimate power over them. Using his supposed authority granted by Tempest to keep them from seeking community elsewhere.

Keeping them from ever questioning his decisions by making their ultimate punishment—exile—look worse than anything they could possibly endure within Skyhaven's borders.

The press of her boot over one of those wolf-pelt rugs made her sick.

The nausea only worsened as she made her way out of the lodge's main sitting room into one of the narrower, shorter halls. There were no windows here, only kerosene lamps mounted on the walls; three in a row on each wall, leading her straight to the unadorned wooden door at the end of the hall.

Her mouth dried out, but she swallowed her panic, ignoring the way it burned going down.

*I am the Eye of the Storm, the peace within chaos, the power within peace. He cannot touch any piece of me I do not offer.*

She had survived one trip down the stone stairs beyond that door. She could do it again—she would.

They only had to make it long enough for Aeris to erase Kallias's connection to Tempest…and for Finn to recover the relic.

Still, she held her breath as she opened the door and took the first step. She did not let it out again until she reached the bottom.

All at once, a flood of familiar smells assaulted her—damp, salt, stone, fear. It took a moment for her eyes to adjust to the blue-tinted darkness—no lamps down here, only torches carefully set in sconces, two to each of the four walls. The flames burned green and blue, not red or gold—a result of the torches being soaked in saltwater and dried out again before being lit. It was more of a cellar, almost a cave, the walls and floor both made of rough stone. The far left wall showed off a dark hole twenty feet tall, a yawning mouth with only shadow beyond, and spilling out from it was a pool shaped like a…

"Stormcloud." Aeris's voice drew her attention away from the water. He stood at the edge of it, and despite her rage, her fear…her useless heart still stuttered at the vivid glow of his blue eyes lit by the torches, his amiable smile, the gentle way he watched her.

But her body remembered the whips. The nails clawing her eye out of its socket. The ice that glazed over those beautiful eyes as he listened to her scream.

Two other members of the community knelt at the foot of the pool, staring downward intently—a brown-haired boy and a blonde girl, no older than sixteen. She came to stand at the opposite side of the pool as Aeris, peering down into it. Kallias was resting near the bottom, and her heart stumbled again at the sight of his closed eyes, at the manacles of stone that clamped over his wrists and ankles to keep him pinned below. Even so far down, she could just barely see the rise and fall of his chest.

They'd begun without her.

"How long has he been under?" she whispered. This wasn't what they'd done to her.

"Ten minutes." Aeris crossed his arms, frowning down into the shadowy depths. "He spent two of them struggling—instinct, I assume— then started breathing. He hasn't lost consciousness yet."

There was a question buried in that statement. "Tempest blessed him with the ability to breathe underwater." And thank the *gods* for it, too—what was Aeris thinking? "Why were you trying to drown him?"

"I asked him what he thinks of when he pictures Tempest. He said that Tempest often sends him dreams of drowning…and when he's awake, all he can think of is consuming water. His magic makes him thirst beyond reason." A one-shouldered shrug from Aeris. "It seemed the closest thing to a sign we had. I thought maybe if he actually drowned, it would sate the thirst…make the magic flee, seeking out someone else to satisfy it. Then we could revive him after."

Kallias hadn't told them any of that. Her throat tightened. "And?"

"And I'm still waiting, obviously." He sighed in frustration, scratching at the column of his throat. "If this doesn't work, we'll have to try something else. Maybe…"

"No." The word flew from her mouth before Aeris even had the chance to suggest the thought she saw brewing in his eyes.

She had lied to Kallias. She knew exactly what they'd done to her that day to rid her of her magic. And that was *not* an option.

When Aeris looked at her, his pale brows furrowing, she almost cursed herself. "Stormcloud," he said, so tender it made her furious, "you know I had no choice in what happened that day, don't you?"

She ground her teeth together. "Don't you dare try to claim innocence. You had a choice."

"I couldn't have stopped him."

"You could have *tried*."

"And what do you think would have happened to me?" Aeris's eyes flared, and the temperature of the air around them dropped from comfortably cool to utterly frigid. His hair stood a bit on end—so did hers. "You think it would have helped? To question the Stormspeaker's judgment is sacrilege. I would have been tied to that whipping post right beside you."

Her chin threatened to tremble. She steeled it with half a thought, taking a step back from the edge of the pool. "If it had been you instead of me, I would have gladly taken any blow if it meant saving you."

She didn't know the nature of the storm that gathered in his eyes. Only that it forced the hair on her arms to reach for the sky, a buzzing sensation pouring down her back like a hundred bees crawling beneath her clothes. The surface of the pool rippled outward, lapping at the rocky sides, splashing over the edge to soak the toes of her boots.

"Then your faith was not as strong as I believed it to be," he said.

"Stormspeaker!" called one of the other Skyhaven wielders before Raquel could stutter her way through an accusation of *wolfshit*, the boy leaning forward to hover one hand over the surface of the water. "He's starting to struggle again."

The floor fell out from beneath Raquel's feet. She practically flew back to the edge of the pool, squinting to see past the still-choppy water. Her breath froze in her lungs at the sight of Kallias no longer breathing, his eyes wide with terror, flailing as he tried to pull himself free of the manacles—to no avail.

He shouldn't have been drowning.

*He shouldn't have been drowning.*

"Let him up," she said, straining for calm.

Aeris didn't move. "This is what we were waiting for, Stormcloud. We have to let it happen."

"He's *dying*!" Damn *calm* to the pits. "Let him up!"

Aeris's expression didn't change—and in that lack of response to her order, she saw that she had been wrong. Horribly, miserably wrong.

Aeris certainly possessed the cruelty his father had once chosen as his favored weapon. But he had softened it, gentled it, kept it hidden in a velvet sheath until the time came to wield it.

And now, fueled by jealousy, he held that blade to Kallias's throat.

"Someone restrain her," he ordered quietly.

The curses that flew from her mouth would've knocked her mother clean dead. She tried to dive into the pool, but something solid slammed her backward— not a body, not a weapon. A pillar of stone that burst up from the ground and drove itself into her like a battering ram, knocking her back against the wall with an impact that bashed all color out of her vision. Ears ringing, still-bruised ribs roaring in pain, she beat her fists uselessly against the barrier that held her flush against the wall, gasping against its weight, each breath shallower than the last as the rock continued to press in just below her chin. Over its edge, she caught sight of the boy who'd called to Aeris holding his hands out, his brow wrinkled in concentration.

Gods, she hated elemancy.

"Aeris." What she meant to be a roar came out as a thin, wheezing moan. "Stop."

"It's for your own good, Stormcloud." Aeris's voice sounded hollow and tinny in her ears, black spots dancing in her visions. "And for his."

"For *yours*?" She coughed, her palms scraping against the rock as she shoved at it, a growl pitching into a cry as she fought with all her strength to make it *move*, gods damn it—

"Stormspeaker!" The girl this time. "He's unconscious."

Disbelief numbed every bone in her body.

With the very last of her breath, with everything she had left to give, she let out a scream that would have brought the entire lodge down if she could still wield the power of storms at her fingertips: "*Get him out!*"

For a moment, the only sound in the room was the drumbeat of her pulse in the hollows of her ears.

Then a splash. A glimpse of soaked hair darkened from gold-threaded auburn to dull cinnamon.

Without warning, the rock pillar eased back from her, relieving the pressure on her lungs and heart. She pushed away from the wall immediately, her boots squeaking on the damp floor as she sprinted to the side of the pool—to Kallias, who'd been dredged up from the bottom with bleeding wrists and ankles, his lips pale and tinted with blue.

"Kallias." She pressed her fingers to his throat, her breathing speeding up when she felt how…*warm* he was. Colder than most, cold as death, yet warmer than he'd been in weeks. She couldn't find his pulse. She *couldn't find his pulse.* "Don't make me do this again, you incompetent *asshole*, I'm not doing this again!"

"What tender words from a bride to her husband," Aeris deadpanned. He leaned toward her ear as she started jamming her palms against Kallias's still chest, lowering his voice: "You know, I didn't believe a word he said. Not knowing how you feel about Atlas. But that look on your face, the way you screamed for him…you *do* love him, don't you?"

She wasted a moment of precious time to turn and drive her dripping wet fist into Aeris's face.

The crack of knuckle against cheekbone was a balm to a sore she hadn't known she was still carrying, filling her with satisfaction purer than a bottle of Nyxian liquor.

Aeris slowly turned to meet her gaze again, expression utterly incredulous, blood tricking from his left eye.

"Mock me again," she rasped, returning her hands to their work, "and I promise you, magic or no, I will make you regret it."

The boy and girl Aeris had brought with him advanced, but he held both his hands out to stop them. Not a word spoken—just his palms facing outward, his eyes narrowed on her, keen as a hunting hawk.

"Go on, then," he murmured. "Save your prince."

There would be a price to pay for the mark she'd left on his face. And there would be time to worry about it once Kallias was breathing again.

This was the third time her lips had touched his, but only the second time it had been necessary to save his life. Maybe she could pretend the other time had been necessary, too. Life or death. Maybe he would have keeled over dead the next second if she hadn't shocked his heart back to life with her kiss. Nobody ever needed to know otherwise. It was her word against his, and she had the distinct advantage of not being hated by most of this kingdom, so—

His chest jerked beneath her hands, and she barely managed to move in time before he curled to the side and vomited up mouthful after mouthful of brackish river water.

Relief. Wrath. She didn't know whether to apologize for bringing him here or yell at him for going along with something so ridiculous without her or Finnick there to help.

Though, if she was being honest…no, she knew exactly what she was going to do.

"You're an idiot," she fumed, bracing his shoulder before he could collapse. "You're an *idiot.*"

"I know," he groaned between coughs.

"Don't ever make me do that again."

"Noted," he agreed. "No more almost dying. I promise."

"Good." Once she was marginally sure he wasn't going to pass back out, she shoved him into a sitting position and scooted back, wiping her soaked hands off on her pants. "Because next time, I'm making Finnick kiss you."

Another gag. "If it ever comes to that," he wheezed, "do me a favor and let me die."

"Not a problem." Not exactly *convincing* after she'd just saved his ass for the third or fourth or gods-knew-how-many-times by now, but she had to go for it anyway. It was a matter of pride, of principle. "Did it work?"

Kallias blinked hard, teardrops of water running down his pale cheeks, his lips only just beginning to take on some color. He sat back in his dripping wet clothes, the cloth hanging off of his body like the awning of a tent sagging with rainwater, and she might've laughed if she wasn't still aching, shaking, freezing with terror and burning with rage, a storm in and of herself.

He held his hand up. Flexed his fingers to call the ice.

Nothing. Water dripped freely from his fingers.

He tried again.

Nothing.

He swallowed thickly—smiled—even laughed. But there was a gleam in his eyes that didn't speak of joy or liberation…a gleam that looked like grief.

"It worked," he whispered. "It's gone."

That should have coaxed a smile to her face, too. It should have made her pits-damned *ecstatic*.

They could leave. Once Finn acquired the relic, she could leave this place in the past for good. Right where it belonged.

So why, watching Kallias stare at his hand with that odd look in his eyes, did she feel the gentlest pinch of dread deep in her gut?

# CHAPTER 14

# FINN

Aeris's cabin was pitifully easy to get into.

That was the problem with cult leaders, though—always too confident in the devotion of their disciples to worry about sensible things like *locks* or *guards*. Or even a little bell to act as an alarm, for the gods' sake. The most difficult part was not laughing out loud as he twisted the doorknob and slipped inside, closing the door behind him without even a squeak to alert the rest of the village.

Honestly, if it was this simple to do, he needed to start infiltrating more cults.

"That could be fun," Occassio said cheerfully, already lying on her back with her legs braced against the bed's rosewood headboard, jamming the sharp heel of her crystal shoe into the eye of an intricately carved relief of a man Finn assumed to be Tempest. She watched him upside down, her curls tumbling across the ultramarine velvet bedspread. "More fun if you let me play along, though."

Finn scowled at her, moving to the ivory desk shoved against the large four-paned window on the left wall. "You're already more involved than I want you to be."

"Nobody likes a sore loser."

"I haven't lost yet."

"Well, you're definitely not in the lead."

He grunted rather than replying, tugging on his gloves and carefully sifting through the objects in the first drawer built into Aeris's desk. Plenty of baubles—figurines of Tempest, pendants carved with Tempest's symbol, particularly shiny river rocks, even a fully intact and surprisingly large conch shell—but no relic.

"You really think he'd leave something so important in an unlocked desk?"

"He left it in an unlocked house," Finn pointed out. "Feel free to leave if you disagree with my methods, Fidg."

Occassio scowled. "I think we can leave that name behind, don't you?"

"Oh, apologies." He turned and leaned back against the desk, offering her a grin and a sweeping bow. "Feel free to leave if you disagree with my methods, *Cassi.*"

Her scowl deepened, but even outside the softer guise of Fidget, it didn't frighten him. He knew by now that it was her smiles he should truly fear. "You know, most men kneel before deities. They don't mock them."

"You know very well I'm not most men. Isn't that why you like me?"

"I don't *like* you. I need something from you." She sat up, spreading her arms in frustration. "You think I'd be sitting here watching you botch the easiest job of all time if I didn't have to?"

"I was under the impression you enjoy driving me mad, so…yes."

And there was the smile. She chuckled. "Fair enough, Trickster." When he blinked, she'd vanished from the bed and now stood directly in front of him, holding one hand out. "May I?"

He hesitated, then gave a stiff nod.

She took his wrist in her hand, frowning at his wristwatch—the only other one he'd made besides the one he'd given to his father. "You've already taken too much time, I'm afraid."

As soon as she let go of his wrist, the doorknob clicked.

Panic bolted through his body. But before he could run or hide or even curse, Occassio pulled out that smug little grin he hated so much.

"Here," she said, covering his wristwatch with her hand this time. "Let's try that again, shall we?"

***

Aeris's cabin was pitifully easy to get into.

That was the problem with cult leaders, though—always too confident in the devotion of their disciples to worry about sensible things like *locks* or *guards*. Or even a little bell to act as an alarm, for…

Wait. Hadn't he just…?

"You look confused, darling."

He closed the door behind him, scowling at Occassio, who sat cross-legged on the ultramarine velvet bedspread, her head cocked to one side. "Why are you here?"

"Bored." She shrugged primly. "How 'bout you?"

"Looking for a divine relic. Ever heard of them?"

"Mm, can't say I have." Her eyes trailed him as he moved to the ivory desk, pulling out his gloves, and…

Déjà vu struck him between the eyes, a stabbing pain shooting straight to the back of his skull.

"Not that drawer," Occassio said dismissively. "Try a different one. And hurry, will you? You're wasting time."

He turned to glare at her over his shoulder. "By all means, if you have somewhere to be, don't let me keep you."

"But I do so enjoy your company."

Finn scoffed softly, turning away and tugging on his gloves. His fingers shook. Everything shook.

"Stop," he muttered.

"I'm not doing anything."

The shaking worsened. The ache sharpened. "*Stop.*"

"I'm not *doing* anything," she insisted, hands spread innocently in the air. "I already told you: the harder you fight, the worse it gets."

"Then stop *making me fight you.*"

A longsuffering sigh. She stood on the bed, bounced on her heels a bit, then did a cartwheel—an honest-to-gods *cartwheel*—off of it, hold her hand out patiently until he set his palm to hers. She closed her fingers around it, frowning at his wristwatch.

"Out of time again," she murmured as the doorknob rattled. "But I'll take the blame for that one. I distracted you. Again, from the top!"

***

Aeris's cabin was pitifully easy to get into, but even so, just opening the door took effort with his stiff, unyielding hands. It took three tries to turn the knob, pinning it between both sets of paralyzed fingers and twisting his wrists, and afterward his head hurt so badly he could hardly see for pain.

Five seconds in, and already this was going poorly.

Every step jarred his bones, a pervasive wrongness clouding around him until he caught himself looking over his shoulder every five seconds, heart pounding, the weight of hundreds of invisible eyes pressing into his back. Paranoia danced in his stomach until his breakfast sat up and threatened to evict itself from the premises. He wanted to run. He couldn't run.

He'd never been in this cabin before. He'd lived entire lifetimes within its walls. *How long have I been in here?*

When he approached the desk, his eyes caught on a flaw in the woodwork— a series of scratches, too uniform to have been left accidentally, curls of white paint left behind where something had dug its way into the wood.

Something wasn't right.

On a whim, he drew his dagger, pressing the tip into the wood and dragging a new scratch into the row.

It matched perfectly.

Fractals of fear burst outward in his chest, but he bore down on the shivers that tried to wrack his body, forcing himself to breathe evenly as he counted.

There were over two dozen tallies cut into the desk.

*Breathe*, he ordered himself. *In. Out. Again: Breathe.*

The back of his neck tingled.

He whirled on his heel, catching Occassio's wrist in a grip so tight that the mirror bracelet she wore cracked beneath the pressure. She hadn't been reaching for him, he realized a heartbeat later—she'd only been standing there, watching over his shoulder. Shards of glass dug into his fingers, weeping hot blood down both of their wrists, but he never broke her gaze.

Her smile was innocence incarnate. "Hello, Trickster."

"Whatever you're doing to me," he rasped, tightening his grip when she tried to pull away, relishing the mind-clearing bite of broken glass, "*stop*."

"I'm trying to *help* you." She turned to look over her shoulder. "You have less than two minutes before someone catches you, and you keep using them *wrong*. Would you rather I didn't—"

"I don't want your help." Every word seethed with hatred no matter how hard he tried to grapple his mask in place. Calm was out of reach here, in this moment he'd relived gods-knew how many times before he'd recognized something was wrong, before he'd started tallying his time in this cabin. "Go find someone else's mind to lurk in."

Her lips pursed, and all color leaked from her irises, her gaze flashing blinding white. "Fine," she sighed. "Good luck with your minute and thirty-two seconds."

Oh, he'd be just fine without luck. "If you really want to help, why don't you go distract whoever's out there?"

"So you *do* want my help?" She glanced at the door again, tapping diamond-sheathed toes against the floor. "One minute, twenty-five seconds."

"I want you out of this cabin. Look, are you going to make yourself useful or not, Fidg?"

"Anything for you, handsome." She tossed him a wink and skipped backward to the door, giving her curls a quick ruffle and smacking her lips to even out the gloss she wore. Glitter fell from her hair, floating gently to the floor in shards of rainbow. "Honestly, I was thinking of playing with Aeris a bit anyway." Her mouth screwed into a knot, like she'd stuck her tongue to a salt-rimmed glass expecting to taste sugar. "Men like him are why I got into this gig in the first place."

He opened his mouth to ask, but she raised her hands above her head and rubbed them together. More glitter rained down over her—so much his vision of her was obscured—and when it all finally drifted to the floor, Occassio no longer stood before him.

Instead, he was staring up into the golden eyes of a man even taller than Kallias, dressed in furs and leathers that still didn't manage to disguise how brawny he was. His shoulders were broad, his skin the same rich brown as Occassio's, though missing her distinct freckles. He had a weather-beaten look to him that brought to mind the mountains they'd traveled alongside, but someone who wasn't Finn probably would have called him handsome—ruggedly so, though bordering on unnatural. His jawline and upper lip were covered in a carefully groomed dark beard, and when he smiled, his teeth were white as the snow outside.

His hair was glossy black and textured; though not outright curly, it flowed forward before rearing back at the front like a cresting wave. In spite of the air being completely still in the cabin, the furs on his shoulders and the hair on his head stirred ever so slightly, as if caressed constantly by some intangible wind.

"Let me guess," Finn said. "Tempest."

Even with such a flawless illusion, he now recognized Occassio's smug grin anywhere, on anyone. She bowed, those furs swaying along with her. "What do you think?" she asked in her own voice, then frowned, clearing her throat. When she spoke again, her voice had deepened to a thunderous depth, a pure bass tone that could've probably carried all the way back to Atlas. "Sorry. What do you think?"

Finn glanced down at his watch. Hopefully she couldn't see the bead of sweat trickling down his temple. "I think I have twenty seconds left."

Her familiar pout looked decidedly ridiculous on her brother's face. "C'mon. Scale of one to ten."

"Four. Get out."

Now her jaw dropped near to the floor. "*Four?*"

He spread his arms in a *what do you want from me?* gesture. "I've never seen your brother!"

"I just grew a foot and a half, and you call it a *four.*" Occassio scoffed under her breath, cracking her neck in a way he *did* recognize; Tempest had done the same when he was in Kallias's body. "You're lucky I enjoy making my brother look bad. I'm about to buy you five minutes. Use them wisely—this is your last try."

With one last sultry wink and a snap of her fingers, Occassio vanished faster than a wisp of smoke in damp alley air, and he was left with a scratched-up desk, his skull aching like something was trying to gnaw out the back of it, and no idea where he'd already searched.

"Shit," he announced to the cabin.

The cabin didn't reply.

Muttering quiet curses to himself, keeping his wandering thoughts busy by trying to come up with some he'd never used before—*Occassio's glittering dandruff* was about to become a new favorite—he closed his eyes and covered them with the heels of his palms, casting himself back into the murky depths of lost memory.

No one knew him better than himself. Where would he have searched first?

The desk—it was safe to assume that had been picked through thoroughly. He would have searched it for hidden compartments; probably would've searched the walls, too. But anything after that would have depended on how long it took him to find the scratches in the desk and go through the exact same thought process he was going through right now.

"All right, Finn," he murmured. "Five minutes. You're a religious zealot with no eyebrows who doesn't lock his door. Where does he hide the things that matter?"

It was just a puzzle. He loved puzzles. He could solve them in his sleep—and *had* on one occasion, when his mother had caught him playing chess against himself in the middle of the night. According to her, he'd silently resisted being put back to bed until he'd played himself to a stalemate draw.

His eyes caught on the chess set arranged on a small table a couple feet away from the bed. There was only one chair beside it.

If there was one thing he'd learned after a lifetime of power, it was that it came hand and hand with loneliness. He only knew how to play chess alone so well because he'd done it plenty of times awake, too.

How often did that set get used?

He hurried over to the table, which was barely large enough to hold the chess set at all, and sat down in the single chair. Gloves on, fingers finally steady, he carefully picked through each of the pieces, examining them for chinks or hidden screw caps or false bottoms. Nothing. His fingers only found glazed wood.

Until he tried to pick up the white king.

The piece didn't budge—it clung to the board beneath it, which in turn clung to the table. But when Finn twisted it, it obliged his advances, and deep within the bowels of the table, a series of clicks purred like music to his ears.

"There you are," he breathed.

He ducked down to peek beneath the table just as a compartment dropped open, a square-ish maw revealing a small suede pouch tucked against its lip.

"You're a genius, Finn," he mumbled as he swiped up the pouch and pocketed it. "Oh, thank you, Finn, you're too kind to—"

*Time's up, Trickster,* Occassio's voice sang in his head—not accompanied by her face this time, thankfully. *You can gloat later.*

"I can gloat more than once," Finn said. All he received in response was an undignified snort.

Once, that might have made him smile.

He clicked the compartment closed, made sure everything else was left exactly as it had been before, then hightailed it out of the cabin. When his boot crunched into the snow, heat welled up behind his eyes—tears he didn't understand, a wave of relief so potent it nearly drove him to his knees.

It made him wonder how long he'd truly spent in that cabin.

How many tries Occassio had put him through that he *didn't* remember.

# CHAPTER 15

# ANIMA

The stones from the Erudi River were always her favorite.

The pebbles teetering on the rotting floorboard in a pile before her were objectively perfect—smooth and round and carrying hues of blue and purple. They were soothing against her soft hands, a bit of roughness to balance out the tender touches of plant and feather and fur that dominated most of her days. Rock was lifeless, and it didn't bend to her as easily as most things.

But, eventually, it did bow. And better—it danced.

She giggled as she swept her hands up, those pebbles following her gesture, arranging themselves into the rough sketch of a person, hands and feet and legs and arms all assembling to their proper places. The rock-friend bowed to her as she twitched her finger, and she bowed back to it, grinning with joy until—

"Ani! Stop that!"

*Mora's panicky hiss broke the magic; the stones clattered back to the floor, lifeless and dull once more, and Ani's laughter died in her throat. "Mora, I was just—"*

*"You can't play like that out here, remember? Anyone could walk by and see you." Mora scooped up the pebbles and ushered her toward the door, a warm hand on her back, worry honing her voice into something sharper than Ani was used to. "No magic by the windows."*

*Ani bit down on her quivering lip, reaching out to accept the pebbles as her sister dumped them back into her palm.*

*She would not cry. If she cried, it would only make Mora and Braeden fight again, and she was so tired of them fighting.*

*She shoved the lifeless stones into her pocket, and she did not play the rest of the day.*

"Ani."

She wasn't ready for another scolding, not so soon. She curled away from the light, the voice, desperate for the gentle reprieve of sleep…

"Ani!" Sharper this time, but still quiet, the barest hiss under someone's breath. "Come on, Goddess Great, I need you up. We don't have a lot of time."

*Goddess Great.* Only one person in the world called her that, and it wasn't her sister.

She opened her eyes…no, that wasn't right. She did not call them to open, but they were open nonetheless—and when she tried to blink, they did not obey.

Porcelain chilled the palms of her hands, the lip of a sink basin clutched between her fingers. She was staring at herself in a mirror, its frame tarnished silver and its glass smudged with what looked like years of grime, but it wasn't her looking back. Those eyes were greener than the magic she had been blessed with, not gold; and though it was the same face she had grown used to wearing, it had adopted its old sharpness once again, a countenance better suited to wolfish snarls and taunting smirks than soft smiles and shy blushes.

"Wake up," Soren said to her, lip curling to bare her teeth. "We need to have a talk."

Everything was muddled, groggy, her mind coated in the same tarnish as that mirror's aged frame—a grimy film that turned everything gritty and tasting of rust. *What happened?*

Soren hesitated. "You killed Arthur, Ani."

Panic and horror thudded to life in her core as the memory of the mercenary's twisted neck came back to her, her heart beating its wings like a bird trapped in a box. But she forced herself to breathe…whatever that meant in this state. Soren's lungs didn't respond when she tried, but it made her feel calmer nonetheless.

*I…I remember. I didn't mean to.*

Something new stirred across the miasma between them…a trickle of feeling that almost felt like *guilt.*

"Ani," Soren said quietly, "he hurt us. You think I blame you for what you did?"

*I killed him. Just like…just like Vaughn…*

"You did exactly what I would have done." Tension riddled Soren's voice, but not the kind of tension that accompanied dishonesty—and Soren wasn't one to coddle through lies, anyway. "Maybe not in method, but…look, that's not what I…I need to talk to you about something else."."

That didn't bode well at all. Soren had never been one for *talking. What happened?*

And something *had* happened—she could see it, *feel* it in the slump of Soren's shoulders. Nothing like her usual slouch, a posture of casual comfort, the confidence to rest in her own body.

This was a boy of twenty-two bent near in half over a broken desk pilfered from some neighbor's refuse, silently counting out a pile of mismatched coins that never seemed enough. This was a boy of twenty selling trinkets strung together with driftwood and sea glass, charging a silver coin for a prediction of the day's weather. This was a girl of nineteen bent around a broom as she swept the altar of a church she wasn't allowed to bend the knee at except to polish its floors. This was a girl of seventeen transforming into a hundred different people with the help of stolen cosmetics and scavenged costumes and hours spent practicing new faces in front of a cracked mirror—

"Ani."

Soren's voice wound her spiraling thoughts back to the present, a spinning wheel turning in reverse. *Sorry. I'm here.*

"We're back in Nyx, heading for Andromeda." The shock of that—of just how many days she'd missed—didn't have time to settle before Soren continued, "We've stopped at an inn for the night, but—"

*I thought we were going to Ursa.*

"Ursa has been closed off. No one in, no one out." Soren's hands flexed around the edge of the sink, her nails clinking against the stained porcelain. "Rumor is the one man who escaped to tell his tale was rambling about chaos and spoiling for a fight he couldn't win."

Those words took Ani's stomach and threw it off a ledge with no bottom, a free-fall into pure disbelief…utter *betrayal.*

Brae had promised her. He had *promised* he wouldn't do this, had promised he would keep his magic in check…

Another lie. Another trick.

How had she ever believed she'd outgrown the naivete of her first life? She had lived with Cassi long enough, for gods' sake, how could she *still* not see the signs?

A dark, quiet rumble spread through this wisp of being she had been shrunk into…a subtle tremor that built and built until the quaking had overtaken her whole form, agony so powerful it somehow didn't hurt at all. It was too strong for her to comprehend; too deep for her to truly feel.

Pain only existed if it could be differentiated from how the rest of the body felt. This was not pain.

"Ani." Soren's voice was tight, strained. "Ani—Ani, stop!"

But she couldn't stop. There wasn't enough of her to contain this darkness, this *wrath*, and it was leaking out of her, it was overflowing from this space this cage this *hole* she'd been buried in—

No. That wasn't her anger.

Blood—it was blood. Twin rivers of it flowing from Soren's crooked nose, painting her panting mouth in scarlet, stark against the sudden pallor of her skin. Her freckles could have been spatters of ink for how dark they looked against the pale.

"Ani," Soren gasped, "stop, or I'm going to call Elias."

And if she called him, he would bring yet another reminder of just how many times she'd fallen for a sibling's false promises.

So Ani tried. She tried to breathe, tried to remember *soft* and *gentle* and *nurturing* and not *foolish, foolish, foolish.*

Life. She was the Goddess of Life, not of wrath, not of death, not of blood.

Not corruption, violence, chaos.

She was not Mortem. She was not Tenebrae.

"Breathe," Soren choked. "Help me breathe."

And for the first time, when the lungs of this body opened up to take in a breath, it was a breath summoned by both of them. And in their tandem exhale, there was a relief so deep it overwhelmed even the wall keeping their consciousnesses separate.

"Gods," Soren coughed, "you try to help someone—"

*I'm sorry.* She hated the tremor, the truth in that apology. *I didn't mean to hurt you. I didn't…I didn't mean for anyone to—*

"I know." Abruptly, Soren's voice was quiet; serious. "That's why I'm asking for your help."

*Help?* Soren didn't ask for help. Soren helped herself. *With what?*

"My…" A resigned sigh. "Our body is failing, isn't it?"

*I think so.* She'd already begun to suspect that this pervasive weakness had less to do with the lingering effects of the Tallisian drug and more to do with their ongoing conflict. *I don't know how to fix it.*

Soren was silent…something that always set off warning bells on Ani's side of their mind. Normally Soren's consciousness was an ever-buzzing core of activity, a beehive overflowing with thoughts and ideas and idle daydreams. Silence meant a deliberate string of thought, a *plan*, and those rarely ended in Ani's favor.

"I think," Soren said quietly, "we might be able to slow that down."

*How?*

"By coming to an agreement."

She already knew where this would lead. *Soren, I can't leave your body. And I'm not saying that because—*

"I know. Ani, I know. I believe you."

*I believe you.*

The part of her composed of springtime and summer flared gently…a flower bud unfolding with tentative warmth.

Soren—suspicious, snarling, ever-hostile Soren—believed her.

Brae hadn't even offered her that generosity.

Soren cursed, dashing her fingers at her eyes. "Are you *crying?*"

*No.* Maybe. *What do you want me to do?*

Soren looked her in the eye—or, well, she looked herself in the eye. "I'll stop fighting you. I won't try to force you out, and I won't let anyone else try to, either. But you need to let me keep control, and you need to help me figure out what in the *depths* your brother is doing out here."

An alliance between host and goddess.

No such thing had ever been done before. But for all her power, for all her might, Ani was not clever. She was not scheming or strategic or any of the things that might have given her the upper hand in this.

She was not Occassio. She was not Tempest.

She was Annelisa, a girl who'd been trained in goodness by her eldest sister and power by her eldest brother. A girl who'd learned responsibility from her middle brother and silent kindness from her middle sister.

She had done wrong to this princess, regardless of what excuses and reasoning Brae had offered for the breaches of conscience. She wasn't sure yet where she stood in all this, but she knew she didn't stand in the right…not as long as she remained in Soren's head.

*All right,* she said softly. *Deal.*

Soren's fingers loosened on the basin, aching relief splintering through her knuckles. Ani watched nervously as the princess moved to the bath and twisted the rust-kissed knob above its faucet, ducking her head out the door and calling to Elias that she was going to freshen up from the journey before coming back in, shutting and locking the door. Only when steam began to rise and the hiss of running water drowned out all chatter from the inn's common area below did Soren finally say, "Tell me your brother's plan."

And in what Mortem might have named *penance,* Anima did.

***

*Annelisa Rosemary Medeis knew what life felt like.*

*It was the thing she breathed back into mouse bones and ragged fur on her third birthday, her curiosity tumbling into delight as the fur and bones came together to dance for her.*

*Death did not exist for her then—she only knew that the poor little creature was cold, and she could make it warm again.*

*It was the fizzing, bubbly feeling in her stomach as she belly-laughed beneath the merciless tickling of the next-youngest sister, Cassandra's laughter harmonizing with hers as they played chase, daisy petals drifting on the breeze behind Ani's ankles as she ran.*

*And then there was…*

*A cough heavy with phlegm. Sour breath polluting the air in their tiny home. Eyes cloudy with fever, a pale sheen glazing them blind. A voice rough and trembling, rattling and dull, a constant chant pouring from a throat ravaged by vomiting: "Mora…Mora…"*

*"You said no magic," she whispered, wringing her hands as she stared down at the man lying before her. He had such pretty hair, all curly and gleaming like the gold coins she sometimes saw her siblings bring home on very good days, days that ended with candies and cuddles and maybe a new pair of socks. Cassi always knit when she was excited, and nothing excited her the way gold did. "M-Mora, I wanna help, but you said they'll take me away—"*

*"He won't! He—he won't, Ani, listen…" Her sister, already on her knees, turned to Ani and gripped her by the shoulders, her shaking hands encompassing them with ease. Mora's deep brown hair hung in ragged hanks on either side of her face, once-shining locks dulled with dust and sweat, her eyes hollow with horror that bordered on something that scared Ani down to*

*her toes. "He's my friend, Ani. He won't tell anyone about you, I promise, but he…he needs help, and you're the only one that can help him. Do you understand? You are the only one." Her thumb brushed Ani's cheek, dirty callouses scraping tender skin. "You are the most special girl in this whole world, you know that? Sancta made you so special, and you are the only one special enough to save him now. Please, sweetheart. Please."*

*Annelisa Medeis knew what life was. It was the flare of sunfire and daylight that streamed from her fingers and took root in the rivers of disease running their course through the man's body, healing power pushing back the tide of devastating illness.*

*And Annelisa Medeis knew what life wasn't—she knew its warmth lived nowhere in the scalding heat of the bonfire constructed in the center of the village square, kindling and firewood thrown together in the long-dry fountain, a stake driven into the middle. A stake her eldest sister was tied to, brown hair blackening with scorch, the strands already catching with embers floating from the fire dancing at her feet. Her fathomless eyes widened to the whites with mortal terror as she fought and kicked and wailed to the sky.*

*And abruptly, those wails turned to roars.*

*"Sancta!" A thunderous shout echoed over jeers and laughter, Mora's voice reaching to the sky with furious, fearsome demand. "Have I served you for nothing? Have you abandoned me as you abandoned my mother? She told me you loved us, you protected us…prove it!"*

*As the flames devoured Mora Medeis, crowning her in flames and dressing her in char, the screams of the remaining Medeis siblings rang out over the crowd…fury and terror and grief, each trying to fight their way to that blaze, even knowing already that it was far too late for their quietest and bravest sibling.*

*It was too late for them. Even Ani, for all her gifts, could not reach her in time.*

*But a god could.*

*A god did.*

*And when fire bellowed out in deadly harmony with Mora's dying scream, incinerating every person and building and plant to silent, snow-like ash, Ani met Death for the very first time.*

***

*Each of the Medeis siblings survived the cataclysm that wiped out their birth city, and not one of them ever breathed a word of who was responsible for its decimation.*

*When Sancta gifted Mora with her magic, she was not alone—he also gifted Braeden, Peter, and Cassandra with abilities beyond any that had been wielded by mortals before. And to Annelisa, who had already possessed magic, he gave a triple helping of what she'd once had—a power that left her still steps above her siblings in ability and marvel.*

*They were not gods unto themselves. But they were very, very good pretenders.*

*Until Annelisa met Death for the second time. Until her body was crushed within the confines of a carriage, metal and wood twisting into her flesh until bone broke and skin gave, until organs punctured and heartbeats halted.*

*Her magic woke her up a day or so later. But that was long enough to break the others.*

*It was long enough to mangle Braeden's heart even worse than the accident had left her body. When she woke up from death half-buried in dirt, she almost didn't recognize the man who was interring her.*

*Everything went bad after that.*

*Everything.*

***

*A flash of dark curls clustered on a sweating brow, hungry eyes darting along the path of notes scratched across what appeared to be half-burned parchment. Her eldest brother hunched over an ornate desk, his ungroomed facial hair wisping across his jawline with bits of something dark still clotted in it, a tarry streak that leaned crimson when he turned his head toward the light.*

*"We're close, Anima," he promised, glancing to his side and only slightly upward—she wasn't very tall, after all. "I just need Mortem, and we'll be ready."*

*"Mora's gone," said Ani, wringing her hands—brown as summer soil, spattered with the most subtle spray of freckles. As she fussed, petals fell one by one from between her fingers, as if she were playing a game of "Loves Me Not" with an infinite rose. "I went to her temple this morning, no one was there—"*

*"Mortem. And she's not gone. She's in Sanctaviv, trying to gather support against us."*

*Winter chilled the blood in Ani's heart, freezing it between beats. The rose petals falling from her hand withered, dried, died. "Brae—"*

*"She's afraid, that's all. We'll get her to see reason. Occassio is already on her way there."*

*"What about Pet…Tempest?"*

*Tenebrae merely held up his hand, dangling a chain from his fingers…a chain with a shard of ice that did not drip, not even as it dangled over the flame of the candle. Tenebrae's eyes reflected it, a dark mirror to the impossibility swaying side to side before them both.*

*"I already have what I need from him," said Tenebrae.*

***

*A flower bloomed from the very heart of Anima's power, a gleaming thing of deep greens and brilliant sunset streaks and gilded edges that brought her to tears every time she beheld it.*

Occassio's favorite mirror, its surface quicksilver-bright with no reflection, a useless example of its kind; still, she'd fondly called it her "cage" with such sweet poison in her voice that Ani had yet to shake her fear of peering into it.

An ice shard that resisted its very nature, never chipping or melting from its chain, created by and stolen from Tempest's hand through Occassio's special brand of trickery.

A phoenix feather plucked from Mortem's favored mount as it slept, neither of them the wiser as one of Tenebrae's worshippers crept away with the proof of his devotion clutched in his slowly-burning fist. By the time he arrived back to them, his entire arm was charred and scorched, the feather gripped between the barest husk of fingers, his grin gleaming with the feral glee only brought on by Tenebrae's chaos magic.

Ani had healed him of his burns, but she couldn't do a thing for that corruption. Brae had promised her over and over, as she knelt at the edge of a cliff and wept for the man who'd leapt off to hear the wind sing, that it would never happen again.

But when Tenebrae brought out that damned music box, his teeth flashing with the exact same hunger, the exact same nightmarish appetite…even then, she should have known it was a lie.

***

Anima, Goddess of Life, knew life and death both as intimately as she knew her own face.

And what happened the day Tenebrae, God of Chaos, attempted to wrest immortality from the fabric of the world and infuse it into their bodies…that was not death.

That was something worse.

A piece of her magic ripped from her chest, a piece so deep and perfect and precisely hers that they might as well have torn her heart free from her chest, ventricles and arteries exposed and seeping lifeblood. That piece went into the flower she had so lovingly painted stroke by stroke.

The rest of her body followed suit soon after…a rankling in her bones before they vanished from the sheath of her skin. A dissolving of muscle and bone and tissue that rendered her voiceless, bloodless, nothing but spirit and magic shunted between the layers of the world, separated from that which she had been named Goddess over.

She was not alone. Sancta, King over the Old Gods, punished each of the Medeis siblings for their hubris in the measure they were due: Mortem the least, Tenebrae the most.

Gods unto themselves, immortal and all-powerful. But there were no bodies, no feelings, nothing but magic and memories and the hammering of prayers against the thin veneer separating her from the world she loved so much.

But Tenebrae would fix it. He told her so in the in-between, his voice never lost amidst the cacophony of prayers beyond.

*"I'll make it right," he told her, feverish desperation pulsing in the rambling torrent of words. "I swear to you, we are going to be a family again. Whatever it takes."*

*And he did. As they figured out how to take hosts to walk the world once more, he used every lifetime to bring himself closer, to read more legends, to concoct more theories, to cajole their other siblings and test their every limit.*

***

Now they were here, and all he needed were the relics…and for each of them to have a host. A scion. A vessel to anchor their power, their souls, to the world they wished so badly to return to.

He'd had Occassio's mirror—that was gone now, hidden away who-knew-where. His followers in Artem were meant to take the phoenix feather; Elias and Mortem had beaten them there. Raquel, Kallias, and Finnick were on their way to find Tempest's ice shard. As far as she knew, her own relic remained under the protection of her followers across the sea, and Tenebrae's music box…

If what the Nyxian men had claimed was true, then Tenebrae had it. And he was using it, she guessed, to try and draw Soren back into his clutches…to return *Anima* back into his possession.

# CHAPTER 16

## SOREN

Along, long hour later—a delay Soren had explained away to Elias with some half-baked excuse muttered through the door—Ani's horrifying tale still spiderwebbed its way inside her skull, making purchase on every inch of thought she managed to churn out past the pounding headache beginning to form in her temples.

Withdrawal was no joke. She'd always heard it, but had never known it herself—she'd never liked the idea of numbing herself so thoroughly with herbs or small doses of poisons, even after wartime injuries or during the worst of the cramping agony that came to visit once every month. She'd always worried that once she started, she wouldn't be able to stop. Thankfully, this substance had never offered anything pleasant to balance out its annoyance, but it still didn't feel good to come off of it. This was a hangover sent straight from Mortem.

Heaving in a breath that reached clean to the depths of her lungs, she turned back to the mirror, forcing herself to meet her own gaze.

Green. Bloodshot. On the verge of tears…but it was her, not Anima, staring back. Her, not Anima, who reached a hand up to fiddle absently with her too-long hair.

She'd always kept it longer than most of the soldiers, though not for lack of knowledge; back when Ember used to spend much of her time on the battlefield, she'd liked to keep her hair as short as she could without fully shearing her head, but despite her steady weaponmaster hands, she always managed to nick herself on the back of the head at least once. She'd taught Soren how to properly style the back, guiding her hands through the motions of cutting and shaping to her satisfaction.

She'd asked once why Ember didn't just shave it off entirely, and had laughed when Ember admitted that she worried the tops of her ears would get frostbitten without the added protection from her locks.

A fierce ache built in her chest, a softer pain than the irrational hatred welling within her at the sight of the hopeless tangles that hadn't loosened even after two rigorous washes. With everything that had happened, she'd barely had time to miss her sisters. She hadn't seen them since saying goodbye before Ursa, before her injury, before Atlas…before all of it.

She didn't know what Elias had told them. They might not even know she was alive, or…

*Gods.* They might not even know the truth of her origins yet. That her blood ran thick with saltwater the same way her lungs ached for the bite of snow-laden wind…that she was not only third in line to the Nyxian crown, but first in line for the throne of Atlas.

Her hand froze in her hair, and she swallowed so hard that she saw her own throat bob in the mirror.

In her single-minded focus on survival, on finally returning to the family she'd lost so long ago, she'd somehow forgotten that part.

Tenebrae…a false god bent on defying the truer deities that had blessed him. A false god who stood ready to usurp the throne of her birth kingdom…*her throne.*

Before, it had been easy to dismiss, to scoff at—the idea of *her* on the Atlas throne? Worse than ridiculous. Even before she'd remembered them, the shifting of title from Jericho back to her had seemed like a mistake that would eventually be corrected. Now…

Soren Marina Atlas. Princess of Nyx…Heir of Atlas. Their future *queen*.

If there was even a throne left to inherit.

If she even survived long enough to inherit it.

Her jaw clenched, and she stepped away from the mirror with shaking legs, forcing herself to breathe as a wave of weakness tried to overcome her, every muscle thinning with fatigue. She leaned against the wall, bracing herself with her forearm and pressing her forehead into her clammy skin, forcing herself to breathe through the dizziness. The fear that tried to rear its head deep in her core.

She was Soren Marina Atlas, daughter of queens, sister to tricksters and heroes, battlemate to Death's chosen warrior. Whatever Tenebrae had planned for her, it could not be worse than what she'd already endured.

She *would* survive this fight, and every fight that came after. And she wouldn't stop until she clawed her way back to her brothers, even if she had to crawl hand and knee through snow and blood to do it.

One step at a time. And right now, that meant shaking the weakness out of her tired hands and getting herself dressed in something clean.

"Soren?" A hesitant knock on the bathing room door. "Look, I'm trying to give you your space, but you're kind of scaring me."

Good. She was scaring herself a bit, too. "Sorry. Just taking it slow. That damned drug they were giving us…"

Elias had a way of wielding silence like others wielded words. The depth and breadth of it always told her everything she needed to know, and this silence was brim-full with guilt.

"Stop it," she sighed. "I can hear you brooding."

"I'm not brooding."

"In that case, who are you and what did you do with the real Elias?"

A snort, and something thumped against the door—a broad, scarred shoulder, if she had to take a guess. "Just worrying about how the others are going to take this, that's all."

She bit her lip, forcing words out past a guilty silence of her own: "Is everyone else downstairs?"

"The twins have already been banned from three separate card games, and Samhain has no fewer than five offers to accompany patrons back to their rooms tonight."

"And Kriss?"

"Kriss left black eyes on the three who were disrespectful about it."

And the sun hadn't even set yet. "I missed them so much."

A smile in his voice, so warm her eyes welled with tears: "I know. Me too."

"Are you going to get off the door so I can come out?"

He pretended to consider, and she contemplated attempting to ram the door down before he finally said, "Only if you promise not to laugh."

Curiosity piqued, she dropped her hand to the knob, gripping it for a moment without turning. "Laugh at what?"

"You'll see."

As she went to twist the knob, her burning, exhausted eyes caught on the door itself. Its wooden surface had been carved in the likeness of a hulking wolf, two holes where the eyes would be, the hearth-light within the room lighting the gaps in blazing gold.

Her stomach curled inward, a piece of her composure withering. But she resisted the urge to strain to catch a glimpse of her own eyes in the fogged-up mirror; instead, she opened the door and kept herself moving, each step proving that she still held the reins to her own body.

This fear would fade in time. She would whittle it away piece by rotten piece with every word she chose to speak, with every path she *chose* to walk.

But that path came to an abrupt halt when she stepped into the room and found Elias dawdling at the foot of one of the room's two beds, looking for all the world like a little boy who'd done something terribly naughty while his parents had their eyes pointed elsewhere.

"As much as I'm sure you're enjoying stealing my clothes," he said with a laugh that didn't quite ring true, "I thought you might want something of your own."

And when he moved aside to reveal the thing lying on the foot of her chosen bed, her breath utterly arrested.

"When," she asked, stepping toward the bed with one aching step, "did you have time to find *this*?"

For there, laid out on the bed with precisely arranged folds to show off its pattern, was the *ugliest* gods-damned sweater she had ever seen in her life.

"Seems a merchant in this town shares your taste in yarn." There was a smile in his voice, but his mouth didn't match it—nerves bent those lips downward.

She shuffled forward to scoop up the sweater, biting her lips to hold in a curse at the pops of pain in her knees.

A faint, cautious giggle in the back of her head. *It sounds like you're popping corn in your kneecaps.*

*All right, I get it. I have weird joints. If you're not going to heal them, you don't get to make fun of them.*

Ani was quiet for a long moment. *I mean…I could try, but if I'm not in control, my magic won't settle…*

*It was a joke, Goddess Great.* Not her best by any means, but still.

One, two, three tries to heft the sweater over her head only resulted in grating pain in her shoulders and neck. A low growl escaped her throat—good. Better anger than embarrassment. "A little help?"

Elias smiled now in earnest, but it was his gaze's turn to rebel against the emotion he was trying to portray; though he chuckled as he approached her, those eyes grew dark with worry. Even the gold-rimmed one seemed to dim beneath fear's shadow. "You're really hurting that much?"

Soren almost shrugged—almost. She caught herself just as her shoulders hit the edge of an action that would have caused her pain. "Sore from traveling."

It was a poor excuse. They both knew it. Still, he allowed her the small dignity of not arguing. He merely helped her dress, pressed a kiss between her brows that softened every edge of her lingering dread from the conversation with Anima, and whispered, "Before we go down, we need to have a talk."

Tension rippled through her, but she merely glowered up at him…more *up* than normal. Had he gotten *taller*, too? "That's my least favorite way to start a conversation."

"Well, I'm about to change your mind."

"Go on, then. Astound me."

His lips thinned, another sure sign a conversation she wouldn't like was coming. He stepped back a pace, dragging in a breath that shook at its tail end—

And his finger looped through the ring hanging on the chain around his neck.

Now her heart stopped.

"I…" he began, then stopped, blowing out a breath of frustration that stirred the tips of his hair. "Gods damn me, this wasn't how I wanted to…"

Oh gods, he was doing it.

He was actually doing it.

"I didn't want to rush it," he was saying, but she could barely hear him above the pounding of her pulse, above the rush of joy filling her heart near to bursting, her scowl oh-so-slowly curling into a grin. "And maybe this is bad timing,

I mean—" He gestured around them with either a chuckle or a throat-clearing, his fingers trembling at the tips, his smile shallow and shifting with anxiety. "It's certainly not the location I had in mind, but I hope—"

"Elias," she interrupted, and he stopped breathing like his body's default state was dying, "ask me the damned question, or I'm going to ask it instead and rob you of a very passionate, dashing, swoon-worthy speech."

A snort, and he wiped at his brow with such profound lack of subtlety she almost laughed. But something told her that this laugh, out of all of them, might just break his heart. "You think I'm that eloquent?"

"Based on information I received previously, I *think* you've been rehearsing this in your head for at least a few years, so you should be well prepared by now." Her laugh came out wet and shaky, but for a good reason this time—the best reason. "Ask me."

With that demand—with that *challenge*—his eyes sharpened from nerves to determination, to the look of a man who had just sighted the end of a path he'd run for so long he'd forgotten anything existed outside of it. The look he always got when she dangled a dare in front of him…ever since the very first.

*Anima,* she said, *can you give us a moment?*

A pause from the other side of the ever-thinning veil. *Oh. Um…I think so. I'll try. Let me just…*

Some of the pressure that normally pressed against the barrier between them lessened. She guessed that was as much "privacy" as they were going to get.

Elias's fist tightened around that ring. Tugged it up and over his head, his broad fingers making surprisingly quick work of the delicate clasp as he slipped the ring into his palm.

His knee hit the dusty, pockmarked, stained floor of this second-rate inn. The air smelled of old cloth and burned-out candles and long-spilled whiskey. Her every bone ached, he bore new scars in so many places she couldn't count them, and her hair might as well have been a game of cat's cradle…

And it was perfect.

All of it perfect, because he was Elias, and she was Soren, and it had never mattered where they were or how they looked or how badly the odds were stacked against them.

She belonged to this man, and he to her, tied together by blood and braids, loyalty and love, and something stronger than the very Death he served.

"Soren Marina Atlas," he said, his Nyxian accent embracing her Atlas name with such tenderness she might have wept if not for her overwhelming glee, "you are the most gods-damned annoying human being I've ever known."

"That's not very romantic."

"For once in your life, you awful, cruel, beautiful woman, will you *please* shut up until I finish talking?"

"Sorry." She wasn't. But she bit her unavoidable cleverness back, caging it behind her teeth.

"You are the most annoying human being I've ever met," he tried again, grinning in spite of himself, his eyes shining with joy like she'd never seen, "but there's no one I'd rather have at my back. No one I'd trust more with my life and my love. No one I'd rather have walking me home. So, Soren Marina Atlas…I'm asking you to marry me."

Oh, this man was unbearable.

"Elias Tiberius Loch," she said, stroking a thumb over his cheek to rub away a tear that had escaped ahead of its cue, "I'm saying yes."

Then the ring was on her finger, his hands were buried in her hair, her back was pinned to the wall, and he was kissing her so breathless she had to wonder why she'd ever bothered kissing anyone else.

# CHAPTER 17

# RAQUEL

They needed to pack up. They needed to run. And they'd started—once Kallias had felt well enough to bathe off the underground river and get himself changed into dry clothes, the two of them had begun gathering their things in a hurry. But when Finn had marched in with his pack and thrown that little bag on the bed…

They'd all stopped to stare at it. They'd been staring for two minutes they didn't have to spare.

"Did you open it?" Raquel asked.

Finn grimaced. "Depths, no. Relics and I, we don't get along."

"Well, someone should," Kallias croaked. Even after his hot bath, he hadn't stopped shivering, a series of near-convulsions nothing seemed to soothe.

"Otherwise we might get out of here and open the bag to find Aeris's…I don't know, his collection of pebbles or something."

"Nah, that was in a different drawer," Finn said.

Ridiculous boys. "I'll look," she said. "Kallias, get as far back as possible, just in case. Finnick, watch him."

The younger man's nose wrinkled. "I really do prefer Finn."

"Noted." She pointed toward the back wall. "Back up."

Finn pushed his hand into Kallias's chest, moving him back—then throwing his other hand up to catch Kallias when he stumbled. Finn's expression twisted from amused to dark calm in an instant. "What did Aeris do to you?"

"I'm fine," Kallias muttered. But he covered Finn's hand with his own, gripping it for support. His lips were still frighteningly pale.

"That's not what I asked," Finn said through gritted teeth. "What did he *do?*"

Kallias met Finn's gaze, and Raquel nearly shivered at the piercing look in his eyes…his eyes that were once again green, only the barest tint of blue leaking in. "What did Occassio do to *you?*" he countered softly.

Finn's eyes darkened further. He merely adjusted so his arm was wrapped around Kallias's back, ready to catch him if he fell…or if he lunged for the relic. Raquel didn't know what effect the object would have on him, especially with his magic supposedly snuffed out, but she wasn't willing to run the risk.

She sat on the bed, the springs creaking beneath her, and she gingerly scooped the silver suede pouch into her hand.

The moment she touched it, lightning lanced through her sternum, and her entire chest lit with skyfire.

The gasp that ripped from her lungs was nothing short of exultant, rounding out into a sob before it was over.

*Magic.*

"Raquel." Finn's voice. She barely registered the caution in it.

"I'm fine," she promised, not sure if the wobble to her voice was from tears or laughter. It had been so long since magic walked the halls of her hollow body. "It's fine."

Distantly, she knew that wasn't quite true; and she hadn't even meant to lie, not really. But her words knew what her mind hadn't yet concluded: if they suspected something was wrong, they'd take this away from her.

They couldn't take it away from her. Not again.

Reverently, she coaxed the drawstring top of the pouch open, fingertips barely creeping inside its confines.

Her fingernail scraped against ice.

Thunder exploded in her ears, a glorious layering of screams and roars that built into music, the chorus of a storm just barely born.

*Raquel Angelov. I remember you.*

Not just storms—the earth beneath her bent to cradle her feet. The wind coiled to embrace her body, lifting her hair off her back. She couldn't breathe deeply enough to taste it to her satisfaction, the crispest air she'd ever had the privilege to breathe. That ice inside the pouch began to crawl upward, outward, following the path she'd provided with her finger—

A hand struck hers hard enough to knock the pouch to the floor. "Raquel!"

Finn's shout shattered the singing of the storm in her head, the magic scattering like shrapnel through her mind, dozens of tiny agonies punishing her for her hubris. She swore, stumbling backward while clutching her head, and strong arms caught her from behind—arms that still trembled from their own ordeal.

"Raquel," Kallias said urgently into her ear. "*Raquel.* Are you with us?"

It took a moment for her to find her voice. "I'm with you. What…"

"You touched it, in spite of us yelling for you *not* to, and I don't know what happened after that, but you wouldn't talk to us. And you had a look in your eyes I didn't like." Finn scooped up the relic and popped it back into his pocket, scowling at her and Kallias as if they were his own personal punishment. "I think it's best if I hold on to this."

"Agreed," she and Kallias said together. Perhaps the fastest they'd ever agreed on something. And for them to be agreeing that Finnick of all people should hold the key to an immense, unimaginable power…

Either it was the only right decision or the absolute wrong one. But she'd always been a disciplined gambler; she didn't often place her bets in places that weren't near-guaranteed to bring a profit.

If she knew one thing about Finnick Atlas, it was that his interests did not lie with the god of storms and seas; a disposition she and Kallias did not happen to share. The relic was safest in his hands…no matter how much hers ached to hold it. Perhaps *because* hers ached to hold it.

And gods, did it *ache.*

"Five minutes," she croaked. "Pack up and get ready to go. We want to be far away from here before Aeris even gets a *hint* we might have touched this."

She'd barely finished her sentence before there was a sharp rap on the door.

"Miss Angelov, Princes Atlas," said a reedy voice she only recognized from the ordeal this morning—the boy who'd accompanied Aeris during the ritual. "The Stormspeaker requests an audience with you. *Immediately.*"

Raquel exchanged a look with Kallias before they both turned their eyes to Finnick, who gave an exasperated shrug and mouthed *Don't look at me!*

"We'll be right out," Raquel answered faintly. Gods, why could she never sound strong in the moments she needed it most?

"What did you do?" Kallias hissed the moment the boy's footsteps faded down the hall.

Finn pressed his hands to his chest, eyes widened for dramatic effect. "Me? I stole a gods-damned deific relic from right beneath a cult leader's nose in less than five minutes, that's what I did. What did you two do? Oh wait, I remember— one of you *drowned*!"

Raquel's blood ran cold. "We didn't tell you that."

"Did you leave any trace?" snapped Kallias, ignoring them both. "Anything at all?"

Finn opened his mouth as if ready to snap back, but she watched as he faltered over the words, a slight pinch to his brow belying his uncertainty.

That wasn't a good sign.

"Enough." Raquel rubbed her shaking hands together. There was no point arguing now. Aeris had summoned them—their only choices were to run, potentially fighting their way out against dozens of Tempest-blessed zealots, or to honor his invitation. "We don't know why he's asking for us. There's no reason to assume—"

"There's every reason to assume," Finn countered, finding his voice again. "It would be foolish *not* to assume. I know you have a soft spot—"

"Don't think you can taunt me—"

"It's not a taunt. It's the truth." Finnick's words held all the softness of a mountain cat's claws. And as far as truths went, she'd rather face any of the ones she'd been hiding instead of the crooked, blade-bodied boy in front of her. "He's dangerous enough that the Trickster Goddess herself felt the need to pay him a little visit, and believe me, most aren't deemed worthy of that. So let's assume this is a very bad sign for us. What's our plan? Do we fight, do we flirt with risk, do we stall? Give us a heading and we'll follow it, but you better be damn sure that it's our best bet. We don't have room for a loss."

"Wise words," she muttered.

Finnick held her gaze. "I have my moments."

"Raquel, we're looking to you," Kallias said. His eyes bore into her, serious and scared, his hand absently scratching at his sternum like he was checking to make sure he still breathed. "Stay or run?"

Instinct screamed to run. Reason cautioned her to stay. And somewhere in the war between, she realized there wasn't a choice at all, not really.

To run would likely leave them all dead anyway, their bodies littering the snowy forest floor. To stay…

"Let's see what he wants," she said.

And though both princes looked decidedly uneasy—and Kallias, perhaps outright afraid—they did not fight her.

For the first time, she desperately wished they would fight her.

***

"I have a very important question to ask you."

That much was clear. They'd been forced back down into the lower level of the lodge, villagers coming to flank them as they walked, two silent guards to each of them. Kallias was shaking again, his teeth chattering with cold. As they came to a halt at the edge of the pool, his arm pressed against hers, clammy and riddled with gooseflesh. His knuckles brushed hers, one finger hooking around hers in the barest imitation of a squeeze.

"It's all right," he breathed in her ear. "You're not alone."

"Don't," she whispered back as Aeris threw an incensed look at their hands, his eyes blazing blue, his lips a crack in the ice that had frozen his face in an expression of cold, quiet rage. She tugged her hand away, pinning it behind her back, out of Aeris's sight.

Jealousy could kill. And right now, Kallias didn't need a bigger target on his back than what he already wore.

"One of you," Aeris said, voice deathly soft, "has overstepped the boundaries of my hospitality."

"If we made a misstep," Kallias said, meeting Aeris's glare with a look of cautious calm, "I apologize for the infraction. We're new to Nyxian culture, but it's no excuse. If you could correct us—"

"Oh, no, nothing like that. You've been model guests. At least, you were…until one of you thought to take something very precious from me." His eyes swept over them again, probing, desperation barely contained in the bat of his eyelashes. "Where is it?"

If Mortem was truly merciful, she would have dragged them all to the pits right then.

Instead, Finn spoke up with his usual lazy confidence, the Second Prince incarnate, even daring to wear a hint of Aeris's glower on his own face. "We haven't even been here long enough to *start* deciding whether we wanted to steal from you." He paused. "Unless you mean the soap in my room, but I really was under the impression it was complimentary, and I assumed you wouldn't want it back anyway after the *unholy* amount of dirt I had to scrub off my—"

Finn's voice broke off, and at first, Raquel thought he might have finally run out of hot air to spew. But when she glanced at him out of the corner of her eye, her heart jammed against her ribcage.

One of the villagers behind the Second Prince now held a polished silver dagger at his throat, freezing him mid-taunt.

"I won't ask again," Aeris said. "Where. Is. It."

The steel had barely settled against Finn's throat before Kallias stepped forward, hands up, eyes fixed firmly on Aeris. "I took it."

"Kal," Finn hissed sharply, then exhaled quietly in pain as the dagger pressed in deeper. Blood slid down the column of his throat, a sanguine trickle that could turn into a waterfall at any wrong move from them.

"I took it," Kallias repeated without hesitation. He took another step toward Aeris.

His hands were still trembling.

Every inch of muscle in her body went taut.

"I…I had second thoughts too late. I regretted severing my connection the moment the ritual ended. I…I wanted it back. I *need* it back," Kallias continued, stepping forward again—putting himself between them and Aeris, separating himself, offering up an easy target.

He was trying to give them space to escape.

*Oh, you utter bastard.* Someone had to teach this man how to stop trying to die for people, *damn* it.

She didn't want his sacrifice. She hadn't asked for it. Sacrifice meant repayment, an end to his blood-debt to her, and that meant his life no longer lay in her hands. That she no longer had the right to hold his death at bay with a claim she'd staked so long ago, sealed with a handshake between her and a princess on a snow-covered mountain cliff.

Aeris eyed him with nothing less than venom. "I asked you where it is."

Kallias held his gaze. Said nothing.

"Put him on his knees," said Aeris.

Raquel's stomach crashed through her feet, falling into the very heart of the world.

*"Put her on her knees." Stormspeaker Caelum, her father in the ways that mattered, her dearest mentor, her leader…he looked down at her with a curling sneer, as if she was nothing more than a mule deer carcass rotting in the village square. Nothing but a worthless, disgusting thing that had made the decision to die where it would be most inconvenient for everyone.*

*She was not dead. She did not want to die.*

*"Please don't," she sobbed as her friends, her family, caught her by the arms and shoved her against the stone floor, her knees tearing open as they pushed. The pain was worse because she knew, she knew it was nothing compared to what was coming. "Please, I'd give it back if I could, I—Aeris, Aeris please Aeris I don't know why he picked me, I don't know—"*

*"Someone fetch the whip," said Caelum. "Someone has to teach her not to steal what is holy."*

"No." The word had no voice the first time, but the second time it was a roar. "Aeris, no!"

Aeris ignored her cries as the two villagers who'd been guarding Kallias gripped his shoulders and guided him to the ground. One of them punched a fist upward, and a pillar of rock shot up a few feet. Aeris jerked his chin, and they produced a rope, binding Kallias to the pillar. Then they cut the shirt from him, letting it fall in a heap around his legs.

He didn't fight—he went to his knees with all the dignity in the world, his chin high, his expression entirely free of fear.

It was the face of a man used to taking punishment. And even when the girl who'd announced his death earlier came forward to hand Aeris a many-stranded whip, the steel tips rattling against the stone with a familiarity that struck her square in the stomach, that face did not give way to dread.

She was going to be sick.

Finn's breath caught in a harsh gasp. He jerked forward, heedless of the knife at his throat, and the trickle of blood thickened to a stream. "No. Kal, no— hey! Don't. Stop. It's me, all right? I stole it. It was me."

But this wasn't about who had stolen it. This wasn't about the truth. Raquel knew that the moment Aeris met her gaze across the common space.

This was about punishing her. And he'd chosen Kallias to cause her the most pain.

"Don't." Again, her voice failed her.

Aeris's only answer was to dip the whip into the salt-laced pool.

She realized the intention behind it half a second after Finn did; that was the only reason she heard his outraged intake of breath over her own.

Then Finn seized the wrist of the woman holding him and bent it back until the sickening snap of bone echoed through the cavern.

The woman had barely begun to howl in agony before Finn twisted with sight-boggling speed, plucking the dagger from the woman's hand with deft fingers and driving his clenched fist into her throat. As she reached up to cradle her neck, gagging, Finn dropped to his knees and took advantage of her open torso, swiping the dagger in a blow so quick and vicious that he was moving before the wound even began to bleed through the woman's thick tunic. By the time she'd fallen to her knees, Finn already had spun around to face the man who'd come up behind him, dropping onto his haunches and hooking his legs around the man's ankles to yank them out from under him. The man's skull cracked against the rock, and he went instantly limp.

Raquel jolted forward to help, but two sets of arms wrapped around her from behind, forcing her to the ground with an impact that sent pain singing through her jaw up to her skull. She blinked away the dizziness to see Finn too had been thrust to the ground, pinned not by arms but by stone, manacles of rock fastening his wrists and ankles and neck to the floor. Still, he struggled like a wild animal with the teeth of a trap buried in its leg, eyes wild with a rage gilded in madness, his teeth gritted as he craned his neck to seek out Aeris's eyes.

"This is a mistake," he seethed to Aeris. "Let him go. Let us all go."

Aeris had the nerve to smile. "Or what? You'll kill me, Second Prince?"

Finn smiled back. A dark, beautiful, horrible smile that pulled every one of Raquel's instincts taut with sheer revulsion.

That smile was a glimpse into an abyss no one should wander into.

And that was before the laugh.

It started as a chuckle, a hushed thing that could have been misunderstood as a sigh or a cough. But it built and built until it was no longer a chuckle, no longer quiet—it was full-blown laughter that flung itself into the cave walls with reckless abandon, a cracked tone to it that spoke of insanity.

"No," Finn said softly, the laughter ending all at once. Only the lunacy remained, a silvery gleam in his eyes that reminded her of moonlight. "No, I think killing you would be too kind."

The silence that followed afterward was eerie, the air still carrying the memory of Finn's cackle. And to his credit, Aeris *did* look relatively unnerved.

But it didn't stop him from stepping forward and bringing the saltwater-soaked whip down on Kallias's bare back.

The first rip of leather and metal against flesh tore her heart from her chest. Kallias's body seized, his back arching, but he did not scream.

Another strike. Another convulsion. No scream.

Another strike, harder than the last, the slap of blood against stone drowning out the entire world. Finn might have been shouting curses. She might have been too. But none of it reached past the sound of Kallias's ragged, agonized breathing. None of it distracted her from the way he fought to sit straight as his body tried to sag, his furrowed brow pressed to the stone pillar, his teeth gritted so tightly she could see his jaw twitching beneath his beard.

Even on his knees, he held himself like a king.

"Stop," she said.

Aeris brought the whip down again, and this time Kallias did fall, his breath punching free in a muffled groan as he collapsed flush against the pillar. Rivulets of blood wept from his back, marking scarlet paths down his torso before raining down on his ruined shirt.

"*Wait!*" Raquel surged up, but the hands pinning her shoulders down might as well have been made of lead. She gritted her teeth and pushed back anyway. "Aeris, Aeris—wait. *Please.*"

The whip fell—but not on Kallias's back this time, though his flanks twitched in an instinctive wince when the steel tips clicked against the ground. Aeris met her gaze impassively.

She'd sworn to herself she would never beg again—not for herself, not for anyone.

Kallias's face was pressed to the pillar, but he tipped his head a bit to catch her gaze. His eyes were glazed with anguish, but still he shook his head and mouthed *no*.

*No, Raquel.*

"Let me." This was a defeat, but it didn't have to be his to bear. Not this time. "Let me take it for him."

"Raquel, *don't*," Kallias moaned, his face contorted nearly beyond recognition as he forced himself back up off the pillar, his biceps flexing, his arms shaking with the effort.

"You don't tell me what to do, Atlas." Even her venom lacked bite. She'd brought them here—had placed her confidence in herself and her ability to keep them safe. This was her fault. Her punishment.

Aeris came to stand before her. He bent low, lowering his voice so it only found her: "You will take his punishment for lying to me. And then you will tell me where my relic is."

"Tempest's relic," she whispered. "Not yours. Do not mistake yourself for a god."

He caught her chin, pinching so hard it would likely bruise. He leaned so close that his lips brushed hers as he whispered: "With that relic, anyone can be a god, Stormcloud."

The fervency in his voice reminded her of Zaccheus, of Elias in the worst of his grief, of *heresy* and *sacrilege* and faith fermented into something darker.

"I take the punishment, I tell you where it is," she rasped, "and you let Finnick and Kallias go afterward. You do what you want with me."

With a nod and a gesture from Aeris, all nausea and terror fled. In its place was calm.

Her fate was sealed. There was nothing to fight, nothing to fear.

She had only to endure and survive.

*I am the Eye of the Storm, the peace within chaos, the power within peace. He cannot touch any piece of me I do not offer.*

He was not taking this from her. She offered it freely, and in that sacrifice, there was still power.

They untied Kallias and hauled him up, casting him to the ground between her and Finn. He reached toward her, hand shaking, but Aeris reached down and pulled to her feet with terrible gentleness, pressing a kiss to her forehead.

"Brave," he murmured against her skin, and she shuddered against the urge to shove him away. "But foolish. Nothing has changed."

"Ambitious," she whispered, "but cowardly. Yes, it seems nothing has."

His grip on her arm tightened. "Tie her up."

They obeyed, her two guards forcing her to kneel in Kallias's blood. While they tied her wrists, she craned her neck to look for the princes.

They'd let Finn up—how he'd talked them into that, she didn't have the faintest idea, but he was kneeling beside Kallias now. His ankles were still pinioned to the floor with stone, but he was muttering angrily into Kallias's ear while he tore off the scarf draped around his shoulders and pressed it to the inflamed welts on Kallias's back.

Kallias wasn't even listening. His eyes were fastened to her, tortured and helpless, his fingers flexing against the stone like he wanted to crawl to her.

*It's all right,* she mouthed to him. Again and again and again. *It's all right, it's all right.*

He shook his head. His lips barely moved, trembling, bloody where he'd bitten them to hold in his screams: *Raquel.*

Just her name. Again and again and again. *Raquel.*

Aeris did not grant her the mercy of a swift cut like he had Kallias. Instead he knelt before her, undoing her shirt button by button, his touch tender and adoring and utterly cruel. He exposed her as a lover would, fingers lingering and worshipful. She wanted to vomit on his finely crafted tunic.

She would not scream. Not after Kallias had borne the rabid teeth of the whip so quietly.

Besides, these walls still remembered her screams from her first punishment. The ground likely still remembered her blood, her tears, her writhing body. She would give it something new to remember.

It would remember her silence.

And it was silence that she clung to with all her might as the whip flayed open her skin, layering new wounds atop old scars, salt burning into her blood like a branding iron.

# CHAPTER 18

# KALLIAS

**E**very sickening *thwack* of steel-tipped leather against Raquel's skin was worse than any agony he'd ever endured on his own body.

Worse still was the silent, unblinking focus with which she took every blow, not so much as a gasp or a whimper escaping with each strike Aeris rained down on her bare skin. Already she'd taken more strikes than he had, and still she refused to collapse. She wouldn't look at him—no matter how desperately he tried to catch her gaze, she only looked forward, her lips pressed into a self-muzzling line, her body shaking with the effort of holding in her cries.

Dead. Everyone in this room, everyone who'd ever laid a finger on her was *dead*.

"Finn," he breathed, interrupting Finn's ranting while his brother stanched his wounds, "give me the relic."

"Oh, sure, of course," Finn muttered. "Maybe when Mortem's fiery morning breath goes cold—"

"I'm serious," Kallias choked. "We have to get out of here."

"Raquel's getting us out of here."

"You really think he's going to let us go like he promised?"

Finn shrugged one shoulder, leaning over to help Kallias sit up. He couldn't tell if Finn's fingers were coated in his blood or the blood of the dead cultist—the cultist his lazy, squeamish, scholar-minded younger brother had just murdered with all the efficiency of a practiced killer.

They were going to have a long, long talk once they got out of this place.

"I think he doesn't give a damn about us," Finn murmured. "And I think we can get out of here on our own."

"I'm not leaving Raquel."

"She volunteered."

"I am *not leaving her.*" The next strike sent Raquel lurching against the pillar, her eyes rolling into her head before she shook herself back to her senses, and panic stole all feeling from his own body. "Give me the damned relic, Finn."

Still his brother ignored his command. "I'm not trading your life for hers. You take this relic, and Tempest takes you."

"It's not your choice."

"It's not yours, either."

The next time the whip fell, Raquel slumped against the pillar and didn't get up.

Terror strangled him, and he had to choke out his next words. "Finn, *please.*"

Silence from his brother. Then: "Swear to me you won't give in to him. No matter what he says, no matter what he threatens or promises, you will *not* let him take you."

"I promise." Gods, he would have sworn anything he asked for at this point. "Give it to me. Now."

He didn't even see Finn move—didn't see where he'd had the relic hidden. But suddenly the suede pouch was nestled in his own hand, a hint of frostbite pulsing in the cage of his fingers.

There were only two moments in Kallias Atlas's life when he'd felt time stop. When he'd known that his next choice would shape the rest of his life for better or worse, and nothing could change its course once time began to move again.

The first was when he saw Soleil on the battlefield in Ursa, fighting under a Nyxian flag.

The second was here, now, with godlike power clenched in the hollow of his palm.

This was entirely different than staring down a glass of wine, his tongue and throat and mind yearning for its cloying touch, and forcing himself to say no—and yet, exactly the same.

Addiction was addiction. Once he tasted this power again, his thirst for it might never be sated.

And for just a heartbeat, just one in that moment of stillness, he hesitated.

But then he heard Raquel whimper. A sound so raw with agony that it utterly shattered his heart.

Anything. For her, anything.

He opened the pouch and pulled out the relic.

His blood turned to ice in his veins, and white flashed across his vision, blinding him in the blink of an eye.

Power drove into his body as a battering ram hauled against an unyielding gate, and every one of his bones buckled beneath its weight. Yet there was no pain, none at all—nothing but the zing of lightning and the roar of thunder and the thrill of an ecstasy so all-consuming that he momentarily forgot where he was. What he was. *Who* he was.

He was no longer prince or brother or man. No longer Kallias or Kal or Atlas.

He was the ice that grew from the hinges of rooftops like the fangs of a colossal beast. He was the wind that blew ships out to sea and carried sailors home. He was the thunder that shook windowpanes in their frames and drove little children to huddle in their parents' beds, begging to be soothed with tales of the gods playing games just above the snarling clouds.

He was the lightning that painted the sky in vivid strokes of lavender and ivory. He was the stone beneath his knees. The sand between his toes. The seawater that lingered in the welts on his back.

He was the one who spoke for the storm now.

And the storm was *pissed off.*

The blinding flash of power settling in his body faded just in time for him to see Aeris drop the whip, horror and rage taking turns with his face like children bickering over a shiny toy.

"*Stop him!*" he roared.

Or at least, he tried. But before he could even get through *stop*, Kallias reached out a hand—

And tore the air straight from his lungs.

The horrible retching sound Aeris made as he fell to his knees and clutched his chest should have sickened him. But nature, as it turned out, wasn't bothered by much.

*Welcome back, Prince.* Tempest's voice came stronger than ever, thick with amusement—and perhaps a hint of relief. *I knew you'd change your mind.*

"I didn't do it for you," he muttered.

*Of course not.* Tension replaced amusement. *I don't take kindly to people abusing my blessings, Prince. Shall we teach him a lesson?*

Kallias cracked his neck, standing to his feet, fueled by the power tumbling through every limb. Cold crept up his back, numbing the fiery pain.

His eyes met Aeris's. The Stormspeaker's gaze widened, and the fear Kallias saw there filled him with vicious, unfamiliar glee.

"It would be my pleasure," he rasped.

And with half a thought, Kallias Atlas unleashed himself on his enemies.

# CHAPTER 19

## RAQUEL

Fire and ice raged through her body, a war she hadn't asked to fight in being waged on a battleground built of pain.

She couldn't open her eyes.

Every thought swirled in sluggish patterns like oil poured into water, refusing to blend into something coherent. Every sense was dulled and dreamy, some kind of half-sleep shielding her from the worst of her wounds.

Maybe the half-sleep was the beginning of death.

Death had never dared creep too close before—she'd never offered Mortem more than base respect for what she could do, and Mortem in return had seemed willing to give her space. The only time they'd crossed paths was after her exile from this very village, when she'd fallen asleep in a shredded shirt, using a snowdrift as a bed, a never-ending river of blood flowing down from her empty eye socket.

She'd dreamed of wolves that night, and had woken to strands of silvery fur caught in the fabric of her clothing.

But there were no wolves now, though there *was* a hint of howling just beyond the miasma of sleep muffling her senses. Instead she drifted like a snowflake bobbing in the wind, only the support of stone against her cheek reminding her that there was still a world beyond this gentle pocket of reverie.

After a time, the howling stopped. Something cold pressed against her jaw, cradling it with a tenderness she wasn't used to. Her head lolled into it, shuddering at its caress. No one had handled her with gentleness in so long…

"Raquel." The wind whispered her name, anguished and pleading. "Raquel, open your eyes, look at me. Look at me, let me see your eyes."

She tried—she tried, but her eyelids felt frozen shut, and she was back in the woods again, sleeping in the snow, her heart hurting worse than her wounds ever could.

"Please, please…" Could the wind tremble with emotion? Could it sob in her ear like she was breaking its heart? "Come on, you beautiful terror, let me see your damned eyes!"

"Kal," said something else—not the wind. Something colder. "Kal, we have to go."

"We have to get her up, I can't carry her…"

"She's not going to be able to walk. Look at her back."

"Then what do we do? Give me ideas or stop talking!"

"Oh, *now* you want my ideas?"

"Stop." She barely recognized her own voice, slurred with pain and tasting of salt and iron. "You two…ridiculous."

A laugh, breathless and wobbly with hysteria—*Kallias*. "There she is. Wake up, you. We're getting out of here."

The pad of his thumb brushed beneath her eye again—she realized a heartbeat later he'd been wiping away her tears, a constant stream fueled by the ruined flesh of her back. "Can't."

"Oh, don't start that."

"Kallias, *look* at her." Finnick. She recognized him now, even with his voice swimming in her ears. "There's no way we're walking out of here."

Even as distant as she was, a word came to mind—the memory of something close by. "Boats."

"What, Raquel?" Both of Kallias's hands held her now, one supporting her neck, the other curled around her waist. Even this close to tumbling over the edge into Mortem's pits, the icy touch of his hands against her bare skin sent goosebumps erupting over her body. She barely felt the bindings on her wrists snap, freeing her from the pillar, and as badly as she wanted to, she couldn't keep from collapsing against Kallias, limp and shivering with shock.

"The boats." It took all her concentration to form her moan of agony into words. "The river."

"The fishing boats. Kal, the boats—" Finn's voice grew distant and echoing—either he'd moved further away or she was drifting into a daze again. "There's a current leading down the tunnel. If we can sail down the river…"

She tried one last time to raise her head, to open her eyes, to seek out the prince who held her against him like he was afraid she'd slip through his fingers. But all she could see behind her stubborn eyelid was the faintest flicker of gold.

And then, nothing at all.

# CHAPTER 20

## SOREN

Soren had yet to convince herself she wasn't dreaming by the time she and Elias managed to tear themselves apart long enough for him to escort her down to the inn's common area.

The explosion of sound might have been overwhelming to anyone who had not missed this exact tumult caused by these exact people every day since she'd been removed from it. As Elias had said, the twins were in the process of claiming their winnings: Andrei gathering the money, Nikolai subtly snatching his marked cards back from their hands and nudging them up his sleeves. Samhain and Kriss were tag-teaming at the surprisingly crowded bar counter now, coaxing free drinks from the various patrons already seated and mouthing their running total to each other as they went—Samhain had received five, Kriss three. Frigga and Rian were watching patiently from one of the booths against the far wall, Rian silently signaling to Samhain which drink he wanted next. And Jakob and Varran were watching it all from their shared booth, Jakob's arm looped around Varran's shoulders, the two of them scanning the tavern with the practiced assessment of men used to needing to deescalate situations before they turned into a bar brawl.

"Are we going to tell them?" Soren asked out of the corner of her mouth, bracing Elias's back with her ring-adorned hand to keep it out of sight.

"I don't really think we have a choice," Elias sighed.

"I don't think they'll notice on their own."

"True." He reached back to grip her hand, pulling it away from his back and kissing the knuckle with the ring. "But I don't know if I'm going to be able to stop myself from telling everyone who'll listen that you just agreed to be my wife."

His *wife*.

Prickles of delight danced a jig up her spine. "Never call me anything else but that again."

His laugh warmed every inch of her. "We're not married yet, smartass."

"I don't care, jackass. Call it practice."

"There you are!" called Jakob across the tavern, grinning—then raising an eyebrow when he caught sight of her garish outfit. "Mortem save you, what bet did you lose?"

"Not everything is a bet." She dropped into the booth across from him, jamming her heel into the toe of his boot and scowling when it didn't give, not even an inch.

"Are you trying to play footsie with me?" Jakob looked at Varran. "She's trying to play footsie with me."

"Her funeral," said Varran without looking up from his soup. "I think you shriveled one of my lungs when you took off your boots last night."

Jakob cuffed the back of his battlemate's head, and Varran gagged as his spoon jolted into his mouth. While he was busy choking on soup, Jakob patting his back and grumbling apologies, Soren leaned in. "I'm going to tell you a secret."

"Is there *another* kingdom you're the secret Heir of?" Jakob put his free hand over his chest, his cheeks going a bit sallow. "Please, gods, I can't take anymore drama."

A smile crept across her lips, and she slowly lifted her hand to the light, wiggling her fingers to ensure the ring sparkled properly.

Jakob blinked. Varran stopped choking, though that could have been a coincidence.

"I'm going to lose my shit," Jakob announced. "I am going to *fully* lose—"

"Please don't," Elias groaned.

"Ah, ah!" She shot her hand out and caught Jakob, pinning his arm to the table as he tried to stand—possibly to climb up and give a grand announcement himself. "Think this through, Captain. This is an opportunity."

Eyes gleaming, he glanced around at the rest of the company still knee-deep in their shenanigans; then he looked to her, dropping back to his seat and propping his bearded chin on his hand. "I'm listening, Princess."

"Speaking of bets," she coaxed him, mirroring his posture, positioning her hand with the ring to keep it in sight, "I think you could make some good money if you started a pool on this subject now."

"Don't encourage him," Elias and Varran said at the same time, but she ignored them, holding Jakob's ice-blue gaze.

*Though its ice-blue eyes pierced into hers with feral intent, though its teeth were long as a paring knife's blade, there was no fear—only adrenaline, a building urgency that heated her veins and urged her to run faster, faster, faster—*

Breath caught in her throat, a silent gasp she only just managed to swallow down, burying it behind her smile.

Dreams and nightmares. She was tired of them both.

"You make a very good point," he pondered aloud, stroking his chin with deliberate slowness. "I suppose we'd share the pot?"

"Seems only fair. As long as you don't embarrass Elias with a huge scene right here in the middle of a pack of strangers."

"Hm. Wouldn't want to alarm your *fiancé*, now would we?" Smirking slyly, he eased back against the padded backboard of the booth, lifting his glass of whiskey to his lips and sipping. "When will you break the news?"

"After we reach Andromeda, I assume." She glanced at Elias, who nodded while pushing a glass of water toward Varran, who took it with a silent thumbs-up of thanks. "I'm guessing Elias will want his family to know first, and I…I should tell…"

Her mother.

The enemy queen.

All moisture fled her mouth as those warring thoughts crossed her mind, and she swallowed hard against the dryness.

*That's complicated,* Ani sympathized, a soft flutter of voice that still almost startled her out of her skin. She'd nearly forgotten the goddess was there.

"Worse than, Goddess Great," she said…out loud, she realized too late.

Varran frowned at her. "Excuse me?"

So the fiancé conversation would wait. But there was another that could not.

"Gather everyone in our room," she said to Jakob, and his spine straightened at the order—so rarely did that occur, though she technically outranked him as Princess. Even the third-in-line princess. "They need to hear the truth before we get home, and they need to hear it from me."

Jakob frowned but obeyed immediately, standing in a swift motion that halted every single company member where they were, all eyes darting to him. He gave a quick wave of his hand, and they all extracted themselves from conversations with either apologies or final curses or parting jokes as they gathered at the base of the stairs, filing up one by one as Jakob muttered the room number to them in a hushed voice.

Elias gripped her shoulder and pressed a kiss to her temple, murmuring into her ear, "You don't owe them the whole story, you know. Not if you aren't ready to tell it."

She closed her eyes and took a deep breath, savoring the familiar smells of Nyxian whiskey and fresh-cut wood, hearty stews being cooked in the tavern's kitchen and candles burning on every table. "I need to tell them the truth. Atlas is part of me. I can't...I can't pretend to hate it anymore."

"I'm with you," he promised, rubbing her upper arm, the yarn heating with the friction of the gesture. "All the way."

*All the way to Atlas?*

The question chilled the undercurrent of her blood, the low dread of a realization only just rearing its head...a realization that came too late.

Elias had asked her to marry him. And that was what she wanted, more than anything—that would never be in question. It *hadn't* been in question for longer than she cared to admit. His presence at her side was so cemented in her mind that when the threat of the Viper venom had come into their lives, all ideas of what her future held had been the first thing to fall to its deadly bite.

But he was here now; so was she. There were things they still needed to solve, things that might yet head off the culmination of what this ring promised, but no matter where they went from here, they went together.

But could she ask that of him? Did he realize just what it meant to bind himself to Atlas's heir?

Did he realize that Nyx could no longer be her home?

The moment that thought crossed her mind, she dug her fingernail into her leg, letting it pinch until the reassurance of choice loosened her breath.

The Atlas throne was hers to reclaim. But once she did, there would be no sharing titles, no pretending that her mixed name was enough to allow for mixed loyalties. She would be Queen, and he…

To be married to her was to be King-Consort of Atlas. To marry her was to never call Nyx his home again.

He'd already chased her there once. Could she ask him to do it again? After all he'd already lost?

"Do you need help?" came his voice again—too quiet for the others to hear, a rumble of words coated with concern.

She'd halted at the foot of the stairs, the tips of her boots barely brushing the bark-edged rosined wood, and she was…staring.

Staring, and doing nothing. Like a puppet waiting for her strings to be tugged.

"No." She gripped the railing and squeezed it—once, twice, and again, just to prove she could. "Sorry."

Maybe she was thinking too hard about this. After all, it might not be strictly traditional, but Atlas did have two other heirs…one she knew for a fact would be happy to take the throne, should she offer it.

The crown was a problem for another day. For now, the truth of her origins was enough to untangle.

They made it up the stairs, Soren silently fuming at every attempt her knee made to buckle, every ache that pinged in the seams of her joints, every protest her body made against the weight of two souls.

*Sorry,* Ani whispered miserably.

*It's all right. You didn't know this would happen.*

*That doesn't make it right. This is all…* Ani shuddered, a wave of anger, of *shame,* jittering Soren's bones. *I want* my *body back.*

*I know the feeling.* It was an effort not to roll her eyes.

*At least yours is still here.*

Their conversation was cut off by Elias slipping around her to open the door, a gentlemanly gesture she almost laughed at. She moved into the room; Jakob and Varran were sitting on the bed, and the others were scattered about, but all of them were looking right at her.

Waiting.

Nerves fizzed at the edges of her fingertips and the tip of her tongue, but she refused to bend before their curious, concerned looks. This wasn't one of Finn's tricks or cons. She didn't have to perform—she only had to tell the truth.

But to do it while looking into these faces—faces she had seen spattered with Atlas blood on countless occasions, faces that had laughed and mocked the soldiers they'd killed, faces that lit up at the prospect of Atlas defeat, Atlas death…

Something began to burn deep in her belly.

"Jakob," she said, "how much do they know?"

"Very little."

Good. It would be easier to tell when she didn't have to contend with someone else's account."Everybody should sit. This is going to be a long story, and you're not going to like it."

# CHAPTER 21

# SOREN

For the first time, Soren Marina Atlas told her story from beginning to end, memory leading to memory in one unbroken chain: the story of a girl born Soleil, raised by both sea and snow; the story of a woman who was taken home and taught her true heritage, reuniting with the family of her birth.

Here, Kriss flinched a bit, an orphan in her own right; Rian's expression was comically open, spelling out his disbelief loud and clear, while Samhain and the twins listened with only the barest blinks giving away a hint of reaction. And Jakob and Varran, who already knew most of it, only made faces when she spoke of Finn.

She told them of her brothers, and though she could have—and maybe should have—she did not hide her love for them. Her fear for them. How Kallias had gone out of his way to warn the kingdom of her heart what was coming; how Finn had tried to get her to run with him when he escaped the palace. And when she was done, Elias told his own tale, a far more succinct story of goddess-given blessings and fire-touched trials and a trek through the Tallisian woods.

"So," Samhain said slowly once Soren sat down, her head leaning into Elias's side; he stayed standing, absently running his hand over her hair. "You're Soleil Atlas. The dead princess that started this whole thing."

"Yes."

"And you didn't know until they took you?"

"No idea."

"I'm sorry, are we actually buying this?" laughed Andrei, who sat forward with a jackal's grin. "You have to be concussed if you think we're going to—"

"Andrei," Jakob interrupted, "stop talking before you make an ass of yourself. I heard this same story from Princesses Yvonne and Ember themselves, and Elias as well."

"So? Maybe she's Atlas, fine, but I don't believe for a second she's got a goddess in her," Andrei scoffed. "If you expect—"

"Ani," Soren cut him off, "care to show them?"

Andrei stuttered, his young face contorting in confusion. "What did you just call me?"

Elias stiffened behind her. "Soren…"

*What if we have a fit?* Ani's voice trembled with anxiety. *Soren, if I hurt you—*

*I'm not going to fight you this time. Call it an experiment.*

*I don't like experimenting with what your body can handle!*

Her body. Ani had called it *hers*—not theirs.

*Ani. I'm trusting you.* She closed her eyes. *It's okay.*

With unbearable, flinching slowness, Ani's consciousness crept toward the wall, pressing close to it—it felt like pressure, like someone pushing open a door in her skull, but Soren forced herself not to fight. When that door opened, she pictured herself letting Ani in before letting herself out, the feeling leeching out of her hands and feet, her limbs…

And before she had time to truly panic, it was over.

A great shudder seized her, and Elias cursed, his hands going to her shoulders, ready to catch her—but she did not fall.

*Ani* did not fall.

Their eyes opened again, and Ani lifted their hand in a meek wave—a wave that sent daisy petals scattering to the floor. "Hello," she whispered. "I'm, um…I'm Anima."

Andrei and Nikolai swore in tandem and scrambled back until they hit the wall, both presumably taken aback by her now-golden eyes. Samhain's hand went to her mouth; Rian, Kriss, and Frigga each put their hands to their weapons. Varran reached up to clasp the symbol of Mortem hanging around his neck, Jakob leveling a thoroughly murderous glare at Ani despite her trembling in every limb.

"Let her back out," Jakob snarled.

"She asked me to show you," Ani defended, and the annoyance in her voice lit Soren up with pride. "You heard her."

"That's not enough." Kriss's disbelieving sneer prickled at Soren's temper; Kriss was one of the more difficult members of the company, though she and Soren had never had a real spat. Soren's energy had always been directed to antagonizing Elias, and Kriss had enjoyed pushing Kaia's buttons when she was alive, so their interests mostly aligned. "Prove it."

"Her eye color changing isn't enough?" Even Samhain, paragon of patience, seemed exasperated on Soren's behalf.

"It's all right." Ani carefully approached Kriss, who tensed in every limb, her crooked fingers wrapping tightly around the handle of one of her twin axes. "Here…let me help."

Kriss's breathing sped as Ani cautiously reached out, hovering one hand over Kriss's elbow. "What are you doing?"

"Proving it." Ani glanced up at her timidly. "May I?"

Kriss's throat bobbed, but she nodded once, a clipped gesture that belied her fear—but Kriss was always the last one to back off from a challenge, determined never to be seen as a coward.

Ani's fingers closed around Kriss's elbow, probing her dark sleeve, and Kriss flinched; that elbow had been shattered in a training accident years ago, and it hadn't healed properly. Joints were tricky, and even their skilled physicians could only do so much.

A flash of green light. An audible pop. Kriss's shout of pain, a cry that brought every solider to their feet, weapons out—until she blinked, sitting back down herself, a look of utter shock on her face as she lifted her arm. Bent her elbow. Twisted her arm back and forth, her eyes gleaming the longer she went without pain.

"Holy shit," said Kriss. "That's mad."

"That's magic." Ani smiled. "Good enough?"

"Good enough." Kriss looked up at her now…cautious still, but with a hint of respect. "You gonna put the princess back, *Ani?*"

Ani paused, and Soren's heart arrested as reluctance crossed the wall.

And then the door opened. Ani closed their eyes. *Let's try this again?*

The moment the door was there, Soren couldn't help herself—terror swelled behind her, an urgency whispering that the goddess could change her mind at any moment and shut her back into her cage, forcing her into silent servitude, nothing but a cobweb strung at the back of her own skull—

She forced herself through, and a flash of pure agony shocked through her body.

Elias caught her with a curse. "Soren? *Soren—*"

"I'm okay," she panted. "Sorry."

"Well," said Rian—calmly, though he was staring at her as if she'd grown a second head—"great. So where does this leave us?"

"Kallias, Finn, and Raquel are handling Tempest's relic," Elias said, his voice filled with confidence Soren wished to the gods she could share. "Mortem's relic is…protected. Occassio's as well. Arborius guards Anima's relic, and being that Tenebrae's people only just infiltrated Artem, I'm hoping they haven't made it as far as the island yet. But if what you say about Ursa is true…"

"Tenebrae's people are here," Soren finished. "They have his relic, and they're using it here…gods know why."

"So we hunt them down," Samhain said with an ease Soren envied—as if the task would be nothing but another patrol, another battle against an enemy they had the potential to defeat.

"We don't know yet," Elias hedged. "First, we need to tell Ravenna herself. But once a plan is in place, Soren and I *have* to go. I promised Kallias."

Rian snorted. "And what loyalty do *you* owe to an Atlas princeling?"

Elias held Rian's stare without bend to his back or shame in his eyes. Only stark honesty. "I told you. I owe him my life."

Rian's lip curled. "A life-debt to an Atlas bastard. Lovely."

"A life debt," Elias's teeth bared in wolfish warning, "to my *friend.*"

The company shifted, silent thoughts traded between eyes teeming with emotions Soren could barely keep track of—displeasure, worry, understanding…even some anger. Rian and Andrei had yet to release their weapons. But Kriss, surprisingly, had shaken off her hostility, still moving her arm around in silent wonder; and Samhain had her hand on Rian's shoulder, a wordless warning for him to keep his temper in check.

"Well," Rian said, sparing a glance at Elias's formerly wounded shoulder, "you'll want to pay that *life debt* back in short order, won't you?"

Soren's jaw dropped. For him to be so callous about the Viper bite—

"Rian!" snapped Samhain before Soren could haul off and punch out his teeth, and he flinched like a kicked wolf pup. But Elias didn't avert his stare. He merely reached up and pulled down his sleeve, revealing his healed-over scar…and his fully-tattooed arms, the flames climbing over every inch of skin.

And within those tattoos, the flickers of golden-red heat that ever burned within him.

"Not as short as you might think," he rasped.

Varran's eyes nearly blew from his sockets, his grip tightening on his token. Samhain's hold loosened on her battlemate's shoulder as she stared at Elias's exposed shoulder and bicep.

Soren scowled at them. "Stop ogling my f—*ffffriend.*"

Jakob let out a laugh that sounded more like a mule's bray. Elias looked down at her with a raised eyebrow. "*Friend?*" he mouthed.

She threw one hand helplessly in the air, mouthing back, "I panicked."

"She's right. Enough poking and prodding," Jakob said—bless him. "Put your shirt back on, Pious. Nobody wants to see that."

"I do," Soren said.

"Take a lap," Jakob retorted.

"Bite me."

"But that's Pious's job."

"Enough, all of you," said Varran with a groan. "This is a lot to take in, and it's all going to look better in the morning. Get your rest. If someone is mounting an attack on Nyx, our news can't wait. We need to pick up the pace tomorrow."

And when they arrived, she would need to be ready. Not just as Nyx's returning princess, an escaped prisoner of war…but as Atlas's heir. Their ambassador. Their protector.

Gods, why couldn't Kallias be here instead of her?

"I want to make something clear," Jakob called out, all amusement fleeing from his face. "No matter our feelings about Atlas and certain members of their ruling family, Soren is a victim in this. She didn't choose her blood, she didn't choose to be taken away and raised here, and she didn't choose to be taken back. What she *did* choose was to tell you all her story, and I expect you all to respect that she chose to share her truth when she did not have to. If I hear any of you causing trouble with her over this, I will not hesitate to throw you out of this company. We're family—all of us. Blood changes nothing. Am I clear?"

All mutters silenced at once, and one by one, each member of the company nodded in acknowledgement. They filed out slowly—Rian and Andrei ignoring her entirely, though Nikolai offered her an apologetic eye roll as he trailed after his twin. Samhain gave her a hug and a quick kiss on the forehead, promising to get Rian to see reason, which was far too ambitious a task for any one person to take on. Jakob and Varran both patted her shoulder as they walked out, Frigga too, and Kriss…

Kriss dawdled in the doorway, looking down at Soren, her posture bent in a way that almost seemed…awkward.

"That was pretty great, what the goddess did," she said begrudgingly. "Tell her thanks."

Soren smirked. "She can hear you."

"Well, don't *laugh* at me, it's not like I'm used to…" Kriss grumbled under her breath, then sighed, scrubbing a hand over her hair. "Fine. Thanks, Ani."

And with that, the door slammed shut behind the warrior, and everything was quiet.

# CHAPTER 22

# FINN

As was becoming the pattern, that went about as poorly as it possibly could have. And Finn had a *fabulous* imagination, so if he couldn't come up with a way it could have gone worse, he knew they'd royally sunk their ship.

Between him and Kallias—the latter only keeping his footing by repeatedly soaking and freezing his back to numb the wounds, a move that would've left him with horrifically damaged skin if not for the relic hanging around his neck—they managed to get one of the fishing boats that Kallias *hadn't* torn apart with his magic into the water. Raquel lay unconscious in the prow, turned on her stomach to slow the bleeding from her back. He'd stolen a thick cloak from one of the cultists—

the very, very dead cultists—and draped it over her to keep her warm, but the cold would be the least of their worries if infection settled in the wounds.

At least the saltwater Aeris had whipped them with might help prevent that.

While Kallias climbed into the boat, Finn turned to look over his shoulder at the damage wrought behind them.

The power that had torn itself free from Kallias had *decimated* the underground sanctum. Piles of discarded rock lay scattered around the cave, chunks of the ceiling and walls Kallias had called forth with nothing but a gesture and a roar. The six cultists that had been guarding them were all dead—two by Finn's hand, the others cast against the walls with broken necks or cracked skulls, his entire body flinching at the glassy eyes and contorted bodies he encountered everywhere he turned.

Aeris himself had not been so lucky. He hung from the cave wall—literally hung from it, fastened into the stone by five glistening javelins of ice. They were just beginning to melt in his body, diluted droplets of blood sliding serenely down his impaled throat.

He wouldn't be speaking for anything ever again. And as badly as Finn's hands shook to take in the grisly sight, looking at his brother's back—and at Raquel's inert form—he couldn't find it in him to feel horrified at the violence his gentle older brother had unleashed with half a thought.

Though he did have to wonder how much of that rage, that raw killing instinct, had truly been *Kallias* at all.

Footsteps on the staircase finally stirred him into action, and he leapt into the ketch, cursing as it bobbed beneath him. Despite his parents' best efforts to the contrary, he'd never been comfortable on boats. The rest of his siblings had been born with sea legs. He'd been born with rooftop feet and a complete distaste for riding anything that moved without his prompting.

And a stomach that did not care *one bit* for the toss and turn of ships.

"Once we get out of here, I can sail us to the nearest city," Kallias panted, his brow carved with lines of concentration. He should've been face-down on the deck of the ketch beside Raquel, not rushing about tightening some things and loosening others and doing gods-knew-what to get them moving. "The Vela runs past several, if I'm remembering the map right. It's big enough that a lot of Nyxian cities use it for inner-kingdom trade."

"I don't need a geography lesson," Finn snapped, leaping to help when Kallias barked in pain and nearly lost his grip on a rope. "Just tell me what to do to get us out of here."

Both of them had now taken on the burden of godly relics, and Raquel was dead to the world—in a manner of speaking. There was no telling how long he and Kallias would be in their right minds, and if either or both of them failed…

He swallowed. Hard.

They could do this. They'd both been raised for this, even if Finn had never had a taste for it.

So he followed the instructions Kallias gave him, forcing himself to ignore the sickly feeling already beginning to whirlpool in the vat of his stomach, and focused on getting them out of this damned cave.

***

Three days. That was how long they sailed without seeing another human being.

Three days with no food, their only water summoned by Kallias from thin air—a new power of his granted by the relic, it seemed.

It probably should have unnerved him. It said something that it didn't.

Raquel hadn't regained her senses since losing them in the cave. The closest she came to consciousness was thrashing in pain, letting out guttural moans in place of words, her eyelids fluttering as she gazed around blindly at her surroundings. Despite the cold, her skin burned with fever, and she kept trying to throw off the cloak keeping her from freezing to death. Kallias often had to leave the steering of their stolen ketch in Finn's inexperienced hands to drop down and soothe her, running his cold hands over her clammy brow until it smoothed beneath his fingers, her left eye just as glassy as the right as she stared at him without seeing him.

Finn had never seen Kallias quite this fussy, this tender. He would've made fun of him for it if he wasn't too busy trying to keep their ship from crashing into the banks of the river.

"Look at you go." Occassio, as always, sounded amused—she'd taken to pacing the sides of the ship like a tightrope walker, laughing wildly with every wobble and near-plunge into the depths of the river below. She'd actually bothered to put effort into the charade of reality today—she was bundled up in a thick woolen coat dyed her signature shade of purple, lined with fleece and bound tightly to her body. Its hood was up, only a few stray curls escaping from beneath its mantle, but her boots still showed off her favored sparkles—the laces were capped with pearls, and a myriad of colorful gems crusted the fine leather at the toes. "I didn't know you possessed such rugged talents, Trickster."

He ignored her. They were in too close quarters now to risk being seen talking to himself.

She sighed. "You're becoming less and less fun."

Still silent. He would not give her the satisfaction of making him look like a fool.

Again.

Hunger gnawed at his stomach, a sensation mostly unfamiliar—he'd never been truly *hungry* before, had never gone longer than a handful of hours without eating. Now, teetering on day four of nothing but water, his stomach was starting to truly rebel. Soon it might persuade his muscles to join it, and once he lost his strength…

He swallowed hard. Braced himself against the rope wrapped around one arm.

That was a worry for later.

Kallias finally came back, eyes hollow with worry and stride beginning to falter. As much as his magic had helped with his wounds, he wasn't Anima-blessed—he wasn't healed, and though shock had lent itself kindly to the endeavor of their escape, he wasn't going to last much longer in this constant state of exertion.

"We can't go much longer like this," he said before Kallias could open his mouth.

Kallias shook his head, gaze darting back to Raquel. "She needs treatment. And to get out of the cold. You're not looking so well, either."

"Speak for yourself. You look like a fish two days dead."

Kallias's mouth faltered toward a smile, but failed before achieving it. "Are we going to talk about what happened in the cave?"

Tension slithered along his shoulders, but he kept his tone light, noncommittal. "You did what you had to do."

"I don't mean what I did. I mean what *you* did."

He tightened his grip on the rope. "I did what I had to do, too."

Kallias eased his hand over the rope, staring at Finn until he finally relented and let go. Kallias started adjusting things with an air of absentmindedness, his focus never truly leaving Finn. The welts on his back were still red and inflamed, some of them leaking fresh blood, but he barely flinched—and he had yet to complain about the cold, though his skin had been exposed long enough that he should have been frostbitten thrice over.

"You lied to us," Kallias finally said, voice hushed.

"I never really—"

"You lied to *me.*"

Finn's heart stuttered at the hurt in his brother's voice.

"I thought you could barely handle a practice sword, let alone gut a person like a fish without breaking a sweat," Kallias continued, averting his gaze to focus on his task. But his hands still shook, his eyes sharp with emotion. "You let me think you were helpless all this time."

Finn hesitated. "It was for a good reason."

"What good reason could there possibly be for letting me believe that, Finn? For letting me think you couldn't protect yourself? Do you know how many nights I've lain awake *worrying* about you? Wondering how I could get you to safety if war ever came to Port Atlas's gates? Did you ever stop to think for even a moment that I could have used your *help*?"

A wry laugh burst out of him against his better judgement. "Oh, you've had my help. You have no idea how often you've had my help."

"So tell me! Tell me the truth, for once in your life."

Occassio, still balancing on the edge of the tossing ship, chuckled darkly. "Oh, this oughta be good. Do you even remember what the truth is, Finn?"

The truth was he had no idea where to even *begin* telling his brother the reality of who Finnick Atlas was. He'd never had to tell anyone before. Soleil had figured it out on her own. Jericho had barely gotten a glimpse before Tenebrae took over. Occassio had known all along.

And out of everyone, out of anybody who still believed the lie…Kallias was the one person who might be horrified by what lay beneath the masks.

Finn had endured more pain than most in his time. But he didn't know if he could endure *that.*

When his silence dragged on and on, a gate slammed down over the hurt in Kallias's eyes. He scoffed quietly, turning his back to Finn. "Fine. Keep your secrets. Not like you're the first to keep things from me."

"Kal—"

"Don't. Either tell me the truth or stay quiet."

The silence between them stretched on long enough that it would have been easy to let it last. Easy to walk away. Easy to let Kallias stew in his hurt feelings until he moved past it on his own.

"I was twelve when I went into the city alone for the first time," Finn rasped.

Kallias's gaze darted to him, going wide for a moment before he seemed to school his features back into calm. He nodded once, but said nothing—just listening.

Every word dug like thorns into Finn's tongue, truths hidden for so long they screeched in protest at being thrown out of their home. But he forced himself to keep going—to tell Kallias the story of Finnick Atlas, con man and thief. To lead him down the winding, shadowy streets of his journey from frightened boy to bored swindler to Port Atlas's sole remaining defender.

Every success. Every failure. Those memories remained untouched by Occassio's wicked magic, and as wrong as it felt to give voice to them, it was almost a relief to find those roads of memory were still pristine as ever.

Kallias hung on every word, his body working to keep the ship moving while his attention remained fastened to Finn. He flinched at the darker stories, which always made Finn hesitate; but he laughed at some of the more ridiculous ones, especially the ones involving him parading as Jaskier.

"That lordly prick deserves it," were his brother's exact wheezing words.

By the time Finn finally came to his misadventures with Occassio, reluctantly sharing the details of his worst and final failure, Kallias merely listened, his expression solemn and unreadable.

When it was over, Finn waited, his lungs refusing to take in air while Kallias held his silence. Only the winter wind spoke for a time, a low moan that numbed Finn's ears in spite of his knit cap, and he almost wished Occassio would distract him with her chatter. But she'd vanished at some point during his storytelling, leaving no trace behind, and he wasn't foolish enough to try and summon her back. If he could even figure out how.

Then, finally, in a voice so low Finn nearly couldn't hear it: "I should have been there."

Finn snorted. "You were there for most of it."

"But I wasn't *there* for you. I didn't…" Kallias shook his head, a pained laugh escaping him in a puff of vapor. "I should have seen it. I should have *known*. You were always sneaking off, always distracted…I just figured you were getting into trouble. Jericho and I had a bet going on whether you were gambling or drinking."

"Which did you have money on?"

"The gambling. I know you don't drink."

Awkward silence smothered them for a moment, a shared memory of shattered glass and terrified screams stretching like a tightrope between them.

Finn cut the rope with a quick throat-clearing. "If it helps, there was some gambling involved. So Jer owes you some money."

"It does, a little." Kallias was quiet for a moment. "I'm sorry, Finn. I'm sorry you felt like you had to hide this from me."

Finn's stomach pinched. "You're not...?"

"Not what?"

"You're not angry at me?"

"Angry?" Kallias laughed hoarsely, raking a hand through his ice-crusted hair, pinning it back from his eyes so he could look at Finn unhindered. His cheeks were flushed with wind-beaten color, his lips not even slightly blue despite the killing cold they sailed through. "Finn, you've singlehandedly run Atlas's underbelly in our favor since you were a *kid*. You taught yourself how to rule a kingdom without ever wielding your crown or throne. You protected us better with your words and a fancy costume than I ever have with my sword. Angry? I'm gods-damned *proud*."

It had been a long time since Finn had been rendered speechless.

Even longer since someone had said they were *proud* of him. And never, *ever* had anyone said they were proud of the truth of him—never had anyone seen the full measure of Finnick Atlas, shadow and all, and looked at him with *pride*.

No one but Occassio, and that had only been a well-wrought fiction.

"But I failed," he croaked. "I let Occassio get in my head. I showed my hand to Tenebrae."

"You held up under the influence of a goddess known to drive men mad," Kallias countered. "You picked a fight with the god of chaos and escaped with your life."

"Barely."

"*Finn*." Kallias reached out and caught his shoulder—it was like being touched by an ice sculpture. "Stop trying to convince me to be ashamed of you. It's not going to happen."

Before he could untangle the knot in his stomach enough to reply, his eyes caught on something over Kallias's shoulder.

"Kal." His heart dropped, and he pointed toward the horizon. "Ship. There's another ship."

For a heartbeat, when Kallias turned and peered in that direction in utter silence, Finn had the horrible thought that this might be one of Occassio's tricks, her visions that his eyes seemed all too vulnerable to. But then Kallias swore, ducking to snatch up the extra cloak Finn had taken from the cave and throwing it over himself, tugging the hood over his hair. "That's a frigate—smaller than most, but there's likely a crew of at least twenty. We'll be far outnumbered. Pull up your hood. Can you manage a Nyxian accent?"

He affected his best Nyxian impression, taken directly from Soleil's mouth. "I think I can handle it, yeah."

Kallias blinked. "That's almost creepy."

"Thanks."

"What else can you do? Can you sound Lapisian? What about—"

"Can we focus on the task at hand, please?" Finn tugged down his hood and adjusted his stature, adding a limp to his leg and a bit of a hunch to his back. "I'll be happy to show off once we get past this ship."

Kallias nodded in silent affirmation, though his gaze lingered on Finn's costume briefly, as if taking in a stranger. Then he surged into action, navigating the ship as Finn would a card game, pulling at strings and reading bluffs in the current until they'd moved enough to be well out of the approaching ship's path.

But none of that mattered. Not when the approaching frigate—a vessel with *Starsinger* painted across its hull in rich navy paint, the *S's* designed like playful sirens—flung grappling hooks over the edge of their ketch and yanked them to a lurching stop in the water.

"Hail!" called a mockingbird voice, warbling and confident. Its tenor song crossed the river between them as easily as a duck cutting its way through a still pond. "Who is so bold as to cross paths with the *Starsinger* in a Skyhaven ship?"

"We don't want any trouble," Finn called back in his best Nyxian accent. "We have an injured woman in our company, and we wish to see her tended, that's all."

Evidently, his leaning toward stirring these sailors' potential chivalry was the wrong move. That mockingbird song only trilled with laughter. "Right, of course. And since when has Skyhaven cared for the fate of its women?"

"This isn't going well," Kallias muttered to him.

"I noticed that, thank you." Then, raising his voice again: "What business do you have with a simple fishing ship?"

"No business at all with a fishing ship." This time a figure leapt up on the side of the *Starsinger*, nimble despite the thick winter gear he wore, a white-toothed grin beaming like sunlight against snow. A knot of satin-smooth black hair was loosely tied at the base of his neck, and despite this winter kingdom's weak attempt at sunlight, his skin was gleaming bronze, hunting-hawk eyes fixed on Finn and

Kallias with a gleam that set of every alarm Finn had ever possessed. "A bit more business with Atlas princes captaining a stolen Skyhaven vessel."

"Right," Finn snorted. "We're Atlas princes, and you're my pet goat's uncle."

The captain—at least, Finn assumed he was the captain—gave a careless shrug, drawing a dagger and carefully paring his fingernails down with it. "I have a half-brother or two wandering around the kingdoms. I certainly wouldn't be surprised if one of them fathered a goat."

"How do you know who we are?" Kallias cut in, waving tiredly at Finn when he shot him a venomous look that shut most people's mouths upon receiving it.

"I know the look. You, you're actually quite good, I'm impressed—" the captain gestured to Finn, "—but you, pretty boy…you reek of royalty. Sorry to break it to you. Care to come aboard?"

Finn and Kallias glanced at each other, then back up at the captain.

The stranger's grin only grew. "Fine, fine. I know your face, First Prince Kallias. You can guess how later. Care to come aboard?"

It didn't sound like the kind of question that offered the option of a *no*.

# CHAPTER 23

# KALLIAS

"A lot of good that accent did," Kallias said.

Finn only rolled his eyes, as if the accusation didn't merit a reply. And maybe he could have said it more kindly, but manners were a bit of a struggle when one felt like they were withering to dust.

Every inch of his skin crawled with all-consuming yearning, and if it weren't for the agonized, feverish moans of the woman in his arms anchoring him in place, her brow furrowed so deeply that he half-feared she'd split skin, he would have flung himself to the current's mercy rather than come aboard this ship.

This ship manned by traitors and deserters…himself among them now.

This was the first time he'd ever heard so many Nyxian and Atlas accents mingling together in laughter instead of battle banter or wounded cries. The pirate tending a cut on Finn's skull was Nyxian, her accent biting and clipped, though her eyes held nothing more dangerous than irritation as Finn flinched away from her ministrations. From what he could tell, the crew was a fairly even mix…Nyx and Atlas existing in effortless peace on this vessel.

His rage guttered a bit. He tightened his hold on Raquel.

"Well!" The captain of the *Starsinger* came swaggering back to them after chatting with more of his crew, clapping his hands and offering them a razor-thin grin. He'd stripped down to a fur-lined studded leather vest, showing off thickly-tattooed arms and shoulders—even his neck sported considerable ink. Sirens with jewel-toned tails twined around his biceps, waves flowed up his shoulders to crash against his collarbone, and a sailor's rope coiled around his neck, ending in an anchor resting at the base of his throat. His sleek black hair was knotted up at the top of his head, showing off rows of piercings down the shells of his ears, glimmering bits of color Kallias assumed hadn't been acquired legally. He knew the look of a pirate when he saw one. "What an honor to be hosting royalty on my ship. It's been some time. I'm surprised to see salt-bloods this far inland— don't you Atlas princes think you own the sea?"

Kallias ignored the slight. What he *did* take note of was the fact that the captain moved his hands along with his words every time he spoke—not only him, but the rest of the crew, as well. He'd learned enough sign in school to understand most of it, though there were a few here and there he didn't recognize. "And who do we have the honor of being hosted by?"

The captain doffed an imaginary hat. "Captain Patch of the *Starsinger*. I would say I'm at your service, Prince, but it took quite a bit for me to get out of it, so I'll avoid dipping a toe back in."

It took a moment for him to catch up. "You're Atlas?"

"I was. Even fought your war for a bit, till I got tired of it. Deserted, stole a ship with a couple friends, started picking up others trying to get away." Patch spread his arms out, gesturing to his crew milling about the deck. "Everyone you see here is Nyxian or Atlas, all soldiers escaping the fight. Except Morrow, who got kicked out of Lapis for being too ugly."

A man with brownish hair and an impressively groomed mustache tossed a middle finger toward Patch, calling, "It was treason, actually."

"Close enough!" Patch grinned.

"What's Patch short for?" Finn asked.

"It's short for none of your business," said the captain.

"It's short for Patrick," said one of the other pirates.

Patch shot them a betrayed look. "You. Plank. Walk."

"You're hilarious, Captain."

"We could get you imprisoned with what you just told us." Finn changed tack, catching the pirate woman's hand to stop her from continuing to poke at his head. "Why confess to desertion?"

"Because I want you to understand that I've no qualms about slitting your throats and dropping you overboard if you turn a stink eye on me or my crew. We owe allegiance to no one. Either you're a problem or you aren't. I suggest you aren't." Patch's eyes fell to Raquel, and for the first time, his grin flickered to something more concerned. Sympathetic. "If you can agree to those terms, we're happy to help with her injuries. We have a medimancer on board."

It went against every instinct to bow his head to traitors. But Raquel's moans and mutterings had quieted since they'd been brought aboard, and not in a way that reassured him—her eyelids had stopped fluttering, her chest rising and falling in stuttering jerks, and no matter what he tried, she wouldn't rouse.

Besides, they were all traitors to something. The high ground wasn't exactly his to claim.

"Whatever you require from me, you have it," he rasped. "Just help her."

Patch nodded. "Follow me," he said, turning on his heel and striding off without waiting for Kallias to stand. The captain waved upward, and a petite girl split off from where she was adjusting the rigging, her golden skin and chestnut hair salted with snowflakes. Despite the bitterly cold weather, a crown of blossoms twined through her hair, a tiara of dandelions and wild carrot flowers that didn't belong in Nyxian snowstorms.

"This is Elowyn," Patch introduced, still moving his hands while he talked; the girl smiled and waved. "Do you speak sign?"

"I do."

"Good. Makes everyone's life easier." Patch turned to Elowyn. "This was done by Skyhaven, so go slowly." When Kallias started to protest, Patch held up a hand before adding, "Skyhaven purposely leaves wounds that are difficult to heal without leaving behind permanent pain. Do you want her well?"

"Obviously."

"Then slow and steady it is, Your Highness."

Slow and steady didn't feel plausible right now—not with Raquel's breaths getting shallower and shallower every moment. But he had no other choice. Once again, they were outnumbered and out of options.

So when Elowyn led him belowdecks, taking him to the sailor's quarters and directing him into an empty cabin, he followed without protest.

The cabin was modest—a cot nailed to the left wall, a lantern filled with what appeared to be enchanted gold crystals mounted on the back wall, and a trunk also fastened tightly to the right wall. It smelled of wood and sea salt, and a shiver of longing hooked the base of his spine and tugged, an uncomfortable jerk that nearly pulled him from Raquel's side.

But it didn't matter how desperately he was craving water and wind. He wouldn't leave her in a stranger's hands.

"Put her down," Elowyn signed to him, keen hazel eyes taking in Raquel's limp body with worry. He obeyed, gently stretching Raquel out on her stomach, pulling her hair up to keep it out of the way.

Elowyn carefully removed the cloak covering Raquel's body, and Kallias's breath caught so sharply it hurt.

Her back was inflamed and horribly bruised around her wounds, ridges of torn flesh carved deep into her, the stench of infection turning his stomach so viciously he nearly gagged.

Elowyn's face twisted in anger. "This was more than punishment," she signed. "This was done with intent to break her."

"I know," Kallias signed back. "Can you help her?"

"I can." Elowyn squeezed his arm. "Hold her hand. Be ready if she wakes."

He could do that much. He moved to crouch beside Raquel's head, taking her hand and holding it in both of his. It burned between his palms, but he refused to let go.

Elowyn smiled at him. "While I work, why don't you tell me how you two met? A Nyxian warrior and an Atlas prince…that must be quite the story. Just keep your hands where I can see them. I might not catch every word, but I'll get the gist."

Quite the story, indeed. "It's not the most pleasant one."

"Some of the best stories start out poorly. Otherwise, the happy ending might not be as powerful."

The idea of endings didn't sit right while Raquel looked so ill. But it was either talk to this pirate healer or be reminded of Jericho while the green-tinted magic of medimancy got to work repairing Raquel's back, and he didn't want to think of his sister right now. Didn't want to hate her for what she'd doomed them to. Didn't want to get sick with worry thinking of her all alone in Atlas, being hunted by a god that was likely far crueler than the one breathing down his neck.

He hated her for betraying them. He feared so desperately for her life that it was getting harder and harder not to give up on everything else and rush home to plead with her to stop. And the fight between those two instincts was going to tear him apart if he gave in to it here.

So he clung to Raquel's hand and signed with his free one, telling Elowyn how they'd met, what they'd gone through since: death threats, life debts, breakfasts spent negotiating and verbally sparring, how they'd banded together to help Elias through his grief, and how that had led them to Nyx…and to Skyhaven, where everything had gone horribly wrong.

He was in the middle of regaling the wonders of Havi's baked goods and coffee when Raquel suddenly jerked, her hand curling inward to claw at his, her nails digging into his palm as her face contorted in pain.

Elowyn lurched closer, the glow of her magic intensifying as she focused. Raquel bucked against her hold, and Kallias surged up to pin her down, catching her when she tried to throw a punch.

"Raquel! It's me, it's Kallias. Hold still. She's helping you."

"Get off," Raquel snarled, her eyes dull despite the tears gathering in them. She fought harder, her body surging up again and again, but she was frighteningly weak—he barely had to brace himself to keep her down. "Aeris, let me *go!*"

His chest caved in. He adjusted his hold to try and be gentler, cursing quietly under his breath. "It's not him, Raquel. He's never going to hurt you again, do you hear me? I have you. *I* have you."

Finally, her eyes found his, and her struggles slowed a bit, her breath coming in ragged sobs. She blinked, her brows bending toward each other as her head lolled back on the cot. "Kallias?"

Relief swept his stomach away, and he crouched once more, brushing her sweat-soaked hair out of her eyes. "It's me. You're all right. We found a healer to help you."

Raquel closed her eyes once more, and fear surged through him so powerfully he nearly collapsed to his knees. "Hey, uh-uh, no—none of that." He thumbed away a tear, tangling his hand in her hair and giving her a soft shake. "Eyes open, Officer Angelov."

He waited as she forced them open into a glare, leveling him with such a baleful look that he almost smiled. But that urge fled at her next words, breathless and tired: "You didn't leave me behind."

"What?"

"You could've left me there." Her next breath rattled, and she flinched against his hand. "You should have."

"*Never.*" The word cut his tongue. "Never, Raquel."

"I slowed you down."

"You took this for me. You really think I could have left you there with him?"

"You used the relic." She gazed at him with dull eyes, but tears kept overflowing, rolling down to soak into her pillow. "We can't take that back."

Fear tried to jam itself into his windpipe, but he forced it out. Now wasn't the time for fear. She needed him here, not somewhere in the unseeable future.

At least, unseeable for anyone but Finn.

"I don't regret it," he whispered. "Not at all."

Finally, her lips curled into a faint smile. "That's because you're a fool."

"It's because we have a deal." He leaned a bit to catch her gaze again. "Nobody kills us but each other, remember?"

She snorted, her chuckle trailing into a caught breath as Elowyn's magic flared again. Raquel's nails dug into his skin, but he didn't flinch. Didn't tear away. These negligible slices of pain were nothing compared to what she'd taken on his behalf.

"I think," she gasped as fresh blood dribbled down her sides, "we're past pretending we're still enemies after this, Atlas."

His stomach fluttered—with nerves, this time. Ridiculous to be nervous talking to a woman who was likely so lost in agony that she didn't know what she was saying. "I didn't want to make assumptions."

"I know. I hate that." Another wobbling breath, and she shifted a bit. "I hate how good you are. It makes it so gods-damned impossible to despise you."

"Sorry."

She laughed outright that time. "Sorry for being too good to hate?"

"No." He did get on his knees then, clasping both hands around hers again. "I am sorry for what I did to Jira."

Her hoarse breathing ground to a halt.

"I robbed you of a sister," he croaked. "I know that pain. I've carried it nearly half my life. And I wouldn't wish it on anyone. It was war, and it wasn't premeditated, and I would be lying if I said I've lain awake at night agonizing over it. I wish I could tell you I have. Jira deserves justice, and you deserve to give that to her. I was wrong to act as if you don't. And I do...I do remember her face. Now that I've seen you, now that I've been thinking back, I do remember her."

Barely a flicker, not even enough to call a memory, but enough that he could recall vicious coffee-dark eyes and a knife that had sunk itself in his back after he'd believed his enemy was already dead. "She nearly took me with her. I have a scar…"

He took her trembling hand and slid it beneath his shirt collar, down to a thin line of scar tissue like a series of stitches embroidered into his skin. The remainders of a serrated knife that had buried itself so deep that Jericho had told him over and over how lucky he was to not be dead or paralyzed from the neck down.

"This was the closest anyone ever got to putting me in the dirt," he croaked. "And she was already dying when she landed it."

Raquel's eyes glittered, and he couldn't read the emotion in them. Her finger ran down the line of his scar, fervid and shaking, her touch stinging like a brand everywhere it lingered.

"Are you lying to me?" Her voice was deathly soft.

"No. She never stopped fighting, not even at the end." He squeezed her hand. "Just like her sister."

Raquel's hand shuddered once more, then went limp in his grip at the same time Elowyn eased back, her eyelids heavy with exhaustion. "I've done what I can for tonight," she signed. "I'll come back in the morning. For now, she should rest."

"Thank you." He looked back to Raquel, clearing his throat and starting to stand. "I'll leave you to sleep. If you need—"

Her hand shot out and grabbed his wrist.

"Don't go," she whispered. "Don't…don't let him find me again. Don't."

Kallias's chest tore in two. He knelt beside her again, shifting her weak grip so he was grasping her hand. "He will never touch you again," he vowed. "And if he tries, he'll lose his hands first. Then his tongue. And when you're done making him suffer, I'll freeze his head in a block of ice, and we'll throw it in the nearest chamber pot to thaw."

He would tell her the truth—that Aeris was quite irreversibly dead—later. Later, when he could apologize properly for taking that kill from her deserving hands.

Her laugh, quiet and weak but utterly genuine, nearly undid him. "You're terrible."

"So you tell me." He leaned over and pressed a kiss to her temple. "Rest. You're safe."

Her eyelids began to droop, but she fought hard, her eyes glazed with midnight fog. "You won't leave?"

"Only if you ask me to go." And if anyone else tried to make him, they would quickly find out just how well this spoiled Atlas prince knew his way around a sword.

Her eyes finally sank shut, and though it worried him, he didn't protest this time. Her chapped, pale lips moved, just barely: "You're beautiful."

And then she was asleep, leaving him to stare uselessly at her with his jaw dropped to the floor, her fingers still twined loosely in his.

# CHAPTER 24

# ELIAS

Andromeda was a city that sang.

Not in voice, maybe, but in rhythm—the clopping of horse hooves against cobblestone streets, the creaking of carriage wheels, the harmony of ever-winter wind curling its way beneath eaves and alleyways. This was a city built for sled races and snowball fights, hot coffee in carry-cups and thick socks shoved into boots, friends huddled together to shield each other from the biting cold and snowmen balanced at the lips of fountains built to freeze.

This city was not unlike Delphin in many ways, only it was in possession of twice as much splendor; the entire city glimmered and twinkled, starlight crowning every rooftop and doorframe in the form of crystals carved to catch the light.

And Elias had *missed it*. He didn't realize just how much until they set foot inside the city limits.

As they began their journey through the outer streets, Soren did not walk as she normally did in the city of her raising, the city he'd seen her *literally* navigate blindfolded once on a dare; instead of striding the streets as if she was the one who owned them, she tucked into his side, hood up and head down, a fugitive in her own home.

It broke his heart. But he knew why this was a necessity, why this could not be the triumphant return he'd imagined for her when they were first plotting to escape Atlas. This was not the entrance of a conquering princess, an escaped prisoner of war returning home a hero…this was the Heir of an enemy kingdom returning to her captors.

Soren might hold love for both kingdoms, but both kingdoms might not hold love for the truth of her. He couldn't blame her for not being ready to face the eyes of their people just yet.

In truth, he wasn't sure he was quite ready, either. For while he might not hold love for Atlas, he did hold love for two of its royals, and that was enough to make this very complicated for him.

Not to mention, should Soren choose to honor her blood-claim to Atlas's throne…the ring on her finger bound him to that dais, too.

The rotten-lemon flavor of fear flooded his mouth, and he swallowed hard against it, bundling her closer to his side.

What would that make him? Prince Elias *Atlas*? One day *King-Consort* Elias Atlas?

He had no love for that kingdom; he had no wish to make his home there. The salt air, the constant hint of fish, the sticky heat, the riotous overwhelm of color and sun and noise…he'd be perfectly happy never to see it again. But the only alternative to that future was one where he and Soren lived a kingdom apart, and that…that was a life he was entirely unwilling to live.

Nyx was his home, but she was his heart. He knew which one he could survive without.

Soren looked up a bit to catch his eye, frowning at whatever she saw there. "You're thinking too hard. What's wrong?"

"I'm worried about you." A lesser truth rather than a lie—that was the only way he could fool her.

The crease between her brows softened. "I'm fine. Just…" A shaky breath. "I've missed it. Being here. I never thought I'd see it again."

Heart in his throat, Elias rubbed her arm, allowing himself a quick kiss to the crown of her head. "Neither did I."

"Do you think my sisters are here?"

He paused, considering. They'd been in Delphin weeks ago, but by now… "I wouldn't be surprised. They were only in Delphin to organize a rescue for us, and once I went to Artem…"

Soren's breath caught a bit, and the pain filtered back into her gaze, her brows coming together once more. She gripped the clasp of her cloak. "They were?"

"It took quite a bit to convince Ember not to come along herself, actually."

That pain softened into something hollower, lonelier—a desperate wish he'd seen in himself on many occasions these past couple months. "I want to see them."

"I would be surprised if they weren't here by now." He paused. "They spoke with Kallias. It was…less violent than I expected."

A brief, startled laugh, and Soren wiped at a stray tear. "How did they get along?"

"Kallias was terrified of them. I'm honestly shocked it didn't end in a proposal."

Another laugh—much more Soren-like than the first, a snorting cackle that eased some of the tension in his shoulders. "Something you and he have in common."

Elias blinked. "Excuse me?"

"Because you both swoon in the presence of angry women," said Jakob over his shoulder.

Elias looked to Soren, who gave the daintiest possible shrug and a genteel flutter of her eyelids.

Well. It wasn't like he could argue. And even if he'd wanted to…

That was the exact moment they turned onto a new street, and his lungs seized up.

Not just any street—the street his feet knew better than any other, because they'd taken their first wobbling steps across those bricks. He'd been raised in the shop that sat a bit apart from the others, fenced in by wrought-iron bars and guarded by two kerosene lamps mounted on either side of the gate. Thorny vines and scarlet roses twisted between the bars—flowers that by all rights should've been long dead in this unholy weather. Instead they flourished, stretching layered petals up to embrace the falling snow, cradling frozen droplets in their centers. Loch Ironworks.

"Elias," Soren whispered, urging him with a gentle check of her shoulder, "we can't yet."

He knew that. But he could already smell it—the smoke of the coals burning inside, the stinging tang of metal on the back of his tongue, the incense his mother always kept burning beside her workstation. Smells he thought he would never experience in anything but memory ever again.

Desperate longing bore down painfully on his chest, the strength fleeing from his knees in a way he hadn't experienced since the poison had been burned out of his blood by the will of his battlemate and the borrowed power of a goddess.

Even before he'd left after the Ursa battle, riding madcap after his captured battlemate with some foolish notion of rescuing her, he hadn't been home in some time. Not that he hadn't wanted to; things had just become so busy in the barracks, it had gotten harder and harder to sneak away to visit home. And beyond that…after his Viper bite, there were conversations his mother wanted to have that he wasn't ready to face.

All of that was over now. He was healthy; he was home; he had his battlemate back. And right at that moment, the thing Elias wanted most in the world was to see his family.

But Soren was right—they had to see Enna first. Their queen was owed a report…long past owed. He'd been so removed from being a soldier for so long it was hard to even remember when that kind of thing mattered—when he'd actually thought about his duty to his kingdom, to his queen.

Oh gods, he'd started this whole thing by committing *treason*.

"But we'll come back," he heard himself say, still unable to unroot his feet from the ground. "We will."

"We will," Soren promised, shaking his arm a bit. "You think I'm walking out of this city without a meal from Sera Loch?"

"I think you can't afford to," Rian mumbled, giving her a frank once-over that twisted Elias's temper in the worst way.

Soren had never needed him to fight her battles, so he bit his tongue. But satisfaction still simmered as she leveled a glower at his cousin, her hand tightening around his arm as if to warn him against acting on her behalf. "I could still kick your ass, Loch."

"Sure." With a snort, Rian turned and walked ahead, his cloak shifting—

Soren dipped so quickly Elias thought she might have fainted—until she snapped back up, pitching something through the air with swift, focused precision.

A snowball exploded in a starburst of white powder against the back of Rian's head.

Rian froze in his tracks, as did the rest of the company. Slowly, he swiveled on his heel, staring at her in disbelief.

Soren raised her eyebrows at him as if to ask what the big deal was, her chapped lips pursing, a challenge roaring to be answered in her eyes. But behind that…

Elias's heart sank at the desperation playing peek-a-boo behind her confident mask.

"Make no mistake, Rian," she snarled—nothing playful there to soften her tone, nor the finger she stabbed toward him. "Mock me one more time, and you'll find out exactly why a goddess chose *me* as her host."

Something in his own blood rose to that challenge—a singing heat that called the taste of smoke to his tongue, his fingertips aching with barely-withheld flame.

A dark, soot-soft voice whispered in his ear, a warning: *Careful, Elias.*

Only when Mortem's words fully registered in his mind did he realize he was *actually* smelling smoke—not just from the forge, but from Soren's sleeve, where he'd tightened his grip to hold her back. Tendrils of smoke floated up from beneath his fingers in a quintet.

He let go immediately, but Soren didn't seem to notice; she kept her gaze fastened firmly to his ignoramus of a cousin, her face set in a mask of authority and fearlessness. But either she didn't share Finn's affinity for such theatrics, or he simply knew her too well to fall for them—he saw every crack and flake in its exterior, every mark of exhaustion bruising her face in shadow, every tremble of that hand that had thrown the snowball.

Elias wrapped one arm around her once he was sure the fire in his own hand had died, hugging her around the shoulders from behind, leaning into her ear to whisper, "Easy, smartass."

And to his relief, she seemed to let it go. She waved impatiently at Rian before letting her hand drop, muttering something under her breath even Elias couldn't catch.

The rest of the trip to the palace was uneventful and quiet within their own group, though the streets hardly lacked for people. Though it was early in the day, hardly when the city showed its best face, there was no real lull in activity; Nyx was a lively place at any hour, no matter how often he'd entertained himself by testing just how many silly things Kallias would believe, including the idea that all Nyxians were nocturnal.

Even as they entered the castle's courtyard, the soles of his feet ached to turn and run back to the forge. But he steeled himself—this was not the moment to indulge in his own wants. This was about Soren, and she could not afford for him to be distracted now.

This was going to be a difficult, dangerous meeting. No matter which way Soren chose to lean, toward nature or nurture, this conversation with Ravenna would be…well. Either it would go well or it wouldn't, but no matter what, he wouldn't let anyone lay a hand on his battlemate.

The castle itself was a comforting sight despite his private misgivings—an impossibly tall structure that stretched so far into the sky that he couldn't see its top for clouds. It was pitch-dark and multi-layered, spired and star-spattered, glass windows shining like clusters of moonlight in the walls. The entire structure shimmered like it was built from the night sky itself.

And in spite of everything, Soren relaxed a bit as they approached the entrance, as if she'd only just let go of the vigilance she'd held since they'd left the guardhouse. Like she only now believed herself safe.

"Welcome home," Jakob called over his shoulder; there was a gruff edge of emotion in his voice as he glanced at them, a muscle quivering at the edge of his jaw. "Gods, I really didn't think I'd ever get to say that."

Elias glanced at Soren; when she gave him a nod, he released her and caught up to Jakob, clapping him on the shoulder and bumping foreheads with him. "Thank you," he croaked, "for bringing us home. And I'm sorry for whatever part we might have played in those gray hairs you seem to have sprouted."

With a growl, Jakob shoved him off, smoothly transitioning into a rude gesture. "I meant Soren, obviously. I had Varran pray to Mortem every night that she'd grant us sweet peace from *you*."

Before Elias could even decide whether to laugh or "salute" him back, they reached the doors…and the guards waiting for them there.

Jakob stood at attention, but did not bow—he owed these guards no fealty. Ranks didn't transition well between soldiers and palace guards, and there was a sort of private animosity that lingered beneath grudging mutual respect. Elias, as a frequent visitor to the palace, had never risked anything less than friendliness with those in the guard, but Jakob had no need for such caution.

"Captain Jakob Petrov and his company, returning from patrol near the Tallisian border. I must see Queen Ravenna immediately." And when both guards gave him a look of utter reproach, he leaned in closer, whispering something under his breath.

Elias only just held back a wince when their gazes flashed in tandem to him, then to Soren, still hooded and hidden in his shadow. With considerable haste, they seized the wrought-iron handles of the towering castle doors, towing them open with a shout of notification to those manning the turrets above.

A rush of warm air surged out to greet them, heavy with the scent of jasmine and sugar and hearthsmoke, and Soren caught her breath beside him, a hand pressing to her chest as it heaved in a deep breath.

The last time they'd set foot in this palace together, it had been after he'd received their orders to depart for Ursa in the morning—and she had been refused permission to go to Arborius to seek a cure for his Viper wound. They had spent that night together in the midst of a winter storm, her complaining about his incense burning, him complaining about her icy feet, her tugging out that little poison-study book she'd been trying to hide from him when she thought him asleep, her fingers stroking his hair back until he fell asleep in truth.

Warding off nightmares, he'd told her then. In truth, he had been praying for a miracle…praying for a cure to make itself known without her having to make such a dangerous journey to find it.

He clearly hadn't prayed hard enough.

"Come on." He rubbed her back as they crossed the threshold. "Let's go find your mother."

Soren's eyes dimmed and darkened—with pain, with longing, with anger. So many emotions he couldn't hope to sort through the storm.

"No use putting it off," she whispered. "Let's go."

But as they stepped forward, one of the guards held out a hand of warning before Soren, her eyes gleaming with unshed tears.

"Princess," she said in a hushed voice, "I am endlessly glad to see you safe and sound, but you should know…"

Soren's brow furrowed. Tipping her hood back, she faced down the guard. "Tell me."

The guard hesitated, the pieces of her armor scraping together as she shifted uncomfortably.

Her next words sent a torrent of nausea shooting from Elias's stomach to his throat:

"The Queen is currently presiding over your funeral."

# CHAPTER 25

## SOREN

*H*ome.

The word might as well have been etched behind her heart; with every thud, the blood-beat in her head echoed it, a desperation begging her to bypass all this pomp and circumstance, to run until she found her mother and sisters and launched herself into their arms and wept herself dry.

But this was not her only home, and the other was depending on her for its salvation. That weight forced her shoulders back and her head high; that urgency forced her feet into a marching clip.

After all, it would be terribly rude to be late to her own funeral.

"You have to realize," Jakob's tone was sharp with haste as he hurried to keep up with her—despite the pain in every joint, she was in the lead now, Elias at her side and Jakob on her heels— "that Elias told us you were dead, all right? Dead-dead. Deader than a rock on a pyre. Deader than Rian's love life. Deader—"

"You knew about this?" she hissed. "And didn't think to drop a quick, Hey, by the way, your funeral is today! Care to crash it?"

Jakob sighed. "Honestly, when we ran across you two, I thought the delay would make us miss it anyway. The period of mourning was set to end while we were gone, but…look, it's on me, Soren, you can't blame Queen Ravenna—"

"There are a whole gods-damned lot of things I'm blaming her for at the moment, Jakob!" Starting with causing her first funeral and ending with presiding over her second.

"Soren," Elias said, sounding a bit out of breath himself as he picked his pace up to a jog, his cluster of charms tapping against his chest, "maybe we should think twice about causing a scene?"

*Maybe he's right*, Ani chipped in nervously, her tone warbling like birdsong— it always did that when she was anxious. Fear shouldn't sound like music, but oh well. Another superiority the goddess could claim over mere mortals.

"On the contrary," she muttered, both to Elias and to Ani, "I think a scene is exactly what I need right now." In fact, it was the only thing that might soothe this rageful sensation boiling in her tossing ship of a stomach.

She was utterly, entirely sick of being dead. Utterly, entirely sick of being grieved.

She was more alive than she'd ever been, depths take her, and she was going to cause as many scenes as she needed to until everybody gods-damned knew it.

That slow-burning seethe in her gut consumed her so entirely that she barely even noticed her surroundings at all—her feet knew their own way through these soaring, closed-in black marble loggias, and she'd attended enough events that she knew exactly which chamber this particular one would be held in.

It didn't matter to her that she was tracking slush and mud and pine needles all over the plush white carpet. Didn't matter that a chorus of gasps and curses and shocked prayers to Mortem echoed around her as she tossed her hood back, revealing her travel-roughened countenance to black-clad palacefolk. Didn't matter that there was the faintest melody floating through the air, carrying with it that discordant tone all funeral dirges used to set the proper mood of mourning.

Her anticipation grew with every step, with every note of that thin song that tweaked her eardrums the wrong way.

No more mourning. No more lies. Soren Atlas was alive, and she was going to make it everyone else's gods-damned problem.

Violin scratched past her eardrums, a mournful groan that wormed beneath her skin, a spined and crawling creature of noise that tickled her just the wrong way in her very marrow.

And the only thing that fended off that sensation was the forceful shoving of the door to the Nyxian throne room, all the tingling energy in her arms thrown out into the space beyond, replaced by a satisfaction as a series of scandalized gasps echoed, rising to the rafters in layer after layer.

The Nyxian throne room could not have been more opposite to Atlas's; mainly because it was a throne room only in that there was a handful of chairs set apart from the rest.

Four chairs—one for the Queen and each of Soren's sisters. The fifth was buried in so many bunches of roses she could barely see the plain black velvet of the cushion beneath.

There was no dais, no gold, no sparkling chandeliers or ocean views—there were rows and rows of cushioned seats fanned out in every direction, each currently holding a familiar face decked in mourning veils or sorrowful stares slowly turning to horror as they took her in.

She'd seen much the same look on the faces of Atlas folk as they fled from the undead clawing their way through Port Atlas. She'd seen much the same look on Ramses's face when he first beheld Soren in the private dining room where she'd eaten her first real meal after returning to Atlas.

She did not see that look on Ravenna's face as she rose from the chair positioned at the front of the room, her gown sewn from such deep black silk that it seemed she wore a void in place of cloth. She did not see that look as three girls of varying complexion and countenance rose from their seats in turn, Yvonne first, Ember second, Auralee last.

Ravenna wasn't the cold, merciless queen Soren's birth kingdom believed her to be, and in spite of everything, that much had not changed in Soren's estimation of her. Ravenna had not yet seen forty years; there were no silver strands in her hair, no wrinkles on her face, no shake to the hand she braced against the arm of her chair as she pushed to her feet. No cruelty in her countenance, no chill that accompanied her presence. She had never been the shrieking winter wind or the deadly impassivity of a blizzard; she was the crackling fire that welcomed one to settle and sleep beside its warmth in safety. She was a lullaby hummed beside a slow-dimming candle, a promise that the dark of the night was not a threat, but a shield.

She was a young queen, younger even than Adriata; she'd only been twenty-five when her late father set the ocean kingdom ablaze and dealt the Atlas family a never-healing wound. But there was grief worthy of a lifetime in her midnight eyes as she stared at Soren…stared as if she could not quite believe what she saw, as if a ghost had marched into her throne room and declared the castle properly haunted. Grief that melted into desperate, desperate hope the longer she held Soren's gaze, waiting…just waiting.

The music stopped, leaving behind only a memory of whatever emotion had pushed her into this room without giving anyone the generosity of a warning. Without giving herself the generosity of a moment to breathe, to think, to plan this moment the way a true princess and Heir ought to.

And in that single moment of holding her mother's gaze, Soren realized she'd made a mistake.

She wasn't ready for this. Not yet. Gods, she could barely keep herself steady on her aching ankles and blistered feet, let alone hold her head high and keep her composure beneath the broken eyes of the woman who raised her.

"Soren!"

Auralee's scream shattered the trance that had overtaken the room, and before Soren could decide whether her legs would allow her another step, her youngest sister crashed into her so hard she thought a rib might've snapped beneath her clutching embrace.

It took less than a second for Auralee's tears to soak through the sweater Elias had bought her—less than five for Yvonne to catch up, yanking Auralee back from her with a hiss of warning, and for Ember to rip a knife from her bandolier and set the tip to Soren's clavicle, her eyes blazing with equal parts grief and rage. Her sister never bowed or broke in the face of a fight, but in the face of this one…there was a quiver to her chin. A hint of silver in her eyes.

"Em, wait," Soren choked, but that steel only bit down harder, a fang in the mouth of a hunting wolf.

"You have a lot of nerve," hissed the Artem-born weaponsmith, her tar-black blade biting uncomfortably deep into Soren's skin, "marching my sister's body in here like you own the place."

Honestly, why was this everyone's reaction to seeing the dead come back to life?

*It was your reaction too,* Anima grumbled.

*Those ones were actually* dead, Soren reminded her.

*We are at your funeral, Soren.*

*Touché.*

"Em," she rasped again, "please move the knife."

Ember didn't move the knife. "Don't say my name like you know me, Goddess." Then, over Soren's shoulder— "Elias, why did you bring her here?"

Before Elias could answer—and before she could come up with some way to escape her sister, one of the only people she couldn't win a wrestling match with before all of this chaos—a new chorus of shouts and sobs started up from near the front of the room, a gaggle of dark-haired heads leaping from and over chairs and sprinting toward the door with admirable haste.

The loudest sob of all came from just behind her, and a dark blur hurtled past, colliding with the murder of crows coming their way…also known as the Loch family.

"You're home!" squealed a girl no older than five, throwing elbows and tiny leather boots every which way until her siblings parted for her with a chorus of pained grunts and protests. She flung herself into Elias's arms and nuzzled her little face into his cloak, her eyes squeezed so tightly shut her entire face screwed up with them.

Something dull and steel-tipped thudded straight into the center of Soren's heart…something that hurt worse than Ember's knife.

It was only too easy to picture a different little girl, redheaded and older by a handful of hourglass grains. Only too easy to picture a different older brother clutching her close and silently weeping for joy.

Soren's gaze slid back to Ember, whose countenance had not softened even slightly.

"This is about to get really complicated," she said.

Ember scowled. "For you, maybe."

"For all of us." Soren flicked her gaze to the Loch siblings. "Between you and them, there's too many *E* names to keep track of."

"Emberlyn, that's enough."

Ice crackled to life in Soren's veins, and she raised her head a bit, meeting her mother's gaze once more.

Ravenna put a hand on Ember's shoulder, her fingers flexing in a gentle squeeze… also known as the first step in Ravenna's motherly countdown to obedience. And with reluctance so great Soren could practically hear it rusting her sister's joints, Ember painstakingly lowered her knife.

The next breath that whooshed into her lungs was not one of relief from pain. It was bracing for more.

*Mama.* The word burned at the tip of her tongue, an ember that had been smoldering since the moment she slipped away into sleep on the battlefield of Ursa. It was a plea that had been buried for so long…first out of dignity, then out of impossibility, and now…

Now, it scorched with the seething heat of accusation.

"Soren," Ravenna said softly. Crackling fire. Sweet-sung lullaby. Funeral dirge. "I see you, sweetheart."

A stray violin bow struck a sour note. That burning ember leapt free of Soren's tongue, but it took a new form now: "I know what you did."

All the winters in the six kingdoms couldn't numb the pain that broke Ravenna's composure into shards of serrated emotion, the pieces flashing in so many different shades Soren couldn't name them all—guilt, certainly, but grief, too. Resignation, acceptance, and…and love. Still love, even though the truth finally stood unmasked between them.

"Come," Ravenna said. "We'll talk upstairs."

Venom stung Soren's lips; she spat it out. "We'll talk *here*."

Now the Queen's gaze steeled. "We will talk *upstairs*. Now."

The salt and sea in her blood did not want to obey. Did not want to bow. But the part of her that was snow and stars was still Ravenna's daughter, enough to feel properly rebuked.

And even the more rebellious part of her understood that she was being petulant; of course they couldn't have this conversation in a room full of gawkers, every word being squirreled away for the gossips and the rumor-mongers of the city.

She caught Elias's gaze over the heads of his siblings—the concern there, the longing, finally loosened the bindings of her stubborn temper.

"Fine," she muttered. "But let Elias stay here."

"Of course. His mother will want to see him, I'm sure—I think she snuck out to get Auralee a handkerchief." Ravenna smiled, briefly; when Soren didn't return it, she let it fall. With a flick of her hand, she summoned a woman wearing an ensemble of black velvet and intricately-etched silver steel armor. The woman's hair was meticulously curled, strands of gray streaking through the brunette locks, and her brown eyes took Soren in with equal love—and equal guilt—as Ravenna. A whole new bud of betrayal bloomed to life in Soren's gut, and she squeezed her hands into fists, forcing all that feeling into her fingers until they shook with barely contained fight.

Not her, too.

Ravenna gripped the woman's wrist, leaning in to murmur in her ear: "Clear the palace, then meet me in my office."

Sierra Korazin, battlemate to the Queen and General of the Eclipse Guard, gave a swift nod and salute before turning back to the room and directing the castle guards in the rapid dissemination of the gathered mourners. No bow—Sierra might not have been equal in rank to the Queen, but battlemates never bent before each other. They were equals in heart.

Just as that thought crossed Soren's mind, a hand brushed the small of her back, her only warning before Elias's voice murmured in her ear: "You're shaking."

Blowing out a slow breath, she forced her fists to uncurl, trying to flex the tremor out of her fingers. "I didn't expect to be so…"

"I know. It's all right. Fair warning, my family's—"

Before he could say anything more, the knot of Lochs suddenly descended upon her—gently, even Emma, so Elias must have told them to be careful with her.

Normally, that might've miffed her. It bothered her that it didn't.

"We thought you were dead," sobbed Eliana and Elinora in tandem, the twin sisters wrapping their arms around her middle and burying their heads in either shoulder. Ezra and Erin, boys born a mere year apart, clung instead to Elias, but they both beamed at her with equal joy. Emma wrapped all four limbs around Soren's leg and promptly started rattling off every single thing that had happened since she'd last seen her—including such momentous events as having eaten a muffin that morning—and Evanna, who had trailed Ember with a hand resting over her hip, was regarding her with cautious disbelief.

"Elias?" Evanna asked carefully.

"It's all right," Elias said quickly, offering Ember an apologetic look. "I…it's a long story. But it's all right. It's her."

It seemed his word was the only confirmation needed. Because between one blink and the next, Soren found herself not only smothered by every Loch sibling, but by her sisters, as well.

Ember had her face buried in Soren's hair, weeping silently and planting kisses along her temple. Auralee was lost somewhere in the crush of Lochs, but Soren could hear her crying, a sound that never failed to crack her heart in half. And Yvonne…

Yvonne reached out and held Soren's face in both hands, pain and apology written in equal measure on her countenance.

"We didn't know," she whispered, wiping at Soren's cheeks—gods, when had she started crying? "We didn't know, Soren, I swear to the gods. I'm so sorry. I'm so sorry."

All at once, every emotion that had built and built and built for all these months…all of them boiled over beneath the pleading eyes of her eldest sister.

"They're alive, Yvonne," she sobbed, and Yvonne shushed her softly, pressing her forehead against Soren's. "My family's alive, and I forgot them, I *left them*—"

"It wasn't your fault." There was no doubt in Yvonne's voice; not even a waver of uncertainty. "I spoke to Prince Kallias…to your brother. I know it wasn't your fault, and so does he."

Soren sniffled, worming her arm out of the group hug to wipe her own eyes. "I heard he didn't do so well in front of you."

Yvonne smiled slightly. "Actually, he was quite impressive. He held himself like a prince ought to."

Of course he had. He'd always been the best at commanding a room, whether he knew it or not.

"Elias claims he nearly fainted when he laid eyes on you and Ember."

Yvonne rolled her eyes, gesturing down at herself with one hip cocked. "Well, we can hardly blame him for *that*, now can we?"

Laughter—harsh, awful, and almost healing—broke free from Soren's chest, and she sagged into the web of arms around her, letting herself be held.

Letting herself, for just a moment, rest in the embrace of her heart-family.

# CHAPTER 26

# SOREN

She had been away from Elias enough since Anima had taken hold of her in Port Atlas's temple; it should have been easy to urge him away from her side now, to leave him behind with his clamoring siblings while she was escorted to the second floor of the castle…but it wasn't.

It did help that Yvonne stood to her right, Ember to her left, and Auralee behind her. Yvonne's posture directly mimicked Ravenna's, head up, back straight, the future Queen making no secret of who these marble halls would belong to on the far-off day when Queen Ravenna would either lay down her crown or pass into Mortem's care.

Soren had never envied Yvonne that crown…in fact, until recently, it had been her biggest relief that she would almost certainly never wear anything heavier than a heap of hairpins on her head.

Now she carried something so much weightier. And her shoulders already ached from the burden.

The fate of Atlas depended on her, a girl connected to it only by threads of blood and a few short years of memory. It was treacherously little to build a war campaign on. Hardly enough to give her authority to initiate a negotiation of this caliber.

And that was what this was—a negotiation led by a person tantamount to collateral damage. A piece of kindling coming back to the firestarter, pockmarked and scorched and trying to cleanse itself of the ashes clinging to its scarred surface.

*That's not true,* Ani protested—she'd been quiet for a while now, but her voice floated in sharper than usual, like she'd grown a thorn or two while she sat and listened. *And you know it. Where is this coming from?*

Where *was* it coming from? These kind of thoughts, dark and dismal and tinged with the frantic energy of someone desperate to run…they weren't like her at all.

She swallowed hard, giving a hard shake of her head—maybe a good shuffle was all she needed to come back to herself.

This was not a battlefield, for gods' sakes. This was her home. This was her family. Ravenna had never hurt her, and that wouldn't change now.

So why was every muscle locked in the rigor of anticipating a blow? Why did her fingers long to be holding a blade, a shield, anything to protect herself with?

Why were those gods-damned violins still moaning their melancholy song after she'd effectively ended her own premature funeral?

It was only when they crossed into Ravenna's office, the guards shutting the door behind them once Sierra joined the gathering, that the troubled edge to her thoughts finally soothed. The familiar smells of incense and petrichor cooled the battle-ready heat building in her muscles, untying the knot in her stomach just enough for her to sink into one of the chairs arranged before Ravenna's desk, her palms sliding against the cool, smoothly carved birchwood until the fingertips of her left hand came across the subtle ridges carved into the apex of the chair's arm.

Beneath the pad of her finger was an *S* she had slowly carved throughout years of being summoned to this room. Whether to receive lectures, orders, praise, or to simply spend time with her busy mother, she'd spent enough time in this chair to make a fairly deep divot using only her fingernail as a tool. She set that nail back to task now, a calming rhythm of sensation that kept her hands busy so her mind could be free to focus.

Sierra circled the desk to stand beside Ravenna's chair, leaving the other two chairs on either side of Soren free for the taking. Ember hovered behind Soren rather than sitting, agitated energy radiating from her like a mountain cat on the prowl; Auralee sank into the chair on Soren's left, and Yvonne into the chair on her right. After a heartbeat, Auralee and Yvonne rested their hands on her arm and wrist, respectively; Ember's hands slid over her shoulders, bracing them with firm reassurance, her weaponsmith's callouses rubbing against Soren's raw scrapes even through her sweater. Still, she didn't have the heart to pry her sister's hands off of her; in fact, without that quiet faith, that promise of support, she might not have had the courage to say what she did.

"Tell me the truth." To her relief, her voice rang out strong and sure. "All of it."

And in the practiced tandem of two women who had fought back-to-back and side-by-side since well before Soren was born, Ravenna and Sierra told their tale.

Much of it she had already guessed—orders delivered to Ravenna in the form of a paper slid across her father's ebonywood desk, no words exchanged for fear of listening ears; King Byron had descended deep into paranoia in his years of reckless warfare and greedy snatches of power, and if Ravenna's rare stories about him rang true, she had not heard her own father's voice for five years prior to his final words.

Similarly, if whispered barracks legends rang true, those last words had been "Good girl," choked through blood that stained his violent grin as he died on a knife he'd gifted to his only daughter on her sixteenth birthday.

Ravenna had received her orders from her father, a death sentence to the Atlas Heir written in ink that ran red as blood. That paper was nothing but ashes by the time she exited the office; appropriate, considering the weapon her father had recommended for the job.

Sierra picked up the narration at this point, Ravenna lost in staring at her own desk, tracing a dent in the ebony surface. The Queen's battlemate whispered of orders shared with precious few; only King Byron's personal retinue of assassins, the Ichor Blades, were to accompany the then-Princess to attempt to cripple Atlas beyond recovery.

And in so many ways, despite only managing to rid Atlas of one royal, they had succeeded.

Ravenna—along with Sierra, the youngest member of the Ichor Blades— had plotted their own betrayal far from the keen ears of their comrades as they made the dangerous journey into the very heart of Atlas, the group traveling in two pairs and a trio, staying in separate inns and speaking in varying accents to avoid being noticed. And every night of the journey, they traded notes back and forth, burning them afterward with the flame of a borrowed lantern—a tool from the King's own book.

An assassination plot infected with the hope of a rescue. A quiet defiance of Ravenna's father's orders, a small rebellion she could only mount in the privacy of her own mind. Even her position as Byron's sole heir—the only daughter of her late mother, Queen Esmeralda—would not protect her from his violent tendencies if she was to be discovered in defiance.

A host of black-clad, flame-wielding assassins descending on a celebrating Port Atlas. Orders burned to ash over weeks, imprinted in Ravenna's mind as she waited beside one of the curtains in the ballroom, a vial of oil in one hand and a flickering torch in the other.

A silent cue that came and went. A screamed warning of fire before the fire had even started—Sierra, hidden amongst the crowd, giving everyone the chance to run in the seconds between when Ravenna was meant to set the fire and when she truly did.

And in spite of all of it, in spite of the planning and the plotting and that soft, subtle rebellion Ravenna had so carefully executed…in spite of it all, Princess Soleil still did not escape that ballroom.

Now Ravenna finally raised her head…now she met Soren's gaze, blackened eyes silvered along the lids. There was no quiver in her chin or crack to her voice, but when she spoke, it was with the weight of one who had carried guilt and sorrow for so very long that it almost hurt more to set it down.

"I wouldn't let you die," she whispered. "You were only a child. I used to play with you at summits while Adriata…while your mother negotiated with my father. She and I—and Ramses—were friends back then. Good friends. And even if we hadn't been…you were *children.* My father was a madman. I couldn't defy him outright, but I could ensure his plan failed." A beat, then a lower whisper: "I *thought* I could."

A storm of emotion swirled in a miasma around Soren's heart…clouds in varying shades of anger, of gratitude, of love and hate, of adrenaline and exhaustion. The war for her reply was fought just beneath her breastbone, and when the victor finally scaled the column of her throat to form the words she needed to say…

There was simply no fight left to have.

The Heir of Atlas, kidnapped from her family and raised in a kingdom not her own, should have wielded her righteous anger to buy Atlas the help it needed. She should have demanded reparations be paid in the form of weapons and warwork on their behalf. She should have stood before Ravenna as an equal.

"You took me from them," she whispered. "I understand why. I even understand why you kept me away. But why…why didn't you *tell me?*"

Ravenna hesitated. "It's not a noble reason."

"None of this was noble." No, it was all a viscous stew brought to boiling over the fire of desperation, knit together by spur-of-the-moment decisions that built into a situation so thorny and tangled it couldn't possibly have been escaped. So many people had a hand in tying this knot, it was a wonder they'd even gotten this far into untangling it.

Ravenna offered her a wet, shaky smile. "I was afraid. Afraid if I told you, you would go running off back to them without waiting for an explanation…which, well, a whole lot of good *that* did. Even then, every time your birthday rolled around, I promised myself this would be the year…every time you woke up half-asleep and crying for someone whose name you couldn't remember, crying for Mama without wanting me, crying for your papa…every single time, I promised myself I would tell you. But I always talked myself out of it, and the timing was never quite right…maybe it never would have been. And, selfishly…" A pained laugh. "Selfishly, sweetheart, I was never ready to lose you."

The cold sensation of a clammy hand wrapped around hers. Her battlemate's dazed, feverstruck eyes flashed through her mind.

*"I chased you all the way here. Now I'm asking you to walk me home."*

Had she not committed the very same crime? Had she not clung to someone without concern for their own needs, too scared of life without them to let them go like she should?

Anger and understanding. They locked horns, waiting for her to put her own weight behind one or the other.

She would be a fool not to believe the sorrow in Ravenna's face. A fool to let her anger blind her into thinking this had been done with malicious intent. And future queens could not be fools. They did not have that luxury.

*She* did not have that luxury any longer.

But that didn't mean she had to forgive her. Not today—and maybe not at all.

So she said nothing.

"We'll solve this," Ravenna promised her after several moments of silence, voice hushed with what sounded like lingering shame. Good. "All of it, together if you wish. But for now, you've come so far and rested so little…go with your sisters. Get seen to by a physician, and take the night to rest. I'll have your story from Elias for now. Everything will be clearer in the morning."

It wouldn't. The morning sun had solved nothing thus far, no matter how many times people tried to say otherwise to her. But the idea of rest after this ridiculous, draining day left her nodding in spite of her doubts, a cramp in her stomach reminding her she hadn't eaten in hours, either.

Yvonne stood up, helping her to her feet. "Come on. Let's get you fixed up."

Too tired, too heartworn to do anything but obey, Soren followed the three of them out.

***

A visit to the physician, a visit to the kitchens, and a hot shower later, Soren sat at the foot of Ember's bed, staring at herself in the mirror as she nibbled halfheartedly at a cinnamon bun.

Yvonne was cursing mildly as she attempted to untangle Soren's hair, mindful of Auralee's listening ears. Auralee herself was snuggled into Soren's side, and Ember was rebandaging wounds that had broken open from the strain of getting herself dressed after her shower. The soft silk pants, dyed a beautiful shade of dusty pink, strained a bit against her thighs and hips—silk had little give, after all—but they were the only thing gentle enough not to pain her sensitive skin. Though the matching silk top lay across her knees, for now she wore only a soft lace brassiere, giving Emberlyn access to her wounds and bruises.

After a good twenty minutes of Yvonne's cursing growing more and more harried, the eldest Nyxian princess finally threw the comb down with a growl. "I need a break," she announced, flexing reddened fingers, staring at the mark the comb had left behind with a pronounced scowl. "This could take days."

"Here. Let me look." After tying off one of the bandages, sending a dull spike of pain through Soren's arm, Ember got up and took Yvonne's spot.

Silence reigned for a good two minutes. It wasn't hard to watch her sisters' expressions in the mirror: Yvonne frustrated, Ember reluctant and resigned. The longer those ragged mats brushed against her neck, the longer she thought about the length Anima had coaxed out of the strands unnaturally, the worse her skin crawled. She had her body back, at least for now, but that hair was a reminder that some pieces of her were Anima's and Anima's alone.

Those pieces had to go. They *had* to go.

She turned to look at her elder sisters, a disgusted shudder rattling her spine as the tangles in her hair rubbed against the nape of her neck. "Cut it."

Yvonne's brows furrowed. "What?"

But Ember's tense jaw relaxed—like that necessity had already occurred to her, and she'd only been afraid of breaking that news to Soren. She expertly ran her fingers through Soren's curls, fiddling around with the various knots. "We'll have to take most of the length. Is that all right with you?"

"Yes." Desperate. Reckless. One-two-three taps against her leg. "Please cut it."

Yvonne hesitated, but Ember must have seen the building frenzy in her eyes…hopefully she didn't see Soren's tapping fingers, the way she blinked and breathed and fidgeted in clusters of three, the way she kept glancing to the mirror to ensure no gold had leaked into her irises. Ember reached to her bandolier and drew out a set of small, sharp scissors, less of a weapon and more of a tool.

"Turn around, sit straight, and hold still," Ember ordered, and despite her crawling skin, despite wanting to ignore the order just to prove she could, Soren obeyed.

Ember's hand settled at the base of her neck. Lingered. Hesitated.

"If you want me to stop at any point," she said, "tell me, and I will. No matter how uneven your haircut looks."

A laugh, halfhearted as it was, settled Soren's nerves a bit. She adjusted her posture, hugging her knees to her chest and fixing her eyes on her own gaze in the mirror. "I trust you."

"Good." Ember squeezed her shoulder, then got to work—a soft snipping sound and a slow disappearance of weight from Soren's back the only signs she had indeed begun cutting. "In the meantime, will you do us a favor?"

Soren frowned. "I guess." Though what favor she could do in this state, she wasn't sure.

"Tell us about your other family—your brothers and sister." Ember caught her eyes in the mirror, cracking a rare smirk. "I want to know which rumors are true…and where we land among the ranks of favorite siblings now that they've doubled."

That time, her laughter was wholehearted, strong enough to shake the last of the uneasiness from her belly. She took a bite of that heavenly cinnamon bun, savoring the mix of spice and sweet on her tongue, rolling her eyes toward Ember as Auralee giggled. "It's not a competition. But if you want to know…"

And for the next couple hours, as hair drifted silently to the bedspread and Ember and Yvonne worked in tandem to shape her curls anew, Soren told her sisters of her birth family…of Finn's cunning and caution, his odd penchant for hot chocolate in wine glasses and the soft spot for his family he so viciously tried to hide; of Kallias and his natural gift for leading and love, his fierce dedication to their people, his insistence on carrying every burden so those he loved never had to feel the weight.

She told them of her blood mother, Adriata, and how she was once a doting and devoted mother before war broke and reshaped her into something marred and merciless, a queen so desperate not to feel the grief of losing another child that she'd pushed all the others away.

She told them of her father—here, she had to clear her throat several times, taken off guard by just how much she missed him and how hard she wished she had not wasted the time she'd had in Atlas.

She told them of Jericho and Vaughn, and there she began to shake so badly they had to take a break from cutting for fear of nicking her skin. They held her hands as she spoke through gritted teeth of Jericho's grief twisting her in different ways, worse ways than Adriata; how in her fear of losing the man she loved, she'd made a deal with something so dark and dangerous that its threat now shadowed every kingdom, every family, every good or terrible person alike. How it had not been ambition or cruelty that led to Jericho's betrayal, but a love so deep and dear that Jericho had not been able to bear the idea of death sundering it.

A fear Soren knew only too intimately.

Silence fell well before the last tangled curl did. But when it was over, Soren lifted her eyes to the mirror…and found a different woman looking back.

Not Anima—the goddess had stayed quiet for some time now, lost in her own thoughts, and there was no glint of gold in the green of her eyes. But the woman who looked back at her now…

The cropped halo of curls that danced around her head was beautiful…a frenzy of gilded fire only barely tamed. When she reached up to run a hand through it, no knot or tangle caught her in place…and when she ran that hand downward, the strands came to their end at the nape of her neck, not a single strand weighing on her back.

Soren Marina Atlas. For the first time, she looked like the woman she'd become…the woman she'd grown into. The woman she'd chosen.

Relief flooded her so powerfully she nearly bent forward. Instead, she sagged back, leaning into her sisters. "Thank you."

Yvonne dashed a stray curl away from Soren's eyes, pressing a kiss to her temple. "Of course."

"We'll leave you to rest," Ember said, nudging Yvonne and giving a meaningful look to Auralee, who reluctantly peeled herself away from Soren's side. "You can stay here until you're ready to head back to your room."

They swept up the shorn hair in short order, each kissed her forehead, then made their way to the door…

And something sharp hooked into Soren's lip, tearing a plea from her mouth: "Stay."

The three of them turned to look over their shoulders, varying shades of concern on their faces.

Silently, Soren cursed herself. But she'd already asked; if she tried to laugh it off, they wouldn't believe her, anyway.

"Stay," she croaked, gathering her knees even closer to her chest. "Just until Elias comes back. *If* he does." He might have decided to sleep at the forge tonight, and she wasn't about to have anyone send for him. He deserved a night at home as much as she did.

"Of course," Yvonne said firmly, tossing her silvered hair over one shoulder…a ploy to hide how she dashed a tear from her own cheek. "Of course we will."

It only took a few seconds for the bed to be filled with sisters, each talking over the other, sharing stories or jokes or arguments as they nestled together. And even as Soren's anxiety eased, even as she relaxed enough to start making jokes of her own, a pulse of pain…of sadness…lingered deep in her mind.

A sadness she didn't think belonged to her.

# CHAPTER 27

# ELIAS

Elias's mother had yet to let go of him, and he couldn't say he minded…even if he hadn't managed to take a real breath in several minutes.

Sera Loch was a woman wrought from midnight and new embers, her hair and eyes rich black, her skin russet brown. Her face was built for the forge, all smooth planes and wide-set bones, and the wrinkles that creased her mouth and eyes only said that she'd smiled more than most in her life. And now she was weeping, alternating between berating him for leaving without saying goodbye and singing praises to Mortem for his safe return.

And in spite of his own joy at their reunion, a thing he never thought he'd get to experience…he could not help the panicky energy building within his restless fingers, an impulse to run and track down Soren chanting in the back of his head, his heart already half-sure that something terrible had happened to her in his absence.

Or, perhaps worse, that their reunion itself had been nothing but one good dream in a string of several nightmares. A cruel imitation of a reprieve, sent to break him in the way no nightmare had yet managed to do.

His mother must have sensed the tension stretching his skin; she finally pulled away, scanning his face with piercing precision, digging straight to the heart of him before he had time to try and hide it. "What's wrong?"

He swallowed hard. Tried to steady himself so his voice would not shake. "So many things that I'm not even sure where to start, Mama."

"And Soren?" Her eyes darkened. "Is she all right?"

His voice pulled taut against the swell of worry in his chest. "It's a long story, Mama."

Her grip tightened. "Tell me everything."

***

As expected, his no-nonsense mother offered him exactly one solution: a trip to the temple he'd been trained in.

"If anyone has your answers," his mother had promised him, "it's Priestess Kenna. Dinner will be waiting for you when you come home."

*Home.* What had once been a hopeless wish now lingered just hours away: a night at home with his family. A long evening spent listening to his siblings bicker while his cat napped in his lap. His mother's cooking heaped into his mouth until he could finally, finally forget the flavor of fish.

But first, he had to make his way through the wrought-iron gate before him…and the ebony temple waiting beyond.

He reached out one gloveless hand, letting out a breath that did not fog, even in the bitter cold. The fire ever-burning in his veins had sapped what moisture might have turned his breath to clouds.

It should have unnerved him—might have, if he hadn't gone through exactly thirty-two more absurd things in the handful of months since he'd been home last.

His bare palm pressed to the gate; the cold metal stung for only a moment before it warmed sharply beneath his touch, such a rapid heating that the iron groaned a bit.

His mother herself had forged the elements of this gate—the iron imitations of flames at its base, the rose vines dotted with thorns twisted around every bar to discourage trespassers. Those thorns were three inches long and sharp as any needle; they were not kind to those who tried to set boot to bar, no matter how well those boots may have been reinforced. Samhain and Rian had learned that the hard way one night…despite all the warnings he'd given before finally giving up, allowing them to do what they wished.

Of course, he could have opened the gate for them. But if there was one thing he couldn't stand, it was people trespassing on holy land.

With a deft twist of his fingers, muscle memory drilled into him by years of tenancy here, he triggered the secret mechanism hidden in one of the metal roses to unlock the gate. Cogs whirred, something clicked, and the gate swung open before him, taking its thorns with it.

Every step he took through the courtyard, snow melted beneath his boots, leaving a trail from the gate to the temple steps themselves. Beneath that snow, the land was bare—no plants grew on Mortem's ground. Life simply did not thrive in the realm of Death.

And right at this moment, Elias was gladder for it than he'd ever been.

He'd only just set foot to the first step when the temple's door swung open, shedding snow from its threshold. A white-haired head peered out from behind it, and he tensed for only a moment before recognition hit: a woman stood there, her pale, crinkled skin draped around icy blue eyes, robes of deep black and vivid red hanging loosely from a form even thinner than he'd last seen it.

Age continued to rob her of strength and stature, but even so, at the age of nearly one hundred and five, Death had yet to do worse than tiptoe around the hem of Priestess Kenna's robes. The initiates had always whispered about it, and the boldest—usually those who had been forced into the service and held no real reverence for Mortem herself—always started the new year with a betting pool on when the Priestess would die.

Elias had staunchly committed to one constant bet: that she simply would not die. The repeated victories were how he'd afforded to pay for his Winter Fair presents every year.

"Elias Loch," she greeted him, her voice grave as ever…though if he squinted, he could imagine a hint of fondness in those piercing eyes, the ghost of a smile haunting her thin lips. "I heard you were dead."

He raised an eyebrow as he bent his head, the gentlest of bows owed to one his senior and superior. "Did anyone take bets?" he said toward the ground, not daring to joke with her while looking her in the eye.

Even so, he heard that immaterial smile creep into her voice. "Of course. We can't seem to break them of the habit."

"Did anyone win?"

"You know I am above such things, boy." A pause. An aged chuckle. "I only returned the favor and told them you certainly were not one to die easily. Now come here. Let me look at you. I sense something new."

She had no idea.

Ears heating—with self-consciousness now, not magic—Elias ascended the stone steps, following his mentor into the temple.

The moment his boot passed the threshold, the four torches mounted on the walls flared with muffled roars, flames licking toward the ceiling before settling once more at Priestess Kenna's hurried wave. Orange and scarlet light roiled across the onyx-carpeted floor, illuminating runes dyed into the tufts, what Priestess Kenna had always called *old magic*. Similar runes to what he had tattooed on his neck and shoulders to ward off Occassio-tainted magics, but more of them, many with functions he couldn't hope to guess at.

The Priestess turned to face him, eyes wide, face somehow paler.

"You've been to Artem," she said.

No point in denying it. "Yes, Priestess."

"You underwent the trials?"

"Yes, Priestess."

"And you survived. Not only survived, but…" She approached him now, her wizened hand reaching to shove his sleeve up to his elbow, revealing his completed tattoos. Her eyes flashed to his, recognition sharpening them. "The Phoenix Priest."

It was all he could do to dip his head in a slow nod, swallowing the nerves that bundled themselves together in his stomach.

She dropped down so quickly that a shout of alarm rose in his throat, and he jerked forward to catch her, stopping just in time as he realized…

She had not collapsed out of shock, not like he'd thought.

She'd fallen to her knees before him. She'd bowed her head to *him*.

"Mortem's cleric," she whispered, with a reverence that made his bones shiver. "She chose you."

"You don't—" He stumbled over his words, stunned to stammering by the shock of his mentor bent before him. Priestess Kenna barely bowed to the *Queen*. "Priestess, please, it's not—"

"It is." The authority in her voice, as always, rendered him silent. "Do you understand what you are, boy?"

A goddess's instrument. Mortem's chosen warrior. Halfway responsible for the fall of Mount Igniquit to Tenebrae's insurrectionists.

None of these things he said to the Priestess. To her he said, "Anything I am that is worth praising, I am because of your teachings. You don't bow to me, Priestess. Please."

"This is why you were always my favorite, you know." With a grunt, she hefted herself back to her feet—Elias helped her with a hand on her elbow, which she allowed with a dismissive glance. "Too humble for your own good, but it proves you have a rare heart."

"I'm just afraid that if you get stuck on your knees, I might lose the bet this year." She bopped him on the head with her knuckles, and he grinned in spite of himself. "I missed you too, Priestess."

"Don't get sentimental on me. These old eyes can't take tears any longer." Patting his arm, she bent her elbow around his with a huff. "Very well, boy. Escort me to my office. You have the bearing of someone with many questions to ask and bad news to share, and I'd prefer to hear both sitting down."

The temple was plainer than he remembered, though that was likely just a shift in perspective—after all, when compared to the chapel in Mount Igniquit, very few temples could compete. Carpeted floors and thick-curtained windows to chase out the Nyxian cold; the scent of incense thick in the air, an overwhelm of scent that would have left Soren bedridden with a headache from Infera; plain chandeliers hanging from the vaulted ceilings, attached to thick wooden beams stretching across the upside-down V shape of the roof.

Kenna's "office" was more of a den—there was a rug stretched across the carpeted floor sewn from false wolf's fur, a crackling fire in a black stone hearth, and two midnight blue couches filled with a motley assortment of thick, misshapen pillows. There was a rocking chair ever-present at the side of the hearth, placed just so to receive the most warmth, and this Kenna sank into with a sigh of relief.

"Go on," she urged when he dawdled, unsure if he should sit as well; with the heat smoldering beneath his skin, there was every possibility the couches would catch fire if he tried. "Tell your story."

And gods, what a story he told.

Candlelight whispers and hidden poisonwork books and a princess determined to save him against all odds. Battlefield screams and dead grass and his best friend in the world choking on her own blood. Sleepless journeys and Atlas clothes and his battlemate being called a different name. Slow-coming death and Atlas princes and the sound of his own neck breaking.

Death.

The woman he loved, gazing at him with golden eyes and a stranger's smile.

The rest of the story he told faster—the mountain, the trials, his crisis of faith. She never looked at him with reproach or reprimand, which he was immensely grateful for. Some part of him had expected her to be ashamed of him for wavering, but she only said, "Faith untested is easy, and easy faith means nothing. Keep going."

The journey home. The waking gods. Anima and Occassio, Tempest and Mortem, all of them taking their sides and staking their claims…

Tenebrae at the root of it all, his chaos seeping into the beating hearts of every kingdom, seeking purchase within their most precious places…or people.

And lastly, he told her of the girl and goddess in one, Soren and Anima twined together in a single body. That though the goddess seemed amicable to sharing, the body was not so inclined. And to Kenna…only to Kenna…he whispered of the deepest of his fears still lingering after living through so many these past months. He whispered how afraid he was that after getting Soren back, after everything the two of them had fought through to find their way home to each other…that even still, even after everything, he would lose her to the very thing that had nearly taken him at the beginning of all this. A simple weakness of the body.

It felt so silly and small for that to be her fate after surviving so much worse. But the world didn't care for what felt silly and small, and it didn't care what worse things they had already endured.

"A girl and goddess in one," mused Kenna. "It's never happened, Elias."

His heart sank. "I guessed as much."

"Still. I'm old enough to know there's a first time for everything. It doesn't help us much here, but if we…" Trailing off, Kenna muttered to herself as she hauled herself back to her feet, tottering carefully to the bookshelf to the left of the hearth. She ran one gnarled hand down the spines until her fingers hooked in the cracked leather binding of one, tugging it out and hugging it to her chest as she limped back to the chair. Sitting and opening the book, she flipped straight to one of the many dog-eared pages, muttering to herself as she squinted at the text.

Impatience teased the tip of Elias's tongue, threatening to make demands that she rush, which would surely get him thrown out of the temple posthaste, Mortem's blessing or no. But he leashed that urge, saying instead: "I don't recognize that book."

"You wouldn't. It's a tome on the godly relics." Her eyes slid to him, faintly accusing. "You can understand why we try to keep it out of the hands of students."

His throat tightened. Almost unconsciously, his fingers brushed against the feather hanging over his heart, a spark of heat kissing the tip of his thumb. "I do."

"Hmph." Several moments later, Kenna shut the book with a thud that threw his heart against the wall of his chest. "The bloom at the heart of the forest."

He blinked. "What?"

"Come on, boy, I know you're quicker than you act." Kenna set the book aside, scowling at him in a way that sent him straight back to seminary school, sitting ramrod straight in his seat and trying to resist answering every question that was directed to the class.

"It's Anima's relic," he said, trying not to glow when she nodded in approval. "But what does that have to do with Soren?"

"Anima's relic is more powerful than the others," Kenna said with a slight scowl, a twisting of her lips that spoke of distaste. "It contains the power of creation…the ability to create life from nothing but the imagination. Sancta, blessed fool that he was, trusted too deeply in the innocence of a child. Children grow up. Ambitions, fears, foolishness…they all leak in eventually."

"Creation." A word that felt too big to describe a form of wieldable magic. "And how does that help us?"

"Reunite the goddess with that element of her magic, and she can create any form she likes." An arched brow. "One separate from that princess you've been making eyes at so long I feared I may indeed die before you got a ring on her finger."

Now he blushed in earnest. Now he grinned in pride. "That's not a worry any longer."

"Good." Wonder of wonders, Kenna winked at him before sobering once more. "Find the bloom in the heart of the forest…in the heart of Arborius…and you may be able to persuade the goddess to make herself a body. But I warn you, Elias…Anima is not to be trusted. Even Sancta was fooled by her sweetness, but gentle hearts can still commit horrific sins. Horrors committed out of love are still horrors."

Gods, didn't he know that. "What would you have me do?"

Kenna gazed at him, those ice-blue eyes placid and stern. "Do not trust her, no matter what face she wears, no matter who asks you to try. The gods, Elias…they are beautiful and dangerous and endlessly powerful, and it is impossible to guess where their devotions may lie. They can be persuasive and charming…they can fool even the most suspicious and clever of men. Keep on your guard. I don't like the smell of the story you've wrought tonight."

He didn't like it any better, but he didn't bother saying so. "So…Anima's relic. Arborius. We were heading there anyway."

"Good." A pause. "There's one more thing. Close the door."

That didn't bode well, but he had never disobeyed her before.

So despite the chill that crawled down his back…a thing no chill had dared to do since he'd walked through fire in the belly of a mountain…he shut that door, sitting at Kenna's feet, as ready to listen as he would ever be.

And the secrets she whispered to him threatened to steal even that gods-gifted fire from the hearth of his heart.

# CHAPTER 28

# SOREN

By the time Elias slipped into Ember's room—directed by a gossipy servant or guard, no doubt—Soren had nearly fallen asleep in the knot of arms tied around her. Three rhythms of breathing brushed against her awareness in the form of air against the shell of her ear, the up-and-down of someone's chest, and the utterly horrific snores rattling from Yvonne's pert little nose.

Elias smirked faintly, making his way silently to the side of the bed and leaning over to brush a light kiss against her forehead. She closed her eyes, savoring the smell of snow and smoke on his clothes. She'd always hated the scent of smoke in any other context, but Elias wore it differently. "Ready to go to your room?"

"Only if you carry me," she sighed, reaching out and offering her best dramatic swoon she could manage without knocking heads with one of her sisters.

With an eye roll that felt just as much like home as the arms of her sisters, he awkwardly bent over and around their sleeping forms, hauling her up with surprising strength and unsurprising gracelessness, given the way he had to stretch to reach her.

She pinched his bicep. "Have you been working out?"

Another eye roll. "If lifting Kallias's emotional baggage counts as working out."

"Remember when I wanted him dead?"

A raised eyebrow. Elias nudged the door open with his foot, stepping into the hall and shutting the door again before replying. "Remember when you stabbed him in the leg?"

Ah. She'd forgotten about that. "I should probably apologize for that."

"He did kidnap you after. I see it as even."

"And how does he see it?"

Elias smirked faintly. "He says you only landed the blow because he tripped."

That *bastard*. "I'm not sorry anymore."

"I didn't think so." He looked down then—and froze midstep, a wobbling halt that tweaked her stomach with unease. "Your hair."

Self-consciousness so rarely reared itself in her that she wasn't quite sure how to wrap her hands around it…how to hold it so it couldn't make her small. She cleared her throat, resisting the itch to reach up and ruffle the curls to make them look a bit longer. "I needed something different."

He studied her with a frown, silent for so long that she could just begin to catch strains of violins playing somewhere in the lower floors of the castle…maybe those funeral players had decided to perform for those who'd lingered after the funeral itself was abruptly canceled.

"Well?" she demanded, self-consciousness simmering into irritation the longer he stared. "Is it bad?"

Elias snorted. "Soren, you could shave every curl off and still be the most beautiful woman in any room. It suits you. I just…"

"What?"

"You look more like Finnick than I realized, that's all."

She considered that for a moment. "So you think Finn is the most beautiful—"

"Stop," he groaned. "I don't want to think about him right now. Or ever."

"He's going to be your brother-in-law, you know."

He blinked. Went sallow in the skin. "Oh, *Mortem* save me."

"I think you have bigger problems—"

"No, no, that's very much the foremost of my problems just now. Can I get that ring back?"

"No takebacks. Besides, you get Kallias, too."

Elias's teeth sank into his lip—she couldn't tell if he was biting back a groan or a smile.

The rest of the walk to Soren's room was quiet, and she couldn't find the words to make it otherwise. Each step down this hall teased old memories to the surface…memories she hadn't realized she'd retained. Memories of storming down this very hall the night before they departed for Ursa, coming back from a failed attempt to convince her mother to let her go to Arborius in order to filch a cure for her dying battlemate.

She remembered dashing tears from her eyes, forcing herself to breathe despite the hysteria trying to tug sobs free from her chest. She'd had to stop in one of the public bathing rooms to run ice-cold water over her eyes, determined not to let Elias see her cry; if he saw her crying, he wouldn't rest until he knew she was all right, and knowing Elias, that could take all night.

He'd needed his rest then more than ever before. Even knowing he would be on the battlefield the next day had scared her straight to her bones.

With a blink and a shake of her head, Soren tugged herself back to the present with a soft curse.

That night had been lived by a different girl…a girl Nyxian to her core, carrying hatred for Atlas and love for her battlemate, knowing nothing would ever come from the latter.

The woman who'd returned…she only held hatred now for those who threatened her and hers, no matter their kingdom or crest. And as for the battlemate…

Well. Looking down at the ring sparkling boldly on her finger, for the first time, she found herself perfectly happy to have been proven wrong.

"Wait," she said, and Elias paused in the center of the hall, tense in every limb. She eased a palm down his arm, offering a smile that would hopefully reassure. "Let me down. I want to walk in myself."

Elias hesitated, his fingers flexing against her arm. His throat bobbed. "Are you sure?"

"Would I have asked if I wasn't?" He flinched a bit, and guilt immediately softened her tongue. "I'm sure, jackass. Put me down."

He obeyed, but he didn't release her fully until she knocked his hands from her shoulders herself, scowling at him. "I can walk."

"I *know*," he mumbled.

He didn't sound like he knew.

"Hey." When he didn't look up, focused on her legs—which, admittedly, were wobbling a bit—she reached out and gripped his chin, tipping it up until he looked at her from beneath pitch-dark lashes.

She cracked a smile, letting herself indulge in the thrill of that shared look, letting him see everything she'd never been brave enough to let out before. "Listen here, lover. I don't know what you did with my best friend Elias, but I'm going to need him back."

His eyes darkened, but not with anger—his mouth cracked into a grin. "Call me that again."

She pitched her voice mockingly upward, fluttering her lashes as she pouted at him. "My bestest friend in the whole wide world?"

"*No*, smartass." He came closer, invading her space so utterly she was forced to back up, a movement they made in tandem until her back was pressed to the wall, his head bowing until his nose nearly brushed hers. "The other thing."

"Elias." A joke, a sigh, the only other word she could remember just then. Her heart thudded against her ribs, trying to leap from her chest into his hands.

"No." Closer. Closer. She could taste the smoke on his breath. He came so close that his lips brushed hers, forming the word against her mouth, the barest beginnings of a kiss: "*Lover.*"

"You like it?" Even her voice hardly dared to make an appearance, afraid of frightening him away. "Thought I'd try something new."

"Can I kiss you?" His voice, on the other hand, had deepened to a growl…a rumble that shook her straight to her core.

Daughter of queens, undone by twilight eyes and a hand that still traced her face with timidity, like it wasn't sure yet if it was allowed to do so.

"For you," she said, "that answer is always yes."

That answer had always been yes, even before either of them had the courage to ask it.

But there was someone else she had to ask.

"Just…one second," she added.

Elias blinked, that heat in his eyes banking a bit. But he nodded, easing back to give her space. "As many as you need."

She shut her eyes—not that it was necessary, but it helped her to focus…especially when Elias was gazing at her that way. *Ani?*

*You want to kiss him again, right?*

*If it'll make you uncomfortable, we won't.*

A pause. *Soren, it's your body. I'm not going to tell you what to do with it.*

Her heart pinched. *Her* body—there it was again, Anima no longer calling it theirs. *Thank you. But you're just as stuck in here as me—I'm not going to force you to—*

*Soren,* Ani groaned with a laugh, interrupting her. *I've figured out how to duck out pretty well now. It's fine. Just…be with him. Be happy.*

A smirk curled across her lips, and she waited for Ani to, as she said, duck out before she spoke again: "All clear, jackass. Do your wor—"

Between one breath and the next, her entire world became smoke and smolder, the taste of fire on the lips that embraced hers like they'd waited an eternity to do so. A startled laugh leapt from Elias's mouth like a flying ember as she dragged her teeth lightly across his lip.

"What?" she mumbled into the kiss, hardly noticing as they practically fell through the doorway to her bedroom. Dull promises of future bruises bloomed across her arm as she knocked into the threshold, tugging Elias in after her.

"I didn't know people actually did that," he admitted.

"Did what?"

"Bite." She snorted, and he scowled, pulling back from her. "Don't *laugh!*"

"I'm not!" She was. "I'm not. Get back here."

He rolled his eyes, but tugged her back into his arms.

In one blink, he'd eased her on her back on the bed, his broad shoulders silhouetted against the skylight cut across her bedroom ceiling.

In another, those shoulders were bare, his shirt tossed somewhere on the floor, and his fingers were undoing that pink silk top, button by pearlescent button.

In a third, he was pressing kisses from her navel to her neck, ferocious heat catching and spreading from every place his lips touched…

And when she finally closed her eyes, his lips finding hers once more, the keening of violins broke through the haze of desire blunting the edges of her jagged fears.

She broke the kiss off, cursing filthily—Elias jerked back, alarm wiping away his own heated look. "What? What happened? I heard something crack, did I hurt—"

"It's those damn violins!" She shoved up from the bed, barely remembering to scoop her silk shirt up from the floor and tug it back on, buttoning it haphazardly as she limped to the door. "Didn't anyone tell them the funeral is cancelled?"

"Soren, careful!" The bed creaked behind her, Elias's steps approaching quickly. "I can hear your knees popping from here, gods—"

With a pulse of…not rage, but something darker, something like a hunger pang, she reached out and threw the door open, not caring that she was only three-quarters dressed and still flushed with lingering passion. She stormed into the hall, stomp after unsatisfying stomp, her bare feet making hardly any impact on the floor.

"Someone tell them to stop playing!" she shouted, seething as yet another mournful groan reached her ears. "I'm alive, for gods' sakes! Sorry to disappoint you, but—"

"Soren!" Elias's voice sharpened to a snap; she barely heard his socks brush against the floor before he stormed up behind her, twisting her around by the shoulder with a roughness that nearly startled her out of her craze. "Stop. Stop."

He was pulling her. Pulling her away, pulling her back, forcing her to move where she didn't want to go—

"*Let go of me*!" Her scream struck a discordant harmony with the next violin note, every vein and bone and freckle shrieking with her, a feeling almost like pain, almost like need, almost like—

"Soren!" Elias released her, hands raised, but there was a frenzied look to him as well, a twitching in his fingers she'd never seen before. Elias was never twitchy. "Do you hear that?"

"Hear *what*?"

"Bones. I can—" His throat bobbed, and his gaze ran down her body, probing the same way he did when searching for injuries after a battle. "I hear bones cracking."

A snarl burst from her chest, and she reached up to claw at her curls, her ears, anything to make the sound *stop*. "I can't hear anything over that damn *music*—"

"Soren!" Elias snatched up her hands and pinned them to her sides, refusing to let go even when she thrashed. "Soren, stop—stop! Listen to me. *There's no music*."

Somehow, even past the racket, the utter untruth of that statement froze her in place. She blinked at Elias; he blinked back.

"Elias," she said, shivering as another roiling wave of hunger crashed over her body, "what are you talking about? They haven't stopped playing since the funeral."

"There was no music at the funeral, Soren." Elias shook her a bit, eyes wide with urgency. "There wasn't any music."

Soren blinked. Breathed. Tried to bear down on that writhing call inside her.

That…that wasn't right. But it was. It had to be, because…

Because Nyxian funerals never had music. They were silent affairs, leaving room for whatever way grief chose to express itself in the moment.

But Atlas funerals did.

Soleil's funeral would have.

She blinked at Elias again. He blinked back at her.

"Are you cracking your knuckles?" he whispered—such a ridiculous question to ask so urgently, but she couldn't find it in herself to laugh.

"No."

He nodded once, as if he'd expected that answer. Without another word, he turned away.

"What's happening, jackass?"

"Cover your ears," he snapped, moving down the hall—in the direction the music was still coming from, a cacophony even harsher on the ear now that she recognized it for what it was. "Cover them *now*!"

"If we cover them, we won't be able to follow it!" she choked, but she obeyed anyway, chasing after him with a curse. "Elias—"

"Stay here." Muffled, but still intelligible, barely.

"Not a chance in—"

"*Stay here!*"

When Elias told her do to something, it was hardly ever harsher than a snap. This wasn't even mild enough to be called a command; this was a roar, a snarling thing of fire and fury and the golden flare of a goddess's power in his gaze.

And it was enough to leash Soren to a dead halt, heart pounding, breath caught.

Elias blinked, looking down at his palms…his fingers, where flames had sprouted, spectral claws flickering in the air. With a harsh swallow, he flexed his hands into fists, burying those flames within.

"Stay," he said again…a plea, this time. "Where it's safe. Please."

She could do nothing but stare and try to breathe, to force her fingers not to scratch and claw at her skin until she dug out the keening need for…for *something* winding through her very blood.

And when Elias ran down the hall, disappearing around the corner, she couldn't even form the words to try and call him back.

# CHAPTER 29

# ELIAS

*E*ach of the six kingdoms were founded by a god or goddess, Priestess Kenna's words floated back on wings of phantom dread as he sprinted through the halls, chasing a sound he would much rather run from…the sound of a spine snapping, shearing bone a percussive melody that followed him around every corner of the castle. A sound that thrashed and shrieked beneath his skin, birthing some wild, wretched hunger he couldn't outrun.

*Each kingdom, except for Tallis. These were the enemies of the gods. But the other five, those were first ruled by a god or goddess in their turn…Tempest over Atlas, Mortem over Artem, Occassio over Lapis, Anima over Arborius.*

A louder crack—in his ears, in his head, so sharp his hands flew to his own throat with a choked cry, convinced his neck had come apart at the seam where it had once been healed. But there was no pain, no encroaching darkness.

Magic. It was only magic…that damned music box.

Not real.

*What about Nyx? Weren't we under Mortem's jurisdiction?*

*No. We adopted her and Tempest as patrons after the gods ascended, but they did not form this kingdom. In the early years of the gods, Tenebrae was king over Nyx.*

The noise returned, over and over, a thousand limbs breaking in chorus around him as his limbs themselves tried to bend the wrong way, as his blood soured and spoiled, as thoughts not of his own making began to seep from the corners of his mind even he hadn't known existed.

This wasn't madness. This was hunger. This was need.

A craving for chaos.

It was too gods-damned quiet in this hall. He could hear every single flake of bone as it splintered, every minute crack as it rent apart. He needed to drown it out. He needed—

He needed to scream.

A breath hurtled into his chest, so deep and full that every sense came to attention. And when he went to exhale—

*Enough!*

Mortem's familiar voice tore through the racket, leashing his scream before it even had the chance to form.

And everything went silent.

Not perfect silence—there was a ringing low in the pit of his eardrum, like something had exploded somewhere close by and burst his inner ear open. He staggered, blinking, looking down—

And found he was standing in fire.

Black, unnatural fire.

Just like the Artemisian insurgents had wielded.

Whirling, he turned to see a marked path where he had been—scorched footprints lined the hall, the smoldering remnants of his socks left far behind. Heat boiled at the back of his throat, a taste of acrid char dusting his teeth, and his clothes…

His clothes were smoking.

Elias clapped a hand over his mouth, his stomach souring now instead of his veins, dragging in a clotted breath through his fingers and coughing out what looked like ash.

If he'd let out that scream…

*You need to hurry.* Mortem's voice again, grim and urgent—if he didn't know better, he would have called it *horror. Even my power won't stand long against that relic.*

"Where do I go?"

*Chasing it is useless. The music box is designed to throw its voice. Go back to the princess. Cover your ears. Don't uncover them until I say so.*

"But if the others hear—"

*The others are not blessed with the magic of ruination, Elias. You will do more harm than good here if you stay.*

"And Soren?"

A pause. *Gods are immune to such magics of the mind and heart. Anima can't fall under its spell, but it seems that so long as Soren is in control, that grace doesn't extend to her. Go!*

The floor clung to the soles of his feet, an aching urgency begging him to continue the chase. To burn his way through all the chaff until nothing but the culprit he sought remained.

To melt through every drop of dross, heedless of the victims he would catch in his wake.

But that was the urging of chaos. And Elias Loch had lived long enough in the shadow of discord.

The woman he loved waited in the wake of his near-destruction, and no appetite could overrule the craving for her nearness, the desperation to secure her safety.

So despite the groaning in every bone, Elias turned away from the chase.

And he ran.

# CHAPTER 30

## SOREN

Soren had never liked the quiet.

She liked it considerably less when it was accompanied by bits of cotton shoved in her ears and Elias pacing at the foot of her bed instead of cuddling her in it.

"Elias," she said; when he didn't turn to her, she leaned over and waved her arms akimbo until he finally turned to look at her. "This is silly."

He frowned, mouthing, "*What?*"

She gave him a look, shaping her lips painfully slowly: "*This. Is. Silly.*"

Elias shook his head with a huff of breath that stirred the hair at his brow. "This is safe."

"It's been hours." And even if it hadn't been, the cotton was starting to make her ears itch. She slid a finger into her ear, popping out one of the cotton plugs, sighing in relief as the ambient noise of the night flooded back in.

"Soren!" Elias's hand reached her ear before his voice did, a panicky gasp as he fumbled to put the cotton back. "Soren, we can't—"

"Elias! Elias, stop. Listen." She caught his wrist with one hand, reaching up to pluck out his wad of cotton with the other. "Listen."

He froze in place; she could've sworn even his pulse paused beneath her fingertips. But there was no violin music sweetening the air, no mourning song crawling beneath her skin and scratching; there was only the quiet whistle of the wind beyond the window, and the soft murmurings of the night shift of palacefolk doing their work. No one else, it seemed, had heard the relic.

No one but them.

*The bearer can choose targets, if they wish,* Ani whispered. The goddess had suggested Soren let her take over until the threat of the box had passed, but with the memory of uncontrollable disquiet still raking over her bones, Soren couldn't bring herself to agree.

Even if it was safer. Even if it was smarter.

"It's all right," she coaxed Elias, ignoring Ani, tightening her grip on his hand—it was shaking so badly that a pang of true concern rippled through her. "It's all right, Elias. It's gone."

Gods only knew where it had been, but presently, all she cared about was that the violins had faded to a hush.

"I can't…" A shaken, tearful breath. "Soren, please put it back. I can't…"

"Hey." She let go of his wrist and held his face instead, brushing her thumb against stray tears that escaped the corners of his frantic eyes. She gentled her voice, the tone she only used on wounded things, on frightened people. "Talk to me, jackass."

His face crumpled, and with some gentle guiding from her, he crawled on the bed alongside her. He wrapped her in his arms and buried his face in the crook of her neck, his tears soaking into her skin—they scalded a bit, but she refused to flinch away. Not when her battlemate was so clearly rattled.

"I'm so sick of this," he muttered. "I'm sick of watching the gods race to see who can take you away first."

Pain ripped through her heart, and she took his chin between her thumb and forefinger, forcing him to meet her eyes. "No one is taking me away."

An empty promise, perhaps, when she could feel her strength eroding away even now, even in this state of rest. But she held his gaze like it was the undeniable truth, because he needed that. Needed *her*.

They were taking turns being the steady one these days. And it was her time to carry him tonight.

He swallowed thickly, trying and failing to smile at her. What ended up forming was something a bit on the miserable side. "I keep waiting to wake up from this. Ever since the temple, I've had these dreams…dreams where you were here, alive, and then…just as I started to believe it was real, you'd fade away. You'd die again, or you'd turn into her, or…" He ducked his head, pinching the bridge of his nose, drawing in another harsh breath. "I don't want to wake up from this. I don't want it."

"Then don't." A simple answer, but those were what she was best at. She drew him closer, running her fingers through his hair, resting the hand that wore his ring over his heart. "A never-ending nap sounds great to me."

A grating laugh. "Soren, that's called *dying*."

"Believe me, it's not." She kept stroking his hair—then paused as her fingertips brushed against an unfamiliar texture. A shorter patch where the hair had once been longer. She hadn't noticed it before.

She frowned, pulling back and craning her neck, trying to catch a glimpse of it. "Where's your mourning braid?"

Elias stilled. Swallowed so hard she could hear it. "They…it burned. During one of my trials. Kallias could only save the cloth." He pulled out the chain around his neck, showing it to her—she'd seen it before, but hadn't asked about the charms on it. The feather, Ani had explained; the ring was now gone, perched on Soren's finger; and now that she took a closer look, she recognized the braided circle of black cloth as what had once made up the cord in his mourning braid for his previous battlemate. But the other braided cloth…

She touched it, and his chest halted beneath her hand. "What's this one?"

Nothing. Not a word, not a breath.

When she looked up, the question ready to hop off her tongue again, the words died as she took in the gutted look in his eyes.

"Oh," she whispered.

*They,* he'd said at first.

Two mourning braids…for two lost battlemates.

Elias hauled in a long breath, pulling away from her embrace and propping himself on one elbow. He gripped the chain with his other hand, running his thumb over the braided cloths, his jaw flexing as he stared at them.

"You were gone," he said quietly. "I owed it to you."

It took several moments for her to muster up her voice. And when she did, all that came out was, "Well…it's a good thing you kept your hair long then, huh?"

Elias choked—a gasp that turned into a laugh, the kind of laughter people often offered to Soren's darker jokes. "You are awful."

"I don't know what to say!" she groaned, poking at the braid again, a shiver running down her spine. "Gods, it's like watching my own pyre."

Elias released the chain to reach out to her, ruffling her hair. "What happened to yours? It was already gone when Anima showed up in Artem."

Soren's throat tightened, humor going sour to the taste. "Anima took it out. She, um…she didn't know what it was."

*Sorry*, Ani whispered.

*It's okay*. It wasn't. But this was never going to work if she kept holding things against Ani that couldn't be fixed now.

Besides…she and Jira had shared their goodbyes. She'd made peace with that one loss. Maybe when they met up with Raquel, the older Angelov sister would have a way to help her create a new braid. Either way, there was nothing they could do about it now.

Elias's mouth twisted into a knot. "I'm sorry."

"So's she. It's fine. It probably would've ended up having to get cut out anyway."

Elias grunted in what might've been vague agreement, but with the way he avoided her gaze, it was difficult to tell. His fingers just kept fussing with that Atlas-blue bit of cloth.

She reached out, settling her hand over his. "Elias," she whispered. "I'm not dead."

A long breath out. "I know."

She curled her fingers around his. "Then there's nothing to mourn, is there?"

Another deep breath. Finally, he slid his fingers out from beneath hers, gripping the back of her neck and pulling her in to kiss her forehead.

"No," he agreed. "There's not."

She took the braid in both hands now. "May I?"

After his nod of assent, she got to work, picking at the slightly scorched piece of cloth until it came undone, slipping free of the chain. And all the while,

Elias watched her—not her hands, but her face. As if ensuring she would not disappear the moment the braid came apart.

They both had a long way to go. They both had wounds that were still healing—some that might never be healed.

But this was one thing she could fix. And if it kept his mind off the chaos that had just ensued, if it kept him from panicking until morning came, then she was happy to take on the task.

Even if it really did feel like watching her own pyre.

Even if holding that cloth in her hand made her fingers tremble.

# CHAPTER 31

# KALLIAS

Three days of sailing, and Raquel had not woken.

Three days Kallias had not slept, bathed, or taken a full breath.

Three days his eyes burned from fear of blinking, afraid that she would draw a breath that rattled a bit too deep, that cut a bit too short, and she would draw no more when he opened his eyes again.

Elowyn had finally drained herself of her strength after days of measured, careful healing sessions…and while she'd promised him over and over that Raquel was not actively dying any longer, his nerves couldn't be convinced.

She might not lie on the edge of death any longer, but it lingered near…Elias's goddess might be with him, off in Tallis or gods-knew-where by now, but it seemed she did not hold the leash of that which lay under her jurisdiction. It wandered, loose and collarless, slavering over Raquel like a hunting hound starved, pacing the boundary of her sickbed with rot-tipped teeth and blood-craving claws.

And all he could do, as cursed as he was to forever be useless, was sit at her bedside, cling to her clammy, bruised hand, and pray to whatever powers lay beyond these fickle gods that death would not be the thing that took Raquel Angelov away from him.

Because something would. Whether it be hatred or duty or the simple fact that they belonged in different kingdoms, something would eventually call her away from his side. He was already on severely borrowed time in her company.

He could bear it. Any of it. So long as it wasn't death.

"Kal." The impatient voice of his younger brother cracked the ice of those gloom-coated thoughts, drawing him back to the present: to the cozy atmosphere of the infirmary cabin, to the sensation of Raquel's hand pinned between his, to the blue-tinted black of her hair that cascaded over the one paltry pillow like the midnight sea, to the blood-caked bandages wrapped with care over her torso. "Anyone home? If you don't answer me this time, I'm smacking you upside the head, and I won't feel bad. I mean, I'd smack you anytime and not feel bad, but especially—"

"What, Finn." Gods, he was tired.

"Patch says Elowyn isn't going to be ready to do another healing session till at least tomorrow. She's worried about infection setting back in, so we're stopping for a supply run." Finn paused. "He wants us to come along."

"I'm not leaving her."

"Patch didn't phrase it like a question."

"Neither did I."

"Look, no offense, Prince," said the aforementioned captain, popping his head in over Finn's shoulder, "but I absolutely refuse to have you on my ship a moment longer without you visiting a bathhouse. You smell like a stray tuna from last week's catch that got stuck under a barrel, and believe me, I know that stench intimately as of this morning."

Finn turned his head to look at Patch. "You need to fire your deckhand."

"Already threw him overboard." Patch jerked his head at Kallias with an easy grin he couldn't help but envy. "And if you don't smell like lavender and lemon and whatever else you royals use to avoid taking on the stench of the common folk, you're next in line for the plank. I prefer patchouli, myself."

"Is that what Patch is actually short for?" Finn asked. "Patchouli?"

Patch poked a finger in Finn's face. "You're lucky I only pick fights with people my own size, Prince Junior. Now out."

With a roll of his eyes, Finn actually obeyed, muttering something under his breath as he vacated the doorway, leaving Patch standing alone. The pirate leaned against the doorframe, spanning the doorway with the full spread of his arms, those colorful tattoos almost dancing in the lanternlight.

"I'm serious about you coming into town," said Patch—but his mocking tone had fallen away, replaced with something more honest. "You're filthy—and I say that with the utmost respect, of course, Your Highness. You're at risk of dirtying her wounds just by sitting there. And in all honesty, we don't have the coin for extra medicine. It's going to be up to you to bargain on your woman's behalf."

Kallias shut his eyes, drawing in a sour breath that only proved Patch's point…he desperately needed a bath and a breath of fresh air. Even still, he'd promised Raquel. "I told her I wouldn't leave unless she asked."

"Romantic." Before Kallias could retort, Patch jerked his chin at Raquel, crossing his arms over the tooled leather of his fur-lined vest. "Tell me, is she the romantic sort? Or does she tend to fall in favor of logic?"

A hint of heat flushed in his cheeks. "Quite decidedly the latter."

"In that case, once she's back in her right mind, I can only assume she'll be more grateful that you chose to get her healthy instead of sitting around keeping promises she likely won't remember you made." Patch jerked his head back over his shoulder this time. "Up and about, Prince. I'll leave my fastest crew member here with Elowyn with orders to come and fetch you if anything changes."

He hated that he couldn't argue. He hated the idea of Raquel waking in a room filled with strangers, but what Patch said rang true…if Raquel had been in her right mind, she would have told him to go.

Didn't mean he had to like it.

"Fine," he said, rising to his feet, the blood rushing back to his legs in a painful gush of pins and needles. "Lead on."

***

"Hand me the coinpurse," Finn fumed as he walked in step with Kallias, snatching at that exact item, which was quite firmly trapped in Kallias's grasp. "You're going to get us robbed."

"Right," Kallias snorted, holding it above his brother's head, out of his reach. "Finn, there's four people on this street, and two of them are at least seventy."

"Eighty at the lowest, but that's beside the point," Finn griped. "I've met very formidable ladies well above a hundred, Kal. Age is just a number."

"If age is just a number, what do you call arthritis?"

"Not as big of a deterrent to pickpocketing as you might think," Finn grumbled, crossing his arms and giving a dramatic shiver. Kallias would have made fun of him for it if he wasn't so concerned by the fact that the cold *wasn't* bothering him, even with his wet hair and Atlas-born constitution.

No, the only bit of cold that touched him was the shard of ice buried beneath his borrowed coat, not even a trickle of meltwater dampening the shirt he wore underneath.

The bathhouse, as much as he'd resisted the visit, had been a welcome relief…not exactly a luxurious experience in a town as small as this one, mainly a semi-private tub and a bar of soap in exchange for a bit of coin, but it had been enough. The sensation of clean hair alone was worth the cost.

Of course, his whip wounds had stung so badly he'd had to stick a towel between his teeth while he washed them, and the pain and effort and steam had left him dizzy and exhausted, but it didn't matter. He was clean.

Now to get Raquel's medicine.

"How are you at bartering?" he asked Finn, interrupting his rant about Kallias's lack of propriety surrounding their coinpurse.

Finn shot him a venomous look. "You're not even listening, are you?"

He merely jingled the coinpurse. "You want to hold this or not? Can you barter?"

Finn eyed the burlap bag mutinously, his teeth worrying his lip as he pondered—then, with a curse and a huff, he snatched the bag from Kallias and tucked it away. "Well, I'd be better at it if you hadn't just flashed exactly how much coin we have to everyone in the street. Odds are some shopkeeps caught a glimpse too, but I'll do my best."

Kallias glanced past his brother to take in the rest of the street. There were only a handful of shops here in Rosewater, a Nyxian town too small to hold any kind of military presence, but he still felt more comfortable relying on Finn's uncanny way around a Nyxian accent than trying it on his own tongue.

"Apothecary," he said. "That's where we should—"

"Do you honestly think I don't know what an apothecary is? Good gods, Kal." And with that, Finn marched down the street, leaving Kallias to trail after, trying to tamp down the feeling that he might not actually know his brother that well at all.

As they entered the apothecary—a quaint little shop with a sign that announced its name as *The Herb Garden*—the rush of warmth dizzied him enough that he had to stop in the doorway, bracing himself against the doorframe, pinching the bridge of his nose.

"Aw, c'mon," said a cross voice from somewhere in the store—not Finn. Younger. "Smell's not that strong."

Kallias opened his eyes and peered across the store. Most of the space was dominated by rough-hewn wooden shelves that hadn't been properly sanded or stained, but in contrast, the contents of the shelves were organized meticulously— each bunch of herbs and bottle of poultice was tied with a different color pastel ribbon, and each type was sorted onto a different shelf, a label that identified the product in swirling script mounted on the edge of each shelf. Many of the labels had two dots and a curve at the end of the specific ware's name…the approximation of a smiling face doodled in ink.

The clerk at the counter did not have a smiling face to match, and judging by his gangly build, sullen slump, and complete lack of enthusiasm at their entrance, Kallias had to assume he wasn't the owner.

"Forgive my brother," Finn said cheerfully, striding up to the counter and propping an elbow on it, slumping forward a bit. "He's sensitive to smells. Tell me, do you have anything here that can ward off infection in wounds? He got himself thrown from his horse, and his back's all torn up. I think he'll heal fine on his own, all told, but my ma insists we get him something strong."

Kallias tried not to blink, but that Nyxian accent, the specific cadence…

Finn hadn't specifically *said* he'd modeled his Nyxian accent off of Soleil, but if he hadn't, the inflection was eerily similar.

The boy scowled at them, dark hair falling over his blue eyes as he rolled them. "You'll have to be a tad more specific. Lots of things can help infection."

Finn's smile didn't falter, even as Kallias's temper began to rise. "Look, we came all the way from the next town over. I know herbs as well as the next person, and my mother didn't give much direction. Is there anything you recommend? You are the shopkeep—"

"I'm just watching the store for my sister." The boy dashed his knuckles beneath his nose. "If you don't know what you need, I can't help you."

Finn's smile dropped, and he leaned closer, his palm sliding along the counter. "That's no way to speak to a paying customer, my friend."

When he pulled back, a small pile of coin sat in the center of the counter.

The boy gave a skeptical glance at it. "That all you got?"

Finn narrowed his eyes. "That's more than enough for any tincture I buy back home."

"Well, you're not back home, are you, *friend?*"

*Now* something changed in Finn's face—and scarier than that was knowing that if Finn hadn't wanted him to see it, he wouldn't have. But just as he moved to intervene—a little faster when he saw Finn's hand creeping toward some hidden sheath—the bell at the door dinged again, a voice near-matching in pitch ringing out over the shop. "I'm here! I brought you some—oh."

When Kallias turned around, Finn a heartbeat behind, he caught sight of the new arrival—a girl who appeared to be about the boy's age, her ebony skin sparkling with what appeared to be rhinestones scattered like freckles across her cheekbones and the bridge of her nose. A cloud of tight black curls framed her face, snowflakes still melting in them as she came to an abrupt halt partway into the shop, a cloth-covered basket over one arm.

A crash drew Kallias's gaze back over his shoulder—the boy had straightened so abruptly he'd knocked over the stool behind the counter, his pale cheeks now raging red. "Er—I—hi! I mean, sorry, I just—they're just customers. I have, um, customers."

The girl smiled at them both, taking a hesitant step back. "I can come back later, if—"

"No! No, it's fine. I'm just—I'm just wrapping up." The boy flashed them a smile so fake that it nearly sent Kallias laughing—would have, probably, if he wasn't so desperate to get back to Raquel. "I'm sorry, um…what did you two say you needed?"

Finn seemed distracted now, his brow furrowed, his gaze still on the girl—which was fine, honestly, because Kallias suddenly had an idea.

"The truth is," he began, letting the exhaustion, the earnestness, the fear whirling inside him show, meeting the boy's gaze as he fumbled to keep his grip on a vague Nyxian accent, "someone I care about very much has been badly hurt.

And if I don't get this medicine for her, I'm afraid of what might happen. Please, I will give…anything. Anything to help her. Can you help us?"

Finn's eyes darted to him, mouth tightening in warning, but the girl drew in a breath, her hand pressing to her chest. She looked to the boy with wide eyes, every feature primed with something close to a plea.

The boy glanced to her, then cleared his throat, giving a firm nod. He rounded the counter, striding to a shelf near the back and plucking a thick, sizable glass jar from it; he came back and set it almost gently in Kallias's grasp, giving him a look that played at something dutiful. "This should be exactly what you need." Another glance over Kallias's shoulder at the girl, and he added, "No charge. Just happy to help."

"Oh, I couldn't possibly accept…"

"Just take it," the boy interrupted—then quickly softened his tone. "Please. I wouldn't feel right doing anything less."

"Thank you." Finn swiped the coins from the counter—then, when Kallias gave him a look, he sighed and placed half of them back down. "But our ma will ask questions if we bring it all back. Take something for your trouble…and enjoy your lunch."

As they left the shop, the girl rushing to the boy in a flurry of movement and gushing words, Kallias gripped Finn's shoulder.

"What happened in there? You got distracted."

Finn shrugged him off, stuffing the coinpurse away. "I…the jewels on her face, they just reminded me of something. Forget it. How'd you know that would work?"

Kallias kept walking, gaze fixed straight ahead—straight in the direction of the docks. "The way he looked at her…he'd do anything to impress her. Make her happy. So I gave him something impressive to do."

A low chuckle, and Finn nudged him in the ribs. "We might make a con man out of you yet."

***

The second they set foot on the ship, Kallias was running.

Not because he heard commotion—but because he didn't. The deckguard was missing, the air too still, some tension thickening the air he didn't like.

Something was wrong.

He descended belowdecks in a single jump, finding his way to Raquel's cabin, the poultice the shopkeep had sold them clutched firmly in his shaking fist.

If he walked in there to find Raquel worse...

If he walked in and saw a body wrapped in a blanket, no breaths stirring the still air...

The god trying to take his body might not have been infecting his mind with madness, but if Raquel had drawn her final breath alone, he thought his mind might crack open all on its own.

His own breath trapped deep in his chest, he flung open the door—

And his feet froze to the floor.

Raquel was not bundled in blankets, lifeless and lost.

No. She was standing—standing at the side of the bed, her hands spread before her, sweat coating every inch of her exposed arms and shoulders. They'd bound her torso tightly in bandages and linen, preserving her modesty as best they could, but any skin he could see shone with the condensation of exertion and fever...maybe even fear.

Because when he looked in her eyes, Raquel was not looking back—not consciously, anyhow. There was a glaze to her good eye that matched the glass in her prosthetic, and when she regarded him, it was not with sharp wit and restrained ire—it was with pure, simple confusion.

"Raquel." He handed off the medicine to Elowyn, who hovered cautiously in the corner with Patch's deck-guard standing beside her, the healer cupping her wrist in a way that suggested injury. Having seen the way Raquel reacted when waking from the throes of her fever-fugue sleep, he didn't have to think too hard to figure out what had happened. He moved toward Raquel with his palms turned out, keeping his voice low: "Raquel. It's all right. You shouldn't be standing—"

"You weren't here," she said; so soft, so shaken, that it utterly sundered his heart. "I couldn't...you were gone, I couldn't..."

"I know. I'm so sorry—"

"I thought he took you," Raquel said—her shaking hand rose to harshly wipe a tear from her good eye, her chest heaving unevenly, her other hand patting at the place on her hip where her knives normally hung. "I thought he took you again."

He should never have left her. Logic or not, reason or not, he should have clung to her hand until she gave him the command to leave.

Who was he, to have given in so easily to some *pirate*, as if those orders could possibly hold sway over the vows he'd sworn to this woman? Who was he to have broken a vow to the only general he would ever swear fealty to, the only person to whom he would willingly choose to bend the knee?

"I am so sorry," he whispered; not that those words could ever be enough. He dropped to his knees before her, raising his hands toward hers. "I am so sorry, Raquel—"

Her knees hit the floor as well, pressed right against his. Her hand cupped his chin, forcing him to look up, to meet her foggy, fever-fire eyes.

"You don't get on your knees," she whispered. "Never again. Not for anyone. Promise me."

He mirrored her, sliding his hand over her burning cheek, stroking a thumb over the scars dashed across her missing eye. "As you order, Officer Angelov." And before she could speak again, he added, as gently as he could manage with the lump forming in his throat, "I'll stand. But only if you stand with me, do you understand?"

She locked eyes with him, her feverish hand still pressed to his cheek…and nodded.

As he stood to his feet, he pulled her up with him, supporting her when her legs wavered beneath her, a shudder shaking her sturdy frame. And the moment he eased her back onto the bed, she drifted back into sleep, her hand falling away from his face.

"You," signed Elowyn as she approached, her bright eyes focused on Raquel's slack features, "are underestimating how much she cares for you, Prince Kallias."

His throat tightened, and he merely signed, "Perhaps."

Delirium—it caused all kinds of strange things to pour out of peoples' mouths. He would give it no true hold in his heart.

No matter how deeply her words might have struck him.

He already knew he'd lost himself, deeply and truly and irrevocably, to the woman sleeping before him. That much was not a surprise.

But it would be another kind of delirium to believe she might feel the same…to believe she might give up kingdom and crest to…what? Love a man with no title, no means, no livelihood to his name…or to love a prince from afar, his hand heavy with another ruler's ring?

No. He would blame it on delirium, on fever and illness and the mild madness that sometimes came along with them, and he would assign it no further value.

To do anything else would be unfair. To her…and to himself.

# CHAPTER 32

# ELIAS

The morning saw a meeting with Ravenna, Jakob, the princesses, and a handful of other high-ranking Nyxian officials…even Kenna had sent a representative in her stead, a dark-haired, onyx-skinned man named Valerian who stood to inherit custodianship over the temple when the Priestess did indeed pass on. The man had always been serious, but as Elias and Soren broke the news of the relic, he looked grimmer than Mortem herself.

"We need to evacuate the city," Elias said finally, tired of watching them all look amongst themselves for answers that weren't there. "I saw this in Artem…not the relic itself, but the effects of Tenebrae's corruption. The worship of him, his blessing…it stirred half of Artem to revolt, and that was without the help of the music box. I can only imagine the results will be more severe."

The memory of the tarry flames shooting from Zaccheus's palms—and the matching ones that had licked at his own heels the night before—still haunted him. Not just in his dreams last night, but in his waking hours. To bear the blessing of a goddess and still not be immune to chaos's corruption…

His throat bobbed, and he forced himself to breathe in. Breathe out.

He'd lit the candle on Soren's nightstand this morning, just to check—the same half-melted candle that had been there the last night they'd spent in this castle together. It had blazed to life without issue, the flame clean and bright and golden-red.

He was not Zaccheus. And he wouldn't wait around to become like him, either.

"I agree," Soren said, though she didn't lift her gaze from the war table's surface. Spread out on it was an intricately detailed map, swathes of blue and green marking oceans and rivers and forests, dimples representing mountains and hills and obstacles to the crossing of armies.

The war map was a familiar sight to him, complete with scale markers and wooden figurines that mimicked soldiers…but it was different now. Those Atlas cities, they were more than names and targets. He could see the faces of the people who lived in them, could see the smiling innkeeper woman who'd welcomed him in one of the smaller towns when he was traveling to save Soren, could see the little girls twirling ribbons in the air as they raced through the Port Atlas streets.

Soren, too, looked a bit lost as she traced her fingertips along the curve of the Atlas shoreline in an absent arc, not seeming to realize that every eye in the room was on her…not all of them friendly.

"Oh, good," grunted one of the generals. "Of course an Atlas would like to see our capital abandoned."

Tension tugged Elias's shoulders straight, a retort jumping to his lips; but before he could even breathe in, Soren's head snapped up, spearing the general who'd spoken with a glare that withered even the bravest of warriors. A glare that spoke of blades cloaked in shadow and blood spilled in the dark.

She had never looked more like her brother…more like her sister.

Elias's stomach turned.

"I would like to see our…" A pause. A clearing throat. Soren sat straighter, anger softening to something milder. "I would like to see your people safe. And I'll remind you, General Hann, that *my* people are already suffering beneath

Tenebrae's boot, whether they know it yet or not. If you'd like to join them, be my gods-damned guest."

Pride and unease played tug-of-war with him as he watched Hann scowl, clearly unconvinced. Soren had spoken like a queen, yes, but…

Queen of a different kingdom.

*Your people.*

It had to happen sooner or later. He understood that.

Didn't make it any easier to hear.

Didn't make it any easier to realize that he wasn't sure he could ever say the same.

*Your people.* His people. Nyx would always be his, even if it couldn't be hers.

Was this why Kallias struggled so deeply with the idea of leaving his people for another? Had he recognized the impossibility of no longer calling them *his*, of having to chain his long-held loyalty to a kingdom he hardly knew? Had even hated, perhaps, at one point?

Pits, he wished Kal was here now. He was the only one who might even begin to understand how Soren's words had started to tear a piece of his heart away.

Gods willing, they would be smart enough to skirt Ursa entirely if they saw a blockade, and were already well on their way to Sirena, relic in hand, Tempest's hold on his friend firmly beaten back.

Another breath in. Another breath out.

He couldn't worry about battles he wasn't there to fight. He had his own war to wage here, his own Atlas royal dealing with the unrelenting grip of a god. Kallias would be fine. He trusted his friend to follow the plan…and failing that, he at least trusted Raquel to keep them on task.

There were very few people he believed capable of standing strong against Kallias's nobility and Finn's…exact opposite of that. Soren was one; Raquel was the other.

By the time he was done breathing his way through that train of thought, Soren was talking again, eyes fixed once more on the map: "Anima and I think this is a trap for us…for her. If we're right, Tenebrae won't care how many flee the city, so long as we stay. He won't chase you all out. It's the best way to draw him out of hiding…or whoever he has doing his dirty work. I highly doubt he came here himself and left Atlas to its own devices."

"Whoa, wait." Elias circled around to lean across the table, catching her gaze. There was a glint of gold sparkling around the center…a blink here and there, barely enough to notice, but enough that his heart sank. "You're suggesting we use you as *bait*?"

"I'm saying I'm tired of hiding. We've already seen how he plays his games, Elias." She speared him with a look Soren so rarely wore: a look of pure, untouched solemnity. "He manipulates people with those they love until they're too desperate to do anything but play by his rules. I'm not giving him that chance again. Are you?"

Bitter fear coated his throat, and it was all he could do to shake his head.

No, he wasn't willing to give Tenebrae that chance. Because if it was his mother, or Kenna, or his siblings–if it was *Emma* left trembling on a cold temple floor, her sweet face filled with fear and agony beyond her years, her rose-printed dress soaked in blood and blackened ichor…

He would hand Tenebrae the keys to the kingdom himself.

But that didn't mean he had to like this plan.

Ravenna, seated at the head of the table, seemed to be trying to catch Soren's gaze as well, the pain in her eyes mounting the longer Soren ignored her. But finally, the Queen swallowed, steeled, stood. "We begin evacuating now. Quietly. Families first. Send soldiers out to replace the shopkeeps—it'll go unnoticed longer if we keep the businesses open. Whoever has the music box, they're likely castlefolk, yes?"

Elias gave a quick nod. "More than likely."

"Should we be looking at any new faces?"

"Not solely." He chewed on the inside of his cheek, trying to think. "He's been at this game for a while. He could have plants in every kingdom…long-standing ones. Gods only know who they could be. But evacuate the palace last, regardless. Give everyone the option to stay on. By then, the majority of the city will have fled; whoever it is, they won't be able to stop it, but they likely will choose to stay if they know Soren hasn't left. It'll narrow down the pool of suspects."

"I don't love it," said Jakob, scratching his beard with a frown. "But I can't see a better way, either."

"Honestly, we've been at the point for a while where there are no smart plans," Soren admitted with a long sigh, blowing her curls off her brow. "Only less terrible ones."

"I've heard worse." Jakob stood with a slap of palms to the table. "I'm staying."

"Me too," said Yvonne, raising her chin in defiance when Soren shot her a reproachful look. "You don't tell me what to do, little sister. A queen doesn't abandon her people."

Soren's gaze darkened, a silent flinch—but she dipped her head in resignation. There was no arguing with Yvonne, not even for another queen-blooded warrior. She wore all the ice of the Nyxian tundra in her eyes…and all the sharpness of the bladed skates they used to traverse it in her tongue.

"I'm staying," Emberlyn agreed. "I grieved my sister once, and once was too much. Besides…" A gleam lit her eyes, softer than the weaponsmith usually allowed. "Elias tells me representatives of Artem could arrive at any time. I should be here just in case."

"You can't all stay," Soren protested. "That ruins the whole gods-damned point, Em!"

"Actually, she's not wrong," Elias countered reluctantly. "If Havi and Safi arrive in the midst of all this…if they bring anyone else with them, it would be good to have their former diplomat here. They weren't too trusting of us when we arrived; they only let me stay because of Mortem's mark."

"Auralee will go," Ravenna said finally; the youngest princess, thankfully, had been excluded from this meeting. "There's no reason for her to stay, and…and it will provide a safety net."

*A safety net.* Reassurance that if the city was truly to fall, the line of succession would survive somehow. Nyx would still have a queen…albeit a young, woefully unprepared one.

Without meaning to, his eyes slid to Soren. She met his gaze with a pinch of her lips, missing nothing; when her throat bobbed, he gripped her shoulder and squeezed, the best show of support he could offer just then.

"I'll stay as well," Ravenna continued quietly. "A queen belongs on her throne, regardless of what threats come close. If this was Atlas, I would meet them face-to-face—I will give the gods no lesser honor." She sat back down, back straight, head high. "Everyone but my girls and Elias, leave us. Begin the evacuation. Any soldiers and guards who will stay will be rewarded handsomely, and those who choose to leave will do so with my blessing. Let me know what we number by the end of the day."

With bows and murmurs of assent, the group cleared out of the war room…all but Yvonne, Ember, Ravenna, Soren, and himself.

The second the door shut, Ravenna's gaze flitted to Yvonne. "You should go."

Yvonne held her gaze without blinking. "I've made my decision, Mama."

"You're not wrong. A queen doesn't abandon her people." Ravenna leaned forward, not breaking her daughter's frigid stare. "But you aren't queen yet. And you need to be doing everything you can to assure you survive to one day change that."

Yvonne's jaw tensed, a flicker of muscle jumping beneath her pale skin. She tossed her starlight hair over one shoulder. "So Ember can stay, but I can't?"

"I don't like that, either, but Ember is of more use here than there. You…you have a reason to go. Not just your own safety, but the safety of our people." Gaze softening, pain and pride sanding her sharp edges down, Ravenna squeezed her eldest daughter's hand. "They're going to be frightened, being forced out of their homes. They'll need someone they trust to lead them. And I trust no one with them more than you."

At that, Yvonne's stony exterior chipped a bit, torn desires—conflicting duties—stirring a storm in her once-stoic gaze.

"Queens don't abandon their people," Soren said softly. "You need to go, Yvonne."

Yvonne looked to her, and her dark eyes filled with tears. "I swear to the gods, Soren, if you die *again*—"

"Not a chance," Soren snorted, and then the two were in each other's arms, Yvonne's circling her protectively despite Soren being an inch or five taller. "Did it once. It was kind of awful."

"Only kind of?"

"Well, it did get me proposed to."

"That would've happened anyhow," Ember snorted, joining their embrace. "He got that ring to me ages before the Ursa battle."

Soren touched her forehead to Yvonne's, then pulled away, stalking to him and grabbing his hand…purposely avoiding Ravenna. "Come on. We should go help your family pack."

Elias caught Ravenna's gaze, doing his best to convey a silent apology as Soren dragged him out. For half a second, he thought to pull her to a halt, to make her look at the Queen, but Ravenna merely smiled. Shook her head. Mouthed, "It's all right. Go."

And with reluctance strung throughout every vein, Elias followed his future queen out, leaving his other behind.

# CHAPTER 33

# ANIMA

*Chaos tasted like black licorice. It was the only candy Brae ever brought her as a child, the only kind unpopular enough to be thrown out at the end of market week rather than sold, and she tasted it every time his magic infected the air around him.*

*Chaos smelled like burnt coffee softened with sour milk. It hung rancid and heavy on the panting breaths of the woman who had been coughing up tar and blood for two days straight, the woman who'd drank a corrupted cure from one of Anima and Brae's joint worshippers. Off in the corner, the perpetrator herself only giggled, her delight increasing with every wretch and plea from the blighted woman's mouth.*

*Chaos sounded like screams. Like laughter. Like shouting and shattering and singing off-key, off-beat.*

*Chaos desired nothing in particular; only that peace and quiet be avoided at all costs. Only that discord never ceased its saber-toothed song.*

*Brae had never liked the quiet.*

*Once, on a night when he was just a little too tired, just a little too truthful, he told her how peaceful their mother's face had looked when she died. That even the pain of the fire and the screams of her children could not keep her awake. That peace had given her permission to sleep.*

*Peace, he'd told her, meant death.*

*And it would never find itself welcome among him and his.*

"Ani." Fingers snapped in front of her eyes—Soren's eyes. And Soren's fingers, actually. The princess sounded annoyed…though, that wasn't exactly uncommon. "Focus. I don't know what I'm looking for here."

*Sorry.* Forcing her awareness back to the thin barrier between them, swimming through the tarry slog of old, tainted memories, Ani forced herself to take in the view.

They were standing in the twentieth nondescript bedchamber they'd searched this morning; Soren's way of passing the time as the slow evacuation of Nyx took place. It had been three days of carefully filtering people out, replacing them with soldiers who'd offered to evacuate last. Yvonne was already gone, as was Elias's family. Others were still deciding whether they'd stay or go.

The truth was, Ani doubted they were going to find anything in these abandoned rooms that could provide them with a proper lead. Anyone who'd agreed to vacate the palace wasn't likely their perpetrator…but she also guessed that Soren knew that.

This wasn't a real search. This was just a way for Soren to keep her hands busy; a way to keep the helplessness at bay as her people fled their city.

But that didn't mean it had to be all useless.

*Maybe…* She hesitated. *Maybe let me try?*

Every muscle in their body stiffened. Soren's hand froze beneath the mattress she was currently sweeping for hidden objects, the weight pressing her palm to the cold wooden frame. "I don't know if that's a good idea."

*You thought it was a good idea with your friends.*

"That was necessary. They wouldn't have believed me if we didn't show them."

*But it helped,* Ani reminded her. *We didn't have a fit. Maybe it…I don't know. I just think it might be smart to practice.*

Soren drew her hand out, flexing her fingers one by one, staring unseeingly at the stitching pattern in the bedsheets. "This…isn't easy for me, all right? Giving up control again."

*I know.* And she hated that she had to ask, but if Soren was right…if their body was breaking down faster because of their resistance to each other… *We don't have to. I just thought it might help.*

The tension between them shifted…from defensive to resigned. Soren blew out through rounded lips, standing up only to flop herself onto the bed, spreading herself out on the quilt. "You're right. Okay. Just…give me a second."

A second was the least she could offer, so Ani settled on her side of the wall, imagining herself sitting with one ear pressed against it…the same way she and Cassi used to sit by the bedroom door and listen to Brae, Peter, and Mora argue with each other about how to split their meager coin that week.

Finally, that "door" opened up…just a bit, almost tentative, like Soren was afraid Ani would shove her way through. "Gods, Elias is going to kill me." A pause, then a sigh. "All right, come on in."

*This is weird.*

"You're telling me."

With as much gentleness as she could manage, she slipped past Soren in the doorway between control and absence. This time, as focused as she was, she could sense Soren brushing past her…a presence fierce and unfaltering, playful and protective, underlaid with such strength of will that Ani suddenly felt foolish for ever thinking the princess would simply fade into nothing with time.

And then, with a snap of sensation flooding her with clarity, she drew in their next breath with a harsh, startled gasp.

*Careful,* Soren said as she sat up in a surge, gripping the blanket beneath her as tightly as she could, fingers reveling in the brush of varying cloth textures against them. *You're okay. Breathe.*

"I'm okay," she agreed; her tongue tripped a bit clumsily over the second word, and she teased it with her teeth for a moment to test for numbness. "I'm all right. Are you?"

*I think so. Just…tired, I think. You make it look easy.*

"Well, it's easier than collapsing in spasms." But Soren wasn't wrong—her muscles ached as if she'd just swum thirty laps, and every breath caused her head to pulse with a throbbing pain…like a tension headache. "I think it's working!"

*Good to know.* Soren did sound a bit breathless, as much as a half-tethered spirit could; but before Ani could voice her concern, the princess added, *What do you see?*

Not much more than Soren had; at least, not in this room. Nothing *felt* magical. "Seems clear. Where are we going next?"

*A couple more rooms downstairs, then the kitchens. I told Elias I'd meet there after he's done meeting with Ravenna.* She paused. *We should switch back before we get down there, though.*

"Do you think it's safe to switch again that soon?"

A long silence followed. *No. But I...* A shiver from the other side of the veil; a hint of swelling agitation. *I can go a bit longer. I just don't want to scare him.*

It wasn't about that; Ani could tell that much. But she didn't push; she just swallowed, curling her fist over her pounding heart. This was Soren's fear, not hers, but the body didn't know the difference. She barely knew the difference. "All right."

Every moment she spent in Soren's head made her feel dirtier, guiltier. Like she was treading in stolen space.

Because, well…she was.

She had *never* forced a host before—never. And that Tenebrae hadn't seen a problem with doing that…it twisted her stomach.

It made her *angry*.

When she didn't say anything more—nor did she move toward the door—Soren said, *What's wrong?*

"Your brothers," Ani said slowly.

*What about them?*

"Have they ever…would they ever…" Rot take her, why was this so hard to spit out? "Have they ever locked you up?"

*No.* A pause. *Well, once, sort of. But that was when I didn't know them. When they were afraid I would hurt someone. And to be fair, I absolutely would have, so…*

"So I overreacted, then, in the palace?"

Another pause. Too long to be anything but reluctance.

*No,* Soren said finally. *That was different, Ani.*

"How?"

*Because he didn't lock you away to protect you or others. He locked you away to punish you for saying no to him.*

"No, I-I overreacted." She had—rot take her, of course she had. "It didn't even come to blows or anything."

Tension pulled taut against the back of her head—she had to swallow down a groan. That wasn't a good sign.

*Anima,* Soren said, *has Tenebrae hit you before?*

Silence.

*That bastard,* Soren snarled, and the force of her anger butted up against the wall, a swelling wave of hot, roiling rage. On Ani's behalf. *That power-hungry, abusive—*

"He is not!" The words exploded out of her, faster and fiercer than she expected. "He's—he's protective, that's all, and stern, and sometimes I…"

*Ani.*

Soren had never spoken to her like *that,* with caution, with something like sympathy.

"He's not," Ani whispered. "It's—it's not like that. We're different than you humans. Gods are tougher sorts."

*I can't tell you what gods are or aren't. All I know is that nobody who hurts you like that can love you at the same time.*

"*Elias* hits you—"

*No, no. Elias and I roughhouse. We're battlemates. We spar, sure, and sometimes we get injured, but that's the nature of training. We have boundaries, rules we both respect. If Elias ever tried to hit me as some kind of punishment, he'd be out on his ass. The same if I did it to him. No one should be hitting you for questioning them.*

Ani shook her head, pushing further away from the wall between their shared consciousness until she could breathe again. "I don't want to talk about this anymore."

Soren didn't protest, which should have been a relief. But there was something about her silence that rubbed Ani wrong, something that had her blinking away memories of bruised wrists and stinging cheeks.

He hadn't always resorted to such things to help her calm down. But she'd outgrown the distractions of gentle hugs and puppet shows and candy-coated treats long ago. She wasn't a child anymore. She wasn't *human* anymore.

She couldn't expect him to treat her like one.

*If he ever lays a hand on you again,* said Soren, *he's going to find out why nobody but Jakob and Elias will train hand-to-hand with me anymore.*

A hint of warmth, like the first bud of spring, just barely began to flicker in Ani's heart. "You're going to punch a god?"

*Wouldn't be the first time.*

"Yes it would."

*Not if you count my dreams.*

A giggle loosened the tight panic trying to tie her lungs in a bowknot, and Ani finally left the empty bedroom, letting Soren's muscle memory guide her to the stairway. "You're too much. I—"

"That's what I tell her all the time, too."

That deep voice halted Ani in her tracks, her foot barely brushing the top step, as she came face-to-face with Elias Loch.

Mortem's favored soldier frightened her perhaps more than anyone ever had; though, maybe that was because she still remembered the feeling of his hands trying to strangle her out of his battlemate's body, the sorrow in his eyes so deep and dreadful it haunted her even now.

This morning, his eyes held no grief, only caution; he was wearing one of the dress uniforms she'd seen several of the on-duty soldiers wearing over the past few days, the silver buttons and epaulets gleaming beautifully against the obsidian jacket. The sleeve boasted a design she hadn't seen on more than a handful of other soldiers, though; a full moon stitched in starlight-white thread, two stars stitched beneath it.

"Is…" He hesitated, his boots squeaking on the marble stairs as he raised a hand, scratching behind his neck. "Can she hear me?"

"Yes."

*Tell him his ass looks good in those pants.*

"She says hi," Ani added.

Soren pouted. *You're no fun.*

For the first time that she could remember, Elias grinned at her, and she wasn't sure whether she or Soren was responsible for the stuttering of their shared heart. "She said something awful, huh?"

She couldn't help it; she smiled back. "You know her very well."

"Better than anyone." He paused again, awkward silence settling between them. "I don't, um…did she agree to this, or…?"

She tamped down the hurt that tried to tug on her heart as his gaze scanned her face—presumably seeking any hint of untruth, any sign that Soren was screaming for help beneath. After all, that caution was more than earned. That he'd even given her the benefit of the doubt was generous enough. "She did. We're switching back in a moment, just…"

"Switching? Like you did at the inn?"

Ani shrugged one shoulder, avoiding his gaze, deciding that one particular swirl in the marble flooring was simply too beautiful to look away from. "We thought it…I thought it might help us get stronger. If we learned how to share."

"Share," he said flatly.

"Just until we can find a way for me to give it back permanently without hurting her worse."

"Right." He didn't look convinced. "Is it going to hurt her if you switch back?"

*Tell him no,* Soren hissed.

"We don't know," Ani confessed.

If a soul could facepalm, Soren's did. *Gods' sakes, Ani.*

*I don't want to lie to him!* Ani protested, for Soren's ears…well, sort of ears…only.

*Let me back out. It's been long enough.*

*I don't know if that's—*

*Let me OUT!*

Whatever calm had once been in Soren's voice disappeared—her last word echoed through the wall like a shout, loud and cracked and so suddenly, wildly afraid that Ani didn't hesitate.

She opened the door, and just like before, Soren burst back through—a rush of desperation that locked every joint in their body, their muscles spasming in one single, strong convulsion that sent a pang of dread trailing Ani back into the other side of their head.

They didn't fall…that one shudder was the only sign anything had gone poorly.

But it felt like a warning. Like they'd only just skirted some line they didn't understand.

"Whoa." Elias gripped Soren by the shoulders, his palms incredibly warm…almost enough to burn. Like he'd held his hands over a bonfire for a few seconds too long. "Are you good? Soren?"

"I'm fine, jackass." Soren sounded a little shaky, still breathless…but not bad, as far as lies went. "Let me see your shoulder!"

Brow still furrowed in concern, Elias smiled a bit anyway, turning and letting Soren look at the stitching on his sleeve. "Don't make a big deal—"

"Look at that fresh stitching," Soren crowed—her tone flippant, casual as anything, as if they hadn't just almost dropped into a body-wrenching fit. She threw an arm around Elias's neck, drawing herself up to plant a kiss on his cheek, then on the stitched stars on his sleeve. "Looks like you outrank me now, *Captain Loch.*"

Elias blushed, his shoulders relaxing as he slid an arm around Soren's waist, pulling her in for a proper kiss—Anima did her best to look away, giving them their moment. "It's just a formality," he mumbled toward the floor. "Enna wants to make sure no one argues if I give a god-related order."

"Mmm. And do you expect me to follow these orders as well, Captain? Should I start saluting when you enter the room?"

They kept bantering as they made their way down the stairs, each with an arm around the other, walking in perfect lockstep. But Ani couldn't find it in her to laugh…not with the echoes of Soren's panicked cry still echoing in the recesses of their mind.

The princess wasn't well—in more ways than one. And until they found a way to make this easy on both of them, she didn't think this slow corrosion of their strength was going to stop.

# CHAPTER 34

# SOREN

By the end of the evacuation a few days later, nearly everyone in their company stayed.

Frigga, a mother of two little girls, did leave with her partner, Maven. The twins, Andrei and Nikolai, left as well, though that was less of a choice and more of an order; both by their parents and by Jakob, who refused to keep the seventeen-year-old boys behind. He'd threatened them with removal from the company entirely if they didn't go, and with great reluctance and myriad curses they'd obviously learned from the more seasoned soldiers, they obeyed.

That left Jakob, Varran, Samhain, Rian—whom, she gathered, had only stayed because Samhain had refused to go—and Kriss, as well as a few scores of soldiers and guards who chose to stay behind and accept Ravenna's offer of extra pay and additional honors.

A surprising number of castlefolk stayed, as well as Seamus—whose name was actually Jaxon, which she only bothered to remember because Jakob flinched anytime she slipped—and Alia, who just looked relieved to have familiar faces around. When they first caught sight of them among the remaining palacefolk, Alia rushed to give Elias and Soren both a fierce hug, almost tearful as she greeted them both with, "I'm *so* happy you're alive."

Jaxon didn't go quite that far, but he did offer Elias a sheepish smile. "I hope you understand why I couldn't help you out back in Atlas."

Elias shrugged one shoulder—the one where the Viper bite scar still lingered, hidden today beneath his thick, fleece-lined crimson shirt. "I hope you understand it wasn't an excuse for you to be an ass to me."

Jaxon flushed. "Acknowledged."

The first time she'd turned the corner and come face-to-face with her former Atlas guard, she'd nearly dropped dead from the shock, and again when she caught sight of Alia behind him. But once they'd shared the story of their escape from Port Atlas, as well as Jakob's relation—which finally put to rest that itch in her brain that had always told her "Seamus" reminded her of someone—she'd calmed down enough to demand more answers.

"How did you get away with living in the palace for so long?" she asked…doing her best not to be too disappointed with herself for not being clever enough to put the pieces together herself.

*How did Finn not catch you* was the real question she wanted to ask. But Jaxon answered that with his next words, accompanied by a sneer and a sigh: "Because I was in Finnick Atlas's pocket before I ever got to the palace."

Ah. "Yeah, all right. That's fair."

"Hey!" Jakob jogged up to them just then, flashing a grin at his brother…a grin softened at the corners by lingering wonder, a sight so familiar that it pinched Soren's amusement down until it better resembled loneliness. "Glad to see you all getting reacquainted, but Soren and I have business elsewhere."

A groan wrenched out of her, and she dug her heels into the carpet as Jakob gripped her wrist and started to drag her out of the hall. "Wait, wait, *now?*"

When he'd caught her earlier that morning in the middle of breakfast with Elias and extended an invitation disguised as an order—"Training room soon, you and me. I need to see how bad the damage is."—she hadn't thought he meant *today.*

"The longer we wait, the more that goddess gets comfy, and the weaker your body gets." Jakob frowned at her…not his usual playful scowl. Something shaped like real concern. "It's not going to be easy on you, but I want to try getting you back on a routine. Strengthening your body might be your best bet for holding up until you and Anima can figure out…whatever you two freaks have going on."

"We're working on it," Soren muttered. Only a half-lie—they hadn't practiced switching control again in a few days. Not that Ani had been unwilling, but…

She tapped her fingers against her opposite wrist. One, two, three.

*I'm not a freak,* Ani pouted. Soren could practically see her crossing her arms and turning her nose up.

*You are a little bit. You can puppet dead bodies.*

*I only do that* sometimes, *Soren,* she said—as if that somehow made it less creepy.

Sometimes *is already too much.*

Ani sighed, and Soren smirked as her presence settled back a bit—a sign of defeat if she'd ever felt one. *Back in my day, it was called a miracle.*

"Jakob," Elias called after them, interrupting whatever comeback Soren had been trying to imbue cleverness into. She and Jakob both turned together, but Elias leveled his gaze at Jakob alone, a warning divot carved into his cheek. "Don't push too hard."

"I trust her to know her limits, and I always respect them," Jakob reminded him—not the first time he'd said it, and not the first time she'd seen it proven true. No matter how much Jakob barked and battered them into improvement, no matter how much he'd pushed them in training, he had an uncanny sense for when a trainee—or even a seasoned soldier—had truly hit their furthest limit. He often called it before they had to choose between dignity and defeat, but if it did get to the point where they asked to stop, he always let them.

She trusted no one with the testing of her mettle more than she trusted Jakob. Elias would call it long before she had to, and she might push herself too far on her own. Jakob would know right where to stop.

Elias's eyes flicked to hers now, and she could see it then: the wrestling match he was having with his own shadows, his own secrets.

He struggled—deeply—with having her out of his sight. She'd learned that much over the few days they'd been reunited, no matter how hard he tried not to act on it. And if she was being honest…her own core quivered a bit at the distance, too.

But the only way to prove that fear wrong was to face it.

She forced a smile, blowing him a kiss and her sauciest wink. "See you later, lover."

His cheeks darkened, and he raked a hand through his hair, ducking his head to hide the boyish smile on his face. "See you," he managed—barely. The last word cracked on the way out, and not with any sort of sadness. "*Soon.*"

Chuckling to herself, Soren let Jakob lead her away, trying not to let her nerves swell the way she could already feel her ankles beginning to. This wasn't going to be an easy session.

"Are you trying to kill that poor kid?" Jakob demanded as they walked, releasing her once he seemed reassured she wouldn't bolt. "*Lover?*"

Soren shrugged daintily, twirling a cropped curl around one finger. "He likes it."

"*Likes* it? I think you gave him a stroke."

Perhaps, but it could be so hard to tell with Elias. He was so very easy to fluster. "I think he'll recover."

"I doubt it. He signed up to live with you his whole life."

"He and Varran should start a support group. *How to Live Life With Your Asshole Battlemate.*"

Jakob thrust out a hand, and she grimaced, ready to take the shove she deserved—but then he sighed, reeling it back in, crossing his arms instead. "You know what? I'll save it for the training room."

They arrived a bit sooner than Soren might have liked, even with a stop at her room so she could change; her strength had yet to rally, and no matter how deeply she dove into herself, tossing aside weakness and exhaustion like pieces of clutter strewn across her floor, she couldn't seem to find where it was hiding.

"Just so we're clear," Jakob announced as he slung off his tunic, rolling his shoulders and shaking out his muscles, bouncing lightly on his heels, "drag me to one more meeting before the sun has even risen, and I'll kick you back to Atlas myself. I swear to whatever gods aren't living in your fool head."

Even though it was good-natured grumbling, his jest couldn't dispel the shadow of dread that had wrapped its hands firmly around her heels, refusing to let go, forcing her to trail it through every patch of watery winter sunlight from her bedroom to Ravenna's office for yet another meeting that morning. Afternoon had taken hold of the day now, but the brightness still seemed duller than normal, as if the sunlight reached through a foggy sheathe of fisherman's netting rather than crystalline glass.

Tenebrae's relic wasn't just in Nyx.

It was *here*. Here, and playing a different song to every ear that happened to catch its twisted, torturous melody.

Soren lowered herself to the wooden training room floor, sitting cross-legged, the polished surface slick and cold against her bare calves, her training pants cuffed just below the knee. She'd plucked her favorite shirt from her closet to train in, only putting it on after spending a good thirty seconds trying not to cry over the simple luxury of being able to wear her own clothes.

In a manner of speaking, anyhow. Technically, the shirt was one of Elias's, but she'd long ago cropped it down to allow for unrestricted movement. It was black and breathable, the sleeves cut to strips that looped over her shoulders, the sides cut to allow for air to flow. She wore a simple dark brassiere beneath, modest and comfortable—not that Jakob would have cared if it wasn't.

It was cold in the training room, but that wasn't what tickled the pit of her stomach with a coaxing toward discomfort. It was the fact that nearly every mark on her body—every unhealed scrape, bruise, and otherwise—was now on display for her captain to see.

She had always been proud of her wounds and scars, even the silly ones. But these weren't scars she'd earned; these weren't wounds she'd done something to deserve.

These were cruelties, evidence of every abuse she'd borne since being spirited away from the battlefield by her brother.

There was pride in them; pride that she had survived, pride that while many blows had landed, none had broken her. But they were also reminders of things she would rather forget, and the last thing she wanted was for Jakob to look at her as someone who needed fixing.

She was not the usual prisoner of war, returning home with a tortured mind and unhealed body, hollow eyes and exhausted limbs screaming of the ordeal they had endured. She hadn't earned that label, that trauma. She would not claim what wasn't hers.

It *wasn't* hers. Her compulsive fingers and pockmarked body might believe otherwise, but…but it wasn't. It wasn't, it wasn't—

"Soren." Snapping fingers brought her gaze up to Jakob's. There was no pity waiting for her there, but there *was* a frown, the corners disappearing into his ginger-tinted beard. "You're staring at that floor like it's the sexiest thing this side of the Vela. Slackjaws don't make for good sparring partners."

"Sorry." She pushed her palms against the wooden floor, forcing herself to her feet. Even as she planted them, steady and sure and determined to stay so, there was a quiver in her soles, an itch to tap her toes until she knew they belonged to her.

Jakob gave her a frank once-over. "You've lost muscle everywhere."

"Goddess didn't want to work out."

*I wasn't good at it,* Ani grumbled.

*You have to try to get better, Goddess Great.*

"You've got more bruises than skin." He wasn't wrong; her body was a garden blooming in shades of lavender and charcoal. She resisted the urge to cover them with her hands. "Any broken bones?"

"No." Small blessings.

"Damaged muscles? Infections?"

A shake of her head. A *tap-tap-tap* of her fingers. "Just bruises and scrapes."

"Hm." Jakob crossed the floor and paused in front of her, one hand out toward her arm. At her nodded permission, he prodded gently at her bicep, frowning at whatever he felt there. "Any tenderness?"

"A bit," she admitted. "That's all over, though. It just…aches. Everywhere."

Another *hm*, this one accompanied by the darkening of his eyes, the grim pinch of his mouth. He let go, but didn't back away, pinning her in place with a solemn look—so uncharacteristic of him. "And those mercenaries…did they hurt you in other ways? You don't have to tell me if you aren't comfortable, but if you're afraid to tell Elias or those who report to your mother…I'm here. You have my silence if you need it."

Her throat clogged with emotion, Soren reached out and took his hand, squeezing it. "No. One of them…" The memory of Arthur's leering sneer dug a rod of nausea deep into her stomach, and she heaved a harsh breath in. "He might have wanted to, but the other was at least half-decent enough to put an end to that idea. But thank you."

Jakob's hand flipped, gripping hers tightly. "Is the bastard one dead?"

Anima's flinch tugged every muscle taut, and Soren's breath caught, fear arresting every inch of her until that tension eased away. She blew out a breath, hoping to the gods he didn't hear the way it shook. "Yes."

"Good." Only then did Jakob fully relax, clasping her wrist and squeezing before releasing her. "One less hunt for me to worry about."

A smile teased the corner of her mouth. "You're going soft on me, Jakob Petrov."

"Well, we all know you're my favorite."

"I'm telling Varran."

He snorted. "*Varran* is above favorites, and he damn well knows it. Pick a stick and let's get to work."

The racks of practice weapons stood against the far wall, an array of woods in shades of sand and mahogany and onyx, all cut from Nyx's own forests. Soren plucked one of the sleek bo staffs from its perch, allowing it to slide through her palm until the groove of the sandpaper-like grip scraped her skin. She tightened her hold and hefted it a bit; heavier than it should have felt, harder to lift than it used to be, but workable.

"Good pick." Jakob tugged one off the wall as if it weighed no more than a feather quill, giving it a deft spin; despite his brawn, he wielded any weapon he touched with the artistry of a trained dancer. "Get in your stance."

She obeyed, pleased to find her muscle memory had not faded. "Bring it on, old man."

"Taunts aren't going to work. I'm not Pious." Smirking, her captain settled back on his heels, coaxing her forward with a bend of his fingers. "I don't get riled by Atlas royals. Though your pretty brother certainly gave it his best."

Her nose wrinkled. "Why does everyone keep saying things like that to me?"

Jakob raised a brow. "Have you *seen* him?"

The bo staff answered for her, hurtling straight for Jakob's groin.

Impact rattled the staff, numbing her fingertips to the first knuckle; Jakob had easily flipped his staff to block her strike, giving her a look and a tut of his tongue. "Playing dirty."

She flashed him a broad grin, resisting the urge to spit in frustration. "I don't play any other way."

A snort, then he grew serious. He shoved her staff away, forcing her back a step—then a second and third, her calves failing to steady her the way they ought to. She stumbled back and caught herself on one of the racks, seething heat—not anger, but humiliation—bubbling in her cheeks.

"Your reflexes are slow. Stance isn't steady. You've got the technique still, gods bless you, but your body can't keep up." Jakob tapped the floor with the tip of his staff. "Try to grab my staff."

"I'd rather not. I'm engaged now, remember?" A joke; anything to hide the fact that there was no gods-damned way her hands were going to be able to fulfill that task. Even holding her own bo staff this long had her trembling in every limb.

"Smartassery doesn't leave bruises," Jakob sighed. "Come on, I need to see you try."

*Try.* She *was* trying; in fact, she hadn't gods-damned *stopped* trying since she'd traded her body away for Elias's life.

Humor fled. In its place, bitterness festered. "This was a bad idea." She tossed down the bo staff, the sharp crack of wood against wood echoing through the wide room. She turned her back on Jakob, heading toward the door—

"Not sure what else I expected from an Atlas."

Stillness settled over her body. Not peace—a disquiet that smoldered with something murderous at the edges.

Slowly, she rotated on her heel, meeting his gaze. He had one brow cocked in challenge, his own bo staff braced against his shoulder.

"What is that supposed to mean?"

"I saw it in your scum Second Prince, too." Jakob kicked her staff toward her, the rattling eerily reminiscent of the sound the undead's bones made when they moved. "Cowardice. Turning your back and letting other people handle the dirty bits."

She gritted her teeth. "Look, I know he scared you, but—"

"But? *But?*" Now that challenge morphed into something a bit less affected, a bit more real. "Soren, that bastard didn't *scare* me. He locked me in a drowning dungeon."

Heat flooded her tongue, and she bent against pain and exhaustion to scoop her staff off the floor, salt spray coating the words she snarled next: "That *bastard* is my *brother*. And believe me, a night in that dungeon was the kindest thing he could have done to you."

It wasn't a jab; it was just the truth. She knew full well that Finnick Atlas had a hundred worse punishments for Nyxians caught on his turf. But Jakob didn't know him; Jakob's scowl turned sour and strange, something darker than anger storming the planes of his face. "So brothers beat out blood-vows, now, do they?"

"Why don't you ask *Seamus?*"

A low blow. But he'd gods-damned started it.

A low blow—and he returned one for one as he swung his staff outward, aiming for her ankles, intent on a sweep.

She only barely caught the blow, and even that hurt—pain struck and spread from her wrists to her shoulders, wresting a sharp groan from her. "Ow!"

"Talk about my brother again, and it'll be your ass on the floor."

"Talk about *my* brother again, and I'll bribe the kitchenfolk to put salt in your coffee."

To her relief, Jakob did laugh at that—a punchy, startled laugh, but a laugh all the same. Even so, he pushed forward, shoving until her ankles gave.

"Jakob!" she snapped as she landed hard once again, every bruise calling out in chorus. "Cut it out!"

But Jakob didn't stop. He stalked forward, dragging his staff across the floor, that awful *rattling* all she could hear…the memory of an undead body scrabbling across the bed toward her, its broken jaw cracking open to speak to her…

The next time he struck, a bolt of energy drove through her limbs, a refusal to take the defeat he seemed determined to force on her.

With a growl, she spun the staff around and caught his blow, shoving *him* back; he stumbled, shaking his head with a hardly warranted curse. She'd barely pushed him.

"If we're talking about brothers," she spat, "how about we talk about the fact that *yours* conveniently showed back up right when all this chaos magic started?"

She so rarely saw true, deep anger in Jakob that it took her a moment to recognize it—especially because his voice didn't rise. It fell, so low she nearly lost track of it: "I know you didn't just accuse him of being a traitor."

"You have to admit, the timing is convenient."

"No more convenient than yours."

In all honesty, she wished she could say what happened next was purposeful. She wished she could say that Jakob had truly gone too far, that he'd deserved the blows she landed, that it had been a simple training session between captain and soldier that simply got out of hand.

But with the rattle of undead limbs echoing in her ears, it wasn't that at all.

She wasn't sure exactly when the taunts became true insults—when the staffs were tossed aside in favor of fists, each of them scrabbling for a hold on the other, neither of them holding back the way they should. She wasn't sure how long it took for Anima to wake up, to start screaming *stop it, Soren, stop, it's the box!* in her ear. Wasn't sure how long it took for the goddess to gasp out an apology, breathless and terrified, and tug so hard on the reins of her consciousness that everything flared brilliant, bruising green.

But she did know that it wasn't Jakob's blows that burst the wellspring of her nose, copper and iron tracing warm paths from nostril to chin.

And she knew there was no one to catch her when her body collapsed, writhing, a single choked whimper escaping her throat before everything went dark.

# CHAPTER 35

# ANIMA

The fit didn't last long at all, but it was enough to convince Ani that they were well and properly dying this time.

Her eyes wouldn't open. Her breath caught in her chest, a horrible scraping sound the only bit of noise that could claw its way free from her throat as she spasmed and shook, muscles ripping, blood vessels breaking, hot tears streaming from her eyes and nose—

"Soren?" Jakob's voice—moments ago, she'd seen a hunger for turmoil in his eyes, stoked by whatever sound had crawled its way into his eardrums. But now the noises had quieted, no more necromantic reminders ringing in Soren's ears, and Jakob sounded…terrified. Guilty. "Soren, oh gods, I didn't mean to— help! Hey, *I need help in here!*"

A door crashed open, but the voice that followed didn't match the urgency in that action at all: "What in the pits happened? Look, Jakob, if you were planning an assassination, this isn't a great place to—"

"It's not funny, Kriss!" Jakob choked. "Something's wrong, I don't—"

Kriss. The blonde warrior whose elbow she'd healed.

"I can see that, Captain Obvious. What *happened?*"

Something about the stern humor in her voice…it made her think of Mora.

*Mora.* Her voice wouldn't form her sister's name, but somewhere inside, the little girl she used to be wanted to. Wanted her sister. Wanted to know that this was only pain and nothing scarier.

"I…" Dazed. Lost for words. It took several seconds for Jakob to speak again: "I don't know. We were just sparring, and then…then it got bad, and there was water…"

"Move over," said Kriss, and the shuffle of knees across the training room floor replaced all words for a moment. "My father used to have fits like this.Don't hold her down like that. Move her on her side—there you go. Do you have something we can use to keep her from biting off her tongue?"

A whimper escaped Ani's mouth.

A chuckle—Kriss again. "Good, she can hear us. Am I speaking to the goddess or the girl?"

Slowly, the spasms came to a grinding halt, but every muscle still felt clogged with molasses, every word syrupy and dull: "G-Goddess."

"Good to make your acquaintance again, Ani. Can you tell me what happened?" Brusque, businesslike—hardly a bedside manner to envy. But her hand was warm as it braced Ani's arm.

"The music box." A cough, and a clot of blood coated her tongue. She retched, spitting it out, only just catching Jakob's dismayed groan. She blinked her eyes open to blood-spattered feet. "Sorry."

"Where's Soren?" Jakob leaned down to meet her gaze, his eyes wild with stark terror. "Where is she? Did I—is she—please tell me I didn't—"

"I had to take it back. She…she couldn't stop. She would have killed you." Or Jakob would have killed them, and either way, she needed to be in control for them to have any shot of survival. "She…"

Soren was still there. Her presence was a slumbering weight in the back of their head, forced into sleep by Ani's forceful retaking of their body. But at least she was calm. Quiet. Safe from the song.

"She's here," Ani croaked, and Jakob bent with a long sigh, his gaze hollow and gutted with guilt. "What did you hear?"

"Water. I thought there was a leak, and it just…I got so distracted, I stopped pulling punches." Jakob carded a hand through his hair with a shudder, leaving behind streaks of rust. "Her, too."

"Can you still hear it?" Ani asked.

"No."

Now Kriss looked to Ani. "Do I need to restrain him?" she asked…deadpan, as if the idea didn't bother her whatsoever.

"No." She squeezed her eyes shut as the blood finally stopped flowing from her nose, replaced with a pounding ache in her head. "The effects only last as long as the music box is playing…or if the song gets stuck in your head. That doesn't happen the first time."

But it did happen eventually, if someone was unlucky enough to hear the song one too many times…and that limit was different for everyone. She could still remember some of the songs caught in Brae's victims' heads before their craving for discord pushed them over the edge…some figurative, some literal.

One woman had sung a battle anthem for days on end, even when her voice thinned to nothing but the barest whisper. She'd mounted a single-handed attack on her entire village, stopping only when she was felled by her sister's blade.

One man had started absentmindedly howling to the sky, an echo of the wolves he'd once been attacked by as he made his way home through dangerous woods. He'd found a pack's trail and chased them for days, running and running until he ran himself to death.

One girl, barely older than fourteen, had tortured her own father with a fire-poker for weeks on end just to fill her head with endless, all-consuming noise, rambling about the ever-singing birds outside their home. In the end, she'd been carted off—first to prison, then to a warmonger's employ, where she outlasted even the most seasoned of interrogators in the most brutal of sessions with their enemies. Ani never had heard if she'd met an untimely fate the way so many others had.

Soren heard funeral dirges and undead bodies. Elias heard snapping spines. And Jakob, it seemed, heard the dripping water of Atlas's drowning dungeon.

Ani herself was impervious to the box's magic—she only ever heard its true song, a tinkling melody that played a childhood lullaby, the one gift Tenebrae had clung to from their late mother. The one possession he'd refused to sell off even in the worst of their misfortune.

Chaos was not an angry thing; Jakob had not attacked out of madness or rage. She could see it in his horrorstruck eyes.

Chaos cared only to disrupt peace where it could, however it could. For some, that meant a craving for adrenaline; others, a craving for noise; others still, a craving for conflict. And once the song sank itself into someone's head, corruption taking root in their very essence, it was only a matter of time before it drove them to destruction.

She'd seen what happened when corruption took root in living things. These people…Soren's loved ones, her friends, her *family*…

None of them deserved that.

Kriss bent down to catch Ani's gaze again; she raised an eyebrow expectantly. "Can you walk, or am I carrying you out of here?"

Well, she knew what Soren's answer would be. But Soren was out at the moment.

"Honestly," she admitted, "I don't even know if I can stand."

"Then up it is." And with an unceremonious grunt, Kriss tossed her over one shoulder as easily as one might a sack of flour.

She didn't know what she'd expected when Kriss had said she would carry her, but it hadn't been half as embarrassing as *this*.

"I'm getting blood on your shirt." It was true—the stream was now dripping freely down Kriss's front, staining the cream vest strapped over her deep blue tunic by three silver buckles.

Kriss looked down with a decidedly disinterested look. "Not the first time, not the last."

"Kriss!" Jaik caught up, though he was limping a bit himself. "Either carry her properly, or let me do it."

"It's fine," Ani said meekly.

"It's not. She's not a deer you just hunted, for gods' sakes."

"You're right." Kriss kept walking, smacking Jakob's reaching hand away. "She's a damnsight lighter. Will you relax? You can't carry her any better with your leg like that."

"She's losing more blood like that—"

"Oh, would you look at that? We're here." Casting a look toward Jakob that could have turned an evergreen yellow, Kriss kicked open a door with a careless strike of her heel, revealing a corridor beyond made entirely of stark white marble, pale wood floors stretching on so long that the end of the hall blurred in Ani's vision. The air smelled of crushed herbs, sharp and somehow soothing, a tang that bathed her tongue in verdant flavor and flooded her mind with memories of a cottage built high in the treetops, a roof thatched with the nests of birds and sheaves of other things she'd grown and dried, a steady stream of people who came to her door for rest or sustenance or relief from pain…

But though this smelled like a place of healing, there were no accouterments of her worship here. No dried flowers or paintings or potted plants. No wreathes or garlands or murals.

No trace of the gods at all.

It made sense, maybe—if Nyx favored her deadly sister, it was hardly a surprise they chose to keep her visage out of their healing halls.

Still. It wasn't often that the Goddess of Life was not acknowledged at all by physicians.

A bud of dizziness began to bloom in the back of her skull, spreading its petals one by one until nausea took root in her stomach, a roiling ache that threatened to spill her breakfast on the floor. Within the heart of that bloom, Soren groaned and stirred, groggy as a bear woken from its hibernation.

*Don't panic,* Ani yelped before she could come fully awake. Nothing good would come from a half-conscious Soren getting hysterical within the confines of their body. *We had a fit. You're okay.*

*Nnngh,* was Soren's wonderfully coherent reply. *What happened?*

*Music box. You and Captain Petrov started beating each other.*

Now Soren surged awake, a sharp pain stabbing into Ani's skull—and prickling within every bruised patch of skin. *Is he all right?*

"He's fine," Ani said out loud, forgetting to keep their conversation inward—only just noticing the look Kriss pointed down at her, because she was looking elsewhere, eyes locked on her purple-patterned wrists.

On the twisted, thorny veins that now sprouted from her bruises, a mimicry of bloodpaths wrought in plant matter, the discolored flesh of each vine still wet with blood where they had burst through her skin.

"Oh, rot take us," Ani and Soren said together, Soren's emotions tuning with Ani's vocabulary, different shades of the same voice speaking in harmony.

"What? What is—" Jakob's voice died on the air, his hand hovering over Ani's bruised, battered wrist, eyes widening in mute horror.

Kriss, however, whistled, her eyebrows rising. "That's disgusting."

And Ani, despite herself, couldn't help the nervous giggle that escaped.

*Chaos magic,* Soren said, spitting it like a curse. *Depths, Ani, are we too late?*

*No.*

*Oh, good,* Soren sighed.

*Your body will give out long before my magic bends to Tenebrae's.* Even weakened, even unsettled, she knew that much. This was just a temporary touch, the effect of standing too close to Tenebrae's power. For her, it wouldn't stick.

At least, she thought so.

Now Soren's presence thickened, a thundercloud rather than a cobweb. *Oh, that's so comforting. Thanks for that.*

Ani bit back a sigh, conscious of Jakob's suspicious attention on her…on her eyes, possibly searching for the green shade to return. Waiting for Ani to disappear.

*He's not trying to be an ass,* Soren said—an attempt at consoling, which was almost adorable, considering the circumstances. Soren had no reason to comfort her. *He doesn't know you.*

*Do you think he would trust me if he did?*

A beat. *Well,* I *do. So they're all going to have to learn to deal with it.*

Warmth flooded Ani's heart…mostly because she knew it wasn't quite true. Soren spoke of trust as a certainty, but Ani could feel her mounting fear, her barely repressed hysteria at being trapped once again.

And in spite of it, Soren held herself still this time. Clung to her courage. Gave words to Ani like *trust,* like *I believe you,* like *us* and *we* and *ours.*

*I'll give it back to you,* she whispered. A promise. A vow. *The second I know it's safe. I just don't want to throw us into another fit so soon.*

*I know.* A tremor through their head, their body, their blood. *Help me breathe?*

Ani's chest caved in a bit, but she forced herself—forced them both—to breathe through that emotion. Soren's fear. Ani's guilt.

In. Out. In. Out.

*Control what you can,* Soren whispered. But Ani didn't think she was talking to her anymore.

"We're okay," she murmured under her breath, ducking her chin toward her chest, trying not to wince at the sight of her wrists-turned-trellises. The blood had dried, at least; the trickles had halted, coagulating in ruby beads of color, and once again she had to be grateful for Soren's strong stomach. Had this truly been her body, she might have gagged. "We're okay."

"Are you in pain?" Jakob asked—a curt demand.

"Um—"

*We're fine,* Soren hissed. *Don't make him feel worse.*

"A little."

*Damn it, Anima.*

"Where does it hurt?" When she didn't answer right away, trying to tally all the places, Jakob's voice sharpened to something more like an order. "Tell me how badly I—"

"Jakob," Kriss cut in—sharper, nastier than even Soren had ever sounded. "You're scaring her. Go find someone to stitch her up. Make yourself useful."

"Who died and made you Captain?" Jakob muttered.

"No one yet, but I'll take it, if you're offering. I hear they just handed it to Pious, anyway, and I've got one up on him—I didn't commit treason." She paused. "Speaking of Pious, try to track him down too."

With an eye roll and a curse, Jakob gave a single curt nod before storming out of the infirmary room, the door shutting swiftly behind him.

*Punch her,* Soren demanded. *I mean it.*

*You always mean it.*

Her right fist curled of its own accord, and Ani caught it with her left hand before it could fully throw Soren's punch, yelping as it struck true in the center of her palm. "Ow!"

Kriss didn't flinch at the sudden movement, the sharp sound—she merely laughed, her eyes glittering. "Cool it, Princess."

"She doesn't like what you said to him," Ani mumbled.

"That's nothing new. Only she's allowed to make fun of Pious these days." Kriss held out a hand, one pale brow raised. "Can I see the arm?"

Tentatively, still unsure of this snow leopard's intentions, Ani lowered her arm into her grip. Kriss rotated it with an impressed hmm. "Biomancy shit. Interesting."

"It's not true biomancy." Ani shifted back a bit, grimacing as Kriss's fingers prodded her wrist. "It's corrupted."

"Right. The music box thingamajig. Can it do this to anyone?"

"I don't know," Ani admitted. "This is…new. It's never been able to affect me before."

"Aren't you supposed to be all-knowing or something? You're a goddess."

*Pretender. Powerful, practiced pretender.*

"We have our limits," she whispered. "Especially when we take hosts. Some memories live in the soul, but most…most live in the mind. Many of mine died with each host I took."

Isa first. Then Lilibet. Lotus and Venetia and Orchid. Viola and Ansari and Fearne. Maybe more whose names she'd lost in the in-between.

Each host's lifespan had been cut in half by the burden of godhood, of a soul made immortal, their bodies burning out long before they could even reach half a century.

And now Soren. But her decline had begun so much faster than the others, hastened by her insistence on fighting back.

Her determination to survive against all odds…ironic, that it was the very thing that would bring about her demise.

"That's…fun." Kriss kicked back in her seat, propping her ankles on the cot, regarding Ani with as much reverence as Soren ever had. "Anyway, enough of that. You got any juicy secrets I can hold over my dear friend Soren?"

*Do not answer that, or I swear—*

"She and Elias are engaged," Ani told Kriss, fighting a grin as Soren blew up into a firestorm of curses so vicious they managed to burn her ears even *without* being screamed aloud.

Kriss's eyes popped wide. She lurched forward, gripping her arm once again—upon Ani's wince, she quickly rearranged her grip. "Sorry. Klutz. You better not be freezing my ass, Ani."

Ani blinked. "Huh?"

*It means you better not be messing with her,* Soren said, though there was a seething hiss to the end of every syllable that promised she was none too happy.

Whoops.

Well, she was too deep into it now.

"No, I mean it. Look." Ani held up her hand to show off the ring—a ring that felt all wrong on her hand, too heavy and tool-beaten and fire-touched. These sorts of things, they had always been better suited to the knuckles and wrists and earlobes of her sisters.

Mora liked things that carried the kiss of flame. Occassio delighted over anything that sparkled, whether the pieces were encrusted with cheap crystals or precious gemstones.

Ani preferred flowers.

"Bones below," cursed Kriss in awe, running a rough-padded thumb over the ring. "Is Pious getting paid extra under the table?"

"From what I've gathered, his mother made it."

"Still—"

A knock interrupted their conversation, drawing both of them to look toward the door. They waited a moment—two—three. No one entered.

"Elias?" Ani called cautiously. "Jakob?"

No answer.

"Come in?" Kriss said, like a question rather than permission. She stood slowly, tension bristling through every well-sculpted muscle in her shoulders and arms, and nerves tied a knot in Ani's throat.

Still no one entered. This time, the knocking came more insistently…a *thud-thud-thud* that spoke of something urgent.

A *thud-thud-thud* that didn't seem to be coming from the door.

"You hear that too, right?" Kriss checked, pausing with her palm on the door. "It's not *the curse?*"

*The curse,* she called it, with an eyebrow wriggle that was entirely too irreverent, with a taunting tone that Cassi used to tell stories that always gave Ani the creepy-crawlies.

Rot take her, what she'd give for that kind of flippant wink-and-giggle dismissal. What she wouldn't give to laugh at the way Kriss waggled her fingers and bared her teeth like some snaggle-toothed hag telling fortunes in a twig and canvas hut.

"Get back from the door," she croaked, easing herself off the bed, a gripping ache circling her ankles as she settled her weight on them, pushing Kriss back a pace. Despite Soren's own fairly impressive height, Kriss was taller still, taller even than Elias. Pushing her was like pushing a boulder. "Let me, Just in case."

Kriss's mouth pinched, but she stepped back, running her palm over the shaved portion of her scalp on the left side. "What should I do?"

"Cover your ears." They couldn't be too careful.

The hallway was not empty—when she craned her neck out, she found a man in simple white robes standing only a couple feet back.

And a more familiar man lying on the floor, silent and still, his expression slack in unconsciousness.

Terror and fury shot through their body from head to toe, a javelin of heat striking through from skull to sole.

*Elias,* Soren choked. *Elias—Anima, let me out!*

Ani caught her breath on a pained gasp as a *swelling* pushed against her bones, her brain—the push of Soren growing from cobweb to consumer, her desperation to reach her battlemate extending through vein and sinew, bending and snapping, groaning and shuddering—

Ani did not fight her. If she fought, they would fall too.

Instead, she tried for sense: *Soren. Wait.*

*Wait for what? He's hurt!*

*Hurt,* Ani agreed—there was a streak of rust painted across Elias's forehead, no denying that, but she could smell the iron-scented smoke even from here. *But not dying. Let me do this.*

A pause. Another swell, another shudder—the inhale and exhale of a second spirit. *Ani…*

I know, she whispered. Trust me.

Carefully, she took a step forward—not toward Elias, but to the man in the robes. The man currently standing with his palms braced against the marble wall, his expression arranged in perfect, preternatural calm…

Slamming his face into the wall.

Over and over and over again. *Thud. Thud. Thud.*

"Sir?" Ani tried, approaching with a measured pace, b eetle-like chills skittering up and down her arms. "Sir, stop. You're hurting yourself."

There was no blink. No pause. No sign of pain. Only *thud, thud, thud.*

*Drip, drip, drip.* Blood streaming down his face, pouring from a smashed-in nose and a torn-up forehead and a burst lip.

Nausea tugged Ani to a stop, a twisting in her stomach that tethered her to the floor, begging her to go no further.

*Thud. Thud. Thud.*

She cut that tether of her better judgment. Walked forward, hands out, eyes flinching away from the near-concave mess of cartilage where the man's nose used to be.

*Thud, thud, th—*

Ani caught his head, forcing him to halt his self-abuse, flinching at the give of his battered flesh beneath her fingers. "Sir, please—"

His mouth opened, pouring blood and broken teeth and a scream that nearly blew her eardrums.

"It *itches,*" he wailed, clawing at her hands, at his flesh, ripping and tearing and begging—"Let go, let go let go it itches *it itches it won't stop it won't it won't*—"

Blood flooded from the scratches on her hands with a five-lashed whip of agony, and she released him with a cry, barely hearing Kriss's curse over the *thud, thud, thud—*

*Crack.*

Not flesh. Not cartilage.

Not nose or mouth.

Bone.

Skull.

And the last thing that flashed in the man's frenzied gaze before he fell, skull dented in just the wrong way…

Relief.

Relief, and then nothing at all.

Ani turned just in time to vomit all over Kriss's boots.

# CHAPTER 36

# RAQUEL

The fifth day in the dim sailor's cabin, her fever finally broke.

Memories of the past couple days were hazy—hazy enough that it reminded her of those first couple weeks after Jira's death, day after day of consuming whatever substance she could find that would keep her numb without robbing her entirely of function. She'd been able to drift through her days without any of them leaving an imprint behind, only knowing she was managing well enough because no one ever noticed she wasn't truly there. They'd excused any slips as the fog of a grieving mind, and only her battlemate Lily had noticed something was wrong.

Like always when she thought of Lily, something darker than grief riled deep in her soul—a viscous, living pain that tried to tack itself onto the walls of every limb and tug until she crumbled. And like always, she cut it free and tamped it back down, because she didn't have time for that. She grieved too hard and too angry to let herself feel it now.

When the war was over, when the gods were back where they belonged, she would lock herself in a room and rip it apart until she finally found tears buried somewhere beneath the rage. But not until the war was over.

Grief would wait its turn. She would come back for it when she was ready.

And this haze wasn't quite so overwhelming as that first one, anyway. She knew they'd escaped Skyhaven, and vaguely recalled Kallias sitting beside her and explaining he'd found help while someone mended the wounds on her back.

*Kallias.*

Every time she could remember opening her eyes, he'd been there waiting. But he wasn't here now. Nobody was. Just her and the glow of magic-infused crystals and the gentle dip and bob of a ship beneath her.

She slowly eased herself up, planting her palms on the cot and pushing, bracing herself for agony to lance up and down her back. But to her surprise, though the wounds definitely protested against the movement, she didn't fall— her body complied with her commands, and though it took a couple minutes, she managed to stand up from the cot.

Someone had given her clothes: loose-fitting brown pants that cuffed at the waist and ankles, soft and lined with thick fleece inside. A long wool wrap the color of raspberry jam that she could fasten over herself with a series of buttons; there were no sleeves to wrestle with, but she did discover slits in the sides for her to put her arms through. Her boots had been taken and cleaned—the leather shone beautifully as she slipped them on, suspicion and gratitude at war as she took in the laces. They'd been untied and tucked inside the tongue of the boot so she wouldn't have to bend and tie them, left loose enough that she could slip them on without pulling.

There was nothing to be done for her hair. She could tell it was a mess— there were knots in every layer, and a cooking vat's worth of oil seeping into the roots. But even lifting her hands past her elbows pulled at the skin on her back, and in the end, it wasn't worth the pain.

Not like there was anyone to impress here, anyway. They'd all seen her in the throes of whatever state she'd been in when she arrived here. Whatever she looked like now, it had to be an improvement.

If she was lucky, maybe Kallias would be busy elsewhere long enough for her to get a bath of some sort.

*Absurd.* Maybe Aeris had whipped the common sense out of her.

A canteen had been left on the trunk across from her bed. She scooped it up and unscrewed it, downing three sizable gulps of water before the burn in her throat eased a bit. She set it down, dashing her hand absently across her mouth—then paused.

Between her extended sleep and the dry weather, her lips should have been split and flaking, chapped to the point of pain. But her hand only encountered smooth skin.

When she set the canteen back down, she caught sight of the little tin on the trunk—a tiny silver thing she'd carried with her since leaving home, a homemade lip balm she applied every night. A habit her mother had drilled into her head as a girl to keep split lips at a minimum during Nyx's drawn-out winter.

These people wouldn't know about it, and she'd hardly been awake enough to think about it, which meant…

Her heart clenched in time with her fist, an unnamable emotion swelling up in her chest as she reached down and scooped up the tin, picturing Kallias searching through her bag to find it in the midst of all this chaos, all this danger.

He'd been paying attention.

It was nothing in the grand scheme of things. But it meant *something*.

She slipped the tin into the pocket of her trousers before finally letting herself out of the cabin, taking a moment to adjust to the swaying floor beneath her feet. It had been some time since she'd been on a boat, and never one big enough to have living quarters. Her feet didn't quite know what to do with it.

Still…it wasn't unwelcome, having the water beneath her once more.

Coming up on the deck, she was immediately faced with a sight that threatened to send her right back to bed, a torrent of heat consuming her that could only mean a return of the fever.

Or something worse.

Kallias was halfway up the rigging, a spool of thread clamped between his teeth as he worked to sew a tear in one of the sails. He was shirtless and barefoot and covered in so many gods-damned freckles he could rival the sky for stars. Despite the cold, he wore only loose-fitting pants similar to hers, though his were deep blue-gray that reminded her of the underbellies of thunderclouds. His hair hung loose around his shoulders, a rare sight—she'd never realized how long it was, reaching nearly past his shoulder blades now. He'd trimmed his beard, and his own wounds seemed to have been treated as well—he moved with only the slightest hitch in his limbs, the deep slices carved into his muscled back already paling to scars. The golden-orange rays of the setting sun rolled down his unruly hair like children racing each other down a steep hill.

The gods were truly trying to see her dead, one way or another. She couldn't quite catch her breath.

"He's got a thing for ships," said a voice to her right, and she turned to see that Finn had crept up on her blind side—a move that normally earned the offending party a solid blow to the gut or face. But she was too tired to be teaching lessons right now.

"I can see that. Is it a passion you share?"

"Gods no. Whatever makes the rest of my family mad for the ocean, it skipped right over me." Finn crossed his arms, gazing up at Kallias with an uncommon pinch to his mouth. The shadows under his eyes looked nearly bruised now, a mottled purple that almost mimicked how Soren had looked after her first broken nose. She'd inwardly doubted the truth of Elias's claims toward Soren's true bloodline before, but since spending more time with Kallias and meeting Finn…there was no denying the resemblance. "It used to be tradition for Atlas royals to take solo sailing trips, you know. Sometime before they turned eighteen, they were expected to sail to either Summercove or Phoebus, meet with the royal families there and reaffirm our welcome in their ports and vice versa, then sail home."

"They would send teenagers that far alone?" There were two continents that existed far beyond theirs—one to the southwest, whose closest kingdom to them was Summercove, and one to the northeast, whose closest kingdom was Phoebus. The southwestern continent was known to be a far more peaceful place, made up of four kingdoms each named after a season, rumored to be complete strangers to the concept of war. The northeastern continent was more of a mystery; she hardly knew anything about it, and what little she did know was mainly legend and lore. Stories of girls with fallen stars for hearts and kings crowned in sunlight.

"They would. Only one or two didn't make it back, and it was long before our time." Finn's eyes glittered with memory. "Kallias was meant to leave on his sixteenth birthday. But Soleil died just a few weeks shy of it, and Mama and Papa refused to risk another child for something that wasn't strictly necessary. I think he still wishes he got to go."

"Did your other sister do it? Jericho?"

"She did. She visited Summercove." Finn banded his arms tighter around himself. "Honestly, I'm grateful the war put an end to it. I would've ended up as shark bait, no question."

That, she didn't doubt. "It's refreshing to hear someone own up to their weaknesses."

"Mm. Has Kallias owned up to his yet? Spouted any declarations by your deathbed?"

To her horror, her cheeks warmed. Thankfully, her complexion shielded her from being found out by blushes. "I don't know what you're talking about."

"You're a gods-awful liar."

"He has nothing to confess."

"Except that he's in love with you."

He might as well have thrust his fist straight through her chest. "You're *mad*."

"Yes." Finn's smile turned a bit wretched. "And he's mad for you. I'm shocked he hasn't asked to kiss you yet."

She only had a second to choose between denial and silence; in a moment of panic, she settled on silence.

Finn's eyes widened. "Oh my gods, he *did*. Did you tell him yes? How bad's the damage? Did you two—"

"Will you *shut your mouth*, Jira?"

The *second* that name crossed her lips, the buzz of activity on the deck dulled. Because of her outburst?

No.

Because someone was singing.

A tenor voice flowed smooth as whiskey from somewhere above their heads, and it didn't take long to catch the movement of Kallias's lips. The thread spool was no longer between his teeth, and he didn't seem to be paying attention to the deck below; his focus was fastened firmly on the tear he was repairing, the melody winding from his throat in the distant tones of a dreamer.

A slow, chill-inducing shanty—a song that had often floated to Nyxian war camps on errant breezes crossing enemy lines.

After one chorus, two more voices wound their way into the song…then another…then another. Nearly half the crew began to sing along—never turning away from their tasks, but even so, their eyes grew misty. Some voices wobbled. A couple didn't sing, but instead put their hands over their hearts, staring out across the river with eyes seeking something that wasn't there.

Atlas sailors, war-weary and self-exiled, hearing the song of home.

"I didn't know he could sing," she whispered to Finn out the side of her mouth.

"Me either." To her surprise, even Finn's eyes shone with a bit of emotion.

An introspective silence fell over the deck, leaving room for the river to sing its own song, a babble of currents that never ceased; at least, until Patch surrendered the wheel to one of his people, jumping down to the deck with an impressed whistle and a loud round of applause. "Well, that's one way to bring an evening to close. It's been a bit since we had a night of music. Got any more songs hidden in that pretty head of yours, Prince?"

Kallias dropped down from the rigging, the blush in his cheeks obvious even from here. "I don't do half as well with an audience."

"Understandable. Rowyn!" Patch clapped his hands once more, turning with a flourish to face a sailor with hair dyed in streaks of red and orange and gold, their eyes an amber color that reminded her eerily of god-touched gazes. But Rowyn's eager grin was entirely human, and without Patch even saying another word, they scrambled off belowdecks.

While they waited to see what nonsense this would result in, Kallias made his way over, concerned gaze raking over her with an intensity that almost stirred a shiver. "Should you be up?"

"No one's stopped me," she said. "I feel fine."

"Actually fine, or *I'm going to be a stubborn ass and try to give Kallias a heart attack* fine?"

"My bet's on both," Finn said. Raquel elbowed him sharply, but he only laughed.

"So tell me what we're doing on this ship," she said.

"They caught us on the ketch. Long story short, we made a deal with them while you slept. They're going to sail us out to Sirena."

Warning bells rang in her mind. "Elias is supposed to meet us in Ursa."

"I know. But failing that, he knows to head to Sirena. We can't reach Ursa by the river, and you're hardly up to another long journey on foot."

"So!" Patch called out before she could argue, Rowyn returning with a beautifully polished fiddle carved of rosewood, its edges sharp as the thorns of the flower that went by the same name. In the sailor's other hand was a case, its buckles still closed. "Does anyone dare challenge our reigning champion?"

Kallias nudged Finn. "That's all you."

Finn snorted. "You're joking."

Kallias snagged Finn's arm and held it above his head, ignoring his protests. "You've got a challenger right here, Captain!"

"*Kal!*" hissed Finn, snatching his wrist back, no longer smiling. His eyes were wide with…anger? Irritation?

No.

*Nerves.*

"What?" Kallias grinned, a thing so carefree it made her blink. "You're a brilliant fiddler."

"I'm mediocre at best."

"Right. Lady Ophelia begged Mama to force you to audition for the traveling symphony because you were *mediocre.*"

A snorting chuckle escaped her before she could stop it. Finn shot her a look that could have melted every ice floe on the river. "I'm not doing this—"

"Ah, one of our guests has found his courage!" Patch plucked the case from Rowyn's hand and strode across the deck, ever-grinning as he shoved the case into Finn's hand and clapped him on the back. "Brave, Prince. Foolish, of course, but brave all the same."

As if that didn't describe their entire allyship.

Finn shot Kallias a look that promised something worse than death would soon find him, but Kallias only grinned wider—wider than she'd ever seen before, a teeth-baring thing of glee that snared her breath and held it trapped in her lungs.

He looked…happy.

Had she ever seen him happy?

Once. Once he'd smiled at her like that, his eyes glazed with desire and joy, his cold hands pulling her in for another kiss, passionate and hungry—

"Raquel?" Kallias's fingers against her elbow pulled her from that memory, and she found herself lightly touching her lips. She quickly shoved that hand into the pocket of her trousers.

"What?" she demanded—probably more sharply than necessary. But it wasn't like he wasn't used to that from her by now.

"Watch." He nodded toward the center of the deck, where Finn and Rowyn faced away from each other. This was the first time she'd ever seen Finn show his nerves, his hand plucking uncertainly at the strings of his borrowed fiddle, the bow held awkwardly between his fingers. "You're going to want to see this."

"Did you set him up to be embarrassed?"

Kallias smirked. "Finn can't be embarrassed. Just watch, will you?"

Well, there wasn't much else to do. She watched.

Patch swaggered into the center between the fiddlers, both hands raised in the air, a greedy gleam in his eyes as he took in Finn's unsure handling of the instrument. "All right, ladies and gents and everything in between! Toss in your bets. I'll be your entirely impartial judge for the evening, so keep that in mind when turning out your coinpurses—"

Kallias pitched something into the center of the boat. It landed with a heavy series of clinks right at Patch's feet.

Raquel's blood froze. "Tell me that's not our entire—"

"All in on the Atlas prince," Kallias called casually, crossing his arms over his chest.

How had Kallias even gotten *hold* of their coinpurse? Finn was the one who'd been carrying…

One of Finn's eyelids twitched—something that could easily have been mistaken for a nervous tic, if she hadn't also seen the faintest curl of his mouth.

*Oh.*

Patch's eyebrows reached for the sky, his mouth bending into an impressed *hmm*. "Bold move, Prince. Anyone care to match him?"

With a chorus of laughter and joking mutters traded between ears, three more coinpurses sailed out to join theirs, landing with musical thuds as three voices rang out in favor of Rowyn.

One more landed in the pile—this one thrown by a familiar face, the healer who'd been treating her for the past couple days. Elowyn's hazel eyes twinkled as she signed, "My bet's on the prince."

"Lovely. Seems we have a high-stakes competition tonight. Rowyn, as reigning champion, you're up first." Patch unwound a strip of cloth from around his wrist, raising it in the air and bringing it down with a showman's flourish. "Begin!"

Rowyn didn't hesitate. The amber-eyed sailor immediately launched into a jaunty sea shanty, a wicked-fast melody that tickled at her heels, stirring a long-forgotten knowledge in her muscles: a memory floated through her head of fireside dances, her and Lily and the rest of their company competing to see who could keep their feet the longest despite a long night of drinking, laughter rising above the music as they tripped over each other's feet or collapsed in a dizzy heap or collided with another dancer until only one was left.

It seemed they weren't the only ones to play such games—after a couple traded taunts between pirates, some of them broke away from the sides of the ship to dance to the playful shanty's beat, skirts and cloaks twirling in colorful swirls as Nyxian and Atlas folk alike lost themselves in the music.

But then it was Finn's turn.

Rowyn's melody slacked off into an invitation, a quieter thing made up of harmony rather than melody, leaving space for Finn to leap in. But Finn dithered at the edge of the song, his bow shaking a bit as it touched the strings, and the first note that burst forth was so sour Raquel's tongue curled up.

"Pits," she muttered as the pirates burst into laughter and groans.

"Just wait," Kallias assured her, his confidence never wavering.

Finn lowered his head as if weighed down by the jeers of the pirates, his shoulders curling inward in an affected flinch.

And then his bow started to *fly*.

A chorus of gasps and delighted whoops circled the ship as Finn crashed into the melody, his head snapping up to reveal gleaming eyes and a smug-ass grin, his entire body transforming from wavering nerves to sheer reckless confidence, his feet barely touching the deck as he spun back into the circle to face Rowyn down. While the melody had flowed beautifully beneath Rowyn's skilled hands, it seemed to come alive under Finn's fingers, wrapping itself around ankles and hearts until it almost hurt not to dance to it. As Finn leapt atop a nearby barrel, keeping his balance flawlessly despite the rocking of the ship, Raquel caught herself…smiling.

Not quite as broad as Kallias's, perhaps, but…a smile. A tap to her toes. A wistful feeling weighing down her chest.

A hand pressed to the small of her back.

"Can I have this dance?" Kallias murmured into her ear, his icy breath lifting the hairs on the back of her neck.

"I'll only slow you down," she reminded him.

"Then slowly it is." And before she could find a better protest, he swept her into the ring of dancers, one hand firmly bracing her back below her injuries while the other twined itself with her fingers.

And before she knew it, she was…laughing.

Laughing, and grinning so hard it almost ached as Kallias spun her about the deck, never going too fast or forcing her to move in a way that hurt her. Every step was careful, thought-through, but there was never a hitch to their dance— likely a result of his training in swordplay and battlework, an ingrained knowledge of how to plan a series of movements with only a second of thought.

All the while, Finn and Rowyn traded off melodies, each adding their own unique twist to the same base song, rising in fervor until they were barely inches apart, bows flying at a pace she would have thought impossible. Though everything was a bit blurred as she and Kallias danced, she could hear Finn's own laughter rising above the music, could catch glimpses of his blithe grin.

And then she saw nothing but stars and shadows and an excess of freckles as Kallias pulled her into the shadow of one of the ship's masts, his arms bracing above her head, pinning her in place with her stinging back against the wood. Both of them were panting, her breaths ragged and warm, his steady and cold.

"You were starting to look uncomfortable," he explained softly. "Thought you might need a break."

Now that he mentioned it, she was a bit shaky—her back was twinging, but it wasn't anything close to the agony it should have been after such exertion. Medimancers did truly impressive work. "I'm all right."

"Forgive me if I keep you here a moment anyway. You're shaking."

"I'm *fine*."

"So you keep saying, but I'm still making you take a break."

She blew out a frustrated laugh, knocking her head back against the mast. "Gods, I hate you."

Without warning, Kallias tugged her close by her neck, fingers curling beneath her hair, his winter-pine breath cool against her mouth.

"Show me," he rasped, and she hated herself for the way she trembled. Not with fear, not with exertion. Something far more pleasant…something far harder to bear. "Show me how much you hate me."

She didn't give herself time to hesitate, to talk herself out of this, to remind herself of all the reasons she shouldn't—of all the reasons why he *couldn't*.

She pulled him down and kissed him with all her might. And though he was gentle as he backed her against the mast, he wasn't half as gentle when he raked his teeth over her lip, when he dug his fingers into her hip to pull her flush against him, when he growled her name into her mouth with such desperate hunger that it sent a thrill straight to the marrow of her bones.

She showed him how deeply, terribly she hated him until the music came to a halt, until Patch reluctantly awarded the win to Finn, until the rattling of coins fell into teasing chatter between Finn and the rest of the crew. And once they were confident Finn had retreated from the deck, she kept showing him as they made their way belowdecks to her cabin, fumbling with the latch on the door until Kallias figured out how to lock it while laughing against her lips.

She hated him until she couldn't pretend it was hate anymore. Until he made her forget why this was such a terrible, terrible idea. Until hunger and hatred became something softer, more tender, a loving worship of lips against skin and hands in hair and him murmuring her name with all the reverence of a prayer.

Until he stopped, hovering above her, one hand planted beside her head, the other tracing the contour of her jaw with such tenderness that her entire body erupted in goosebumps.

"I don't want to hurt you," he said, the words barely breaking through the crashing of waves against the hull. "You're still…if my magic—"

She pressed a finger to his lips. "When I want you to stop," she growled, "I will tell you to stop."

The worried crinkles around his eyes softened some, and he grinned crookedly, leaning in to whisper, "As you order, Officer Angelov," against her lips.

Gods, she hated how much she loved that.

# CHAPTER 37

# FINN

"Now *that* was a show."

Occassio's voice no longer startled him, no matter how suddenly it arrived. So he merely sighed as he bent over to untie his boots, the soles of his feet aching from his wild dance across the deck. "I have many talents."

"Clearly." The glittering tips of her bejeweled boots nudged at his. "Enough distractions, Trickster. Are we going to have that talk?"

"What talk?"

"The one where I convince you to let me into your head already."

Kicking off his boots, Finn dragged a hand through his sweaty hair as he turned away from her. Gods, his arms hurt. It had been a good year or more since he'd wielded a bow and fiddle. "We're never having that talk."

Her lilting voice traded banter for blade. "For all you know, we've already had it."

His stride faltered. But instead of giving her the satisfaction of seeing him rattled, he fired off another question: "Why do you even need it? Clearly you can show up wherever you please without it."

"That's not precisely right. I can appear to people when I wish to, but only for a short time before I get tired."

"Goddesses get tired?"

"Crossing between worlds takes incredible power, Prince. Only Mortem and I can manage it without hosts. Why do you think Anima was so out of practice when she started puppeting your sister?"

Honestly, he'd just assumed Anima was a bit on the ditzy side. "Fascinating. But oddly enough, I'm not too keen on making it easier for you."

"This isn't just about me, you know. It's getting worse, isn't it? The memory loss." Her voice came closer, though he didn't hear so much as a brush of her boot against the floor. "How far back can you remember today? A year? Two? Can you tell me the name of your first love?"

A tremor attacked his arms. He bore down on it with a hushed sigh, crossing his arms and crushing his ribs in his own embrace. "I'm not telling you that name just so you can steal it."

"So that's a no."

He held his silence.

"Finn." She rounded his side, looking uncharacteristically serious. She lowered herself gracefully onto his cot, gazing at him with her multicolored eyes, her pouting mouth taut with something he could have named *worry* if he wanted. Maybe *apology*. "It's not going to stop. My magic isn't meant for mortal minds without the safety net of divinity. You have a strong mind—stronger than any I've seen yet. That's why you've held up this well. But even you can't carry this power for long."

He almost barked out a laugh. This was holding up *well*? "If I let you have my body, I'll die. It's not exactly a bargain tipped in my favor."

"If you don't, this magic will kill you anyway." Truth—he could hear it now, how she spoke when she wasn't lying, a rare touch of frustration carried only by those used to not being trusted. "It will steal you away, memory by memory, until you're left with only terror and emptiness to your name. And then, in the end, you'll lose even that."

"The terror?"

"Your name."

If he let that idea sink too deeply into his head, he'd lose whatever tattered strips of courage he still had left.

So instead he said, "You can have it. I've never been all that attached. In fact, I've been thinking about picking a new one."

Occassio scowled. A victory if he'd ever seen one. "Finn."

"What do you think of Arturo? Or maybe Finnegan? Obviously that's a bit close, but it'd change it up enough, I think."

"*Finnick—*"

He sighed forlornly. "A beautiful option, but alas, that's the one I have now."

"Do you ever take anything seriously?" Occassio demanded. "You're losing your mind here."

"Not losing it," he corrected her. "You're stealing it."

"Semantics." She crossed her legs, then her arms, glaring at him like he was a puzzle piece she couldn't find the proper place for. "You were more fun when I was Fidget."

"*You* were more fun when you were Fidget."

"Oh, don't start that. You liked me better when I showed a little truth." Her teeth practically sparkled in the light of the enchanted crystal lamp on his wall. "You think I missed the way you looked at me at that auction?"

He kicked back against the wall, nailing her with his most charming smirk. "You think I missed the way you looked at me up on that lighthouse?"

They held each other's stares for a time, unblinking, unflinching. The memory of champagne soured the tip of his tongue.

Not many people could brag that they'd kissed a goddess. Pity he was more embarrassed of it than proud. What a reputation he could build with *that* kind of rumor.

"I think we can stop pretending any of it was real, don't you?" she said softly. "We were both playing games. We still are. You're just sore because you're losing."

A half-forgotten wound twinged on the dark side of his heart.

It only hurt because she was right: he *had* been playing her, just as much as she'd been playing him. Just another fiddle duel, but one he'd been woefully unprepared for. She'd bided her time, stretching out her harmony to his melody until she found a way to break one of his strings.

But what really hurt was that he'd felt *guilty* on his part. Had been prepared to beg forgiveness from the girl who'd made him feel that he was perhaps not entirely unlovable. That he could be admired for his darker parts rather than feared.

A lie. All a lie. And one he'd foolishly believed.

There was no love left for Finnick Atlas. Not after all he'd done. Not after all he had yet to do.

"Could I trouble you for a truth, then?" he asked.

Her eyebrow quirked. "Sounds like a nice change of pace. Can't hurt to try."

"The story you told me about losing your siblings. How much of that was a lie?"

To his surprise, rather than firing off another fib, she considered for a time, brow wrinkled in thought. "Mm…it's hard to say. There's a sprinkle of truth in every lie, you know that."

"That's not an answer."

"There's not really an easy way to answer. There are degrees of honesty. Some of my lies were more true than others. Some of my truths were closer to fictions." She shrugged a shoulder, flashing a grin that didn't light up her eyes the way he was used to. "Maybe I'm not sure what the truth is, myself."

"You can't lose me with riddles." He tapped his temple suggestively. "Strongest mind you've ever seen, remember?"

"It's not a riddle," she said—too softly. So softly he half-expected to blink and see Fidget's face before him. "But if you care to take a little journey…I could show you."

"I'm not going anywhere with you."

"Tell you what." She shifted around, rolling until she was lying on her stomach, both cheeks squished against the fists she braced beneath her chin. Her sparkly boots kicked up behind her, tapping chaotic rhythms across the wall. "Come with me, and I'll teach you something new."

How did she manage to look so gods-damned *innocent?* And without altering so much as an eyelash? "About what?"

"Your magic. *Our* magic. Something that could make you a little more useful in a fight, at least."

*When Tempest's frosty snot melts* should have been his quick, rude answer. It might've even made her laugh.

"Fine," he said. "One journey. But I don't see where you think we're going to be able to go from here. We're stuck in a ship, remember?"

Her smile curled at a near-sickening angle. "Oh, darling," she said sweetly, "haven't you learned not to underestimate me by now? Someone on this ship has to be half as vain as me, and once we find them…" She cracked her knuckles in a musical scale, a *do-re-mi-fa-so* of popping bone. "We're going to have some fun."

***

They found a full-length mirror in Captain Patch's cabin.

Finn had crept into much tighter, much more heavily guarded places than the cabin of this swaggering captain. But for some reason, every squeak of a floorboard or creak of the door sent paranoia crawling with ice-cold feet over every inch of his neck, trying to tug his head around to peer over his shoulder.

It likely had something to do with the curly-haired shard of diamond striding ahead of him, sequined chiffon dusting the floor, the edges of her body pulsing with hallucinated light. She had a way of tugging at the well-stitched threads of his composure until they split.

Still, he treaded with caution. Magic-induced or not, his paranoia's intention was to keep the snoring captain safely nestled in dreamland, and as much as he would have rather done it self-assuredly, he preferred anxious success over confident failure.

Occassio crept up to the mirror, running her palm over it in the same soothing motion Finn had often seen stablehands employ with their assigned mounts. She looked over her shoulder with a grin that pulled out her double dimples. His thumbprint ached with the memory of the curve of her cheek. "Ready?"

He glanced over his shoulder at the captain, who slumbered on without so much as a snore, his lanky form sprawled out on his considerably more comfortable-looking mattress. "How is he sleeping through this?"

"Oh, he can't hear us." Occassio dipped her finger into the glass, ripples spreading their wings across the silvered surface. "We're invisible tonight, Lord Lionett."

Silence smothered them both as she froze in place, her fingers halfway submerged in the suddenly molten glass; for his part, his heart stretched itself into parts of him he hadn't known it could reach, ventricles twining with tendons until he couldn't tell heartbreak from exhaustion.

"Go on," he rasped. "We're wasting time."

She pulled her hand out, reaching for him instead, her fingertips glimmering with droplets of quicksilver. "Come on."

This was a terrible idea—worse, it was probably a hallucination. Glass didn't oscillate like a pond with a stone thrown into it. Goddesses didn't offer their hands to Tricksters. Princes didn't fall for pranks played by evil deities.

But Finnick Atlas was no ordinary prince. And Occassio was no ordinary goddess.

So he set his hand in hers, and she took it. And before Patch could so much as snuffle, before even an eyelash could twitch, they plunged into the glass as one might dive beneath a cresting wave.

***

Finn opened his eyes to candlelight.

His feet dug into rotting wood, the scent of mildew and rain and smoke assaulting every sense. Surrounding him were the walls of a ramshackle cottage, smaller than even the poorest of Atlas citizens inhabited, barely large enough to hold the fireplace built into one wall and the stove burning against the other. The rug on the floor appeared to be hand-knit, and not with anything expensive— wool, maybe, definitely spun in haste. But despite its humble appearance, it immediately struck him as…cozy. Homey. A place to come when you needed to hide.

"Where are we?" he asked, sensing the presence just behind his left shoulder. Even in full goddess form, even without the façade of Fidget, he always knew when she was close. Reality bent itself around the Goddess of Time.

"Home." The simplicity of her answer surprised him as much as the truth that rang in it, bitter as it might be. "This is where I grew up."

It was hardly what he'd expected of a goddess's origins. "It's…"

"I know." She pushed past him, gesturing vaguely for him to follow. "Keep up."

That wouldn't be a problem—even if the cottage *hadn't* been the size of a dollhouse, his steps were worth three of Occassio's. He followed her into the back room.

There were no windows in the back of the cottage, nor were there lamps— the only light came from a dying pile of candles arranged in a small ceramic tray in the far left corner. There were four thin, ragged bedrolls all pushed together in a square, with one far nicer one in the center. All five had sleeping people nestled inside. None of them stirred when Finn jolted to a halt, nearly tripping over a loose board in his haste to back away, catching himself with a curse on the splintering doorknob. Wooden teeth bit deep into his palm.

"Relax. They can't hear you." Occassio pirouetted through the room on her tiptoes, stepping in the gaps between arms and legs and sleeping faces. "This is just a memory. It's not like when you used *my* mirror."

*Oh, of course. Should've known that, Finn. Because you have so much experience walking through* mirrors.

"Meet my family." She stepped to one of the bedrolls, gesturing down at a girl with gentle features and a tangled braid hung over one shoulder. "Mora." She moved to the left, standing above a broad-shouldered boy with tousled black hair and a hint of sunburn on his nose, his canteen clutched loosely in his hand. "Peter." She stepped left again, this boy closer to a man, his lean form and sharp cheekbones announcing he hadn't had a solid meal in weeks. "Braeden." Left once more, above a girl who was the mirror image of her, only lacking the sparkles and the smiles…and the sharpness. This Occassio's face was softer, sweeter, but tired-looking—she'd curled so tightly into her bedroll she looked like a sleeping cat, her curls dirty and dull.

Her face…

He leaned closer, blinking hard just to be sure…and his breath stuttered.

He was looking into the face of Fidget.

"Cassandra," Occassio introduced more quietly. And then, stepping into the center…

A girl years younger than the rest, no more than six or seven, her smooth chocolate-brown hair plaited neatly down her back. She wore a warm nightgown and was safely tucked into the nicer bedroll, hers the only face that wore any peace as she slept. There was a wilting daisy crown twined into her hair. She had what appeared to be a lump of wax tucked under one arm, loosely shaped like a human being. Some kind of makeshift doll, maybe.

Finn crouched down a bit, searching in vain for any trace of the timid goddess who'd blackmailed her way into his little sister's body. But between the girl being asleep and him not being familiar with her wearing *this* face…there was no telling if she was truly the same Ani he'd walked and talked and dined with these past weeks.

"You were all human once," he ventured. A question disguised as an observation. Sometimes it was best to come at something sideways when Occassio was involved.

"Obviously."

"When did that change?"

"Don't play dumb, darling. It doesn't suit you. I know you already heard that story from the Empress." Occassio made her way back to him, but stayed standing, her eyes lingering anywhere but on her family.

"I heard how you all got your magic. But how did you become…" He gestured to her current self, which even now didn't fully hold its shape. The edges of her bent and wavered a bit, as if she was the reflection in the liquid mirror rather than the person who'd crossed into it.

"That's a much longer story."

"I have time." All the time in the world, so long as he was in the company of the goddess who governed it.

"Fine. Let me rephrase. It's a tale I don't care for you to know." She sat down beside him, hugging her knees to her chest and resting her chin atop them. "Long story short? We received a very abrupt reminder that while we may have been worshiped as gods, we were that in name only. And becoming something more than a name came at a cost we weren't prepared for."

"Your bodies?"

Not so much as a twitch of her features. "Yes."

"And that's how you lost…?"

"Yes."

"But your siblings are alive. So you lied to me about that."

"People don't have to be dead to be lost." She didn't sound sad, only matter-of-fact. "You know that. You saw it with Soleil. Mora and Peter…they didn't agree with Tenebrae's ambitions. I landed on his side, and Ani…Ani was caught in the middle of it all. I haven't spoken to my older siblings in centuries."

He tried to picture that—to imagine having such a falling out with Kallias or Jericho that he held his silence for what amounted to lifetimes. It was a near-impossible idea. "I see."

"I can hear you judging me."

"It's sort of my natural state."

She snorted, almost a laugh. "I know."

The silence that came after was almost warm. Enough that breaking it seemed rude. But manners were the least of his worries right now. "You also lied about showing me what happened."

"I said I'd show you how much of my story was true." She gestured to her sleeping siblings. "I had siblings. I lost them. That's the truth."

He sighed. "You're really just…awful."

Occassio grinned that time. "Awfully wonderful."

"Awfully awful. With an extra helping of awful on the side. A bit of chilled awful for dessert."

"I like my awful served warm, actually."

"You *monster*," he said, and her song-sweet laugh almost made him forget she was trying to kill him.

This was such a dangerous game. More dangerous than he'd ever played before. And it was worse because a part of him—the part that was sick of constant migraines, scared of losing his memory piece by piece, and still half-besotted with this violet-scaled snake—was desperately ready to lose. And this wasn't a game he could win halfheartedly. He needed his entire self in the fight.

If he lost one inch of ground, she would claim the entire battlefield. He needed to do more than resist.

He needed to start fighting back.

By now, he'd learned how to sense the ribbon of Occassio's magic that threaded through him, a piece of power that answered to him and not her. It had aided him in his escape from Tenebrae back in the palace. It had allowed him to hide in plain sight from Queen Esha and her guards, coaxing shadows to bend themselves around him until he was invisible.

He didn't let the plan take shape in his head. Anything that took more than the barest scrap of thought would alert her.

One try. One attack. Just to see if it could work.

Before he could think about it further, he shot his hand out and gripped the back of her neck, throwing his entire strength into his own magic like a wildly-aimed javelin, trying to tug this memory free from her head the way she'd stolen so many of his.

Her scream—of rage, of shock—shattered the world around them, and before he knew it, they were somewhere else.

He was *someone* else.

***

*Occassio*

She had nearly forgotten the world outside the twenty-seven metal rods that circled her.

She'd stopped trying to seek out anything past the gaudy silk covering that shrouded her room, her home, her *cage* ages ago. No sound, no sight, no *help, help me, help me.* Nothing but shivers and scrapes and *all around the songbird cage, the future chased the goddess. Her master thought 'twas all in fun, mad goes the goddess!*

"Shut up!" snarled a voice outside the *room-home-cage.* Something boned and fleshed knocked against the bars, and her breath caught on a giggle or a groan. So she wasn't the only living thing left in the world after all. "Quit that racket or it'll be another week without food for you, pet."

*Pet.* Her lip curled. Pet. Not a pet. She was Goddess, she was Seer, she was—

Hungry.

So hungry.

So she bit down on her tongue until it bled, until it clotted over the unending song warbling from her throat or her head or from the leak in her ears. *Mad goes the goddess, mad goes the goddess—*

"Good girl." Light knifed into her eyes as the shroud lifted, and her hands came up to shield her, but something tugged them to a stop just short of their goal. Something cold and fanged and cruel. She forced herself to squint past the blinding light, to take in her wrists.

Metal and shine and her own hollow cheeks reflected back at her.

Manacles.

She'd forgotten she was chained.

A face appeared just past the bars, a blurry meld of grayish eyes and sneering lips and horrifically white teeth.

"Well?" he prompted, as if he'd asked a question. Maybe he had. Her ears were so distracted with all the other voices these days, it was hard to remember to listen harder to the real ones. "What do I have to look forward to today, pet?"

She smiled at him, the sweetest baring of teeth she could muster. "I'm going to kill you."

"So you say every day."

Did she? Fascinating. At least she was consistent.

"Go on," he urged, rattling the bars. "You want to eat today?"

She did. She truly, deeply did.

So she closed her eyes. Let herself spiral down the paths of her captor's future, shedding light on steps he had yet to take.

"Your morning will be pleasant," she said, flashes of a decadent breakfast flooding her mouth with water, her stomach somersaulting as the smells of butter and meat and pastry danced at the edge of her senses. She chewed absently at the edges of her fingers, the give of flesh beneath her teeth oddly reassuring. A dim memory of a scowling face and a scolding voice interrupted the stream of visions, Mora's hand snatching hers away from her mouth, pleading with her to *stop picking at your fingers at the table, will you, Cass?*

But Mora wasn't here, and her fingers were already decorated with scarlet streams flowing from her wrists. A little extra red could hardly hurt. It was Mora's favorite color, anyway.

"Your afternoon will bring surprise visits," she added, doors opening and closing in her mind, the startled eyes of her captor gleaming in what she vaguely remembered as *sunlight.* "And in the evening…oh, would you look at that!" She beamed at him again, her mouth forgetting to stop in its proper place, stretching nearly to her ears. "I'm going to *rotting kill you.*"

His eyes narrowed with the promise of punishment, and she sighed internally, her stomach groaning in deep mourning.

There would be no food for her today.

***

Finn

Pain cracked through his skull as he flew backward, shattering the glass and landing in a heap on the floor of Patch's cabin, a haze of iridescent fog falling over his eyes as he slumped. Even then, the slumbering pirate didn't stir. But before Finn could do more than start to sit up, something sharp nibbled at his pounding pulse, biting down just hard enough to draw blood.

He blinked away the haze to find thief's-hoard eyes blackened with wrath above him, freckles and fury consuming his vision, every muscle in Occassio's petite body focused on her unforgiving grip on a crystalline dagger.

"If you ever pull a stunt like that again," she breathed, her breath smelling of plums and jasmine and visceral fear, "I will bleed you dry and leave you for your brother to find."

For the first time, he had absolutely no doubt she meant it. Still, he ground out a retort past the pressure on his throat: "I see. So you can dish it out, but you can't take it back?"

"I am a *goddess.*" She pressed so close that her heart hovered above his, their pulses pounding in opposite rhythm but equal speed. "You cannot—you shouldn't be able to—"

309

This was not the façade of fear she had thrown up in an Atlas alleyway to tempt him into putting his more deadly instincts on display…this was true terror, so pure there was no charade it could not cut through, no costume it could not sully, no magic that could mask it from his sight.

Whatever he had done, whatever trick he'd pulled off on a foolish whim…he'd made a goddess afraid.

"What happened to you?" he rasped, the memory of iron bars and bloody wrists melding with the reality of her frantic heart, her ragged breaths.

Her entire being flickered before his eyes…the image of Occassio, Goddess of Time, shivering over the more-familiar face of Fidget—of Cassandra Medeis.

"That was a mistake," she snarled.

He leaned into the caress of that crystalline knife in her unshakeable hand, meeting her gaze without blinking.

"My mistake," he murmured, "or yours?"

That steady hand gave a single, near-imperceptible quiver.

And with a pulse of pain that thrust his head back to the floor, he woke in different place.

Cobblestones dug into the bare soles of his feet as he ran through the lower levels of Port Atlas, white-hot fire burning in his lungs, every muscle screaming as he sprinted for his gods-damned life. Behind him, a chorus of rattling shrieks and suffering moans told him he wasn't running fast enough, that he *couldn't* run fast enough, and no one was coming to save him now—

Somewhere in the back of his mind, his better sense screamed for him to stop running, to remember what this truly was—a trick, a nightmare, an illusion spun by a vengeful goddess with a death grip on his sanity.

But the wails that beat his back along with the heat of the sun drowned out all but the barest whispers of sense. Especially when fingers snagged the back of his sweater, the off-kilter snapping of brittle bones shooting a thrill of sheer terror up his spine.

He knew that sound. Knew those screams.

Knew the *smell* of the arms that wrapped around his torso, tackling him into a painful skid against the street, the cobblestones ripping into his flesh at the same time teeth tore into the back of his neck.

He thought he might have been screaming, or *trying* to scream, but the chattering voices of the undead surrounding him drowned out everything else.

Teeth ripped out chunks of his flesh. Sharpened bone-talons shredded apart his sweater, his back, agony exploding in so many different parts of him he couldn't keep track of all his broken pieces.

There was nothing he could do. No one who could save him.

So he screamed. And screamed. And screamed.

***

"Wake up!"

He kicked and writhed and clawed at the arms wrapped around his middle. He would not die like this, he would not die like this, he *would not die.*

"Stop—c'mon, stop it!"

No. No, he wouldn't stop, he couldn't—

"Gods damn it, it's *me*!" An arm crashed down over his chest, and his eyes flew open to a familiar face, to reddish hair washed silver in moonlight, to…

"Kal?" His raw throat protested even that much of a word. The moment moonlight touched his eyes, a pain like grinding bone drove itself into the center of his forehead, wrenching a groan out of him. "Oh, gods…"

"Are you *insane*?" Kallias demanded, only barely easing up as he forced himself into a sitting position. Anima's leafy pits, every muscle *hurt*, and even that pain didn't compare to the blinding throb in his head.

"What happened?" he rasped.

"What *happened*? You were trying to throw yourself off the ship, that's what *happened*." Kallias's breaths came in great heaves, face pale with terror, hand trembling as it seized his chin and turned him from side to side. "Are you awake? Are you with us?"

*Us.*

Only then did he see Raquel was there, too, positioned near the edge of the ship, her eyes locked on him. She had one arm out, wearing only a shirt that was a couple sizes too large, her legs bare below the knees—Kallias's shirt.

Well. At least one thing had gone to plan.

He reached up to rub his throat, wincing as he swallowed, his vocal cords gritting against each other as he whispered, "Was I screaming?"

"No." But Kallias was still too pale, still watching him with too much fear.

"Then what?" he demanded. "Kal, if I was just sleepwalking—"

"Laughing." The hush of Kallias's voice cooled his irritation in one fell swoop.

"What?"

"I came out of the cabin because I heard you laughing," Kallias said. "Laughing like…"

Like a madman. It wasn't hard to hear the unspoken words.

When he stayed silent, Kallias cursed quietly, sitting up and dragging him up by the shoulders. "I've let you keep to yourself about this whole Occassio thing because I thought you'd talk about it when you were ready. But enough's enough. You need to tell me what's *happening* to you."

"Why?" The word emerged dull and quiet, and he rubbed at his throat again, avoiding his brother's eyes.

"*Why?* Because I can't help you if I don't know what's wrong! You just tried to—"

"Oh, now you want to help?" A dark chuckle rumbled in his chest, a sound so reminiscent of Occassio he might've been afraid if he wasn't preoccupied with an old, long-buried anger. "And how exactly do you plan to do that, hm? You've done depths-all for a decade, and *now* you want to try helping? *Now* you're ready to try and save me?"

Shame dimmed Kallias's gaze, but his brother's hold on his arms only tightened. "Look…"

"No." He knocked Kallias's hands aside, his chest beginning to heave in great waves of anger, building and building until all his composure was caught in the riptide. "No, you don't get to change your mind now. You don't get to spend ten years teaching me not to depend on you and then get mad that I listened. Do you even remember what you said to me that night?"

Kallias cast his gaze to the deck. All the answer he needed.

"*I can't save you,*" he snarled, shoving himself up from the deck, ignoring the dizzy agony slithering through every crevice of his brain. "That's what you told me the night you almost *killed* me. And I believed you. You want to act hurt that I lied to you? You want to act like I should have come to you with my fears, my burdens, my battles? What proof did I have that you were able to carry them?"

"That night was an *accident*," Kallias snapped, standing to his feet with surprising strength—satisfaction flooded him at the sight. Maybe he'd get a real fight from his brother after all. "A gods-damned *accident*, and I've apologized a hundred times, I—what more do you want? A hundred and one? I'm *sorry*. But I was a kid too—"

"What do I want? What do I *want?*" He meant for it to be a roar. It came out a strangled, embarrassing sob. How long had it been since he cried in front of his brother? In front of anyone? "I don't want apologies! I want…I want…"

So many things. *So* many things, and he couldn't have any of them.

"I want this to never have happened," he choked. "I want Soleil to never have died. I want Jericho to not have betrayed us. I want to—I want to stop *forgetting who I am*, gods *damn* it!"

Kallias's eyes widened, the fury draining from his face. "What did you say?"

Everything was pain. His mind quaked with it. His eyes burned. Helpless, uncontrollable sobs smothered all but the softest whisper, forcing him to choke out his next words: "Kal, I can't remember my *name.*"

It was the last thought he had before blessed darkness escorted agony out of his body.

# CHAPTER 38

## SOREN

Ani gave her back control after spewing her stomach contents at Kriss's feet, which felt more like dodging consequences than honoring a promise.

But Kriss, to her credit, didn't complain—she only checked to make sure Soren wasn't going to lose her own senses before helping rouse Elias, whose bleeding had burned to nothing by the time she finally reached him.

"Are you okay?" A hand on his brow. A thumb across his cauterized wound, the clotted blood still slightly warm to the touch. A stiff, shaking, sprig-dotted hand hastily brushing his hair back.

All of it distant, detached, like she was watching someone else fuss over her fiancé.

Nothing new, not really. But Ani's soul was bundled into the back of their skull, shuddering with horror yet unresolved. Soren's consciousness was the one directing the hand, the fingers, the voice, but inside…

Inside, her body felt so far away.

Inside, she kept hearing the crack of the physician's sundering skull.

The crack of Elias's snapping neck.

She didn't come back to herself until Elias came fully to wakefulness, blinking away the fog in his eyes with a flinch and a curse. He gripped her hand, and her consciousness snapped forward like a slingshot released, catapulting her back to her senses. "I'm fine, smartass. Are you? Jakob said—"

"I'm all right, jackass." A *tap-tap-tap* against his temple—an absentminded little proof, one she hadn't meant to give expression to.

Not proof for him; proof for herself.

Elias glanced at her hand out of the corner of his eye, a slight crook to the corner of his mouth, a bit of wire bent into a fishhook curve. He hadn't missed that little twitch, that cursed slip.

She covered it with a smile. A tug against his hair. "Did anyone else hear it? How bad's the damage?"

Elias's eyes narrowed. "You're deflecting."

"Your face is deflecting."

"Soren—"

"Not now," she interrupted—so sharp it hurt on the way out, so harsh she almost checked to see if the tip of her tongue had started to bleed.

She didn't have time for this. Didn't have time for her swollen muscles and her stinging tongue and the too-keen way he was looking at her.

But he didn't push. And she didn't give.

The dead physician was quietly and swiftly taken away, presumably to be given his rites and burned on a private pyre. His family, she gathered from palace gossip, had been evacuated two days ago; he'd volunteered to stay.

Elias was asked to perform the rites, and Ani begged Soren not to make her go, not to make her see that poor man again. So sunset saw Soren sitting on the snow-covered balcony outside her room, cross-legged on a cushioned bench, wrapped in a thick blanket and sipping steaming spiced tea as she kept her eye on the ever-growing plume of smoke coming from the palace courtyard.

*Couldn't you have raised him? Like you did Elias?* Soren asked as she kicked aside the tarp she'd just removed from over the bench. Outdoor furniture wasn't easy to keep in good condition in Nyxian snowstorms, but she managed. And now that she'd seen the arrangement of balconies in the Atlas palace, she understood why she'd felt compelled to have such a silly addition to her near-useless terrace space.

*No.* Ani's voice still fluttered with nausea. *Not like this. Before, in Atlas, when you were…quiet…then I could have. I was fully settled then. My magic had room to grow. Now…*

Now Soren had crowded it out, resisting anything that could have been mistaken as that sugar-syrup thrill of power; anything that might have called flowers to bloom or wounds to heal.

Or dead bodies to walk again.

"Hmm." Soren let her next sip of tea drown the words in cinnamon and cardamom, nutmeg and ginger. The gentle kiss of the tea seeped warmth into her upper lip and memories into her mind—memories of Ravenna teaching her the magic of this particular mix, telling her that spices were measured by heart and by instinct, not teaspoons and weights. "Poor sap."

*I didn't hear the music box that time. Did you?*

"No." No one was around to hear; there was no need to worry about being overheard and thought mad. "Not a note."

*Then he was the target, not collateral damage. A warning?*

"Feels like a step backwards. From threatening us directly to choosing a random innocent?"

*Maybe it doesn't weigh as much on you,* Ani said, her tone faintly accusatory, *but that man died to send a message to* me. *Tenebrae knows…he knows I can't…*

A tremor. A choked whimper that wasn't her own, but was borne on her voice.

Panic set in on instinct, a screaming to fight against that sound, that emotion, the trauma that belonged to the guest in her head, not to her. But she forced herself to breathe. To let Ani speak her piece.

"I hate this," Ani sobbed aloud, and Soren's left fist tightened, her nails digging into her palm. That fist banged against her knee, and Ani growled, so close to Soren's own voice that she might have made a joke if Ani wasn't still talking. "I *hate* this!"

"I know," Soren whispered.

Gods, it was harder to pretend she wasn't mad when the conversations between the two of them were happening out loud.

"I know," she said again, more strongly, swallowing Ani's distress like a bitter healing draught. "I hate it, too. But we can't give him what he wants."

"It would stop this—"

"It wouldn't." Interrupting herself; that was a new one. "It wouldn't, Ani. Don't let him break you."

Another choked sob. Another growl. Then…

"Help me breathe?" Ani whispered.

*Breathe in. Breathe out.*

Soren's heart clenched, and she nodded—a useless gesture. "You know," she said as she dragged in a deep breath, "this would be easier if you were…I don't know."

"Not inside you?"

A dry laugh. Soren rubbed the cold out of her cheeks, blowing a strand of hair out of her eyes as she rasped, "You don't need to make it sound creepy."

The balcony door creaked open behind her, a groan of cold, rusted hinges protesting against being forced to do their job under such conditions. Soren sipped her tea to wash away the lingering words—Ravenna's words, *control what you can*—until the desire to whisper them slipped away.

"That's the fastest pyre burning you've ever done," she said into the wind, ears trained for Elias's footsteps. "Miss me that much?"

"I missed you every day."

A smattering of icicles dropped one by one down her back, turning her spine into a slalom of chills. She twisted around to find Ember standing at the balcony door; her middle sister was dressed in casual clothes today, soft pants that swished at her ankles and dusted away the top layer of snow and a sweater she pulled more tightly around her shoulders as she inched her way onto the balcony.

"Sorry to interrupt…whatever you're doing out here." Ember ruffled the fallen snowflakes from her hair, then gestured to the bench. "May I join you?"

"Only if you don't tell anyone you caught me talking to myself."

"Deal." With a tired smile, Ember picked her way over, settling her feet in Soren's larger footprints to avoid sinking into the snow. She brushed freshly fallen flakes from the bench with a quick flick of her hand, then settled beside her, staring out at the smoke in the distance.

Then, without warning: "Mama gave her signet ring to Yvonne."

Soren blinked, turning to face her sister; Ember's gaze was firmly fixed on the horizon, but her hands were fussing with one of the knives hanging from her bandolier. Ember wasn't often fidgety. "What?"

"She gave it to Yvonne." Ember crossed her arms and slouched back, her shoulder pressed against Soren's, her leather pants and coat creaking with the movement. "She said that if Tenebrae succeeds in whatever he's doing here, she doesn't want him to gain an advantage over other kingdoms by possessing the ability to send out missives with the seal of Nyx's throne."

A strategic move, a smart one; but not one Soren liked. Not an attitude she cared to possess. "He won't succeed."

"I agree." Ember shrugged, frowning distantly as she fiddled with her own bare ring finger. "But you know Mama. Practicality has to win out over hope."

The thinking of a queen. The kind of thinking she should have been engaging in herself.

The words flooded out before she could stop them: "How did you do it?"

"Do what?"

Soren shrugged, gesturing to Ember's tattoos…flames climbing up her arms, much like Elias's, though Ember's were sparser. Less realistic, too; they were artful and delicate, scrawled across her skin like a form of calligraphy. "Leave Artem behind. How did you choose Nyx over them?"

Ember frowned at her. Her dark eyes turned piercing, prodding at Soren's gaze as if seeking answers…answers Soren didn't have for her, because she didn't even know the questions. Finally, in a meaningful tone, she said: "Who told you that you had to choose?"

Soren's heart sank, and she silently cursed it for its stupidity. She stood with a huff, bundling up her blanket and folding it over her arm, relishing the cold slap of reality the winter wind offered. "You know what I mean."

"If I knew what you meant, I wouldn't have asked."

"I'm Atlas-born and Nyx-raised. I love both; I'll always love both. But I have to leave this…" she gestured to the courtyard beyond, wishing her traitorous hand wasn't trembling, "and go back to them."

"You *have* to go back?"

The question struck a sour note in her chest, and she bit out, "I don't have a choice."

Ember made a soft *hmm* sound. "Don't you?"

Not a question that time. A challenge.

Heat seared her throat, a lump of emotion swelling to life. She swallowed it. Hard.

No room for tears. No room for reluctance.

"I'm Atlas's Heir," she rasped. "I let them down for ten years. I can't let them down again."

Ember's voice became a guillotine—rising and sharpening until her words threatened to draw blood. "You let *no one* down. Nothing that happened was your fault, nor was it your choice. You have no penance to pay."

She wanted to argue—wanted to bite back, even though she'd said as much in Ravenna's office, even though she'd tossed that blame fully at her adoptive mother's feet.

There was a difference between saying something and believing it, too. And she could say it was Ravenna's fault all she liked, but if she followed that anger through to its conclusion…

That path didn't end at Ravenna's door.

"I'm the Heir," she said again, but this time it broke. This time it trembled. "Even if I don't keep that title, even if I pass it to one of my brothers, I owe it to my kingdom…to my family. They fought a war over me for ten years, Ember. I killed their people…*my people*."

Ember studied her for a long moment. "I hear you," she said. "I do. But I don't have the answers you need." A shrug. "I never chose. I was born in Artem. I chose to move to Nyx. I went back to Artem for some time, then came back here, and soon…if all goes well, anyway, I'll be going back there. But that doesn't mean I'm choosing one people over the other. No one's asked me to…and if they did, I'd laugh in their face. My loyalties lie with both."

That didn't feel like a luxury she shared. "But—"

"Soren." Ember rose to her feet with sinuous grace, stopping before her, brushing aside some snowflakes that had melted on her cheek. She gave Soren a thin, knowing smile, but sadness waited deeper in her gaze. "No one is asking you to choose. All that matters is where *you* want to be."

Heat flared in her eyes…tears threatening to spill over. "I shouldn't *want* to be here. I was stolen here."

"I know." Ember dropped her hands to take Soren's, squeezing them tightly. "And no one can blame you for being angry. You don't have to—"

"But that's the problem." Every inch of her shook beneath the weight of this confession, the shame of its truth. "Ember, I'm not angry. I don't know what I am, gods damn me, but I'm not angry. I know I should be, I'm *trying* to be, and I just…"

She owed it to her parents, to her siblings, to *everyone* who had carried rage on her behalf for so, so long, to take her turn carrying that fury. It had been placed in her hands by the truth of her blood, but every time she tried to curl her fists around it, to carry it as she ought to…

"I know I should be angry at her," she whispered. "But I think…I think if I force myself to carry any more anger, I'm going to burn out completely."

Now Ember's eyes transformed from dark obsidian to burning coals…so much like Elias when he was feeling particularly wrathful, though his fire had recently become more literal. She framed Soren's face with her hands, stroking her fingers through her newly shorn hair. "Soren," she whispered, "you owe no one your forgiveness…but you owe no one your rage either, do you understand?"

Soren bit her tongue, forcing back a rogue sob. Gods, she'd been crying so much lately. "But I—"

"Listen to me." Ember shifted aside a stray curl, then dropped her hand to Soren's shoulder, gripping her shirt and shaking her gently. "Listen, you stubborn little fiend. Plenty of people find their power in anger…gods know I do. But others find it in forgiveness. Neither one is wrong. Some people have worked hard to heal enough to feel angry about what was done to them…others have spent so long being angry that they need to set it down before they can be whole again."

Her shoulders fell. Bone-deep exhaustion set in. "Em…" Her voice shattered. "I'm so *tired*."

Shame pulsed on the other side of the wall in her head, but she couldn't take the time to try and tell Anima she didn't blame her. She didn't have the energy to have two conversations at once right now.

"I know. I know. It's all right…Soren, you have bigger things you're carrying right now. You don't need to worry about where you'll go after all this is over, not yet. Right now, you need to focus on getting *well*."

Soren swallowed so hard her ears popped. "I'm fi—"

"You're not," Ember interrupted her, utterly unyielding. "Soren, you're not."

And she thought she'd been hiding it so well. "I don't even know where to start."

"Start by not shaming yourself out of it. Start by talking to someone…Elias, me, whoever you like. And start by putting down all the burdens you don't need to pick up yet."

It didn't *feel* like a burden she could ignore…not with Jakob's taunts about her family still echoing in her ears. Chaos-corrupted or not, those words had stung…and though he'd apologized a hundred times just in the hours since, she still couldn't get the way he'd looked at her out of her head.

Worse than that, even when she leaned into the side of her that was Soleil…even if she pretended, just for a moment, to be all Atlas…

Even then, a gentle, half-forgotten dream whispered in her ear.

Even then, her heart ached for a snow-covered roof and a frozen lake and the giggling of children desperately trying to find their skating legs. A makeshift forge and dough rising on the counter and a husband who would be just as happy to spar with her as sleep in with her on snowy mornings. No crown, no throne, no castle…just a home and a sword and maybe some very fine armor to replace the set she'd lost on that fateful day in Ursa.

Because no matter how hard she tried, she could not imagine herself wearing Atlas's golden, glimmering sunburst diadem or sitting on one of those beautiful gilded thrones.

Because she just kept remembering Kallias and the sadness in his smile when he told her he would one day be sent away from their kingdom.

And lastly, it occurred to her that if someone had broken that same news to her, if someone had told her she was to marry Elias and remain in Nyx and only sometimes see the shores she had been born beside…

She might not have minded it all that much.

"All right," she whispered finally. "I'll try."

Ember squeezed her wrists. "Get some rest, little sister. I'll be here if you need me."

Somehow, that promise—unfailing, steady as the steel her sister wielded—made her feel even worse.

Unfortunately, despite her obeying her sister's order and climbing into bed after toeing off her snow-clumped boots, that *rest* wouldn't come for some time. Because the door had barely swung shut on Ember when it flew back open again, admitting Jakob's stretched-out shadow, cast onto her floor by the lights in the corridor.

"If you've come to apologize for the fortieth time," she moaned, lifting her head from her pillow and squinting against the brightness, "then you can save me the trouble and throw yourself off the—"

"You're needed in the barracks." No smile, no laugh, no roll of his eyes. "It's urgent."

# CHAPTER 39

# RAQUEL

"Kallias," she said, watching him pace past her for the twentieth time, "stop it. He's going to be fine."

"His name. His gods-damned *name*." Kallias clawed his hands through his hair with a soft curse, his shoulders squared like he was searching for something to fight. "How long has this been happening? How did it get this bad this fast? How did I not notice…"

"Because Finn would walk over broken glass before admitting he needs help, that's why." She caught his arm the next time he passed by, standing from her seat beside Finn's cot. "*Kallias.* Don't panic. That's not going to help anyone."

He blew out a quivering breath, squeezing his eyes shut and pressing his palm to his own forehead. "I can't lose him," he said, seemingly to himself. "I can't lose…"

"You *won't*."

Empty words, when Finn looked so terrible. He'd collapsed like a snowbank in summer up on the deck, his eyes rolling into his head as blood began to leak from his nose, his ears, his mouth…enough blood that she'd nearly been sick, and she wasn't the squeamish sort. Though Elowyn had done what she could, Finn had yet to wake nearly eight hours later, and Kallias had yet to sleep. Now both princes wore pallor and exhaustion on their faces like expensive cosmetics, no amount of sleep or succor wiping them clean.

They were losing this battle, and it was starting to scare her.

She wasn't a priestess; she was no good with deities and powers that robbed memory from minds and blood from bodies. If it couldn't be downed with a blade, she was useless to fight it.

This was a battle these princes had to fight on their own. And she was no longer convinced they were strong enough to win it.

Kallias finally sat in her abandoned seat, leaning forward and fussily brushing Finn's hair out of his eyes, chuckling roughly. "He's starting to grow a beard. Will wonders never cease."

"I hear sailing brings out the potential in people." She stood behind him, leaning against the back of the chair to take pressure off her still-mending back. "It doesn't suit him."

"No, you're right, it's gods-awful. Should we shave it?"

"I'll leave that choice to you, Atlas."

Silence for a moment, the only sound Finn's ragged but even breaths.

"What did he mean when he said you nearly killed him?" Not a question she intended to ask, but curiosity got the better of her.

He shrugged one shoulder. "Got drunk after Soleil died. Threw a glass bottle at the door. Finn got between the bottle and the door without me knowing, and…" He mimicked an explosion with his hand. "Luckily, he was a quick kid. Ducked in time to avoid it. But for a second while he was lying there on the ground, I thought…"

He trailed off. Teared up. Buried his face in his hands.

"I cannot lose him," he whispered again, raw with terror. "Not him. Out of everyone, out of all of us…not him."

Before she could seek out the words that could ease the pain in him—if any such words existed—there was a knock on the door. Elowyn slipped inside with a smile and a quick wave of her hand, and Patch poked his head in directly after, a bleary look in his eyes like he hadn't slept well either. "Good bloody morning. Nothing out of him yet?"

"Not yet," Raquel said. Kallias didn't even lift his head.

"Well, nothing a little rest can't fix, I'm sure. If you two are interested, we're docking for the afternoon to restock our supplies—might be good for you both to get a little air." Patch's eyes wandered to Finn. "Might be a good idea to pick up some medicine for him, too. Magic's all well and good, but some things require a more natural touch. You got some practice bartering in the last town anyway, and this'll be even better—we're on your turf now, Highness."

It didn't seem likely to her that there would be an herb or tincture that could cure a goddess's torment. But the gleam of hope in Kallias's eyes when he finally raised his head…she found herself reluctant to crush it.

"It couldn't hurt," she agreed.

Though the false hope could.

Kallias was up in an instant. "I'll get ready to go," he said. "Will you stay with him? Make sure he's all right?"

The trust in his eyes when he looked at her…leaving his younger sibling in her hands when she'd spent so long threatening revenge for the death of hers…

"Of course," she said softly, and meant it.

He was barely out of the room when a breathless voice reached her ears: "If you're gonna kill me, at least let me change first. I want to look devastatingly handsome at my funeral."

A snort escaped her nose before she could think better of it. She eased onto the bed beside Finn, surprised at the strength of her relief when he opened his eyes. "Were you waiting for him to leave?"

"Maybe," Finn mumbled, his lips barely moving. "Wasn't quite ready to apologize yet."

"Prideful ass."

"Welcome to the Atlas family." He squinted at her. "Did I hit you last night?"

She frowned. "What? No."

"Then what's that awful thing on your neck?"

She clapped her hand over the spot in question, her face flushing hot as Finn grinned smugly at her, one of his eyelids fluttering in a sad attempt at a wink. "So he *did* leave a little damage."

"Maybe I *will* kill you."

"At this point, you might be doing me a favor."

All amusement fled, and she leaned forward. "Don't try to pull that. That's what she wants."

"Then maybe she can have it." His eyes fluttered closed again, his brows coming together in a pained grimace. "I forgot my *name* last night, Raquel."

"I know. But if you give up, so will he."

He was quiet for a long moment. "He might not. Not if you're here."

A scoff burst out of her, and she crossed her legs, punching his beneath the blanket. "I think you're forgetting more than your name now."

"I think the *hickey* says otherwise—"

"Enough about that! It was one time, all right?"

And that was all it ever could be—a one-time weakness. A mistake. She was a Nyxian soldier with no family worth speaking about and nothing to offer that could entice a prince. And even if she did, she knew how marriages worked in Atlas. Kallias Atlas was destined for a throne and a crown. Not…her.

Never her.

Finn watched her like he always did—with eyes that understood everything she didn't give voice to. Even debilitated and suffering and barely able to remember who he was, he still knew too much about her.

It was a familiar irritation. One that made her desperately wish Jira was here.

"I won't lie to you," he said. "Atlas is Kallias's home. I don't think he could ever be happy if he left."

Her heart sank, which was ridiculous and embarrassing and all kinds of foolish. "I know."

"But sometimes people can become a home too," Finn added. "I've seen it happen."

"Is there a point to this, or is the blood loss making you ramble?"

He blinked. Looked down at himself with mild alarm. "Am I bleeding?"

"You were. Not anymore."

"Oh. Well, don't scare me like that."

Before she could push him, the doorknob turned, and he flopped back onto the bed. In the span of half a breath, he looked as if he'd never opened his eyes at all.

"Coward," she hissed—even as she caught her collar and folded it up to hide the mark on her neck.

He folded his fingers so one in particular stood out. Then, as the door creaked open, he tucked that one away too.

"You ready?" Kallias asked, leaning in with a smile that hung sideways with exhaustion. That seemed to be all anyone wore lately; exhaustion, anger, or fear. It seemed impossible that only yesterday they'd danced across the ship's deck with no cares weighing down their feet, his face filled with a beaming joy that could rival any sunlight she'd ever seen.

She'd thought war between kingdoms was bad enough. She'd never imagined the toll that divine war could wage on the mortals caught in the middle.

"Ready if you are," she said, resisting the old sisterly urge to tattle on Finn— if only because she knew he'd immediately fire back with something far more mortifying on her part. Better to stay on his good side while she could.

Kallias slipped back out, and she took a moment to pinch Finn, whispering, "You'll talk to him when we get back."

"Is that a threat?" Again, his lips barely moved.

"Yes."

"I'll think about it," was his final answer before she followed Kallias out, grazing her hand against the grooves in the door before snagging the doorknob and tugging it closed.

They had yet to reach the ocean, but they were close—she knew it by the way Kallias livened up as they walked off the gangplank, taking in deep breaths through his nose. Yes, better she pay attention to that—not the slight swagger to his step as he walked, his borrowed satchel bumping against his hip. Not the way the sun gleamed off his neatly-braided hair. Not the deep slit that cut down the front of his ash-blue shirt, revealing a muscular chest that had no gods-damned business being attached to a royal.

Truly Atlas's prince. The very air seemed to embrace him as he stepped off the gangplank, playing with his hair as he eagerly strode into the arms of his kingdom.

She would not think about how badly she wished to ruin that perfect braid. How badly she wanted to tear that shirt right off his back.

She'd never held a grudge against a shirt before, but stranger things had happened. She glowered at it mutely as they made their way into the Atlas town of Riverstone.

She should have been more nervous, entering a town belonging to her enemies. But it was obvious Patch and his crew were welcome here; cries of greeting flew from every colorful wooden cart positioned just past the docks, merchants crowding in to be the first to hawk their wares to passersby fresh off their ships. The aroma of fresh bread and fried fish and unique spices made her mouth water, and a hunger cramp spasmed through her middle, distracting her from the tweaks of pain from her back.

Kallias paused beside her as she slowed to linger by the fish cart, closing her eyes and taking in a deep breath of fry oil and batter. "You like fish?" he asked, astonishment dragging his eyebrows up.

"We ate plenty of fish in Skyhaven," she reminded him defensively. "We lived on this river too. What did you think the *fishing boats* were for?"

"I just…Elias hates it, that's all. I figured all Nyxians would be the same."

"That's prejudiced."

His lips quirked. "Coming from you?"

She threw an elbow into his ribs, grimacing as the gesture tugged the tender skin on her back. "Just for that, you're buying me some."

"Raquel Angelov, did you just demand I buy you dinner?"

"Keep being smart, and I'll make it dessert, too."

His smirk turned into a full-blown grin, and he offered her his arm with a gentlemanly bow. "I assure you, I'll be on my best behavior. I'll lavish you with all the food money can buy, which is…quite a bit more now, actually, since Finn destroyed Patch's champion in the fiddle-off."

"I wouldn't say destroyed," pouted Rowyn, who was only a few feet ahead.

"I would," Patch grumbled. "And I'm the judge."

"You know, you could have just picked them anyhow," said Raquel, slipping her arm through Kallias's. Even through his shirt, his skin was frigid, and the sunlight caught on a shimmer of sweat at his temple. "Not like we could have argued with you."

Patch blinked. Dropped his jaw, picked it up, then dropped it again. "Oh my gods, you're *so right*. Why didn't I do that?"

"Because you're an idiot," chorused his crew.

Patch scowled. "This is mutiny. I've been mutinied."

Kallias laughed—a full, hearty, booming laugh that actually startled her with its depth. "I've missed the company of sailors."

"Pirates," Patch corrected with a flash of his blinding teeth. "Don't get all hoity-toity on us, love. You're a prince of the ocean slumming it with the riffraff of the sea."

"And honored to be so," Kallias assured him with a wink.

A scowl formed on her face. She wasn't entirely sure why. "About that food?"

"Gods, you're worse than Finn." But he escorted her to the cart selling fried fish and crisp, well-salted potatoes, and they stood in line with as much patience as her growling stomach allowed. She was a soldier—she'd gone longer than this without a hearty meal before. But it seemed the day of ship fare—and the days of hunger before it while she lay unconscious and injured—had finally caught up, because she could hardly keep from fidgeting as they drew closer, inch by torturous inch.

At least the wait was entertaining. While the cart was where the orders were handed out, a steady stream of tavern servers ducked in and out of the unassuming building the cart was parked in front of, bringing out baskets of food to restock once the cart itself was empty. Each order consisted of two golden-brown pieces of fish and a pile of equally golden potatoes tossed into a small basket lined with paper, a cup of some sort of sauce nestled in the center. And the more people who walked away with baskets, the more her mood soured.

Kallias nudged her hip with his. "You're puckered up like *you're* the fish."

"I am not." She pressed her mouth flat.

"You were."

"And now I'm *not*."

"My mama used to say you'll get wrinkles making faces like that," he warned her.

"Did she used to say that you'll get a black eye if you keep teasing hungry women, too?"

Kallias chuckled. "No, but my papa did."

"Listen to him, then. He's a smart man."

Finally, after what felt like hours—which was actually only twenty minutes, but Tempest save her, she was *starving*—they finally received their own baskets. Raquel immediately dug in while Kallias paid, glee thrilling through her at the crunch of crisp batter beneath her teeth.

When Kallias came over, she swallowed and grinned at him. "Well worth the wait."

He took a step back, as if in shock.

She frowned. "Atlas?"

He gripped his chest in one hand, wheezing quietly, staggering back another step. Alarm shot through her like a crossbow bolt to the gut, and she hurried forward. "Are you—"

"I must be dying," he rasped. "Surely Raquel Angelov didn't just...*smile* at me?"

Mouth gaping, she drove her fist into his stomach, cursing as he burst into laughter. "You *ass*, I thought something was wrong!"

"Sorry, sorry." But he didn't look sorry, all arrogant smiles and starshine freckles while he popped a slice of potato into his mouth. "Are you telling me all I had to do this *whole* time was feed you? That's all it takes?"

She huffed, stomping ahead, knocking her shoulder into his as she passed. "It's a good start. Not scaring me half to death is another!"

In spite of her ire, his laughter didn't stop as they wound deeper into the town, passing wooden porches that wrapped around entire shops or houses and balconies boasting the most beautiful garden boxes she'd ever seen, overflowing with blossoms of all colors and shapes, vivid blues and blushing pinks and yellows meant to make even the grouchiest of people feel a hint of sunshine. This town was bustling for being so small, and she found herself counting all the smiling faces.

It was perhaps the first place she'd been that didn't seem touched by the war at all.

The morning bled into afternoon, which in turn trickled into evening. It felt like they must have bought something at every cart; she even snuck to the florist when no one was watching her. Though Kallias seemed anxious to get back to Finn, constantly looking back toward the docks as if he could see them even in the core of the city, he never lost his jovial mood—which, if she was being honest, was a relief. Since he'd taken on the relic, dread had been creeping along at her heels like an unwelcome stray, rubbing itself around her ankles and purring reminders of how much he'd been suffering under the heavy hand of Tempest's blessing. She'd expected it to be twice as bad now that he wore the relic around his neck, the ice shard bumping between his clavicles with every step, but besides his discomfort beneath the sun, he seemed…fine.

Though she wouldn't put it past him to hide just how deeply the magic had taken hold.

Finally, as the sun began to set, dyeing the world in eye-catching pink, she and Kallias wound their way back to the ship. While he went to check on Finn, she dithered near the edge of the deck, worrying the strap of her bag with overgrown fingernails and quietly cursing her own stupidity.

It was to thank him for saving her life. That was all.

"How is he?" she asked when Kallias came back, looking calmer than before, if slightly irked. There was a familiar divot between his brows that seemed to get deeper every day.

"Still an ass." He dropped down to sit on the deck, scrubbing a hand down his face. "Better that than whatever he was last night, though. He knew my name. Knew his, too. I'm counting that as good enough for now."

"Did he apologize?"

Kallias blinked at her. "What for?"

"Never mind." He really was too gods-damned good.

Lowering herself beside him, grimacing as her tired legs nearly gave out beneath her, she dug a hand into her pack and shoved her purchase at him, refusing to look. "Here."

Silence. Slowly, he took the parcel from her hand, the paper crinkling softly before he said: "Flowers?"

"They're a gift. For not leaving me behind with Aeris."

He was quiet for so long that she finally snuck a glance at him out of the corner of her good eye.

Oh, gods, he was *beaming*. "You got me *flowers*?"

Face hot, she struck out to snatch them back. "If you're going to laugh—"

"I'm not laughing! I'm not. These are beautiful." He stroked the petals gingerly, his grin only growing as he took in the periwinkle-and-navy bundle wrapped in parchment. "No one's ever gotten me flowers before. They're for me? Really?"

"They were the only thing I saw that seemed close to Atlas blue," she admitted. "I didn't know what else to pick."

That was a lie—it was more than that, a sentiment she'd silently deemed silly beyond confession by the time she'd left the florist's stand. It was the name of the plant that had called to her, a silent reminder that their paths would soon diverge.

It was best that way. But still, she'd found herself picturing the future he would return home to…a future of arranged weddings and rings and a throne far away…and had picked the forget-me-nots without a second thought.

Maybe it was better that Jira wasn't here, after all. She'd howl her head off to see her sister, once called Eye of the Storm, once and still heartless and ferocious and cruel-tongued, buying a boy *flowers* in a pitiful attempt to stick herself inexorably in his memory.

And it wouldn't have been pitiful or embarrassing or silly, had it been any other person. Had it been anyone at all from Nyx, or even Atlas, or any kingdom. If it had been anyone but First Prince Kallias Alexandros Atlas, enemy of her people, killer of her sister.

He had gotten on his knees and told her he was sorry without asking for forgiveness, because he knew full well she could not give it. But neither could he forgive her—nor her kingdom—for the death of his sister. And yet he still smiled at her. Protected her. Bought her food.

Kissed her.

Forgiveness was different than acceptance. And she accepted the truth of what he'd done all those years ago: that it had been war, a creature that rendered all into enemies; that he had not seen Jira, fierce-hearted and mischief-making and ever-smiling, but instead an enemy soldier, a cog in the automaton that had taken *his* sister away.

The scar on his spine was proof enough that their confrontation could have just as easily ended a different way.

So no, she did not forgive First Prince Kallias Alexandros Atlas for her sister's loss.

But she could accept that the Kallias she knew now, who held no title nor wore any crown, who sat beside her marveling over a gift as trivial as a bouquet of flowers wrapped in cheap paper, was not the monster she'd spent all these years hating.

It wasn't as tidy a conclusion as simple revenge would have been. But only cowards shied away from the complicated, and Raquel Angelov was not a coward.

Except, perhaps, when it came to flowers and flushes and the feelings hidden behind them.

"I actually, um…" Kallias interrupted her descent down that long tunnel of thought, scratching the back of his neck, his smile crooking sideways with shyness. "I bought you something, too."

Her heart stuttered. "Me?"

She couldn't remember the last time someone had given her a gift.

"If you hate it, you can chuck it in the river," he promised her as he twisted away, digging in his own pack while worrying his lip with his teeth. She could've sworn his hands were shaking, and she had to tamp down a smile.

Kallias Atlas, nervous. It was almost sweet.

The urge to smile vanished when he offered her a small velvet box.

Clearly reading the drop of her features, he groaned. "Oh, gods, it's not that, just—open it, please?"

She took the box, the velvet soothing against her dry fingertips, ridges in the shape of curling waves etched into its lid. She pried it open—

And the entire world went still.

A delicate silver chain. Multifaceted, glimmering sapphires. Jewel petals arranged in a way that was all too familiar.

It was a bracelet. A bracelet with a flower charm…a forget-me-not charm.

She looked up to find Kallias's eyes on her, gentle and sad and raincloud-dark, silver lining his lower lids.

"I know you'll go home to Nyx when this is all over," he said softly, reaching out and taking her wrist in one hand while removing the bracelet from its box with the other. While he talked, he slid the chain around her wrist, opening the clasp with surprising deftness for such large hands. "And I know you'll probably be glad to be rid of me. But I…it's foolish, I know, but…I hope you wear this and remember that no matter what happens, no matter how alone you might feel or be…if you need anything, if you need help or a friend or…anything. It doesn't matter what kingdom I'm in, what title I wear, I will come to you if you ask. Say the word, and you have me."

*Say the word, and you have me.*

So many layers to that statement. So many emotions hiding in his lightning-storm eyes.

So many emotions that matched those hiding in her heart.

"Kallias," she whispered. "You know what will happen when you go back to Atlas. When you take your crown back."

His grip tightened around her wrist. "Say the word," he repeated in a whisper, and she couldn't decide if it was a plea or a promise, "and you have me, Raquel."

There was no word she could say that would make up for a crown, for a kingdom.

So instead she whispered, "Kiss me."

The hope in his eyes guttered, and she knew he understood—knew he heard *goodbye* and *I'm sorry* even though she couldn't voice it. But he cradled her jaw in his palm anyway, pulling her in and pressing his lips to hers with heartbreaking tenderness.

*Goodbye* and *I'm sorry* and *I will never stop wishing for you to change your mind.*

Or maybe that was just her. Maybe it was her heart begging silently for her to make the selfish, foolish choice, to pretend that she could ever replace Atlas as first in line for his love.

Instead, she kissed him back, allowing herself one surrender, one weakness—she tugged the leather cord out of his braid and looped it around her own wrist, pulling the braid apart until only silken waves remained. She tangled her fingers in them and pulled him closer until she could hardly tell where she ended and he began.

*I'm sorry* and *goodbye* and *I wish it could be different.* Trading silent apologies and confessions until darkness stole over the world, hiding the two of them in shadow and secrets, giving them a hiding place to linger in until morning came and brought reality with it.

# CHAPTER 40

# ELIAS

Just as he came back in from the pyre burning, starting to shrug his coat off in the castle entryway and hang it on the hook, Jakob breezed by, snatching his coat and flipping it around to catch his arm back in the sleeve.

"Don't bother," he said cheerily when Elias made a groan of protest—so cheerily that it felt jarring compared to the solemnity of what he'd just come back from.

But he knew from experience there was no arguing with Jakob once he had a direction in mind, and it seemed that he did; before Elias could even formulate the right excuses, Jakob had forced his coat back over his shoulders and steered him toward the door.

"Barracks," he said when Elias tried to stammer out some semblance of a question. "Bonding time. Soren's already there, and I promised I'd grab you when you got back."

"This feels like one of those things I'm going to regret before it even happens."

Huffing, Jakob slapped him on the back, causing him to stumble on his own heels a bit. "Get that attitude adjusted. I want this to boost morale."

"You know, we're technically the same rank now."

"*Technically*, I don't care. Let's go."

"I don't think this is a—"

"You're not getting out of this," Jakob warned. "Don't start with that *a man has died, is this really appropriate, blah blah blah* wolfshit. If we don't get a little fun in, everyone's going to start killing each other in a day or two, no chaos needed."

"There's a curfew—"

"What did I *just say?*"

Elias shut his mouth.

He hated how quiet the city was—in Atlas, this sort of hush in the evening might have been normal. But here, night was supposed to be lively and luminescent, full of chatter and singing and vendor carts decked in colorful lanterns and garlands.

Now, every crunch of his boots against the snow-crusted cobblestones echoed through his head…through the marrow buried in his once-broken spine.

Luckily, it was a short walk down the street to the barracks buildings, looming onyx constructions that had always looked far more foreboding on the outside than they were on the inside. Jakob reached up and slapped the doorframe before opening it—the paint was worn away in that precise spot, faded into a shade just shy of black, the result of thousands of hands performing the same ritual when they returned home.

Elias did the same before stepping inside, warm air buffeting him with the smells of leather and weapon-polish and fireplaces freshly lit. The barracks door opened into a large common room, the darkwood floor peppered with mats made specially for combat training, the midnight-blue walls lined with weapons both false and true, wooden and war-ready. The castle armory was where most barracks kept their war weapons, but the Obsidian company had always been a little superstitious in that way…they preferred to keep their personal weapons close at hand.

In fact, his old sword was propped up there—a silver blade smithed by Ember herself, with thread-thin rose designs etched into the flat of the blade. It had been a gift the year he'd become Soren's battlemate, one far too fine for the occasion, but Ember had insisted.

*You're protecting my sister's back,* she'd said. *I won't see you doing it with any lesser blade.*

He could've sworn the scythes strapped to his back warmed in response to the pang of nostalgia in his chest—a little flare of jealousy.

He smirked faintly to himself. *Nothing can compare to gods-blessed weapons, of course.*

*Hmm.* Mortem's voice still came rarely—rarer than in Artem's mountain, and even when she did speak, it was often with an air of distraction—but it didn't startle him the way it used to. *I'm not the jealous sort, Elias Loch. Don't let your imagination run away with you.*

*Yes, Goddess.* He paused. *While I have your attention, can I ask…?*

*You can always ask.*

The implication was clear—he could ask, but he might not get an answer.

He asked anyway. *Have you spoken to Anima?*

A long silence followed…long enough that he'd given up on a response when she finally said, *No. She's been in Tenebrae's fold too long…she sees me as an enemy.*

*I don't know if that's true,* he ventured, the memory of Ani's sad eyes coming back to him. *She's been different since arriving here.*

*She stole your love's body. You want me to attempt to reconcile with her?*

Uncertainty tried to tie his thoughts in a knot, but he shook them free. *I know remorse when I see it. I know horror. She might not be against Tenebrae yet, but she's not with him, either. If we're going to get her on our side…*

*Ah.* Mortem's voice took on a knowing quality. *You want to take advantage of her distance from him.*

*You know them better than me. But I know control—I know it's much harder to hold onto with distance. It's why Atlas lost Delphin. Our best shot at flipping Anima's loyalties…it's now, when she's out of his reach.*

*You're starting to sound like Occassio's boy. The prince.*

He forced down a shudder of disgust. *Desperate times.*

*Indeed.* A sigh—he almost thought he caught a flicker of flame out of the corner of his eye, a hint of hair the color of a fresh grave. *Go have fun, Phoenix Priest. Your captain is right—it's worth indulging in while you can.*

Fun seemed decidedly out of reach in the wake of those foreboding words. But as he followed Jakob out of the common room and toward the company's sleeping quarters, voices floated from within…Soren's laughter chief among them, cackling and terrible and perfect.

He'd lived too long without that laugh.

Desperate longing nipped at his heels, pushing him away from thoughts of doom and danger and into the desire to see his battlemate, to sit beside her and put his head on her shoulder, to be the one coaxing that laugh out of her.

When he crossed into the sleeping quarters, he found himself walking straight into a mimicry of a memory.

Déjà vu struck him stupid as he stopped and stared, taking in the picture before him: the twin hearths on either side of the room roaring pleasantly, the entire company sitting in a circle, everyone wearing pajamas or otherwise casual clothes. There was a glass in every hand, a decanter in the center of the circle, and a gleam of mischief or calculation present in every eye.

"Truth or dare," Jakob announced with an absolutely wicked grin, sitting down beside Varran. The cots had been shoved aside to make room for the circle in the center of the room, blankets and pillows stripped off and tossed haphazardly onto the floor to provide a comfier seat.

The picture wasn't entirely complete—the last time he'd actually participated in this game, Kaia had been leaning against his side, too sweet to really get the mean spirit of the game…until it came to Kriss's turn, of course. Jira had been whispering with Soren, plotting their dares out together. Raquel, Lily, and Frigga's absence was another heartache, another reminder of the worries he still carried, the fear that Kallias would attempt to brave Ursa even if they saw the blockade in place.

Still, the music box was here now. Maybe Ursa had quieted.

In the present, Kriss sat alone, sipping at her drink and staring off into space; Varran looked distracted, troubled, but he offered Jakob a smile as he sat down and leaned in to mutter in his ear. Samhain and Rian were already yawning, Rian keeping a wide berth from Soren, who sat with Alia and Seamus—no, Jaxon—

gods, that was never going to stop being confusing. Maybe it would stick if he wrote it down.

"There you are," Soren said with a grin as he sat down between her and Jakob, finishing the circle. "Took you long enough."

He heard himself offer some lame excuse about the pyre burning taking longer than expected, but didn't really pay attention—his focus was entirely arrested by her, by the halo of cropped curls lit by firelight, by the crimson velvet pajamas draped over her frame...

By the knitted socks warming her feet.

Someday he'd stop being surprised by her stealing his clothes. "Those are my—"

"Are we really going to keep doing this?" she groaned. "Yes, they're your socks, jackass. I got cold. You had an extra pair tucked away on your cot. You haven't worn them in months!"

"I haven't worn them because I was busy being in *Atlas*, trying to rescue *you*, smartass!"

"I am not going to sit here and listen to the same gods-damned argument for the thirtieth time," Varran snapped. "Elias, cut the shit. We all know you stash extra pairs for Soren to find, and we all know she forgets to bring her own on purpose, and I'm going to throw myself into a pyre if I have to pretend for *one more second* you both don't know exactly what you're doing. Shut up and get a drink."

Elias blinked at Soren. She blinked back.

He didn't grab a drink, but he did get one for Soren. And they didn't speak a word about the socks again, too thoroughly scolded to try.

The game commenced in the normal fashion—as Captain, Jakob claimed the first challenge. A truth directed toward Soren.

"Are you all right?" he said bluntly, leaning forward with his elbows braced on his crossed legs. "Did I mess you up today?"

Soren settled her head against Elias's shoulder, and though she smirked, he felt her hand tighten around his wrist—a hand dotted with sharp bits of plant matter, some cross between thorny branch and twisted vine. "You could ask me anything, and you're asking me if you punched me too hard? Is that why you were so pushy about doing this tonight?"

"He knows it's the only way to get an honest answer out of you," Samhain snorted, tossing her raven hair over one shoulder. "You'd talk through a broken jaw just to convince everyone you're fighting fit."

"You knocked my nose a bit more crooked, that's all," Soren said with an eye roll. "Not that I ever actually got looked at by a physician, since he bashed his own brains in rather than deal with me."

Elias winced.

"Dark," Kriss chuckled, taking a gulp of her drink.

"My turn." Soren nestled closer to Elias's side, releasing his wrist, and he looped his arm around her waist instead. "Kriss, truth or dare?"

"Dare," Kriss said without hesitation.

"You never pick truth," Rian complained, and Elias closed his eyes to hold in an eye roll of his own. "What are you so scared of?"

Kriss looked at him with all the respect of a person examining a spider they'd just squished under their boot. "*Dare*," was all she said, holding Rian's gaze as she stretched the word out like Atlas taffy.

Rian shut his mouth with an audible gulp.

"I dare you…" Soren thought for a moment, longer than she ever thought about most things she said, before grinning. "I dare you to lick the doorframe outside."

"Good one," Samhain crowed, at the same time Varran hid his face and muttered something under his breath.

That was how people lost their tongues in Nyx—sticking them to things that shouldn't be licked *ever*, let alone in saliva-freezing cold—but he kept his mouth shut. Kriss only stood with a sigh, setting her drink aside and reaching up to stretch, cracking her knuckles above her head.

"I'm not *that* tall," she said, "so someone needs to boost me. Jakob?"

"Happily." The Captain started to stand as well, but Varran caught him by the shoulder.

"Absolutely not," he said. "You already screwed yourself up by sparring with Soren. Jaxon?"

Jaxon blinked, an expression of surprise crossing his face. "I…"

"Come on, Petrov Prime," Kriss said, passing between them with a kick at Jaxon's shin. "Time you started pulling your weight, anyway."

Jaxon shot a pleading look to Alia, but she patted his shoulder reassuringly. "Go on," she coaxed.

Jaxon heaved a sigh, but smiled as he leaned in and pressed a kiss between Alia's brows. He stood up and followed Kriss out, and Soren got to her feet with a groan.

"Have to make sure she follows through," she said when Elias shot her an inquisitive look. "Be right back."

Of course. Those were the rules. He knew that. It didn't stop him from snagging her hand, giving it a quick squeeze. "Hurry back."

With a ruffle of her hand through his hair, she left, leaving him sitting by himself with Alia, Samhain and Rian busy discussing the likelihood of Kriss coming back without a tongue.

"So," he ventured, Alia looking to him with a raised eyebrow. "How've you been adjusting to being here?"

"It's hard," she said softly—so honest, without any prodding or persuading. He wasn't used to that. "I miss home. But I'm glad not to be trapped in the palace with that monster." She shuddered a bit, her thin shoulders drawing in, plucking at her own nails—there were scabs all over them, indicating some kind of nervous habit. "The things he could do…the things I heard…it was terrifying. I can't believe he already made it here."

"I know." Elias swallowed dread of his own.

It really didn't make sense that Tenebrae's influence had crossed borders quite this quickly. If even Kenna didn't know where the box had once been hidden—and she hadn't, he'd asked—then someone must have been told where to look by Tenebrae directly.

He cast a look at Alia and her fingers.

They'd already searched her and Jaxon's quarters…it had been one of the first places he'd suggested to Ravenna, and they'd carried it out quietly, not wanting Jakob to know what was happening. But if one of them—or both—had smuggled the music box into the city, they knew better than to hide it in their room.

Besides, bitten nails hardly proved anything, and she seemed steady enough besides. She was an Atlas in enemy territory; he'd been on the opposite end of that equation, and it had nearly ruined his nerves for good. He hardly blamed her—or Jaxon, even—for feeling out of their depth.

Still. As the only Atlas citizens to cross the border in recent memory, it would be foolish not to keep an eye on them.

He couldn't come up with anything reassuring to say to Alia before Kriss returned, the others trailing behind—Jaxon with a look of slight disgust, Soren with gleaming triumph. A muscle in his shoulder relaxed a bit as she shook snow out of her curls, looking no worse for the wear.

"Still have your tongue?" Varran asked; when Kriss opened her mouth and stuck her tongue out, red and a bit swollen but still present, he sighed and pinched the bridge of his nose. "I hate this game."

"Yeah, yeah." Jakob dug around in his pocket, then tossed a bag to Jaxon, who caught it with a frown. "While you're already cold, you and Alia want to grab another thing of whiskey from outside? I stuck some in the snow earlier."

Elias frowned at him as Jaxon helped Alia to her feet, looping an arm around her shoulder as they headed out; the touch immediately seemed to calm her. "We just started, and you're already out?"

"*You* just started," Samhain said with a slight hiccup. "Some of us have already played a few rounds."

"And some of us," Soren added wryly, smirking toward Sam, "chicken out of dares, so they have to drink."

"My turn," Kriss announced as she sat back down, the words a bit clumsier than before. She narrowed her eyes on Soren. "Truth or dare, Princess?"

"Dare," Soren said as she settled back by Elias, her cheeks flushed from the transition between heat and cold and back to heat, her curls still a bit windswept and finger-fussed. He reached over and stroked a wisp away from her temple, and she offered him a soft smile that thudded into his chest like an arrowhead. "Of course."

Kriss's smile spoke of a challenge before the words ever left her mouth. "I dare you to let the goddess play a round."

Elias's blood turned to ice, all thoughts of tender touches and flirting glances vanishing. Before Soren could say a word, he bit out, "That's not funny."

Firstly, because every time Soren and Anima switched, it left Soren with a pinch less strength; strength she needed more than ever.

Secondly, because Soren had never once refused a dare, not even when it put her in potentially mortal peril. And he knew better than to hope she'd do it now.

"It's not a joke." Kriss never broke eye contact with Soren. "Let her play."

"Kriss." His grip tightened around Soren. Heat welled beneath his skin. Noise—not chaos-born this time, but simple rage—buzzed in his head until he could barely hear his own voice. "They've traded twice today already. We don't know the limits."

This was not a gods-damned game. This could be Soren's life. This could be—

"Fine," Soren said—so simply he almost missed it beneath the fury heating his bones like a newborn blade plunged back into the forge. "But if I pass out, it's your ass."

"Soren," he tried, but it was too late; he *felt* Soren's muscles twist sharply beneath his touch, her neck arching back, her eyes rolling up into her head green…and rolling back down gold.

Anima blinked once, twice, haze sharpening to shock, her eyes focusing on the group around them.

Anima scooted awkwardly away from him, bumping shoulders with Alia, who was staring at her like she might drop into a fit herself. "Um…hi?"

"That's a sick joke," Elias snarled, on his feet before he could stop himself, in front of Kriss even when he *could* have stopped himself, pulsing red consuming the edges of his vision like a fever haze. "That was *dangerous*, and you know it—"

"Why?" Kriss shot back, standing up nose-to-nose with him, just tall enough to look down into his eyes. She stepped into his space, snarling a bit herself, top lip curled back to bare her teeth. The joke around the barracks was that she'd been raised by wolves in the northern forest—the truth, he guessed, was that she'd fought enough street fights to know that most any challenge could be headed off by appearing bigger and tougher and not worth the fight.

But unfortunately for her, she'd picked the one fight he'd never back down from, whether that fight was against goddess or mortal.

"This isn't a game," he spat. Smoke trailed out after the words, forming a barrier between the two of them. "This is her gods-damned life—"

"You think I don't know that? Look." Kriss pointed over his shoulder; when he didn't turn, having spent far too much time with Soren to fall for that trick, she huffed so hard he almost expected a twin plume of smoke to escape from her nostrils. "She's not shaking. She didn't fall over. She's *fine.*"

His neck burned against the urge to turn and look. To see for himself. To be absolutely sure she was telling the truth. "Kriss—"

"It's the same as training any muscle, Pious. The more they trade hands, the more the body gets used to it. The easier it is to do without making her sick." Kriss crossed her arms, raising her chin, looking at him down the bridge of her nose. "The less they fight it—*both* of them—the better off they'll be."

He still hated that she'd done it. He hated that she was right even more.

Soren could have said no. He knew that. And under just about any other circumstance, he would have never tried to make that choice on her behalf, but...

The trust he'd once had in his battlemate had cracked apart when she gave her life for his in that Atlas temple—the trust that while she had a deep love of recklessness, she would never be reckless with her *life*.

The fear tunneling into him was stronger than that still-healing trust. The fear disguised as fire, licking inside the core of his clenched fists, desperate to get out—

"I need some air," he ground out, every word gritty with the taste of soot, something explosive and awful clenched behind his teeth.

He turned away. Shoved his way through the door just as Jaxon and Alia reached the porch, shuddering as the scent of burning wood bit into his nose. He ran until he was far enough into the training yards to be sure he would set nothing important aflame, that he was surrounded by nothing but snow and abandoned training figures.

Because he needed to have this fight with himself, not with Kriss, not with Soren—because it wasn't his place to try and control what Soren chose, but the imprint of the grief he'd borne so poorly in Artem tried to tell him it was.

That he had failed to protect her once already, and if he let it happen again, he would not survive it the second time.

If he couldn't be in that room without encroaching on her that way, then he wouldn't be in that room.

With every step from the barracks to the snowy field, he might as well have been stumbling through a desert pit; heat boiled just beneath the surface of his skin, pressure building in his core until power turned into pain, a now-familiar beast roaring for release.

Claws scraped his ribcage. A ragged cry of pain shredded through his heart, his lungs, his throat...

Nightmares cackled in the back of his head—nightmares of Soren wasting away in his arms. Visions of her turning to dust and slipping through his fingers. Reminders of that world-ending moment in the Atlas palace's parlor when she'd raised her head and revealed those gilded eyes, when he'd known in his heart his battlemate was dead...

Elias fell to his knees, threw his head back, and released a torrent of fire into the sky with a bestial roar.

When the inferno was spent, the firestorm so far-reaching that golden light licked the underbellies of the clouds obscuring the night sky, he fell forward on his hands and knees, trying desperately to breathe. A shudder ran down his limbs as trails of fire sputtered down his tattoos, illuminating the grass beneath him...grass, not snow.

*Oh, pits.*

A quick glance around revealed the true breadth of the damage...a vast circle of crisp, blackened grass, visible only as a void in the center of a field otherwise buried in crystalline white.

Taking on guardianship of the relic should have put him in firm control of his magic. He hadn't had such a problem controlling it since it had first made itself known in Artem, since the tavern with Kallias...

*Elias.* Mortem's voice—dark and dangerous. A warning.

"I know," he gasped out, shaking off those memories. Even his words sounded scorched, barely above an ashen whisper. "I'm—"

*No.* Now he heard something else buried in her tone...dread. *Something's wrong. Listen.*

There wasn't much else to do but obey.

Within seconds, he picked up on what she meant—the clattering of armor hastily thrown on. Shouts that echoed all the way into this abandoned field, shouts edged with something feral...not anger, but something worse. The clang of weapon against weapon.

Somewhere beyond the barracks, a fight had broken out.

*Not a bar fight gone wrong?* he ventured hopelessly.

*I don't think we're going to get that lucky,* Mortem replied grimly—a kindred exhaustion lingered in the pause between those words and her next: *Go.*

Out of habit, he fumbled for his prayer beads, smoothing the pad of his thumb against the long-worn wood. Then he lowered his hand. Found the phoenix feather dangling on its chain, its bristles ever-warm, even in the harsh Nyxian cold.

He had already endured his trials. He would not create a new one for himself.

He had melted an automaton down to dross. He had forged Artemesian steel into gods-blessed blades. He had walked through phoenix fire and come out unscathed, unbowed…worthy to carry Mortem's blessing, just as his father had once been.

The worst was over. Soren was not dead; no matter what his fears, his furies tried to scream at him, she was not dead, and he would not let that change.

So he took a bracing breath, holding it until the panic subsided, until that fear tunneled into focus.

And he followed the order of his goddess.

By the time he'd jogged back to the barracks, he was not alone in the field; people wearing the armor of castle guards had surrounded the building, each one brandishing their weapons—or worse, torches—with a hungry gleam in their eye and perturbingly calm looks on their faces.

He knew that deceptive tranquility. Knew that distracted, desperate hunger.

Those gazes were predatory. And they were focused on the barracks where Soren and his friends were still playing their game, blissfully unaware they'd been surrounded.

Nausea of a different kind took deep root in his stomach, knotting its roots around his ribs…a sickness that spoke of wrongness in the world. Something never meant to roam the earth had broken free here. Something that had been banished by what little remained of the old gods' power when it tried to reach too far, claim too much, live too long.

Chaos had come again.

And it was closing in on his battlemate. His friends. His chosen family.

Even as he crossed from grass to snow, his steps were silent. Every footfall melted the snow beneath him, settling his boots soundlessly on the ground. He reached behind his shoulders to unleash his scythes, praying the whisper of steel on sheath would be muffled well enough by the ever-present roaring of the wind.

"Go on, then," laughed one of the women, nudging the man beside her with a careless grin that shook him straight to his toes. "It's too quiet out here. I want to hear them scream."

Death was not a gift he was eager to give out, but he might not have a choice here.

He thumbed the handles of his scythes. Let out a slow breath, focusing on the weight of his battlemate braids over his heart.

The moment the man wound up to throw his torch, Elias leapt from the shadows, a spark thrown from a flint, scarlet and gold roaring down his blades with a guttering hiss.

The guards didn't have time to scream. His scythes sliced clean through their jugulars, but called forth no arterial spray, no gagging on their own blood—the fire singed their wounds clean even as the weapons made their cuts. And where there should have been struggle, suffering…there was none. They simply fell to the ground, as quiet and quick as falling asleep after a long and arduous day—and when he paused to shut their eyes, an old instinct driven into him from his earliest days as a priest turned soldier, he found them already closed.

*I have them.* Mortem's voice came to him as easily as his own now, a quiet promise that eased some of the guilt strumming in his chest. *Go.*

Veins aflame, mind chanting one singular clarion call—*save her, save her, save her*—Elias skirted around the side of the barracks to seek out the rest of the perpetrators he could hear chattering and laughing and muttering outside. The shadows embraced him as he extinguished his blades, smoke and damp muddling his senses as he stalked forward, every sense honing into a hunter's silent focus.

There were more voices…a dozen, at least, maybe more. They were gathered by windows and doors, giggling wildly behind their hands, intoxicated with the thrill of causing mayhem. Death was not a thought in their minds—they did not care that they held it in their hands, that it clung to those torches and blades as surely as it clung to his own. Whatever melody coaxed them into this state…

*Melody.*

Elias halted at the edge where the shadows broke, flickering light from kerosene lamps at the front of the barracks just barely stopping shy of his toes. He tore bits of cloth from his sleeves and shoved them into his ears, watching each armor-clad guard for any sign of impending attack.

Something cold and sorrowful threatened to douse the determination in his chest, something that tasted bitter on the back of his tongue.

He knew many of these guards—had *been* them on more than a couple occasions, taking shifts with any of his friends who also drew the short stick for dungeon duty or gate duty or whatever they needed extra bodies from the barracks for.

He wasn't at war with these people. *His* people. But they had *her*.

He dithered far too long at the edge of the light, a hundred versions of this battle dancing before him; some bloody, some soot-stained…some beginning with what would surely be a foolhardy attempt at reasoning with these magic-corrupted people, innocents who had only made the mistake of volunteering to remain and protect their home.

*Kal*, he thought, wishing his friend could hear, *you have no idea how lucky you are not to be—*

His lungs suddenly expelled a harsh, hitched breath—a sound driven out of him by the impact of a blade burying itself in his back, shoving him down on one knee on the torchlit stone path toward the barracks door, pain exploding in his kneecap as the skin on his back went numb.

The way shock settled in the body had never truly made sense to him, but he was grateful regardless.

"Look lively!" shouted someone from behind him—another guard, he guessed, perhaps one who'd come to join his dead comrades. His shout only just leaked through the mufflers in Elias's ears; he stepped past Elias without fear, clearly confident that his blow had been a mortal one. "Get it started! Someone saw us!"

And with that, this choice—just like so many others—was plucked right from his hands.

Heat branded his back and front, calling tears to his eyes as he lurched to his feet and caught the guard's uniform, tugging him around just in time to see his eyes go wide with terror. That, at least, could cut through the miasma of the music box's influence.

"You should be dead," choked the guard. Elias could barely read his lips by the dim light of the torch he carried in his other hand.

"Believe me," Elias said, tired all the way to his bones, "I know."

And with a thrust of his fist, he stopped the guard's heart.

Not the traditional way, not with blade or blaze…but with the darkest of the magics that ran through his veins, the same power that had allowed him to walk through phoenix fire unhurt, the same power that allowed him to take death blow after death blow and get back up afterward.

*Mortemancy.*

The guard did not cry out in pain, nor did he plead for his life. Maybe he would have, if he'd had the time, or maybe he would have said something horrifying. But just like the guards at the back, his body gave out at every joint and muscle, leaving him in a crumpled heap on the path without so much as a scratch.

Elias raised his gaze to the other guards, fist still extended, knuckles paling around the hilts of his scythes. With a long, measured breath, he lit his palms with fire, setting his blades ablaze once more.

"Run," he murmured, "and you live."

To Nyx's credit, its guards were not cowards. Not one of them turned tail. Not one of them lowered their weapons.

To Elias's credit, he wished they had.

He faced them with his own weapons ready, forcing the power of death to retreat from his fingers, leaving his hands numb, tingling, frighteningly cold. Even the fire in his blood couldn't soothe away the chill of the grave…nor could it drown out the muffled thud of his roaring pulse in his head, the splitting ache that cracked down his once-broken spine, the tang of blood on the back of his tongue.

Mortemancy did not come without costs. So when the guards charged him with rageful cries and hysterical giggles and whoops of magic-drunk cravings, spoiling for a fight, he relied on his blades rather than his blessing.

At first, despite all his training in Artem to learn how to fight without a partner at his back, it was clearly a losing battle. They outnumbered him, the use of his magic had left him half-spent already, and—

And then he heard her.

*"Elias!"*

Disbelief, not fear. Not a scream of terror, but no less a call to arms.

His battlemate was here, her voice was calling to him, and these people were *in his way.*

Reluctance fled him with a sharp exhale, and all the torches in his enemies' hands went out at once.

With a rib-shaking roar, releasing a torrent of fire from his snarling mouth, the Phoenix Priest attacked.

Ducking, dancing, riving throats and splitting open chests, one after the other after the other. And even now, even burning and desperate and mad, Elias did not fight without mercy. They did not feel pain as they died.

If any of them had hurt her in any way, he might regret that kindness.

As the final guard fell at his feet, her eyes fluttering closed as he jerked his scythe free from her sternum, he did not spare a look at the smoking, bloodless corpses he left behind.

He'd warned them.

"Elias!" He heard her again just before she crashed into him—crashed against his back, her spine pressed to his, a blade in her hand and a familiar growl in her voice. Soren—truly her, not Anima. They must have traded back. "Are there more?"

The pure relief of having his battlemate back where she belonged—at his back, the two of them mirroring each other's stances, sinking into each other's rhythm without hitch or hesitation—was enough to nearly make him weep. But he swallowed hard instead, croaking, "Maybe. Did anyone inside hear the box?"

"No. We didn't hear anything until Ani said something about people dying outside." A pause…then a curse, filthy but soaked in awe. "Did you kill *all* of them?"

"Yes."

"By yourself?"

He shrugged.

Soren whistled softly. "That shouldn't be attractive."

A laugh scraped against his throat. "It *really* shouldn't."

"Don't be judgy."

"I thought you liked that about me."

She elbowed him in the back, still rotating in a circle with him, seeking out more assailants as the rest of the company flooded out of the barracks, pairing off with their battlemates—or alone, in Kriss's case—to search themselves. "You're really hot."

His cheeks flushed. Absurd. "It's really not the best time, smartass."

"Not what I *meant*, jackass. Your shirt's on fire."

Oh. He cursed quietly, sheathing one scythe to bat at the tiny flames on his shirt. "Sorry."

"It's fine." She turned to help him put out the flames, her eyes still probing the darkness around them. "All right, great. Another attack centered on us."

"Yes." He heaved in a death-soaked breath, wincing at the scent of burning flesh as he wiped the sweat from his brow. "Coincidence?"

"I doubt it." Once his shirt was put out, she leaned more heavily into him, the slump of her limbs telling him just how badly those trades between herself and Anima had drained her. Her breathing rattled so deeply that he could hear it even over the ringing in his ears. "We haven't gotten lucky enough for coincidences in a…well, ever."

Unfortunately, she was exactly right.

Somehow, he doubted they would ever have the luxury of *coincidence* again.

# CHAPTER 41

# SOREN

After reporting the incident to Ravenna—though *incident* seemed like a thin word to use for the massacre that had occurred outside the barracks, cutting down sixteen castle guards all total, a devastating blow—Jakob ordered all who remained in the barracks to move into the safety of the castle. Anyone who argued was swiftly met with a direct order from Princesses Emberlyn and Soren…and if they still resisted, though not many did, they were given the same order by an exhausted, enraged, thoroughly heartsick Queen Ravenna.

All in all, the week had managed to cram far too many tragedies within its short span…the evacuation of the people, Soren and Jakob's disastrous sparring session, the physician's death, the game of truth or dare, and then the near-burning at the barracks.

Not only that, but all in all, Soren and Ani had exchanged control of their body several times…and only one switch had been involuntary.

All the times they'd done so on purpose, it had hurt. It had been exhausting.

But they hadn't fallen into spasms. They hadn't lost consciousness. And though this morning saw her aching so badly she couldn't separate bruises from healthy skin, though her head pounded worse than any hangover she'd ever experienced, though everything was a bit blurred and bloodshot around the edges when she finally did pry her eyes open…

She was almost…proud.

"I think we're getting the hang of this," she told Ani as she sat at her vanity, unscrewing the top from her jar of curl cream and rubbing it into her palms, dragging it through her freshly washed hair.

*Seems like it.* Ani didn't sound quite as chipper about it, but Soren could sense her across the barrier, which seemed thinner by the day…she wasn't upset by Soren's comment. *I can't believe what happened yesterday. All those people…*

Ani had tried to heal the fallen guards. But though she'd been able to close their wounds, none of them had come back to life, not even the ones Elias had killed with his blades rather than his magic.

Though she'd always been reticent to let Ani use magic in their body, she had to admit medimancy wasn't so bad. Unlike the fizzing energy of biomantic power, medimancy was soft and sweet…warm, almost, but gentler than Elias's harsh flames. More like drinking spiced tea and letting it heat her from the inside out.

She didn't want to imagine what necromancy might feel like. And she certainly wasn't going to find out.

"I know." Soren cleaned her hands off on a hand towel before tossing it into the wicker basket filled with dirty clothes in the corner…a basket that had been sitting since before Atlas. The towel hit the top of the pile, bounced off, and landed on the floor.

After a heartbeat, a bundled-up pair of socks followed suit.

"Depths take it," she mumbled.

*You don't do your laundry?*

"I do," Soren said, not caring one little bit for Ani's reproachful tone, "but I'm not out of anything yet."

*You wait until you're out of everything to do laundry?*

"Not *everything.* Just important things. I—you know what, I don't have to explain myself to you. The last time you had a body, you probably had to wash your clothes in a river."

*What?* Ani demanded. *How else do you do your laundry?*

"Forget it. I'll show you later." She took a breath, glancing over her shoulder to the empty bed. Elias had gone to get breakfast, and in spite of both of them being sore straight to their toes, it had taken every bit of her self-control not to persuade him to stay in bed…or maybe join her in the shower. But there were more serious things on both of their minds that morning, and as little as she liked it, they were going to need all their energy for what the day had in store. They were searching the castle again today; all quarters, no one beyond suspicion. Including her own room.

*Who all knows about the search?* Ani asked.

"Me, Elias, Jakob, Ember, Ravenna, Sierra. All need-to-know." Soren got up and went to her closet, rifling through, scowling as her fingertips catalogued every texture and color. Everything felt abrasive against her sensitive skin, even the softest fabrics…

…Which was what led her to the guest room one floor down, knocking on the door and already regretting it.

When Alia opened the door, bright-eyed and bushy-tailed despite the early hour, her eyes widened. "Princess Soleil—ahem. Sorry. Princess Soren. Can I help you?"

"Maybe." Soren hesitated. "Were you going somewhere?"

"Just got back from somewhere, actually." She studied Soren, frowning a little. "Do you need something?"

"Do you, um…I know you left in sort of a hurry, but I don't suppose you or Jaxon have any…any Atlas clothes? Something cotton?"

Alia's gaze gentled in understanding. "As a matter of fact, we do. Jax is still out, but I don't think he'll mind…" She offered Soren a sheepish smile as she let her in, scratching the back of her neck with a nervous laugh. "I'd give you something of mine, but I have a feeling it would be a bit short."

*A bit* was an understatement. Alia was a terror with a duet of knives, it was true, but she was the shortest person Soren had ever met.

Soren dithered by the doorway while Alia scurried to the closet and started digging, half her body disappearing into the packed closet—surprisingly packed, considering they'd only just arrived. "Where'd all these clothes come from?"

Alia's hands paused on the garments, and when she spoke again, it was even quieter than before. Her left shoulder hitched up—halfway between a shrug and a flinch. "We stopped in Ursa on our way here...before everything went bad. Jakob helped us get some things, and when we arrived here...Queen Ravenna insisted on helping. She was...very kind."

Soren squinted at her, trying her best to read what that gesture could mean. But as good as she was at reading certain people, she wasn't half as good with near-strangers. She wasn't Finn. "You aren't happy about it?"

"No! Oh, no. I'm grateful. She was nothing like I expected, is all." Alia paused, turning to face Soren with a sheepish pinch to her mouth. "I expected her to interrogate me. To put me under guard, if not throw me in the dungeons outright. And Jax...sure, he was sent there by her, but he'd been in Prince Finnick's silent retinue for so long...I thought she'd call him a traitor. But Jakob insisted on us coming anyway. Seems he was right."

Soren's gut pinched. "Ravenna's not really the type."

"I see that now." Alia rubbed her wrists, staring as if she could still imagine shackles closing on them. "It's...strange. To meet a supposed warmaker and have her treat you with kindness. It feels too peaceful. It feels...too quiet, maybe. Or..."

"Like a trap?"

Alia looked at her with relief now. "Yes. You would know, I suppose."

She did. She knew the exact feeling, that foreboding sense of waiting for the other shoe to drop...knowing this kindness could not last forever.

Waiting for Adriata's patience to run out on the Nyxian girl playing the part of her dead daughter. Waiting for Finn to make good on his clear distrust. Waiting for one of those necromanced bodies to finally land the right blow.

Somehow, she'd never really feared Vaughn. Jericho had been well below Finn as a threat in her mind.

She'd been wrong about everything, and she'd remembered them all too late.

Maybe if she'd remembered her childhood sooner, if she'd remembered *Jericho* sooner, she could have reached her before everything went bad.

But it was useless going down that road now. All she could do now was—

*Do you really think that?* Ani's voice floated in, interrupting Soren's line of thinking.

Soren frowned, but quickly forced it into a neutral expression as Alia started handing her options, still talking, oblivious to Soren's drifting attention. *Think what?*

*That you could have reached her.* A gulp—she didn't know how Ani managed to *gulp* mentally, and she wasn't about to ask. *You don't think she was beyond help?*

*Oh, no. I see where this is going,* Soren scolded. *Tenebrae is* not *my sister. You know that.*

Ani hesitated. *Well…technically, he might be by now.*

*You know what I mean. Ani, his actions aren't your responsibility. From what you've shown me, he's been* well *beyond redemption for a very long time.*

*I don't believe anyone is beyond redemption,* Ani whispered. *Even my brother…even your sister.*

Bitterness coated Soren's tongue, and she bit down on it, relishing the acrid call to reality. *She killed Elias.*

Betrayal, she could have forgiven. Making mistakes to save the other half of your heart…she'd done that. She would probably do it again.

But her forgiveness stopped just short of harm coming to Elias.

*And I killed you,* Ani reminded her, *but you're still helping me. What makes us different?*

*You're sorry.*

*How do you know she isn't? Soren, you have no idea how in control she was at that moment. Sancta only knows what Brae was whispering in her ear. What he was threatening her with.* A pause. A break in her voice. *If anyone is to blame for your and Elias's suffering, it's me.*

"Any of those look good?" Alia asked, a hint of concern in her voice. Soren blinked, eyes burning—how long had she been staring into space, mouthing a conversation to herself?

"Sorry. Yes." She grabbed a random shirt and held the rest back. "This is perfect, thank you."

It wasn't perfect, unless one considered it a perfectly ugly shade of bruised purple. The cotton material was loose and soft and far too large, even for her. Those Petrov boys were born bulky. But it would do for the day.

"Thank you, Alia. And…just so you know, you're welcome here. If anyone ever bothers you, please be sure to tell me." She cleared her throat. Forced herself to wear confidence as her crown. "You're my people, too. You have my protection."

Alia was one of those people who never seemed to fully relax; ever since Soren had met her, she'd carried a tension in her body that never fully let up, a bird constantly prepared to launch itself into the sky, and that hadn't changed—if anything, it seemed to have gotten worse since Atlas. But when Soren said those words, she could've sworn Alia's shoulders eased back just a bit; could've sworn she had tears in her eyes when she said, "Thank you, Princess."

If only she could relax, too. Something about this room, the Atlas clothes in the closet, the angry itch of her sleeves against her sensitive skin…

She shook it off, forcing a smile as she backed out the door. "Thank you, too."

As she left, despite her reluctance, she made a mental note to ensure they searched this room first later on.

***

When another hour passed and Elias still didn't return, Soren mustered what energy she had—which wasn't much, seeing as she hadn't been brought coffee yet—and stomped down to the dining hall to track him down.

She'd expected to find him caught in conversation with Jakob or one of the other company members, chatting about the logistics of the upcoming room search. Instead, she found him in the kitchen, standing over an assortment of steaming pans, his sleeves rolled up and an apron tied loosely around his waist.

Well. That certainly didn't help her appetite.

"What do you think you're doing?" She came in and peered over his shoulder at the assortment of tasks he was juggling—eggs frying in one pan, bacon in another, and the smell of something sugary floating up from the oven itself. Water flooded her mouth, and she went to pull her hair into a ponytail on instinct before her fingers brushed the cropped strands. She let her arms drop, wrapping them around Elias's waist instead. "I thought you were bringing breakfast, not cooking it."

"Seems all the cooks chose to leave. Everyone's been making their own breakfast." Elias shrugged, leaning into her embrace a bit. "Didn't want to come back empty-handed."

"Mm. Smart man." She planted a kiss in the crook of his neck and smirked as heat flushed beneath her lips. "I could get used to this."

"Me in an apron?"

"Exactly that."

"If you keep distracting me," he said, "I'm going to burn the eggs."

"I'll burn your eggs."

"Has anyone ever told you that you need to get better at flirting?"

Soren rolled her eyes, pinching his side until he yelped, batting at her hand with the butter-slick spatula. "No one's ever complained before, jackass."

"Oh? Rian didn't have any notes?"

She pinched his ass this time. "You know exactly why I kissed your cousin, so stop pretending to be jealous."

"No one's pretending." Elias turned around with a raised eyebrow, setting the spatula aside and tugging her closer by her hips, gripping her so tightly that heat flushed up *her* neck. And cheeks. And just about everywhere else. "You wanna try that again?"

"Try what?"

"You know what." He leaned down and kissed her, and she leaned up into it, toe-curling delight spreading through her entire body. She and Ani had already discussed this after leaving Alia's room—Ani had promised to "take her leave" until Soren called for her, having grown pretty good at sinking into her own thoughts and ignoring what Soren was doing on the outside. "Unless you want breakfast to taste like yesterday's pyre, you'll stop being so gods-damned distracting."

"Oh?" She broke the kiss and stepped away, boosting herself up to sit on the counter. She cocked one leg up and arched her back, giving him her best exaggerated pout. "You find this distracting? Does this particular shade of rotten-grape purple suit my complexion?"

"You're ridiculous." But he was grinning from ear to ear. "Where did you get that?"

"Jaxon and Alia's closet. Everything else felt like someone shoved sand up my sleeves."

That grin faded, and his throat bobbed. "Are you still in that much pain?"

"I thought death would finally knock the fussbudget out of you." When he kept frowning at her, waiting on something other than a joke, she slumped forward and dropped back to the floor on her toes. "I've had worse."

"Have you?"

"Getting a blade shoved straight through my stomach was a damn sight worse than sore skin, yes." Though at least the blade had only been accompanied by blood and fever, not a second soul. She tweaked his ear as she slipped around him, heading for the pantry. "You're burning the eggs, remember?"

"Soren…"

She ignored his prodding tone as she padded into the pantry, bending her fingers in order from thumb to pinky as she searched for…anything that would make a good enough excuse for abandoning the conversation.

Her eyes caught on a glass container of cinnamon, and she snatched it up with a huff, turning back around and exiting with all the confidence of someone who had accomplished her well-thought-out mission.

Elias cast a skeptical look at the jar in her hand. "I don't think cinnamon and eggs really go together."

"I'm making toast."

"There's already a tray of cinnamon buns in the oven."

Ah. "Well, you should have mentioned that sooner."

"All right, enough." Elias turned to move the sizzling pans off of their burners, extinguishing the flames with a flick of his hand. He pivoted back to face her, leaning back against the counter and crossing his arms over his chest, pinning her with his most soul-piercing stare. "Out with it. Something is bothering you."

The fight drained out of her before it ever really started, and she crossed over to his side, hopping up onto the counter beside him and resting her head against his. "*Everything* is bothering me."

"Mmhm." He looped an arm around her, resting one hand in the dip of her waist while he used the other to pluck a bit of egg from the skillet and test it on his tongue, the corners of his eyes creasing with assessing attention. "Anything you want to talk about?"

As if she could form coherent words between the hand and the eyes and the apron. "Um."

Great. Now she sounded like Ani.

"No," she finally mumbled. There—that sounded like an answer. She nuzzled her nose into his hair, planting three kisses in a row from his temple to just above his ear, where she whispered, "In fact, I'd prefer it if neither of us were talking just now."

"You have morning breath," he said, "and I probably taste like eggs."

"Well, eat a piece of bacon then. It's nature's best kissing food."

"Pretty sure that's mint."

"How did I end up with a fiancé that doesn't want to kiss me?" she whined.

In a flash of movement, his hands gripped her thighs, tugging her forward until his body was wedged between her legs, her knees level with his hips. Heat flooded her again as his head dipped. As his grip wandered.

"I," he murmured into the hollow of her throat, "will kiss you anywhere but your mouth right now. You get to pick."

Her pulse thrummed like a trilling bird, and she hissed a curse as his hands continued to roam, curling around the back of her and pulling her even closer, his nose brushing up the column of her throat. "Gods *damn* you, Elias," she choked, "where has this been all this time?"

His lips curled into a smile against her skin. "Waiting," he murmured, his breath warm against her throat, but raising goosebumps all the same. Her entire body stood at attention for him. "Just waiting for you to catch up."

"When exactly could I have started having…you know, this?" Whatever this was, this stroking of hands that kept coaxing her cheeks to flush another shade darker.

He paused to think, and she'd never regretted asking a question more. Not if it meant he had to stop to answer it.

"When was that first game of truth or dare, again?" he asked.

"*That long?*" How dull *was* she?

"Well," he said, a bit defensively, "you told me right afterward that I wasn't anything to write home about."

Curse her teenaged, vindictive, lying self. "Is it too late to say I'm sorry?"

"Never too late, smartass." He kissed her on the lips this time, despite his conditions, then he sighed, easing away from her. "All right, enough distractions. Tell me what's going through your head."

"I think you'd combust if I told you what's going through my head. Literally." She mimed an explosion with her hands.

"*Soren.*"

"You're the one who distracted *me*, jackass." But he only kept that probing, uncompromising stare on her. She heaved a sigh, trying to shove down the tingling discomfort that crept up between her ribs, reminding her that she'd never been one to willingly admit her fears.

"Hey. It's all right. Tell me." He took her wrist and tried to tug her close again, but this time...

*Like a puppet waiting for its strings to be tugged.*

"Don't." She yanked her wrist away, clutching it to her chest...closing and opening her fist to be sure her fingers were still obedient.

Elias took another step back now, hands up, alarm—and guilt— immediately darkening his gaze. "I'm so sorry. Did I hurt you?"

She looked at him for so long. Too long. All the feelings, all the thoughts and dreams and wishes, crowding in her head until they drowned out all words.

If she didn't say something soon, he would start taking guesses. And knowing him, those blows would land just a bit too true.

"I think..." A breath that quivered as it passed over her lips. She cleared her throat, squeezing her eyes tightly shut, wishing with all her might that she didn't believe her next words: "I think I might be broken."

There was a beat of silence before Elias took a careful step forward, hands still up. "Can I come closer?"

When she nodded, he braced his hands on either side of her hips, leaning against the counter as he frowned up at her. He didn't say anything more; he simply watched, waiting for her to go on.

And before she knew it, everything was gushing out of her, blood spraying from a cut in some verbal artery.

"I can't breathe sometimes. If someone pushes me or pulls me by the hand somewhere, if I'm forced to go anywhere I don't want to go...I stop breathing. Other times I just...I forget, like I'm waiting for someone else to *make* me breathe." She could barely manage the breath she drew in next, and she bowed forward a bit, resting her forehead against his—anything to not have to look him in the eye for this. "And I can't ever stop moving. Which isn't *new,* really, but it's different. It's…it's like I have to prove…"

"Like you have to prove you're still in control," he said softly.

He'd always been a bit too good at finishing her sentences. "I have to tap my fingers, or—or step in weird patterns, or…I don't know. I can't stop. And I…I wasn't a prisoner, not really. I wasn't caged or tortured. I don't…I don't want to call it *trauma,* I know it's not anything like others have endured in this damned war…" Gods, even the word felt wrong on her tongue, shame flushing up the back of her neck. "But I don't know what else to *call* it, and—"

"Hey," Elias interrupted—not gentle this time. Sharp. Angry. "Cut that shit out right now."

Had…had Elias Loch just sworn at her?

"What?" she said blankly.

"Look at me." When she didn't obey, her gaze hooked on the slightly grimy kitchen tiles, he said it again: "*Look* at me, smartass. Please."

She had never been the best at resisting a *please* from her battlemate. Reluctantly, she lifted her chin to find him gazing at her with such fervor that the flaming circle in his eye had nearly overtaken the black entirely.

"You," he began, reaching up to grip her chin, "have been through *so much,* Soren. Just because they didn't cut wounds into your skin doesn't mean you got out unharmed. Trauma isn't just about visible wounds, and you *know* that. Where's this coming from?"

Her tongue went a bit numb in her mouth, and she mumbled some semblance of an answer under her breath—something between *I don't know* and a noncommittal hum.

"Hey." Elias leaned into her, gently carding his hand through her curls, cradling the back of her head in his ridiculously large hand. "You take nothing away from others who have suffered by acknowledging what's happening to you. You nearly died in Ursa. You were kidnapped—more than once, by the way—and forced to live with people you thought were your enemies. You were attacked by gods-damned dead bodies. You were betrayed by your sister. You watched me die. You were violated; you lost all your autonomy, and when you got it back, your body turned against you. Tortured? You've been *decimated.* And here you are, standing, talking…making terrible jokes about eggs. You have the right to call yourself whatever fits best." He paused, cursing again—softly this time, though, almost tender—and he ran his thumb beneath her eye.

Only then did she feel the hot, ceaseless trails of tears running down her cheeks.

"But one thing you definitely aren't," Elias whispered, kissing away the next tear that fell, "is broken."

"I don't know what to do." A hiccupping sob, and she bent into him, burying her face against his shoulder. "It keeps—it keeps hitting me, over and over, at the strangest times—I feel *ridiculous,* you're wearing an apron and making me breakfast and here I am crying—"

"In Artem," Elias interrupted, "I couldn't sleep in beds."

Soren blinked, leaning back to look at him. "Huh?"

"I slept on the floor every single night after what happened in the temple." A cracked, jagged grin, a poorly formed joke told in the middle of a wake. "I couldn't make myself sleep in a bed without you beside me. Kallias tried everything to get me to change my mind, and I just…couldn't. It felt suffocating. Too warm."

Soren sniffled, wiping at her next deluge of tears herself. "I thought you hated my cold feet."

"But I love the little faces you make when you sleep. I love waking up to your snores—"

"I don't—"

"You do, stop it—and I love waking up to you wearing my clothes. No matter how much I pretended to hate it. And when it was all gone…" He shook his head with a hushed huff of breath. "Trauma doesn't care for what makes sense. It's all about survival at first, and after that, the best thing we can do for ourselves is to be willing to seek out better ways to cope…and forgiving ourselves for not being able to do it as quickly as we'd like."

"How do I find better ways?"

"I found out that talking helped. To Kallias, mostly, but Raquel and Havi, too." Elias shrugged a shoulder—the unscarred one. Come to think of it, she wasn't sure he'd ever stopped favoring the once-injured one.

Maybe they were both carrying wounds that no longer showed on their flesh.

Soren cleared her throat, forcing a breath in through her nose and out through her mouth.

*Breathe in. Breathe out. Control what you can.*

"Maybe…maybe I'll talk to Ember again," she whispered. "We started to, but I didn't…I wasn't able to…"

"It's okay. You don't owe anyone an explanation, all right? Least of all me. And you know I'm here, too. I'll always listen." Elias hesitated. "Can I help you down?"

The fact that he'd *asked* warmed her heart more than he would ever know. "Please." Then, before he did: "I want to listen to you, too. All of it. Whenever you're ready."

He helped her down, enveloping her in his arms for a long moment before gently twirling her around to face the stove, wrapping his arms around her waist and planting kisses along her shoulders until her tears were replaced with laughter, until they both gathered plates and went back up to her room, wrapping up in her blankets and picking off of each other's plates as they ate.

And as they ate, they talked. About all the things they'd realized they missed while they were apart; all the strange new habits they'd picked up without noticing until someone else pointed them out; all the nightmares they couldn't quite shake.

Later, there would be another fruitless search of the palace. Later, Ani would beg forgiveness for the fourth or fifth or seventy-eighth time, unable to block out *all* the thoughts and emotions buzzing through Soren's head. Later, Soren would remind her that she had already been forgiven, and ask her if perhaps there was anything *she* needed to talk about.

Later, Ani would tell her about black licorice bribes and sugarplum bruises and a downfall so swift and tumultuous she could barely remember it.

Later, Soren would tell her about daggers plunged into Elias's stomach and threats doused in desperation and her sister's green eyes turning gold as she broke every oath she'd ever sworn over Soren's grave.

But that was later. For now, she had breakfast in bed with her best friend, her battlemate, her betrothed.

And for the first time in a long time, she was able to take a true, deep breath.

# CHAPTER 42

# SOREN

The next week crawled by on rickety, arthritic legs, and Soren was about ten seconds away from going out and starting a bar fight just to get some energy out. No chaos magic necessary; just her being so gods-damned *bored*.

Not that there were bars open to start fights in, but she'd figure *something* out.

They'd searched the castle methodically over the past few days, leaving no chamber unswept, no cupboard unsearched, no person uninterrogated. She and Anima had continued to practice switching control back and forth; by now, it was more of a mental struggle than a physical one. Neither of them enjoyed the feeling of being pushed back into the nether-realm of their head, but they both had to admit it was working—they hadn't had another fit in days, and though they continued to wake up each day marginally weaker than the last, the decline was far less steep than it had been. And the chaos-corrupted biomantic vines had finally withered away, leaving behind gnarled scars where they'd sprouted from her skin.

These scars were different than most. Twisted, strange, like knots in a tree.She couldn't help rubbing her fingertip over them as she slumped at the war table, staring emptily at the dusty map of the six kingdoms.

Huffing out a sigh, she melted into her best approximation of a puddle on the table, planting her face in the wood.

The barest traces of life still flickered deep inside its core, and in dying whispers, it told her of its once-grand existence. How it had once been a tree towering high in the mountains, caped in snow, standing proudly with a crown of ice and—

Soren smacked her hands over her ears, groaning into the wood. "Let go!" she moaned against the lacquer. "Go into the light already, or—or the dirt, or whatever trees see when they die!"

*It's lonely,* Ani scolded her. *It's nearly gone. There's nothing wrong with wanting to be remembered.*

"I am not going to sit here feeling bad for a *tree.*" There were bigger things to worry over—considerably bigger things. "Ani, we need that relic."

*I know. But whoever is carrying it, they're doing so carefully. I can't see traces of chaos corruption on any of them.*

"How long can they keep that up?"

*Depends on how many precautions they're taking. If they hear the melody every time, not much longer. If they're careful enough to not hear it at all…it could go on for a while.*

If she could have slouched any further, she would have. "Fabulous."

A beat. *Your brothers will have likely moved on toward Sirena by now. It might come to a choice soon, Soren.*

A fist closed over her heart. "I know." But the thought of abandoning her company, her sister, even Ravenna… "Maybe whoever it is would follow us out. If Brae actually wants you, anyway."

*If it was only about reclaiming his relic, this all would've been over by now. Without me, his odds of winning are worse.* A note of bitterness washed over Ani's voice, a chilling bite of pine and rot. *Without me, he only has Cassi, and she's known to be fickle. My presence evens the field.*

"Soren?"

Ice clapped her over the head, dousing her in cold as Ravenna's voice reached her, tentative and quiet.

"Yes?" she asked, without raising her head.

"Are you, ah…"

"No."

"I thought not." Ravenna's slippers pattered against the floor; the protesting screech of chair legs came next, and her pant leg brushed against Soren's. "What's the worry?"

A dry laugh rasped out of her throat. Without looking up, she splayed one hand in the general direction of the map. "What isn't?"

"Thinking about your brothers?"

Ugly, rancid anger tried to twist her insides; the first words that leapt to her tongue were *You don't get to talk about them.*

"Yes," she said instead. "And Yvonne. And my…my parents."

Silence reigned over the war room for a moment, the kind of silence that coaxed a ringing sound into one's ears. Then Ravenna's warm hand settled on her shoulder.

"I knew your parents," she said softly. "A long time ago. They were a rare thing in those days—a queen and king-consort united in mind and purpose. Stronger together than apart. They are not a city easily sieged. They won't fall."

"That's what I'm afraid of," she admitted, finally raising her head—only enough to see Atlas's shoreline on the map through the slit of her half-open eyelids. "That Tenebrae will demand they bow, then kill them when they won't."

"Bowing is different than falling," Ravenna said. "Many people bow to bide their time. I did it with my father. Adriata…your mother…she's a clever queen and a cleverer warrior. And your father was never one to favor pride over sense."

"A trait we don't share," Soren mumbled, and Ravenna laughed.

"Maybe not, but you two share more than you might think. I saw much of them in you as you grew up, even without your memories. Adriata's stubbornness. Ramses's smile." A pause. "Soren, I should have told you the truth."

"I don't want to hear another apology," Soren whispered. Not angry. Just tired. So tired of pity, so tired of worry, so tired of guilt.

"Then I won't apologize. All I want to say is…" Ravenna paused again, and at the catch in her breath, Soren realized the Queen of Nyx was fighting tears.

There was a unique trait that so many daughters shared—an absolute inability to bear their mother's tears, even in anger. No matter how justified the rage or how long they had been carrying it, there was no escape from the irrational surge of *feeling* birthed from those crystalline tears, those trembling breaths.

There was no better word for it than *panic,* or maybe *pain,* or some cross between the two—some fearful form of guilt, a frantic wish to snatch their words back and make it all better. The daughterly repayment for kisses on scraped knees and tangles coaxed loose and lullabies sung over and over until sleep finally found its mark.

Soren clenched her fists against the sickening swoop of her stomach, stinging tears needling her behind the eyes.

"What I did was wrong," Ravenna whispered, "and I make no excuse for it. I don't ask for forgiveness…I don't deserve it, and I'm not sure I ever could. I did what I believed to be right, but I also did what I knew to be selfish."

Soren squeezed her eyes shut. Fought down a sob. Fought down the urge to turn and hug her, to tell her it was all right; because it wasn't, and it never could be, no matter how much she ached to *try.*

"What I need you to know," Ravenna whispered, "is that you were never an act of war. Not to me. You were never a strategy, never a bargaining chip. You were mine in my heart, as much as your sisters are. And though I wish…for your sake, I wish things had been different, I will *never* regret getting the chance to love you."

Something inside her crumbled. A foundation to a grudge only half-built, a flimsy attempt at hatred that had always been shaped more like obligation.

An anger that had always felt more like a shadow of Adriata than the truth of Soren.

"It was just supposed to be another battle," she choked. "We were supposed to come straight home. It was supposed to be *normal.*"

She could not regret remembering her family. She could not regret surviving. But she regretted how long she had wasted hating them. She regretted not saying her proper goodbyes, neither as a child nor before Anima's presence.

Hate had never gained her anything. It had only cost her time.

A knot tied in the base of Soren's throat, and she barely choked out words past it: "Mama, I don't know what to *do.*"

Now Ravenna's composure crumbled, and when she reached out, Soren did not have the will to push her away. The arms of her mother wrapped around her until cold was nothing but a distant memory, and she squeezed her eyes shut, hot tears tracing stinging paths down cheeks covered in scattered scratches.

"I should hate you," Soren sobbed. "I should *hate you.*"

"I know," was all Ravenna said. "It's all right."

For a moment, there was silence—silence, because Soren could not bring herself to admit the truth:

That she did not, nor could she ever, hate Ravenna.

That in spite of her memories, in spite of the truth, the only person she wanted to talk to about all her hidden fears was her mother.

"It's my fault," she said—hadn't meant to say. It burst out like a hound freed from its cage, intent on hunting down the truth of the emotion that had plagued her since she'd woken from her journey through her memories. "All of it. I...gods, I kept remembering, Mama. I kept remembering, and it didn't *matter*, I couldn't hold onto it I couldn't fight it and I still..."

And she still couldn't fight it.

One goddess to steal her memories. Another to steal her strength. One setting the stage for Jericho's manipulation by ensuring Soleil Atlas stayed dead...the other meant to help Tenebrae finish the rest of his plans.

Anima might be helping them now, but the damage was done—gods knew when Soren's body would break beneath both souls, and if they couldn't reach Arborius in time to try Elias's half-formed plan to separate them...

Not strong enough to survive Anima. Not strong enough to cling to memories of her family.

Not strong enough to have told Tenebrae *no* when he demanded her body as the asking price for her battlemate's life.

At every stage of this gods-damned plan, she had handed Tenebrae the tools he needed to get this far. To manipulate Jericho, to give Anima a body, and now...

She couldn't slow her breathing, gasps so shallow she might as well have been breathing water. Her fist curled into her shirt, tugging to loosen the neckline, to take pressure off of her chest. "I...I need to go."

Ravenna didn't try to stop her. Maybe she knew there was no breath left in that room for her to breathe, not enough air to fuel the heavier confessions left inside her.

She barely made it into the hall before that lump in her throat choked her entirely, cutting off any attempts at a deep breath. The walls blurred around her as she hurried down the hall, wiping at those same cursed tears that never seemed to dry up, quietly cursing herself and her eyes and that gods-damned whiny table—

As she passed the door to the entrance foyer of the palace, a muffled shout came from beyond, tugging her to a sudden halt.

"Did you hear that?" she whispered.

*We share ears, Soren,* Ani reminded her, with considerably less sarcasm than Soren would've wielded. Still sharper than Ani usually spoke, though. *What's going on out there?*

She waited with bated breath, pressing her ear to the wood—then jumping back with a cry she only just managed to bite down, blood creeping out to coat her taste buds.

The door was *blazing* hot.

Memories blew through her with the force of an oaken battering ram, sticking like splinters in the creases of her mind—an Atlas ballroom, a crooning violin, flames wrapping spined hands around her ankles and calves, dancing about the hem of her twirling skirt.

*Fire.* The castle was on fire.

Knees on the ground. Palms pressed into the carpet. Lungs grasping for any gasp of air they could reach, a retch of panic nearly throwing her down entirely—

She'd collapsed on the hall floor.

"Soren!" Footsteps increased in speed as they came towards her, Ravenna's voice raised in alarm. "What happened?"

"Mama," came her reply, coughed out past the memory of smoke, her eyes glued to the door. "Something's on fire, something—"

Without another word, Ravenna rushed to the door, placing her own hand against it. Her lips drew up in a faint snarl, but her eyes glazed over with focus, thoughts flickering behind them like stars winking in and out.

"Move back," she said, and Soren obeyed, only just managing to force enough strength into her limbs to drag herself up. Adrenaline dug its fingers into her bones and shook them, rattling her straight to her core, thrill after thrill of pure, unadulterated terror anchoring her heels to the carpet.

*Not again, not again, not again…*

Ravenna rolled her shoulders and raised her hands in the air, squeezing her eyes shut.

The air changed—charged not with smoke, not with heat, but with something else. Something pressured and humming and *eager*, an energy crackling across invisible channels, called to this place by Ravenna's outstretched fingers.

Aeromancy—a power she had only rarely seen her mother wield.

With a swift, silent motion, Ravenna threw her hand forward, the energy surging out with it.

The crack that followed both blinded and deafened—a flash of light and sound and *power* that Soren barely managed to shield herself from. When she lowered her arms, the door had utterly split, hanging in pieces off its hinges, and beyond…

Fire, like she'd expected. But within those flames…

"Elias!" she screamed, but her battlemate didn't look up.

He was standing in the center of a torrent of flame, circling around the perimeter, mimicked by a man standing across from him; one of the generals who'd volunteered to stay behind, the one who had made a sideways comment about her being Atlas in one of their meetings. His face was twisted into a hungry smile, eyes empty, hands wrapped around the hilt of his massive warhammer.

Soren's stomach dropped so far, she was half sure it must've taken a dip in the pits of Infera before jumping back up to settle in her throat. At the very least, her scream burned on its way out as she called again for Elias, all thoughts of the fire vanishing.

This was his doing; he would not allow the flames to harm her. But judging by the scattered bodies around him—judging by the scorched tatters of his shirt hanging off his body—he had both dealt death and only just escaped it.

They hadn't tested the limits of Mortem's death-defying blessing. Sure, blood wounds could burn shut, but if that hammer crushed his heart? His *head?* Could fire fix *that?*

She didn't know, and she wasn't like Elias; she didn't have faith, didn't know how to be certain of things she hadn't yet seen—

The general laughed as he advanced on Elias, swinging wildly without form or finesse—nothing like she'd seen him fight before, but that wasn't a blessing. They had long ago memorized the fighting patterns of many higher-ups in the army; if the general had been predictable, she could have made a plan. She could have anticipated where he would go, what he would try.

But this was Chaos carrying a hammer outfitted with gods-damned spikes; this was Chaos flinging that hammer toward Elias's head, her battlemate distracted and searching for her amongst flame and smoke and—

Warmth.

Not burning, not scorch, but warmth—that was what flooded her as she stared at the hammer, at Elias, at the death barreling toward him with nothing in its way.

Fire would not stop a hammer. Blood magic could not halt its path.

"*Stop him!*" Not just her voice roaring that command—Ani's softer tones braided in with it, a tandem scream from goddess and girl.

Sunlight blazed through their veins; light become life, life become verdant vines of power as they threw one hand out…

The magic reached with them. The magic sought. The magic searched.

The magic found.

At first, when one of the dead soldiers on the floor leapt to his feet and staggered into the hammer's path, the crunching of bone and the give of flesh beneath metal made her think that maybe she had been mistaken. Maybe the soldier had not been killed by Elias, though he bore burns that suggested otherwise; maybe he'd merely been knocked senseless and had gotten up to chase the call of what chaos remained. Ani had told her many victims of chaos magic eventually took their own lives by accident.

But then the soldier, his entire skull crushed inward, a mashed-up mess of blood and brain and bone, stood up once more.

He *stood up*. Met their gaze, his eyes half-obscured by his crumpled, broken brow.

His eyes were empty. Dead. Brain matter littered the floor, decorating the tiles in gore, and yet he did not flinch.

He merely stared. As if waiting for an order. As if…

Shivering, shocked, sick straight to her center, Soren's gaze trailed to her outstretched hand.

To the tendrils of revolting green magic that twined lazily around her knuckles, stretched out between her and the dead man like strings on a broken marionette.

So.

Necromancy felt like sunlight.

# CHAPTER 43

# ELIAS

At first, when the sound of crunching bone sounded *so* close to him, Elias was utterly certain he had been killed.

Blood splashed his face and soaked his hair. No pain, but the squishy bits of matter splattered over him told him that something *extremely* vital had been bashed open.

He couldn't bring himself to open his eyes. Gods knew why he could still breathe, why he could still hear and smell and *feel*, but he refused to try and look—refused to have the last thing he saw be his own head in pieces around him.

"Elias!"

Not Mortem, greeting him for his final rest, surely disappointed at how very short his run as Phoenix Priest had been.

*Soren.*

His eyes leapt open to see the hammer swinging toward him again, the chaos-crazed general baring bloodied teeth.

*"Move, jackass!"* roared his battlemate's voice.

He could figure out why he wasn't dead later. First, he needed to obey that order.

He only just managed to duck out of the way, rolling sideways, trying desperately not to think about what exactly he was rolling *through*. Shoving his palms down into the floor, he pushed himself back up in one powerful surge, wasting just enough time to find his battlemate in the fray—

And his heart clean stopped.

Soren stood just outside the room, her hand outstretched, familiar green threads of magic tied around each of her knuckles. And when he met her gaze...

One green eye.

One gold.

"Get over here!" she shrieked—*they* shrieked, Anima's softer timbre layered in with Soren's barking shout.

Heart in his throat, stomach threatening to spill itself out on the gore-streaked floor, Elias sprinted to her side, gripping her by the shoulder. "Soren—"

"Later," she panted, eyes fixed on the scene before her.

"Your eyes—"

*"Later!"*

There was nothing else to do but obey; no time to consider it, anyway, because Hann had lurched around to face them again, expression calm—near gleeful—as he beheld the man tottering before him, blood and brain matter streaked down his broken skull and neck.

Elias's stomach turned upside-down. And when Soren stretched her fingers in the imitation of a puppeteer's talon-like grasp, shouting a command across the room—"Don't let him pass!"—he could only watch in mute horror as the dead man obeyed, limbs jerking in time with Soren's minute movements.

When he dared glance at her face, it did not share his horror. Only a grim, settled sort of understanding. An acceptance.

It was over in the blink of her dual-colored eyes. But she did not grant the general the mercy of death, not yet; instead she guided the dead soldier to rest with one hand while coaxing newly birthed vines to life with the other, asking them in a two-toned voice to bind the general hand and foot and mouth.

Elias had watched her perform far more gruesome acts. Had watched her disembowel an Atlas woman who'd gotten a hair too close to landing her blow in one of his major organs. Had watched her scrub blood and bits of organ from her hair and hands. Had watched her strangle the life out of an assassin barehanded when he'd made the mistake of crawling into Ravenna's chambers while he and Soren were on guard duty.

This sight shouldn't have left him with shaking knees and vomit pooling in the back of his throat. But horror did not care for what had come before; it did not care for what might have been worse, what he was already used to.

All he could see was Vaughn, haggard and shattered, holding half-wilted flowers in his hands and praying for a healing that would never come. All he could see was Vaughn, shouting at Jericho somewhere in the whirlwind of blood and death and confession at that same altar, pleading with her to let him be gone as green magic twined around his fingers.

All he could see was Soren, her skin pocked with bruises and scars, her eyes framed by those same sickly shadows. Her fingers twined in those same verdant cords of magic.

Movement drew his attention away from his battlemate, and he found Ravenna standing beside him. Her hand was outstretched too, as if she'd been preparing an attack of her own—she was Tempest-blessed, though that wasn't common knowledge—but though she hadn't lowered her hand, her eyes were firmly arrested on Soren, her brows furrowed deeply over her dark eyes.

"I didn't know she could do that," breathed the Queen.

"She can't." He swallowed horror despite its rotten taste, forcing sense to take its place. "But Anima can."

Necromancy was a death sentence, but maybe not for its original wielder. Surely Anima couldn't perish from her own magic.

Mortem couldn't burn. Tempest couldn't drown. Surely Anima couldn't rot.

As uninfected guards—a handful of the slightly larger handful that still remained—came and helped with the restrained general, Soren let her hand drop.

The dead man fell with it just before the others came in; Soren stared at the fallen body mutely, her lips pursed, her eyes hollow.

Heart in throat, Elias approached cautiously, measuring his footsteps to ensure he didn't startle her. He reached out and gathered her hand into his, twining their fingers. Her hand was cold.

"Hey," he said softly, giving her a gentle shake. "Are you with me, smartass?"

She only stared, brow bent inward, gold and green eyes fixed on the dead guard. On his bashed-in head, still leaking fluid and worse. On his uniform, so carefully pressed at every corner and fold, not a wrinkle in sight even now.

At his hand, where a golden band shone beneath a veneer of scarlet.

"I know him," she whispered in that shared voice, Anima and Soren speaking together. Every muscle in his body went stiff, but he resisted the urge to throw her hand aside. She needed him; Soren needed him, even if Anima made everything strange and twisted and *hard.* "He taught me and the other recruits in my class how to care for our armor properly. His daughter is in the Moonstone company. He was so proud of her, but you could tell he worried…"

Ravenna came closer, eyes fixed on the general, who was still struggling against his bonds.

"What's wrong?" Elias asked.

"We searched your barracks, didn't we?" Ravenna asked slowly.

"Only half a dozen times," Soren croaked. "Why?"

"That's where I sent General Hann this afternoon. Jaxon was finally ready to debrief us about his time in Port Atlas."

He cursed under his breath. "Ravenna, I swear to the gods, I searched his quarters inch by inch—"

"I know," Ravenna interrupted. "Elias, I hardly blame you. There was never any reason to question him again—him or Alia. But I'd say we have cause now."

He turned to Soren, waiting for her to speak—but she hadn't yet torn her gaze from the dead soldier on the floor.

"Soren."

She finally turned to look at him, blinking away the gold in her left eye, so suddenly serious that dread seeped into his gut.

"I'm not leaving," she said. "Not until this is over."

No one had asked her to, but he didn't say so. "We can't stay forever. Kallias—"

"Kallias will *wait*." She said it like an order, not a hope. A command that Kallias might somehow hear across miles and miles of separation. Fury lit her eyes with driftwood fire, green and wrathful and war-ready. "Tenebrae already has Atlas. He will *not* have Nyx, too."

"What are you planning?" Because he could see it brewing already, the beginnings of one of those *Soren* plans that were notorious for almost getting them both killed. Or worse.

"Find Jakob and get the rest of the company together." Soren turned away from him with a snap of her heel, not wasting another glance on the bloody scene she left behind her as she stalked away. "Tell them it's an order from their princess. And if any of them argues, remind them that we had the highest death toll in the company *before* we were gods-blessed."

"Where are you going?"

She kept walking, tossing her answer over her shoulder: "To find a gods-damned traitor."

# CHAPTER 44

# KALLIAS

Kallias woke to wilting flowers in his hair and a vaguely Raquel-shaped bundle of blankets beside him.

He propped himself up on his elbow, letting his gaze wander over her: the healing scars on her bare back, the soft sound of her sleeping breaths, the glimmer of crystal-light on the bracelet she now wore on her left wrist. Leaning over, he brushed his lips against her temple, breathing in the scent of petrichor and wind, careful not to stir her to waking.

Waking meant facing the truth: that no matter how long he delayed, no matter how well he pretended, a goodbye was fast approaching. Ignoring it wouldn't make it go away.

He'd asked for a reason to stay. She hadn't given him one.

That was that.

As he let himself fall back to his side of the bed, a sudden wave of discomfort flowed over him, a sickly shiver akin to fever chills.

He'd been hiding it well—at least, he guessed he was, because neither Finn nor Raquel seemed to notice—but the awful dryness was creeping back. The magic contained inside Tempest's relic was leeching the water straight from his blood, leaving him constantly thirsty, constantly hot, desperate for relief and finding none.

All at once, the warmth of Raquel's body and the rasp of sheet against his irritated skin was too much. He practically leapt from the bed, shuddering as morning air cooled the sweat on his back.

It was time to stop ignoring his problems.

It was time to talk to Tempest.

He tugged on his borrowed trousers, sparing half a thought to wonder what his mother would think if she saw him now: wearing loose, patchy trousers and no shirt; sailing on a pirate ship filled to the brim with deserters, making friendly bets with its captain; leaving a bed he'd shared with a Nyxian warrior.

Gods, he'd probably re-break the record for her longest rant.

The smile that started to spread at that thought withered quickly as Jericho's snickering grin flickered through his mind. She'd always been sympathetic, but she'd also delighted in watching her brothers take well-deserved queenly tongue-lashings. Probably because she'd rarely earned one herself. Oldest siblings knew exactly how to tiptoe their way around a parent's wrath—and how to ensure their younger siblings never got away with the same.

He missed her. So badly that it almost drowned out the pain of this ever-thirsting magic.

Jericho would have known what to do. She would have known how to manage his magic. How to conquer the enormous task left before them.

She would have, if she wasn't the reason they were suffering through it in the first place.

It wasn't fair. It wasn't right. *Us before all* had never been some trite little saying to him—it had been a heart-vow, a creed, something he would have died rather than break.

Jericho had chosen a different vow: Vaughn before all. Herself before Atlas.

And the worst part of it all was that when he'd placed that bracelet on Raquel's wrist, when he'd looked her in the eyes and whispered *Say the word, and you have me*…he'd made the same choice, if only briefly. Raquel before all. Himself before Atlas.

Raquel's soft rejection had saved him from making his older sister's choice. But that didn't mean it hadn't hurt. It didn't mean he wasn't *still* hurting.

He shook off those grim thoughts in favor of grimmer ones, blowing out a breath as he stepped out of his cabin, closing the door lightly to avoid waking Raquel. It was time to stop running. Time to act like a prince. To face his enemy head-on.

He found a secluded section of the deck and swung himself up on the edge of the ship, dangling his legs over the water without a thought, his body instinctively tensing and bending a bit to accommodate the swaying beneath it. Out of practice or not, he knew how to move with the ocean. The saltwater in his blood had not diluted over these months away.

They had passed from the river to the ocean in the night. Maybe that was why his discomfort had rushed back so potently this morning.

"That's one reason, yes."

Wariness pulled his spine straight, and his fingers dug into the wood so hard that it creaked in protest. He kept his eyes straight ahead even as a presence crept up to his side—like someone was sitting beside him on the edge of the hull.

"Hello, Tempest," he said quietly.

The god's thunderous chuckle made him wish desperately for Elias to be here, god-killing weapon in hand. Or even without the weapon. Anything to have a friend at his back. "Hello, Prince."

"It's getting worse again."

"I know. That's not going to stop." A flicker of grayish fur out of the corner of his eye. A hint of black hair, of ocean eyes, of skin the color of walnut wood. "I would like to be frank with you, Kallias, if you'll let me."

"Please." At this point, honesty was all he wanted. Even if it hurt. Even if it ruined him.

Tempest sighed, and as he did, the wind blew harder—a chilled breeze that carried the scent of pine and river and sea salt. "Tenebrae is not only trying to subjugate your kingdoms. What he has planned will not only be the end of Atlas, of Nyx and Arborius and Lapis and Tallis and Artem. He wishes to walk the earth as a god once again."

"Right." Impatience thinned Kallias's tone to near-snapping. "We knew that. That's why he wants Jericho."

"No, that's why he *needs* Jericho. He needs a host in order to reach his true end, but having a host is not that end." Tempest's voice darkened. "He wishes to regain his first body while retaining his immortality."

"I don't understand—"

"Which is why I'm explaining it," Tempest cut him off. "Gods, royals haven't changed in the last few hundred years, have they?"

Kallias scowled, but he stayed quiet. This wasn't the time to fight, and Tempest wasn't someone to pick a fight with even if it was.

"There are checks and balances to our power. When we were mortal, we possessed great power, but we weren't truly gods—we could be killed like any other human. It wasn't much of a worry—we were revered around the kingdoms, and more powerful than any other magic wielder. We never thought to fear for ourselves." A slight tremor accompanied Tempest's next exhale. "But then we lost Ani. It was an accident…a carriage crash, of all things.

"That was when we discovered her resurrective magic, something connected to her necromancy…it was barely an hour after her death that she revived, her magic saving her, but the damage was done. Tenebrae was determined that it could never happen again. So he sought to make us true gods—immortal and untouchable.

"It wasn't natural, and Mora and I knew the consequences would be far more dire than we were prepared for. We opposed him, but Ani was so traumatized by her death that she fell on his side, and Occassio…" Tempest's voice dipped lower, and Kallias recognized the tone it took—the fond, pained frustration of an older brother worried for a misguided younger sibling. He'd worn it himself on multiple occasions on Finn's behalf. "She was always ambitious, always enjoyed power. And she never said, but I think she saw which side was going to win out. She was never one to side with a lost cause.

"Tenebrae succeeded, but in doing so, he threw off the balance that nature had struck with us—without our powers being tempered by our mortality, the scale tipped too far in our favor. So the old gods set us back in balance by ripping away our bodies. We were more powerful than ever, undying, eternal…with no way to walk the world. No way to live our lives.

"Ani and Tenebrae were closest to the ritual, so their forms were the least corporeal. Occassio was close as well, but her magic allows her to appear in spite of it. I obviously have limited presence, and Mortem does as well, but her magic also allowed her to resist complete removal from this plane. That's how we've existed for centuries as true gods…but it's not enough for Tenebrae. He wants it all—our bodies, our immortality, and our power. Hosts limit our power. Our immortality stole away our bodies. And to have our bodies back, we would have to give up our immortality." Tempest's voice dropped to a near-growl now. "But Tenebrae seems convinced that he's discovered a way to have them all—to make us gods in the flesh, able to rule to world as well as be worshipped by it. And if he succeeds, Kallias, this world will break beneath the weight of our power. Nature is not meant to contain something so out of balance. It will be the end of all things."

As if to drive his dire warnings home, a blade of sheer cold drove itself through Kallias's stomach, setting shivers rattling through every bone. He covered his mouth with both hands, staring out at the ocean…in the direction he somehow knew Port Atlas waited. He didn't need a compass, didn't need a map. His heart pointed just as true.

"How do we stop him?" Even the question seemed pointless. What could men do against gods? Tallis's god-killer was no more than rumor, and if it didn't prove to be more…

"Gathering the relics will slow him down—he seems to require them for whatever ritual he plans to perform. But you cannot stop him." Pity took the place of anger now, apology and truth landing blow after ruthless blow against Kallias's resolve. "Only the gods can stop a god, Prince. I find no pleasure in taking hosts— it's an affront to nature, and I despise it. This isn't about power, and it isn't a trick. If it was not a necessity, I would never ask. But I have a responsibility to stop my brother's plans. I have a duty to those who pray to me for protection. I will not let my people down. I'm asking you to help me fulfill that responsibility—and in return, I *will* protect your people as my own. Your family as if they were mine. You have my vow."

His vow.

There was no way to know if Tempest's word was one he could trust. But though he searched for it with every inkling of his strength, though he begged and pleaded for a hint of deception to shine through…he found nothing. The god's voice never dipped into deceit.

Kallias believed him. And that made this choice even gods-damned *harder*.

"Not today," he whispered finally. "Not…not yet. Please. I want…I want to see my home."

*One last time* was what he didn't say, but Tempest seemed to hear it anyway.

"Of course. There isn't a rush. You have time so long as you keep ahead of him with the relics…I will tell you if that changes." He could've sworn he felt a squeeze on his shoulder, a touch from fingers so cold they relieved just a hint of the heat weighing down his skin. "Take your time, Prince. Say your goodbyes as you go. Do what you must to be ready. You are in control of this, every step from here to home."

He might have laughed if he wasn't desperately shoving back the lump in his throat. This was not control. This was inevitability. The only choice he had was how fast or slow to walk this path to its conclusion.

"And if you wish to alleviate your discomfort," Tempest added, "I suggest taking a swim."

Before he could say anything more, the wind blew once more, a hardy gust that nearly knocked him from his perch. And when he turned to look to his right, there was nothing beside him but empty air.

# CHAPTER 45

# ANIMA

*Chaos came in the blink of an eye, and no one ever knew until it was too late.*

*It looked like the twitch of a lip. A smile that lasted a hint too long. A hollowness to the eye, a shift of the shoulder, a shadow to the face.*

*Chaos was quick. And no one ever saw it coming.*

Still, Ani found she couldn't stop looking for it—couldn't stop picking apart each member of the company as they filed in, lingering too long on every sleepless eye and chew-chapped lip, every fidgeting finger and wandering gaze. But chaos could disguise itself as a lot of things, and she could hardly consider herself qualified to separate ordinary nerves from ill intent.

*What are you going to do?* she asked Soren, who had yet to calm after the earlier…incident.

It hadn't been a plan; it had hardly been a rotting choice. One moment, they'd been separate: Ani in the back, Soren in control.

The next, it had been…different.

Neither in control; neither out of it. Like their souls had melded rather than layered, no longer oil and water but raindrops falling into the same puddle.

*Something pretty stupid,* Soren admitted, tapping her fingers against the maps splayed out before her. She had claimed the seat at the head of the war table, despite Ravenna also being part of this meeting; however, the Queen hadn't seemed perturbed about give up her position. She'd merely taken her seat to Soren's right, leaving the left open for Elias.

Beside him was Emberlyn, who was glancing between her sister and her mother with a look that was harder to read than a Sanctaviv scripture. The rest of the chairs were quickly taken up by the company—Jakob, Varran, Samhain, Rian, and Kriss, who gave a wave Ani somehow knew was meant for her—as well as Jaxon and Alia, who sat at the far end of the table, having been escorted in by Soren herself. Alia glanced at the Queen, who smiled at her; even so, the Atlas girl shrank into Jaxon's side, swallowing as if someone had stuck an acorn down her throat.

Ani couldn't help feeling the same way, even though she wasn't currently in control of swallowing the lump forming in their own throat.

Soren wasn't often nervous.

It didn't bode well, to say the least.

"Everyone, sit," Soren commanded, and even Jakob obeyed without question, his eyes trained on her with the usual order-ready stance of a soldier. "We're getting to the bottom of this. Now."

"How?" Rian demanded; his hair was rumpled, his eyes bleary, as if he'd been pulled out of bed—though it was still early in the evening, especially for Nyx. Maybe he'd been napping. He and Elias, though distinctly separate in personality, looked very similar when they first woke up. "We've already searched the castle inch by inch. Unless a beetle scurried off with the music box—"

"I don't think it's hidden away in the castle," Soren said. Ani flinched at just how sharply the words kicked off her tongue, at just how much Soren's belief in them weighed on her. "I think whoever has it has been moving it in between searches. And I think one of you has it on your person right now."

Ani had walked through houses filled with no one but the dead. She'd had to sleep with a jar of trapped crickets beside her bed for weeks after, the thick silence of those homes-turned-crypts haunting her every moment.

Even that silence was not so absolute as this one.

"I don't want to be right," Soren croaked. "In fact, it's the very last thing I want. But the person who has the relic is sitting in this room…and if you speak up now, I promise you that I will find a way to help you get free of it."

Elias, ever the sensible complement to Soren's risky reaches, was already probing Jaxon's face with his dark eyes, seeking flinches or tells…the others were doing the same to those sitting around them, uncertainty and disbelief warring in their eyes.

In fact, the only person not seeking a traitor in the faces of their friends was Kriss, who said with all the confidence of someone proclaiming an absolute truth: "There is no. Damned. Way."

Soren ground their teeth together, pushing back against Ani's protests before spitting out venom of her own: "Kriss, I don't have time to argue with you."

"I'm not arguing. I'm *telling* you that your paranoia is out of control if you think you can waltz your Atlas ass around and start tossing accusations at *us*. We've been your family for ten years, Princess. None of this shit started until *you* came back."

"A theory that would hold plenty of water, if Elias and I weren't already under the jurisdiction of other gods."

"Right. And we only have you to trust on that matter." Kriss bit her lip, expression softening a bit. "No offense, Ani."

"Kriss, I'm not accusing you, or anyone else in this company," Soren snapped. "There's only three of us in this room who have been in Atlas, Ursa, and now here. Three people who were in Tenebrae's space, who passed through Ursa before its corruption, and arrived here before everything went bad."

Every eye in the room shifted to Jaxon and Alia—well, almost every eye.

"Jakob's the one who acted up," Rian said—immediately followed by a swift slap on the shoulder from Samhain.

"I'll strip down right here," Jakob said, almost like he was hoping they'd agree. He looked Soren dead in the eye, one eyebrow raised. "Say the word, Princess. I've got nothing to hide."

"Gods have *mercy*, Jake," Varran groaned, burying his face in his hands, "this is *serious*."

"If you're going to say it," said Jaxon, his dark tone silencing the mutters floating through the room, "then say it, Princess. I know you're looking at me for this. Just ask."

"It can't be him," Jakob snapped, all humor vanishing like mist. He stood to his feet, already bristling, a wolf ready to defend its packmate with nothing but its teeth. "Soren, I was with him the whole time—"

"I would love to be wrong," Soren countered softly. "Can you tell me I'm wrong, Jaxon?"

Jaxon gazed back at her—at them—but something about the look in his eyes struck Ani wrong. There was guilt there, certainly—she had been wrestling with that particular emotion enough lately to recognize it in another—but not malice. Not unease. Not the look of someone who'd been caught in a betrayal.

Instead, there was sorrow. Resignation. He tightened his hold around Alia's shoulders, his mouth opening…

A squelching sound broke the silence. A sound so familiar to both Anima and Soren that they caught their breath in tandem, gaze instinctively darting to Elias, terror lighting them up from the inside as memory invaded, memory of Artemisian steel plunging into his belly, his blood soaking through Soren's hands—

But Elias was already standing, his mouth forming the beginnings of a shout, his hand going toward his scythe.

Jakob was on his feet too, roaring in animalistic rage, one foot jammed into the table's surface as he vaulted onto it, *over* it, lunging for—

Jaxon, whose eyes bugged with confusion, a heartbreakingly soft whimper escaping his mouth instead of a confession.

Alia, who looked perfectly at ease for the first time since Soren had come to know her. Alia, whose right hand twined lovingly into Jaxon's hair, the left occupied with the knife she'd jammed through her lover's throat.

As blood bubbled over Jaxon's lower lip, as the life sputtered and died from his eyes, Alia sighed in relief. Her eyes shut, her left hand releasing Jaxon's hair; his head lolled forward, lifeless in the space it had taken them all to blink.

Alia said, with all the innocence of a child, "Sorry. It was just so *quiet*."

And as her left hand slipped into her coat pocket, a familiar tinkling melody leaking into the air, Soren screamed, *"Cover your ears!"*

And the whole room burst into chaos.

# CHAPTER 46

# SOREN

As her cry rang out across the table, four things happened all together:

Anima slid beneath her skin, a melding of girl and goddess that imbued her with intoxicating, irresistible power.

Ravenna, Kriss, Samhain, and Elias all jammed their hands over their ears; she was at the wrong angle to catch whether Rian and Varran managed it.

Jakob vaulted the table, catching his dead brother with a scream that drowned out all music, hitting the ground with Jaxon's corpse cradled in his lap. And Alia leapt from her seat, spun down on one knee, and drove her dagger down to the hilt in Jakob's back.

Varran's cry rent the room apart; there was no telling whether the chaos magic had clawed its way into his head or not, no telling the difference, because there was no violence greater than that dealt by a battlemate who'd just watched their other half fall.

Horror bent every one of Soren's bones out of shape, a limb-breaking fear that had only struck her once before—when an undead creature had torn off a piece of Finn's arm with its teeth.

Jakob was down. Jakob, her captain, her friend. He was down, he was bleeding, he was—

He was—

She wasn't moving.

"*Go!*" Ani cried, barreling her entire will against their muscles, forcing Soren to stumble forward—she wanted to freeze, wanted to scream, but there was no time to do anything but run. To go toward Jakob and the pool of blood already soaking into his clothes, light blue wool darkening to purple, his trembling lips vaguely tracing the shape of Varran's name.

Trying desperately to choose his last words. Wishing so badly for the last thing he saw to be his battlemate.

*"Elias. Don't go."*

All of it grossly accompanied by Alia's wretched, hysterical sobs, weeping that didn't match the pure relief stretching her mouth into a macabre smile, tears streaming down her face as she huddled in a corner. Her hands were cradling the music box close to her ear, her steady fingers smoothly turning the handle over and over and over and—

"They're coming," she gasped, giggled, wept—a warning or a promise, it was impossible to tell. "It's too late."

Soren could guess what had happened—the fact that they'd escaped the Atlas palace so easily, without Finn or anyone else catching them, had always seemed odd. Perhaps in exchange for their escape, Tenebrae had asked Alia for a simple favor...perhaps he'd told her where to find his box, or maybe someone else had already fetched it for him by then, but Soren would bet every bit of the royal treasury that he'd threatened their lives to get Alia to comply.

Alia had told her herself...she'd expected the Nyxian Queen to be cruel to her, not kind. To attack an enemy kingdom in exchange for her life...it wasn't exactly a bad deal.

Maybe Jaxon had known all along, or maybe he'd only just recently found out. Maybe he'd thought he could handle it himself; maybe he'd feared they would imprison or execute Alia for what she'd done.

Or maybe it was none of those things. Gods only knew the full story, and gods would only ever know, because there would be no reasoning with Alia now. That look in her eyes…it was a look she had in common with skull-bashing physicians and warhammer-wielding generals. It was the look of someone too far gone to save.

And even when Elias dove to engage with her, drawing her attention away from them, she kept on warbling that broken-clock call: "They're coming, they're coming, they're coming…"

Varran crashed down beside his battlemate at the same time Soren did, his normally stoic expression contorted in childlike fear, his hands struggling to cradle Jakob's head; his palms were so slick with blood he could barely keep his grip. His fingers kept slipping off, painting grisly stripes across Jakob's cheeks.

"Don't," he barked when Jakob's eyelids started to flutter. "Don't you even *try it*, Jakob Petrov!"

Jakob blinked, tears melding with blood. "I…Varran—"

"If you shut those eyes, I will *kill you myself.* Don't talk!" Varran looked to her then, chin quivering, eyes utterly focused despite the music box still playing in the background. A tear the size of a pearl hovered at the apex of his jaw. "Fix him."

"I…" Hesitation stole the words right off her tongue. "I don't…"

"Anima." One of Varran's hands shot out to cup her face, warm skin smearing blood across her cheek, no hint of compromise in his brown eyes as he choked, "*Goddess.* Fix him."

*Ani?* She couldn't find her voice, not with Jakob's blood seeping into her pores. *Ani, please.*

It was the only word she could find as she fumbled for Jakob's hand, willing him to breathe, willing him to *live.*

*Please. Please.*

"I'll try," Ani said—inside and out. *I'll try.* To Varran, she said, "Turn him over," and he did so at once, pushing Jaxon's body aside with his boot.

*He's not dead,* Soren said. *He's not dead, so we can fix it, right?*

*I think so.* Ani's voice was taut, tense. *Let me focus.*

As the gentle warmth surged into Soren's palms, tendrils of green nudging the clean-cut borders of Jakob's wound, she managed to drag her attention up to the rest of the room.

Alia and Elias were tussling now, scythes against a single dagger; still, the tiny guard was holding her own, clutching the music box like a lifeline. No creaking bones or violins dug their way into Soren's head—only the simple tinkling melody, the metal divots plinking through note after note without pause. Ani's heavier presence had to be holding its magic at bay.

Or maybe there just happened to be enough chaos in this hall to sate whatever craving it might have birthed inside her.

Beyond Elias and Alia's pocket of conflict, everyone else was gone—the doors hung from their hinges like gaping, broken jaws, and there were sounds of battle ringing out in the hall beyond.

A battle much bigger than their company alone could manage to create.

*They're coming,* Alia had said.

Shit.

Her attention jolted back to Jakob when his back arched beneath her hands, his voice warped around a cry of agony as Ani's magic mended whatever had been torn inside him. Varran held him tighter, face buried against Jakob's temple, whispering inaudible pleas into his battlemate's ear as Ani did her work.

After a too-long moment, Jakob's body eased out of its agonized rigor, and he leaned weakly into Varran's hold, raising one hand to stroke his hair. "I'm all right," he croaked, his eyes squeezing shut. "I'm all right. Get off your ass and go save our kids."

"If you think I'm taking one gods-damned step away from you—"

"Go," Soren whispered. "Take him and go. I'll take care of the others." If there were any *others* left to take care of.

Varran stared at her for a long moment, jaw flexing. As much as he pretended otherwise, this company was his as much as it was Jakob's—though he bore no title higher than theirs, they'd always known to take his word as Jakob's. Where Jakob fell short, Varran picked up the slack. To leave them all behind now…

It would kill him…would kill them both. But there was no choice. Jakob was healed, not whole—he wasn't dying, but he wasn't in any condition to fight, either.

"What do we do? Where do we go?" Varran finally asked. Looking to her—not as his subordinate or his sister-in-arms, but as his princess.

Where *could* they go?

Her heart sank as realization broke through adrenaline, ice encasing her veins.

This was their last stand. If they didn't end this here…if Andromeda fell…

"Get the others out if you can," she choked. "Get them out of earshot. Once you're out of the city, take shelter in the woods and wait for us. We'll find you."

Varran held her gaze. He wasted precious seconds—precious moments he and Jakob could have used to escape—by whispering, "Will you?"

Soren's throat closed up. She reached out and held Varran's face, wiping a bit of blood from his beard. "This is an order, Officer Abrams," she said softly. "I order you to live. Both of you."

Varran held her gaze for a too-long moment, and if her throat hadn't already been choked with emotion, she would have lost all words at the sight of the tears in his eyes.

Varran Abrams, crying for her.

He pulled her in close, bumping foreheads with her, giving her one last shuddering, broken farewell: "It has been the honor of my life to fight beside you, Soren Atlas."

Soren's chin wobbled, and she squeezed her eyes shut, allowing herself the luxury of a single sob to make room for her own goodbye: "And mine. Now *go*."

"No," Jakob choked, struggling to sit up, his hand grasping for her. He just managed to grip her shoulder, but it took nothing at all for Varran to tug him free, looping that arm over his own shoulders and bringing them both to her feet. "Soren, damn you, *no*—"

She offered him a smile soaked in tears. "Love you, Jakob. Don't let it go to your head."

"Please," he begged, but Varran turned and dragged him out, sparing her the indignity of a last look back.

She'd chosen her path. Varran had his orders. All that was left was to carry them out.

With a harsh breath that put her remaining tears to death, Soren hauled herself to her feet, flexing her fingers into fists. Another sob tried to escape; she pounded one fist into her chest, forcing it down with a growl. "No time for that."

The song of war played on outside the broken doors; Elias and Alia's conflict had migrated past the walls of the war room, but she could hear the crackle of flames and her battlemate's occasional shout.

She took a step toward the door.

*"They locked the doors!"*

*"It's spreading—"*

*"Oh, gods, there's more of them—"*

*"Where is the Princess? Where is Soleil?"*

She stopped in her tracks, memory drifting in on tendrils of smoke.

This was a reckoning. An echo. War doused in flame claiming Nyxian halls, a devastating blow dealt by an Atlas hand.

*War.*

But where flames and ash had once weakened her resolve, brought her to her knees, brought her back to the girl she was…

Today, the fire from her childhood did not frighten her.

Instead, it fueled her.

She took one step toward that door. The flames soared higher within her.

She was not the victim today; neither of war nor of destiny.

Soon, she would have to face her responsibilities as Atlas's Heir; soon, she would have to decide whether she would bend to her heart or her birthright, and whether she even had a choice in it at all.

But today, she did have a choice. Today, she chose to fight for the kingdom that had raised her.

Soren Marina Atlas drew her sword—and Anima gripped it alongside her, biomancy twisting around the blade. When the glowing green energy settled, it left behind a twisted vine covered in talon-sized thorns.

"This isn't going to be pretty," she muttered to her goddess. Her friend. "Are you ready?"

"I'm ready."

"And if he decides to show his face today? Will you back down?"

A beat. Two.

"He's hurting our friends." Anima's voice was darker than Soren had ever heard it. "He hurt you. He hurt *me*. No one else. It ends today."

"For once," Soren croaked, "I think we both agree on that."

Soren and Anima walked out that door just in time to see Elias land the killing blow on Alia.

It was the gentlest death Soren had ever seen—a simple brush of his fingers over her face, one scythe holding her dagger at bay as he shut her eyes, whispering a quiet prayer.

She was dead before she touched the floor.

"Gods," Soren croaked, wiping blood from her face with her sleeve, forcing grief to wait its turn, "that's way faster than a sword. Can you teach me how to do that?"

Elias looked up at her, chest heaving.

Soren stepped forward, heart dropping through the floor. "Elias?"

Not a word.

"Are you hurt?" Another step. "C'mon, jackass, talk to me. Did you see where the others went?"

Still nothing. He only stared at her, breathing hard, as if he couldn't hear her at all.

"Hello? Anyone home?" One more step. One more, and she could reach out, touch him, shake him out of this—

He moved so quickly she had no hope of stopping him.

No hope of halting his blade, which plunged itself toward her chest without hesitation.

All she could do was dodge, and even that only partway.

It was the heat she felt first—the abominable agony of superheated steel sinking into the meat of her right arm, the rest of it going blessedly numb before the heat could travel any further down flesh and bone.

She blinked down at the blade, then up at him, not understanding. Not sure it was real.

Not sure it was her battlemate's face that now wavered before her, muddled by pain and shock and smoke, a shadow against the flames devouring the hall behind him.

"Elias?" she whispered.

He said nothing—only jerked his blade out with such a harsh twist that it thrust an agonized groan from her throat. His eyes were glazed, gleaming—alight with all-consuming, mind-altering hunger.

"You talk too much," he said idly. "It itches."

*Ani,* she said, stumbling backward, swiping up her fallen sword in her left hand, *Ani, Ani you need to heal us, Ani Ani Ani—*

*I'm trying!* There was a note of hysteria in Ani's voice—that probably wasn't good. *It only works so fast!*

*Only so fast* wasn't going to be enough. She could see it—she knew all of Elias's tells. That slight hitch of his left shoulder. The inward curve of his left foot. The barest hint of regret in his eyes, still present even with chaos corrupting his mind.

"Elias," she said, "please look at me."

But he *was* looking. And judging by the way he spun that wickedly sharp scythe in his hand, it wasn't making any difference.

# CHAPTER 47

# ELIAS

He couldn't see.

The girl wouldn't die—the girl with the music box, the girl singing her songs and killing his friends and ruining it, ruining everything, making him hear broken bones and the thud of a head rolling across the ground and Kallias gasping for breath on the floor and, and, and—

Even when he closed the girl's eyes, she fell only to stand again—this time taller and stronger, approaching him without fear, so much noise muddling his head that he couldn't think, couldn't breathe, couldn't see couldn't see couldn't see—

He wanted her down. He wanted her gone.

*He wanted her to be quiet, gods damn her.*

*Somewhere in the back of his head, he could hear screaming. Screaming that sounded like him. Screaming that sounded like* stop it, stop it, you're killing her you're killing her you are KILLING HER *stop it stop stop stop—*

*But killing her would make it all quiet again.*

*Killing her would fix it.*

*So he swung again, and again, and again.*

*He landed blows again, and again, and again.*

*But she never stopped talking. Never stopped begging.*

"Elias," *she said.* "Elias, please, look at me. Look at me."

Soren. But where…where was she?

He couldn't tell. Everything was so loud, so ear-splittingly loud, and he couldn't focus, couldn't find her, couldn't—

"Elias!"

His battlemate was somewhere past *that girl, that girl, the one who wouldn't die.*

*That girl was keeping his battlemate from him.*

*He would not let her keep Soren from him.*

*So he swung, and he swung, and he swung.*

# CHAPTER 48

## SOREN

Magic, it turned out, didn't care to race against anyone, even those who were trying to kill its wielders.

And Elias, scythes blazing, goddess eye barely sparking past the blank ebony disk of his iris, had always been the fastest in the company.

"Elias!" Soren snapped, catching his scythe with the flat of her own blade, her injured arm screaming in pain as she pushed all her strength into keeping that death-touched blade from kissing her neck. "Wake up, jackass, it's *me*!"

Elias merely growled in response, deep ridges creased between his brows, his upper lip drawn back to reveal soot-stained teeth. His gums were coated in black, and as he huffed out a breath, she could have sworn flames flickered in his nostrils. Like a gods-damned dragon.

"Be *quiet*," he groaned, reaching his free hand up to scratch viciously at the outer shell of his ear. Blood immediately began trickling down the side of his neck, and he wiped it away with a shudder, still putting all his weight behind trying to break Soren's guard. He drew his second scythe with that bloodied hand, doubling down on his efforts.

Soren's left knee gave out, smacking against the marble with an audible *crack*. But the pain was nothing compared to her arm—it was nothing compared to the idea that if she faltered for even a second, they would soon be finding out if Elias's death magic could trump Anima's medimancy.

Sweat beaded on her upper lip as she leaned harder into her guard, the heat radiating from Elias's blades nearly unbearable. A feverish flush crept through her cheeks as she tried to catch her breath; tried to find something to say that could drown out whatever cacophony had so thoroughly driven her calm, quiet battlemate into such a state.

"Elias," she panted. "you better snap out of this, or so help me—"

So help her, what? What could she do if the music box had swept him away from her with nothing but a long-lost lullaby?

"Hey, Pious!" shouted a voice from down the hall—cocksure, gruff, alive with the thrill of battle. "Eyes up!"

That voice cut through Elias's focus on her—for an instant, only one, he glanced over his shoulder to seek it out.

It was just enough to allow Soren to shove his blades away, rolling past his reach, screaming against the pain in her arm. She jumped to her feet just in time to catch his next blow, and his next, and his next—

And then they were dancing.

It was the Saltwater Ball all over again: just the two of them, matching each other step for step, twirl for twirl, bend for bend. A cord of connection no weapon could sever, an unimpeachable *knowing* of each other's bodies and rhythms in their very blood.

Only this time, their blades rang out the melody they swayed to. This time, fire formed the boundary of a fighting pit around them, a circle of blazing blue and raging red that cast them both in lurid shades of color.

This time, when she looked into the face of her battlemate and found nothing there she recognized, it couldn't be blamed on a momentary lapse of mind.

This time, she wasn't at full strength. Not even close. And he was stronger than he'd ever been.

Every breath knifed into her chest, her throat trying to close in panic, but she forced herself to breathe anyway. To reason. To *think*.

*Be quiet.* The noise—he couldn't think past the noise.

He was blessed by a goddess; not as intimately as her, but if she could cut him off from that melody…

Maybe it would be enough. Maybe then he could stop.

Because he *couldn't* stop—she could see it even as she whirled and parried and twisted, even the barest glimpses of his shaking hands and tortured eyes enough to tell her that.

She'd had enough. She'd had *rotting enough* of terrible magics and careless gods forcing them into this never-ending cycle of loss.

Not today. Not again.

"Sorry Ani," she gasped in the gap between blows. "This is going to hurt."

*What are you—no, no, Soren, don't—*

Her sword clattered to the floor. Her hands rose, reaching toward Elias as he drove at her once more—

Not to stop him. Not this time.

When his scythes buried themselves to the hilts into her stomach, tearing deep into a just-healed scar…a scar she'd earned on a snowy battlefield, chasing down an Atlas prince she only recognized through rage…her throat caught on a hitched, breathless whimper.

There was no pain, not this time. Only the smell of burning flesh as Elias's blades cauterized the wounds they dealt…only the confusion flooding his face as he stared at her, that golden halo slowly blinking back to life in his right eye.

As she clung tightly to either side of his head, her palms pressed over his ears, drowning out the rest of the world. Saving him from that gods-awful song.

"Elias," she mouthed soundlessly, shoving her forehead against his, *"wake up."*

And the next time he blinked, horror flooded his features instead of hunger.

"Oh, gods." Then again, even quieter, patterned in nausea and terror: "Oh, *gods.*"

"It's okay." Still no breath, no voice. She could barely move her lips to form the words.

*Soren!* Ani's shriek hurt worse than anything else. Everything swayed side to side, darkening at the edges—a familiar sensation by now. *What in the rotting—*

*Stop yelling.* Gods, her head hurt. *You're going to want to take over, Ani. I might need…little bit of…* What was the word? *Magic.*

*What do you—*

"Elias." Her lips felt fuzzy. Loose. "Cover your ears."

By now, darkness was familiar territory; something she no longer feared to tread. So when it held out its hand and offered her a gentler way out, she let it take her.

Not for long. She'd be back to finish the fight.

At least, so long as Ani proved herself worth her worship.

# CHAPTER 49

# ANIMA

She'd already known it, but that stunt had irrevocably proved it:
Soren was a rotting fool.

Ani wasn't quite sure where the transition began and ended—all she knew was that suddenly, she was in control of their body. Elias was shouting. Someone was running toward them from the end of the hall.

And her stomach was on fire.

"Elias," she gasped, "take them out."

Frantic, bloodshot eyes met hers. "No. No, if I—it'll hurt you—"

"I can't heal us if they're still inside us, take them out, *take them out*—"

Before her voice could climb any higher, already halfway up the trellis into hound-whistle territory, that approaching figure who'd drawn Elias's attention caught up to them, bracing a hand against Ani's shoulder. She looked up to find Kriss looking down at her, bloody freckles spattered across her ashen face, her ice-blue eyes perfectly calm. She squeezed Ani's shoulder, lips set in a thin line, brows drawn together in what Ani had to guess was rare concern as she took in Ani's gasping breaths, her bloody torso. There were thick wads of wool shoved into Kriss's ears; her sleeves were torn.

"You heard her, Pious," Kriss said loudly over her shoulder. "Take them out."

But Elias didn't move—judging by that dazed, appalled look in his eyes, Ani wasn't sure he could. His fingers were locked around the hilts of his scythes, stiff and unbending, shock rendering him unable to follow even the simplest of orders.

She eased her own trembling fingers over his, pressing gently against his locked knuckles, her stomach thrusting itself into her throat to escape those wickedly curved blades buried so deep in her body. If not for her, if not for this magic that had convinced so many that she had to be deific…

Thank the old gods for the gift of shock. The pain was gone now; only a buzzing numb remained, the parting present the body gave to its owner to make those final moments a bit more bearable.

"It's all right, Elias," she whispered. "We'll be fine. But you need to let go."

"I can't." No breath. No voice. Only the shape of words formed by colorless lips.

"You have to." The world flickered around her. "You—"

Blinding white agony slammed over Ani's entire world, so absolute that she couldn't even scream.

When she blinked it away, a shaken sob caught in her throat, she saw Kriss holding Elias's wrists, his twin scythes hanging limply in each hand, the blades rusted over with burnt blood.

"Sorry," Kriss said, her mouth puckered in an apologetic knot. She dropped two wads of wool in front of Elias. "But I don't think you have time to wait on him."

"That's okay." Gods, she could barely speak. "If you can hear us, you need to get something better for your ears—"

"Oh, I can't hear shit. I'm just good at reading lips." Kriss offered her a grin that quickly faded. "Get healing, Goddess. Fight's not over."

Ani did as she said, swallowing down a groan as her magic eased itself into the cauterized wounds. "What's happening out there?"

Kriss's jaw clenched, wrathful darkness dulling her eyes from ice blue to something closer to gray. "Most of the palacefolk are dead or corrupted. I sent Sam to the outer rooms to gather survivors. Rian's gone—tried to run me through when I was looking for Sam. I guess he didn't plug his ears in time."

That roused Elias, if only slightly; he raised his head, eyes still hollow as he scooped up the wool Kriss had brought him. "Is Sam—?"

"She doesn't know," Kriss said shortly. "Better that way for now."

Ani couldn't argue with that. "Alia said…said people were coming."

"Haven't seen anyone yet." Kriss shook her head, glancing back at Alia's body with a quiet curse.

"And Ravenna?" Elias asked.

"She was covering Varran and Jakob's backs, last I saw. Not sure where she is now." Kriss tightened her grip on Ani's shoulder when she grunted in pain, squeezing her eyes shut as she forced her magic to keep working. "You got this, Goddess?"

"Yes," she whispered, leaning into Kriss's hold. "Thank you."

"Don't mention it. It's what we do."

Ani nodded, blowing out a long breath as the pain finally began to ease. "Soren's lucky to have you all."

"Not just her." Kriss knocked a knuckle under Ani's chin, making her look up. Her mouth hooked sideways in a smirk. "You're part of this now too, Goddess Great. Whether you like it or not."

Warmth flooded Ani's chest—warmth that had nothing to do with her magic. "It's my honor. Truly."

She had lived gods-knew how many lifetimes, had met thousands and thousands of people, had watched them pledge themselves to her worship or her service…and still, in all that time, she knew in her very core that she had never been privileged enough to know a group of people quite as brave and quite as loyal as Soren's chosen family.

What was the point of godhood, if it kept her from knowing people like this? What was the point of life without end, if it meant she could never risk everything for those she cared about?

There was a love humans could achieve that gods never could—a love shown through sacrifice. And if divinity meant never experiencing that love, never being able to show it for herself...

Did she even want it?

Had she *ever* really wanted it?

As the skin beneath her torn tunic sealed into puckered lines of barely healed flesh, Elias finally seemed to shake himself out of his horrorstruck state. He sheathed his scythes before reaching down and cupping his hands beneath her elbows, helping her stand.

"Soren?" he croaked, watching Ani's lips to read her answer.

*I'm here,* Soren mumbled, her voice only just audible, more a half-formed thought than a true intrusion.

*You realize that if my magic hadn't worked fast enough, you'd be dead,* Ani fumed. Not her—her spirit would have survived, even if this body died—but Soren had no such reassurance.

*I know. But I trusted you.*

Well. That certainly took all the air out of her rage-filled sails. She swallowed hard. "She's here. She's an idiot, but she's here."

Soren's voice floated in again, carrying a smile with it. *Why, Annelisa Medeis, did I scare you?*

Shock branded Ani's bones at the sound of her real name in another's voice.

How long had it been since someone had called her by her name, her true name? How long had it been since she'd been brave enough to share it?

Brae had never let her use it. Any time she tried, he'd scolded her, reminded her that they'd long ago left their human lives behind.

*Just...don't do that again, all right?*

*As you command, Goddess Great.*

Elias gave a single nod, closing his eyes for a moment. He had yet to let go of her, his hands carrying a slight quiver.

Before she could say anything else to reassure him, a baying call broke through the silence that had fallen around them.

The keening, bloodthirsty howl of a hunting wolf.

Neither Kriss nor Elias reacted—both now had wool jammed deep into their ears—but Soren immediately said, *Wolves don't wander this close to the city.*

"Kriss," Ani said, waving a hand; the warrior immediately stood at attention. "Wolves—we can hear wolves."

Kriss immediately drew her axes, a feral grin stretching across her blood-spattered face. "That's new. Shall we?"

Ani smiled despite her dread, nerves fluttering in her belly as another howl cut through the air. "Lead the way." To Elias, she added, "The relic?"

Elias smacked his forehead with the heel of his hand, cursing quietly before spinning on his heel and bolting for Alia's body. He patted her down swiftly, retrieving something from her pocket, then hurrying back to Ani. "Is this it?"

Ani's breath caught as she beheld the item cradled in his outstretched hand—a simple wooden box with a copper crank, childish doodles of flowers and stars and smiling faces drawn all over it.

"Yes." She reached out cautiously, tracing those scribbles with one finger, memory taking her where she no longer wanted to go—to a time before Brae had become *this*, a time when he'd caught her coloring on his most precious possession.

But instead of shouting, instead of punishing her or locking her away or striking her across the face, he'd gently gathered her into his lap and grabbed a pencil of his own.

*"Let's decorate it together," he'd said, and they'd spent the next hour giggling over their creation, Brae drawing all the silly faces she made for him, her doing her best to recreate his favorite flowers with her clumsy fingers.*

"Yes," she said again, pulling her hand away. "Put it away."

But Elias kept his hand outstretched, his gaze never breaking from her. "You should keep it."

Ani's heart skipped a beat. "What?"

"You're the only one it can't corrupt. I…" Elias heaved in a deep breath. "I don't trust myself to carry it. It should be you."

Another gesture of faith. Another unearned trust.

Ani's throat closed, and she carefully took the music box into her hands, tracing the grooves in the wood. "It's not your fault."

"I know," he said.

*He doesn't,* Soren said.

*I know.* But that was for Soren to solve later.

She opened the box to reveal its far more intricate insides; hovering her fingers over it, she summoned thick-barked twigs to life inside, jamming up the gears and halting its clinking song. Kriss and Elias unplugged their ears with quiet sighs of relief.

"Let's go," Ani said, tucking the relic away.

But just as they started to make their way out of the hall, heading for the staircase, the embers buried in the smoldering carpet leapt back to life, a wall of flame halting them in their tracks…

And in the heart of those flames, a silhouette.

A form more familiar to Ani than her own.

Heart in her throat, nearly choking on it, Ani took a step back as the shadow stepped forward.

Bare, soot-stained feet. Skirts so black they devoured any light around them, sewn from the very fabric of the void this particular figure ruled over. A crown of living embers pulsing in her hair, brilliant and blazing and nothing compared to the golden flames glowing in her eyes.

Eyes that were fixed on Ani, cold in spite of their fire, her beautiful face impassive in its judgement.

"Shit," hissed Kriss from behind her, awe—and maybe a bit of fear—hushing her voice to a near-whisper.

Her name leapt from Ani's mouth unbidden, sounding just a bit like heresy when spoken in a stolen voice: "Mora?"

Mora, middle child of the Medeis family, the first of them to become something more than human, folded her arms over her chest—a familiar pose. "I can't stay long."

If Ani had felt anything else upon seeing her sister, it didn't stick around long enough to truly be felt; bitterness swept in so quickly that everything else ended up mired in it.

Centuries since she'd last spoken to her eldest sister, and the first words between them were nothing but a promise that it would likely be centuries more before they spoke again.

Mora—Mortem—looked to Elias now. "You're needed elsewhere, Phoenix Priest."

Elias's posture snapped straight. "What do you mean?"

"He's here," said Mortem.

Ani didn't realize that she'd swayed until she felt Kriss catch her—until the warrior muttered in her ear, "He isn't going to touch you, Ani."

So brave—so sure a mortal could stand against the might of the Chaos God with any hope of success.

Maybe it wasn't just Soren, then. Maybe all Nyxians believed they could stand against deities with nothing but a bad attitude and a single-fingered salute.

"He's not alone," Mortem continued, patches of flame leaping to life along the hem of her skirt, rising and falling with the intensity of her voice, with the clench of her fists. "There are beasts in the city—creatures he's infected with his magic." A cursory look toward Ani's scarred wrists. "You've seen the sort of damage it can cause."

"He blighted them?" she whispered.

Mortem ignored her, her fire-touched eyes looking back to Elias. "You can guess where—"

"Hey," Kriss interrupted sharply. "She asked you a question, Ash Breath."

Silence.

Elias gaped at Kriss, eyes bugging; he'd looked less appalled after stabbing Soren straight through. Mortem's gaze snapped to the blonde warrior, her lips parting slightly—the closest to a look of disbelief Ani had seen on her sister in a very, *very* long time.

Ani, without meaning to, giggled. Then slapped her hand over her mouth, but still—the damage was already done.

Mortem stared Kriss down, the flames in her eyes darkening in color— scarlet bleeding in over the gold.

Kriss lifted her chin. Stared Death in the face and did not blink.

Ani could have cried.

"Yes," Mortem said, drawn-out and seething. "He blighted them."

Kriss nodded once, satisfied—the second Mortem's eyes left her, though, her shoulders loosened a bit. Her next breath shook slightly on the way in.

Ani squeezed her wrist, not daring to speak her thanks.

"You can guess where he set them loose first," Mortem finished, grim rage darkening that fire from crimson to the dark, sanguine shade of blood spilled in the night.

Elias's fingers sparked. "The temple."

"This is why I gave you my blessing, Elias Loch." Mortem settled her hand over Elias's chest; a protective instinct wrapped around Ani's ankles like marionette strings, pushing her forward a step before she tugged Soren's emotions back in line. "Defend my people—our people."

Elias dipped his head, but Ani didn't think she was imagining the reluctance hidden beneath the darkness of his gaze.

Now Mortem looked to her, but her words were handed off toward Elias: "You know better than to trust her with that relic."

Ani gritted her teeth. She stepped forward again, placing herself directly in front of her spectral sister, spitting the words in Soren's best snarl: "I am standing *right here*, Mora."

At the sound of her first name, this time, the fire in Mortem's eyes flickered, faded—showing just a hint of sorrowful brown behind. She met Ani head-on, raising her chin a bit to look her in the eyes—Soren's body was taller than the Death Goddess.

"You chose him," Mortem said quietly. "I have nothing to say to you."

Pain ruptured some small piece of Ani's heart, what part of her had never quite grown out of idolizing her pious, patient older sister. But she didn't let it out—didn't let it show.

She wasn't that little girl anymore. She was just as much a goddess as her sister, and she wouldn't cower. Not today.

"Maybe I'm choosing differently," she whispered. "Maybe I'm choosing someone else."

"You have had *centuries* to choose our path," Mortem hissed. "I came to you, I begged you—"

"Not. You." Ani stabbed a finger at Elias, then Kriss, then drove that same finger into her own chest. "*Them*. My *friends*."

Elias, who had trekked through dangerous woods to find and free her, even when he wasn't sure Soren was truly alive.

Kriss, who'd defended her at every turn, who'd spat insults in the face of a goddess who could drop her dead with a single look.

The rest of this company, who had welcomed her with nothing but Soren's word as proof she was worthy to know.

Soren. Who *trusted* her.

"You and Peter—Tempest," she said, choking a bit on her brother's name, "would still sacrifice them. You would still send Elias to the wolves, *literally*. Tempest is trying to take the Atlas prince—I saw it."

"And you took the Atlas princess," Mortem reminded her. "She may be alive, but she's still trapped. She has to fight you for every moment of control. You have no high ground to—"

Ani shut her eyes. *Soren?*

*On it.*

In a blink—literally—the two of them harnessed their newfound ability to work in tandem, their souls melding with singular, shared purpose.

"Actually," Soren said, cocking their head to the side, "Atlas princess, present and accounted for. But good try."

Fierce, overwhelming satisfaction flooded them at the look of true shock on Mortem's face.

"How," she said.

"It's a long story," Ani mumbled.

"We've gotten good at sharing," Soren added. "Thanks for the warning, but I think we have this handled. So if you don't mind…"

Mortem's expression snapped into that indifferent mask once again. She gestured to Elias, who looked decidedly torn.

"You and I," said the Goddess of Death, "will be having a discussion later. For now, the temple."

Elias's throat bobbed. "Yes, Goddess."

Mortem smoothed her palms over her skirt, fire trailing after wherever her fingers touched. She glanced up at Ani one more time—she could've almost sworn she saw pain there.

"I pray, for your sake, that you've spoken true," she said. "Because I swear, Ani, blood or not, I will not hesitate to put an end to what Tenebrae is planning—even if it involves you."

Ani bit down hard on her broken heart, swallowing the shards that wanted to become pleas for forgiveness—or accusations of abandonment. Instead, she simply whispered, "I know."

Mortem, Goddess of Death, vanished in a fount of smoke. And with her absence, all remaining flames in the hall died out, even the torches mounted on the walls.

With a quick mutter, Elias lit them again before turning to them and Kriss. He gazed into their eyes, a war of his own being fought on his face.

"I don't have to go," he said.

Ani retreated a bit, allowing Soren to take this moment.

A reluctant, resigned sigh escaped Soren's throat. "Yes, you do, jackass." She walked forward to press a hand to his chest, brushing at the spot where Mortem had touched him as if to wipe away her claim on him. "It's Kenna. Go."

"But you…"

"*I* have to track down Ravenna and the others, and *I* will be fine, and *you* don't have the time to be this dramatic," Soren promised. "Go. I'll find you."

Elias gazed at her for a long moment.

Then, without warning, he gripped the back of her head and tugged her close, kissing her with all his might—kissing her like it might be their last.

Ani shrank further into the back of their head, doing her best not to roll their eyes as Soren kissed him back, raking her teeth lightly over his lower lip before pulling back enough for the two of them to breathe, foreheads pressed together, soaking each other in.

"Not if I find you first," Elias breathed.

Soren grinned, wicked, war-ready. "Get thee gone, Phoenix Priest. We have a war to wage."

Elias backed away, pressing two fingers to his lips before saluting her with them. When she flipped him her middle finger in response, he laughed to himself before turning and sprinting away, disappearing down the staircase at the end of the hall.

"So. Tenebrae's here," Soren said. "We know who he's looking for."

Kriss cracked her neck, spinning her axes with a bored sigh. "Then let's do our best to find him first, shall we? I haven't killed enough things today."

"You know, I'm liking you more and more these days, Lupin."

"The feeling's mutual, Atlas." Kriss kissed one of her axes, then walked toward the stairs. "Let's go god-hunting."

# CHAPTER 50

# FINN

This pillow was remarkably good at muffling screams.

He hadn't gotten a gods-damned wink of sleep. What had started as a low pounding in the back of his head had built into—

Pain.

Pain.

*Pain.*

Another scream scraped his throat raw, a ragged sob dragged out at the very end, and he couldn't even dredge up an ounce of shame for the wounded-beast sound of it. His body arched against another nauseating surge of agony through his skull, and he could have sworn something was trying to claw his brain from his head. Talons shredding flesh and bone and innards until all he could think, all he could hope for was *let me die. Please, please, just let me die, let it stop, make it* stop *please—*

There was nothing left. No pride, no courage, no fight.

*Let it be over. Let it be over.*

The layered darkness behind his eyes began to spin, flashes of pink and purple and iridescent white flashing like exploding stars, like…like…

Fireworks.

Color consumed his vision, and for a brief moment, all pain went blessedly numb.

*A voice of rockslides and hurricanes and river rapids. "Only a god can stop a god…"*

*Jewels tumbling into an outstretched palm. Champagne giggles. Wicked, lying lips moving languidly against his. "I already told you: the harder you fight, the worse it gets…"*

*His own reflection staring back at him with golden eyes, his gaze doused in a divine gleam. But that smile…that wasn't Occassio's smile. Even on his face, he would have recognized her.*

*He always saw her now. No matter how well she disguised herself.*

*The world spun, a new illusion crystalizing before him: that jewel-crusted hand pressed to his chest, a glimmering goddess standing between him and some unseen enemy, her voice dark with portents of doom: "You will not have him."*

*Darkness. Another whisper, this one in his own voice: "Only a god can stop a god."*

*Soleil's hand outstretched, a battle waging between her green and gold eyes, her mouth quivering with effort as she wrenched out an order: "Run."*

She'd fought Anima off. Had taken her in and forced her out.

*Kallias's agonized face, tears cutting paths down his pale cheeks, his body bent hand and knee in the sand of an unfamiliar beach. Raquel silhouetted against a seaside sky, her good eye clouded, furious, lightning leaping between her fingertips. Soleil and Elias hand-in-hand, facing a horizon he should have been able to name, his sister's eyes dual-colored and dull with grief, hardened with determination.*

*"Only a god can stop a god." The phrase no longer echoed with sorrow, with apology. It sounded like a clue. Like a riddle he wanted,* needed, *to solve.*

Color faded back into darkness, and he woke with a start to sweaty sheets and shaking hands, his head buried in his pillow, his face sticky and aching from his hours of screaming torment.

When he finally pulled himself up, limbs trembling and breath stinging in his chest, he blinked to find a pillowcase soaked in scarlet.

Nausea surged from stomach to throat, and he scrambled free from his twisted clump of sheets, tumbling off the edge of the cot, his bile hitting the floor at the same time his knees and elbows did.

Not bile.

Blood.

He gagged fiercely, every muscle seizing as he vomited more blood, the liquid thickening to a gravelly texture that scraped painfully against his already-sore throat.

It wasn't just his throat that was bleeding, then. It was his stomach too. Gods knew where else his body could have broken down in the night.

When he finally forced himself to his feet, lightheaded and clammy-skinned and weak in every limb, he did another foolish thing.

Thinking back to Occassio forming her illusions, he clapped his hands together and pulled them apart, willing the empty air to harden into something tangible.

A flicker of pink, then nothing.

He tried again. Another flicker. Fresh blood leaked from his nose, coating his lips in copper.

"Focus, Finn."

Occassio's voice gritted his molars together, and he clapped his palms together so hard that his knuckles ached.

When he pulled them apart, hovering one above the other, a mirrored pane appeared between them, showing him every ghastly inch of his face.

He blinked, forcing his breaths to stay slow and even as he studied himself. His eyes were worse than bloodshot, every vein burst and bleeding, turning the whites vivid crimson. Streams of bloody tears were slowly drying on his cheeks, with matching rivulets dribbling from his nostrils, mouth, and ears.

A cluster of rhinestone-dotted curls sparkled over his shoulder, reflected in the mirror he'd created.

"Oh, Trickster," Occassio murmured. "Look what you've done."

"What you've done *to me*." Rasping, broken. He barely recognized his own voice.

"Please. You think I'm any more in control of this than you are?" A note of bitterness. "Do you think this magic treated me any differently? That I didn't break a hundred times before I learned how to carry the weight? The pain never stops. Not even for me. I've just gotten used to it."

"You expect me to believe that? You're clearly enjoying this."

There was a pause before she spoke again; when she did, there was a new pitch to it. He wasn't sentimental or foolish enough to call it *regret*, but it sounded close. "We all have our parts to play. And I play mine better than most."

He bit down hard on his bloody tongue. Refused to trust what his ears told him. She was a liar, the best he'd come across, and he would *not* let her fool him again.

"Enough of the lies," he rasped, dropping the mirror and hitching sideways to face her—not a full turn, but even that much movement spun his head in circles. "*Enough*, Cassi. Gods, do you even know how to stop?"

Silence. No words—no quick retort, no thrown-knife insult.

"The truth?" It was the softest he'd ever heard her speak.

"If you can manage it without burning your tongue."

The Goddess of Time's jaw ticked, as if the words she dredged up really did sear. And when she finally did speak, it was with the raspy edge of a pipe-smoker. "The truth…the truth is that I have pretended to be so many people for so many centuries that I honestly can't remember who I am. The truth is that my head hasn't stopped hurting since the first time this magic woke up inside me. The truth is that lying is so easy for me that I sometimes don't even realize I'm lying until I'm halfway through a story, and it used to be *fun*, it used to be my favorite thing in the world, and the truth…" She laughed, baring her teeth—a snarl pretending to be a smile. Black eyes stamped with blistering, boiling rage, an anger older than the dirt that crusted his shoes. "The truth is that now…now I hate it."

And it *was* hatred that curled off those words like smoke—hatred so deep and dark that it chilled him in his very core.

But Occassio wasn't done. She took a single step toward him, curls shivering, hands trembling, deep furrows cut between her brows, as if every word was a thorn yanked free from her skin.

"I hate it. I hate every second of it. I hate how lying feels, and I hate that I never stop doing it. I hate this magic and the things it has done, is doing, will do. To me, to my seers, to *you*…" Her voice quavered, a harp string strummed just wrong. "I am sick of *people* and their *cruelty* and their *cages*, and the truth, *Finnick*, is that the only time I have felt like myself in hundreds of years is the night I spent with you up on that *rotting lighthouse!*"

Her words—her *shout*—lashed at him, flaying him open from forehead to sternum, a lance of shock worse than any salt-tipped whip. The taste of champagne and chocolate-covered strawberries flooded his mouth. Fireworks flared behind his eyes. Blood painted his hands.

*That rotting lighthouse.*

He had asked for truth. This wasn't truth. This was just the lie he'd already fallen for once.

She had his head. She wouldn't have his heart, too.

So he said nothing—did nothing. Let those twisted, sugar-coated memories drop to the floor where they belonged, among the dust and the mold and whatever refuse these pirates had picked up on the soles of their boots.

"Finn," Occassio whispered. "I am a villain, I am a liar, I am a wicked, wicked thing. I told you one hundred and sixty-three lies about myself while I was Fidget. And somehow, you awful, clever boy, you *still* managed to pick out the one gods-damned truth that mattered to me."

He hated how she said his name. He hated that no one had ever said it so clearly, so intimately, at just the right pitch to strike the one weak chord in his heart.

He shook his head clear—shook it until she finally vanished, until it was only him in the cabin. Then he grabbed his canteen, shucked off his soiled shirt, and soaked it in water. Cleaned his face until he'd scraped away all the stickiness.

He didn't look back over his shoulder as he changed into a fresh shirt and pushed his way out of the cabin. Looking back would give her the chance to reappear, to beguile him with hallucinations and threats disguised as promises, and if he lost another inch to her, it would be his last step toward surrender.

The sun seared his damaged eyes, but he resisted the urge to flee back to his cabin. Instead, he made his way to the edge of the deck, where Raquel and a group of the pirates had huddled to stare into the sea. Raquel's shoulders were stiff as Elias's sense of humor, and new tension rippled over him in turn.

Kallias was nowhere to be seen.

"What's everyone looking at?" Gods above and *below*, he sounded like he'd drunk down a pint of steel shards and gargled them. His cheerful tone was chipped in so many places he might as well have been spitting the words out in pieces.

*You awful, clever boy.*

Raquel glanced over her shoulder, taking in the state of him with concern that both surprised and warmed him. But she simply jerked her head toward the hull. "He's been down there for hours. Hasn't come up for air once. Like he's a gods-damned fish."

Finn glanced over the hull, his heart plunging swiftly toward his toes when he spotted the auburn flash of Kallias's hair beneath the ocean waves. He'd always been a strong swimmer, but this was different—even as Finn watched, the waves seemed to bend and break in Kallias's favor, fighting for him rather than against, bearing him forward so swiftly that he kept up easily with the ship's pace. With a quick glance, he noticed that they'd dropped anchor—though it couldn't halt the ship entirely at this depth, it was enough to slow them so they didn't leave Kallias behind.

"You're worried about him," he said, turning his attention back to Raquel.

A tense nod was Raquel's only response.

He gave her a quick once-over, his lips hooking upward a bit. "Same clothes you wore yesterday."

The twitch of her jaw was the only sign of her annoyance. "Same joke you told yesterday."

Fair enough. He leaned against the hull beside her, staring down at his brother, his fingers flexing to try and work out the unease nibbling at his bones.

"I don't know what to do." Raquel's hushed confession hardly rose above the crash of waves, the song of sea wind. "It feels like he's slipping further every day. I don't know how to bring him back."

She was right. He didn't have to look into the future to see what was coming. He and Kallias were both crumbling beneath the weight of godly influence, tumbling along the same steep slope Jericho had thrown herself down, and if neither of them could stop before they hit the bottom...

"I meant what I said before," he croaked. "He'll stay for you."

"He'll stay for *you*."

"Why are you so gods-damned determined to pretend he doesn't care about you?"

"Because it's pointless." Her arms tightened their cross as she leaned forward, blue-tinged hair falling forward to shield her face. He'd only seen her wear it down a handful of times, and he knew full well that it drove Kallias mad when she did. "He may not be bound by a crown today, but we all know that won't last. When he goes home and your mother realizes that he did what he did to protect Atlas, she'll be begging him to take it back. He'll go home, and so will I, and—"

"You don't have to."

Raquel snorted softly. "Right. And what sort of life do you think a Nyxian soldier would lead in Atlas?"

He shrugged, scratching behind his ear, blinking hard against the fizz of pink that tried to consume him at the question. He could tell her exactly what that life would look like, but it wasn't worth having a fit right here on the ship's deck. "You could be Soleil's lady-in-waiting."

That time she outright laughed. "Shut your damned mouth."

"No, really! Think about it. Obeying orders, polishing her shoes, acting all demure and sweet…it's built for you."

"I'd hit you, but I honestly think I might crack you in half if I do."

He frowned. Sighed. "Yeah, probably."

"Finn." All amusement drifted away, and she finally met his gaze. The depth of the fear there, the frustration, the *worry*… "I know I have to let him go. But I don't want to let him go for *this*."

"I can't save him either, Raquel." The confession hurt worse than his vomiting episode earlier, but she had to know. This was one truth he couldn't afford to keep hidden. "I'm…I'm further gone than him, I think. It's not going to be long before she breaks me. I need…I *need* you to save him. For Atlas's sake."

Her eyes narrowed.

"If not for Atlas," he amended, "then for me. For him. For Soleil and Elias. Whichever one of us you owe the most to, do it for them. Because if Kal and I *both* lose, you will be hopelessly outnumbered. Gods to humans, we're only up by one, if Soleil can't force Anima all the way out."

She stared out at the sea—not at Kallias now, but at the horizon just beginning to crack open with dawn light.

"I will try my hardest," she croaked. "I can promise you that. But only if you promise, too."

"Promise what?"

"To fight that witch in your head. For Kallias's sake." Raquel shook her head. "You have no idea how much he loves you. How terrified he is for you."

*He should be,* was what he almost said. *Don't call her that* was next in line, even more foolish, even more telling. But saying either would only make Raquel push harder.

"I'll try my hardest," he echoed. "Promise."

She balled her hand into a fist, thrusting it into the air between them.

He stared at it, blinking. "Are you punching me in slow motion, or is that supposed to mean something?"

Raquel snorted. "It's how we seal promises in the army."

"By punching the air?"

With a groan, Raquel took his hand in hers, forced his fingers into a loose fist, then bumped his knuckles against hers. "Gods, you and Soren are so alike. Neither of you can take anything seriously."

"So we've been told." What he would have given to have her here to prove it.

Vow sworn with the morning sun as witness, they both turned back to look down at Kallias, who had yet to come up for air. Finn had the sneaking suspicion it wouldn't be need that brought him back to the surface—no, it would be the blue-haired warrior standing beside him, her fist still closed around the promise she'd made, her eye clouded with something softer than worry as she watched his brother sink deeper into the ocean.

So long as she didn't let him sink completely, everything would turn out all right.

Whether Finn was there to see it or not.

# CHAPTER 51

# RAQUEL

K allias didn't resurface for so long that the crew started taking bets on whether he'd been eaten by a shark or drowned by a siren. Finn fell staunchly on the shark side, as they'd heard no singing—and because sirens were simply not real. Patch, who claimed that the ink infused in his skin was pigmented with ground-up siren scales and made him entirely immune to their song, insisted the "land-loving, small-minded princeling" knew nothing about the sea he supposedly had some birthright to.

Raquel didn't want to play.

When Kallias finally signaled for them to drop a rope ladder down so he could haul himself back over the edge of the ship, disappointing everyone on the crew by being neither devoured or drowned, she approached him immediately, tossing him a ragged towel. "Feel better?"

"Much." He caught the towel, but didn't dry off—he simply stood with it wrapped around his fist, his eyes fixed on her face, frowning at whatever he saw there.

"What?" she demanded.

"Have you ever swum in the ocean before?"

That was so far from what she'd expected to hear that it took a moment for her to remember the true answer. "I…no, I haven't."

He tossed the towel aside—it hit some piece of the sail apparatus and hung there, swaying lightly in the breeze—and offered his hand to her. "Do you want to?"

She hesitated, gazing at his hand, her own clasped around the selfish truth.

Of course she wanted to. The Vela might have carried a hint of the sea, but it was nothing compared to the might of Tempest's truest realm.

To dream of the sea was near-tantamount to treason in the Nyxian army—after all, when it came to things associated with Atlas, the ocean was at the very top of the list. But that hadn't stopped her from wishing to see it one day, quietly, a dream so deeply buried in her heart that even Lily—even Jira—had never known about it.

But she feared what would happen if Kallias dove back in. Feared that he might not resurface this time—not because of sirens or sea creatures, but because of whatever that relic was doing to him.

Kallias's throat bobbed, and his hand flexed before pulling back. "It's all right if—"

"Yes." Gods damn her. The word blurted from her mouth without her summoning it; gods knew whether it was her own desperation or the hurt in Kallias's eyes that had cut it loose.

But she knew that the thump of her heart had everything to do with the near-blinding grin that cracked across Kallias's face, crinkling the corners of his eyes. "Get changed and meet me right here."

She wasn't exactly sure what he meant to change *into*—she didn't have anything designed for swimming in—but the ship's navigator, Aabria, flagged her down. "I have something you can borrow," she called, casting an appreciative look at Kallias's dripping wet, freckled and toned torso. "So you don't have to get your underthings wet."

Ten minutes later—eight of which were spent sorting out the straps on the strange garment Aabria offered her, a single piece of water-shedding fabric in a vivid shade of deep blue, Raquel walked out on the deck, more thankful than ever that she didn't visibly blush.

The army tended to drive all sense of modesty out of you; battlefield triage didn't leave time for preserved dignity, only preserved life. She'd been less clothed than this in front of people she knew better, but that wasn't the issue.

No, the issue was the look Kallias gave her when she walked out.

His eyes had been slowly changing…their color shifting from pale spring-garden green to a deep, impenetrable blue.

But when he turned to take her in, his gaze devouring her from head to toe, a slow once-over that left her unable to breathe…his eyes darkened in a blink. A storm with its sights set on a city; a swirling sky before a hurricane.

"Well?" she said brusquely, batting one of her braids over her shoulder, some foolish attempt to affect casual comfort. "Lead on, Atlas."

His mouth curled into a slow smirk—and when he spoke, the words practically rumbled, a growl of thunder buried in the bass: "As you order, Officer Angelov."

Gods damn him. He knew exactly what he was doing with that smile.

Fuming, flustered, she ignored his offered hand this time—he chuckled quietly before pulling himself onto the lip of the ship's wall in one lithe movement, swinging himself over the edge and plunging into the waves below without a hint of hesitation.

She would not look like a coward in front of him, in front of these pirates…definitely in front of Finn.

But she also wasn't stupid enough to jump from this height without the blessing of a god to preserve her health, so she took the rope ladder partway down before plugging her nose and plunged into the crashing sea after him.

Raquel knew how to swim—every self-respecting member of Skyhaven's community did—but even so, nothing could have prepared her for the immensity, the unadulterated *might*, of the ocean.

The impact stole her breath, and that was before her feet didn't hit bottom—she just kept plunging, nothing but oblivion below and blinding sun above when she opened her eyes—

Then, a hand.

Kallias appeared at her side, gripping her wrist, offering her a reassuring smile as he tugged her back toward the surface.

Better she focus on that—on getting to the top so she could regain her bearings—and not the deep unease as she realized that Kallias wasn't holding his breath at all.

Magic—it had to be. No bubbles escaped his mouth, yet he was breathing—and when she shook off his wrist and struck off to close the remaining distance to the surface on her own, she could've sworn she heard him laugh.

She broke the surface with a gasp, and he surfaced shortly after, his hair plastered around the sides of his neck and face as he grinned at her. "You're a natural."

"Shut up," she gasped, treading water furiously to keep her bearings. The second the air touched her eyes, they *burned*, a gods-awful onslaught of stinging pain that had her struggling to tread water and wipe her eyes clear at the same time.

"I'm serious. You should've seen Soren the first time we got her back in the water—Finn says she almost drowned in our pool, and there wasn't even a current."

In spite of herself, she let out a laugh—then sputtered when the overwhelming flavor of salt seeped over her tongue. "It's so much saltier than the Vela!"

"Pure seawater is definitely a different experience." He caught her wrist, ignoring the glare she shot his way. "Relax, I'm not going to let you sink. Let me show you how to swim."

"I know how to swim."

"It's different this far out in the ocean. You want to move like this…"

For the next half hour or so, Kallias guided her through the motions of deep-sea swimming, admitting partway through that even Atlas sailors didn't often risk swimming this far away from shore. But it seemed to her that he had nothing to worry about—while she struggled to keep herself above the water, the ocean seemed to bend and shape itself to Kallias's body, allowing him to strike in any direction with such impeccable confidence she was left to wonder where his shyer side had vanished to.

Whether that was because of his blessing or because of who he was…that was anyone's guess. But it was a marvel to behold, regardless.

After a bit, once she'd found a rhythm and begun to build her own confidence, he pulled away from her side to watch her swim, his smile fading into something more contemplative.

"What's on your mind?" she asked.

"There's something I need to tell you."

Her stomach tumbled, mimicking one of the waves she tread against. "Go on."

He met her gaze, apology invading his features, crowding out what peace had come over him since entering the water. "Aeris is dead."

Ah.

The tension in her body fled just as fast as it had come on, and she forced herself to nod. "I thought as much."

"I'm sorry," he said—such an absurd statement that she had to blink at him for a moment, not sure if she'd misheard.

"What?"

"I'm sorry," he repeated. "That was your debt to collect. But—"

"Kallias," she interrupted, "stop. I was in no state to take him on, and you had to get us out of there. He never would have let us leave if…"

Those words caught in her throat, the taste of salt in her mouth beginning to burn, the memory of that saltwater whip sending phantom pain skittering across her back.

"You did what you had to," she finished. "I don't blame you for that."

Kallias shrugged, his eyes fixed on the horizon now. "We never should've gone there."

A flinch tried to bend her body away from him, but she held strong, swallowing back the shame. "I know. I'm sorry."

"You're sorry? Raquel, gods, *no*. I should've made the call to leave after you told me what they did to you."

"You tried," she reminded him. "I told you no."

"I should've insisted. I ended up taking on the power of the relic anyway, and…" His eyes darkened again, stormy and sorrowful. "You ended up hurt because of it."

She swam over to him, mindful of the potential of watching eyes on the ship as she put a hand on his shoulder, sliding it over until her fingertips met the edge of his own whip marks. "So did you."

Kallias finally met her gaze; she shivered a bit as his skin chilled beneath her touch, so cold she might have been pressing her palm to a sheet of ice.

"Promise me," he said, "that you won't do that again. I won't see harm meant for me fall on you instead, do you understand? Never again."

"I promise," she said.

Whether she planned to keep that promise was another matter entirely. But it seemed to soothe him; the taut muscles in his shoulder relaxed, and he finally smiled again, a smirk that reminded her enough of Finn to tell her that mischief was fast approaching.

"Don't you dare—" she started to warn him, but it was too late; he wrapped his arms around her, ignoring her struggles and shouts, and dunked her under with him, plunging them both into the hidden world beneath the waves.

# CHAPTER 52

# SOREN

In the darkness, Soren Atlas hunted to the baying calls of bloodthirsty wolves.

The entire city was dark—even the moon had chosen to hide behind a veil of clouds, only the faintest halo left behind to prove it hadn't disappeared entirely. Probably Occassio's little contribution to this fight; still, she'd take it if it meant keeping that particular goddess's attention off of her brother.

Breathing in the frigid night air, letting the taste of ice and brewing storms shake her senses awake, Soren melted into the alley shadows, Kriss silently falling into step behind her. For all Kriss's brash, brazen moments, damn if she couldn't move with utter grace when the occasion required.

Pressing her palm to the brick wall beside her, Soren glanced over her shoulder at Kriss, rubbing her fingertip idly over the brick's texture to calm her twitchy nerves. "You really shouldn't come with me."

Mimicking her posture, Kriss glared down at her, those ice-blue eyes picking up what little moonlight did remain; they glowed like a wildcat's as she said, "I promised Ani. That bastard doesn't get to touch her again."

"She doesn't want him touching *you*, either."

Kriss seemed to chew on that thought for a moment; her jaw worked before she said, more softly than Soren had ever heard her speak, "The people who *should* have protected her—who should *be* protecting her—won't. So someone else has to, and I don't see anyone else lining up to volunteer."

Soren couldn't argue with that. She didn't know what she'd expected from Mortem—except, well, nothing at all, because she hadn't expected to even *see* her—but it hadn't been the cold, near-threatening reception she'd offered. Ani had met her with considerably less hostility than Soren had met Kallias with the first time they'd reunited, and Kallias had been far more gentle.

Not so much the soldier that had run her through, but at least he'd *tried* to stop them.

"Fine," she sighed, quickly rubbing an itch from her running nose, "but if we find him, busy yourself with whatever he brought along as backup. We're a bit harder to kill than you, and…"

She didn't want to say this. Didn't want to make it sound like she cared either way. That was the sort of weakness Kriss might hoard to use at a later date, the sort of thing even Elias might think her foolish for.

But she said it anyway, with barely enough breath to cloud the air before her: "He's likely puppeting my sister's body. It's our fight—mine and Ani's."

Kriss whistled faintly—then cut it off when Soren made a violent gesture for her to *shush*. "That would be Princess Jericho?"

"The very one."

"And where do we think they might be?"

"*There* you are," called a familiar voice behind them—a voice that bore thousands of different memories within it, memories of dress-up games and braided hair, memories of shopping trips and dance lessons, memories of surfing practice and sand castles…

Memories of pleading looks and dark daggers buried in her battlemate's body.

"Nevermind," Kriss whispered. "Found them."

Breath catching, heart burning, Soren and Anima turned together to face their siblings.

Sure enough, it was Jericho who greeted them—her body less plump and healthy than before, sharper and thinner, her wrists near-skeletal and her eyes framed in shadow. Her scarlet hair was tied up in a careless ponytail, clearly functional rather than fashionable. Rather than the flowing gowns she so favored, she wore ruddy, studded leather armor from head to toe, and her arms...

Her arms were bare, stenciled with blackened veins and twisted thorns, each the size of a hawk's talon. Some pointed outward, like they were meant as an extra means of defense, but others curled in on themselves, eternally piercing into her flesh. Trails of dried blood painted her from shoulders to fingertips.

Golden eyes gleamed at them from the dark, and Tenebrae smiled with Jericho's mouth.

Even without the change of the eyes, she would have known him—because Anima knew Tenebrae, and she knew Jericho, and there was no trace of the latter in that cruel, calculating grin.

"Honestly, Ani," sighed Tenebrae—a shiver ran down Soren's back at the mimicry of her sister's voice, a darker cast to it than she'd ever heard. "You want something done right, you have to do it yourself, it seems. You've got too much of a soft spot for these people."

"You're not talking to her right now." Soren stepped forward, unsheathing her sword in one smooth movement, grateful beyond words that her hand stayed steady. She might've died of embarrassment long before the battle if she'd trembled before this monster. "You're talking to *me*."

"Yes, I can tell that, that's why I said it." Annoyance colored Tenebrae's voice. "I can't say I missed you much, Princess."

She planted her fist on her hip, gesturing toward the main street with her sword. "I don't suppose you popped in to try the world-famous cinnamon buns?"

"Actually, I'm souvenir-shopping." Tenebrae tilted his head, gilded eyes skimming hers for any tell, any twitch. She knew the look; she'd seen it on Finn enough times. "Happen to know where I could track down a music box?"

"Piss off," Kriss called, stepping to flank Soren's side; Soren bit down Ani's whimper of protest.

Tenebrae's eyes flicked to her, and his smirk curled just a bit too far to feel natural. "You brought a friend."

He took a step forward, and Soren's muscles shuddered, trying to bend—trying to obey Ani, who desperately wanted to move to shield Kriss. But Soren held fast, doing her best to look bored.

*Stop,* she snapped inwardly. *If we make a move like that, we make her a target.*

Ani didn't answer, but her surge of fear nearly swept Soren's resolve out from under her. She gripped her sword tighter, tapping each finger against the pommel in order.

She was still here—she still controlled what she did and said.

"Enough," she seethed—to Ani as much as Tenebrae. "You wanted us; you got us. I've had *enough* of you hurting my family. *Both* of them."

"It's hardly my fault you happened to be born into a family chock-full of bodies able to host us."

Her teeth gritted so hard it hurt; she was half-sure a tooth cracked. "My *brothers* are not *bodies* for you and yours to puppet. And neither is my sister."

Tenebrae chuckled. "Still defending her. Well, not to worry—you won't have to worry about her any longer. Turns out all I had to do was slip a noose over the necks of your parents and she gave right up." He leaned in a bit, almost like a bow, his ponytail slipping over one shoulder. "Seems she was willing to sacrifice a sister, but not quite so willing to sacrifice them."

A hollow whine built and built in Soren's head, rage so potent it became pain. "If you touched *one hair* on their *gods-damned heads*—"

"Relax, Princess. They're still breathing." Tenebrae tapped at his temple with an annoyed little huff. "Magic, you know—it's so picky. Gods know what would happen if I broke my end of the deal; look what happened when I didn't follow the rules with you."

Kriss stepped forward a pace, setting herself just a bit in front of Soren—she could only see the faintest outline of Kriss's braids, the shaved side of her head, the gleam of one of her axes. "Are you the one I have to thank for half my friends being dead?"

With a roll of his eyes, Tenebrae stepped forward, hand outstretched to Soren. "Enough games, Ani. They're toying with your sympathies. It's time to go."

"I *asked* you a question," Kriss snapped, taking another step forward—

A dark vine burst out of the shadows, thorned and shuddering, wrapping around Kriss's throat like a garrot.

"No!" Ani's shriek burst out of Soren's mouth, and before she could get her bearings, before they could make the transition cleanly, Ani shoved back into control, lurching forward with a shudder and a scream. "Let her go!"

"*There* she is." Tenebrae's voice deepened—Jericho's still, but layered with a rumbling purr, the sound of a mountain about to shed a layer of snow. The warning growl of an oncoming avalanche. "Do you like this one best?"

"Let go of my friend," Ani sobbed—no.

Ani didn't sob. Ani *snarled*. Rageful, wrathful…wolfish.

Like a true Nyxian.

Kriss let out a snarl of her own despite the vine squeezing her throat, drawing blood with hundreds of tiny thorns. She flung her arm in a wide arc, bringing her axe down on the corrupted vine—it snapped like a brittle bone, crumbling where she cut, as if rot had already taken it from the inside out.

But no sooner had she cut herself free than another vine shot out. And another. And another—

"Stop!" Ani roared—not just at Tenebrae.

The vines froze, their tips stopping just shy of Kriss's throat. Slowly, reluctantly, they retracted back to their master, slinking away like scolded hound pups.

Ani scurried forward to plant herself—trembling and terrified, but determined—in front of Kriss. Soren could feel the tremors in their very bones…not just from fear. Their body hadn't forcibly switched hands in a long time now.

*Ani,* she warned, but Ani wasn't listening.

"Leave us alone," Ani said. "*All* of us."

Tenebrae raised an eyebrow, casual as anything. "Even you?"

Their throat bobbed. Ani whispered, "Yes."

Kriss's knuckles brushed against their back—a silent show of support.

Tenebrae cocked his head, observing them carefully. "You want to stay with these…people?"

Soren could hear it in his voice. She could hear it, and she knew then—she knew there would be no saving this. No changing it.

But she tried anyway. She tried, because she had to, because they'd already lost so much, because Ani didn't deserve this. *Ani. Lie to him.*

But Ani did not hear what Soren heard. Ani didn't know what it sounded like when a predator had chosen his prey. Ani didn't know how to smell death on the wind.

Because, though she had grown to love Nyx, she did not know it. Not the way Soren did.

So when Ani said, "Yes. Leave them *alone*," Soren was already trying to drag her body back under her control. She was already trying to lift her sword, to drive herself into Tenebrae's path, *anything* to stop what was about to happen—

But ultimately, no matter how hard Soren tried to pretend otherwise, she was not stronger than a goddess. She couldn't defeat Ani at the height of her strength.

So when Brae lazily brushed his hand through the air—when another vine that had crept across the ground without either of them seeing suddenly barreled itself toward Kriss—neither of them were fast enough to halt its path.

At first, Soren couldn't tell what had happened—the vine snapped forward, but she didn't see where it landed, didn't see what damage it wrought—but Ani's blood-curdling scream told her enough.

And Kriss's quiet gasp—the first noise of pain Soren had *ever* heard from her sister-in-arms—told her the rest.

Kriss's body jerked forward, knocking them aside, dragged by the vine— the vine that had burrowed itself *into* her, *through* her, latching into her body like a fanged snake's grip.

Tenebrae pulled her close with that corrupted vine, studying her pale face carefully. He reached out, hooking one finger into the hole the vine had bored into Kriss's torso.

He lifted that blood-soaked finger to his mouth. Licked it. Sighed in disappointment.

"Pity you have to die," he said. "Chaos would find such a lovely home in you."

Kriss met him eye-to-eye…and spit in his face. Blood and spittle joined the freckles coating his skin.

"Go to the pits and *rot*," she seethed. "I'll be waiting for you."

"You'll be waiting quite a while," Tenebrae said. "An eternity, to be precise."

And with a smooth jerk of his thorn-studded wrist, he slit deep into Kriss's throat, releasing a fount of blood that turned even Soren's strong stomach.

Everything went so, so quiet.

Not a thought. Not a sound. Not even a heartbeat.

Tenebrae tossed Kriss's body aside like nothing—nothing but a broken doll, discarded, already half-forgotten.

"One down," he said with a roll of his shoulders. "Who's left, really? Mortem's boy? The Queen? Those two that fled into the forest? Which should I start with, Ani?"

Soren felt the pain first—a ripping sensation in her throat, the kind of burning that came from a scream so primal it couldn't be contained by simple flesh and blood.

She heard it next—a shriek so piercing it drowned out even the howling wolves, even the roaring in Soren's head, even the pounding of her own heartbeat.

And then...

Then she felt the *power.*

It started in their chest, a ferocious riot of heat and light that painted verdant paths down every limb, lighting her up from the inside out—illuminating bone and vein, rib and organ, outlining her insides in green-tinted sunlight. The magic tunneled through her chest, her arms, her torso, her legs—straight through the soles of her feet. Straight into the street beneath her.

The cobblestones beneath them burst into a cloud of dust, snow, and gravel. In a rush of movement, of light and noise and a groaning that seemed to come from the very heart of the world, they were borne upward, rushing toward the sky, the world spinning as—

As a tree burst up from below the surface of Andromeda, its branches iron-tough, curling into a platform to support Anima, who no longer screamed or cried or wailed.

No. Those were the actions of a girl, and no girl stood there now, steady and sure on this still-growing sentry.

"You," seethed the Goddess of Life, the air itself trembling in fear at the sheer wrath in her voice, harmonic in its many tones and pitches, "just made a *mistake.*"

*Ani.* No answer, Ani, *what are you—*

Something *shoved* Soren—something adamantine and unyielding, a force she could not have hoped to stand against.

One minute, she was there, watching as Anima's power woke something up beneath the skin of the earth.

The next, there was nothing.

# CHAPTER 53

# ANIMA

They were not gods unto themselves. But they were very, very good pretenders.

And Anima, despite her sister being queen over illusions and trickery, was the best pretender of all.

No longer did she stand helpless before her brother. No longer did she face him without a scrap of armor or weapon to her name.

She needed no weapon.

She *was* the weapon.

The bark of the tree beneath her soles began to creep upward at her silent summons, creeping over the toes of her boots, layering upon itself in plate-like formations as it climbed her legs, her torso, her shoulders, reinforcing every vulnerable place. The tree itself became her armor, lending its natural strength to the defense of its creator.

Heat tingled beneath her skin from her toes to the very roots of her hair. Magic—worship-worthy, goddess-making *magic*—filled her body to the brim.

She stared down at Tenebrae, her nails digging into the bark of the tree.

He looked so very small from here.

"There she is!" he crowed, clapping his hands in delight. "Rotting bones, if I'd known that was all I needed to do—"

One of the roots of the tree reared up, snapping outward like a whip, throwing Tenebrae into the alley wall. He caught himself, shoving his palms into the brick—it buckled inward at his touch, exhaling dust and debris into the air.

Anima stepped out of the tree, taking the twenty-foot drop without a sound. Trembling—not with fear this time, but with rage, with *might*—she stalked toward her brother, who continued to beam at her as if she'd just made his day.

"You're magnificent," he said. "You—"

She jammed a hand against his throat, pinning him to the damaged brick. Thorns sprouted from her fingertips, digging curved claws into his flesh, teasing the edges of his windpipe.

So easy to rip it out. So easy to silence him.

"You," she snarled, every word vibrating with the weight of her power, "*killed my friend.*"

Tenebrae smiled at her, but the deeper her thorns dug, the more that smile twisted. It warped and withered until only a sneer remained, a scornful thing without an ounce of pity, of guilt.

"I removed a distraction," he said flatly. "What happened to you? When did these *people* become worth turning on your *family*?"

*People,* he said, with the same inflection one might use to refer to a dead rat found buried in their sheets.

"You promised me." Her magic bucked and roiled within her, begging to be set free. "You *promised*, Braeden. No more innocents."

Now his eyes darkened. Now gold took on a shadow, a hint of something hungry. "Don't call me that."

The ground rumbled beneath her feet. Bits of broken brick and cobblestone began to rattle, a sound like chattering teeth.

Chaos rising up to meet her—chaos writhing against the restraints life had placed upon it.

She gritted her teeth, tightening her grip, more thorns sprouting from each knuckle as her magic built up inside her. It arched itself against the confines of her skin, aching against the limitations of this mortal shell.

"That's enough, Ani," Tenebrae said, so gently—as gently as he once sang her lullabies, as gently as he once told her terrible jokes that left their other three siblings groaning as she giggled hysterically. "I'm sorry. I didn't realize how much she meant to you. But we're *so close* now—we can't give up this close to the end. Occassio nearly has her host; Tempest too, misguided as he is. We have Mortem's relic *and* mine right here in this city. We could do it—we could have our family back within *days*. Just come back to me—help me fix it."

She wasn't a goddess unto herself—she was just a very, very good pretender.

And her mortal heart, weak as it was, broke a bit at the earnest pleading in her eldest brother's borrowed eyes.

His sneer softened back to a smile—kind, hopeful. He eased his hand over her cheek, cradling the place where he'd once left a mottled bruise the size of a fully-bloomed carnation.

*"I promised Ani," Kriss had said—willing to face down a god to keep that promise to a friend she'd only just made. "That bastard doesn't get to touch her again."*

"Help me," Tenebrae said, "and we'll finish this today."

*It ends today.*

Anima gazed into Jericho's face; Tenebrae's eyes.

The girl she was would have bowed. Would have cowered. Would have begged for forgiveness. Would have put everything, *everyone*, aside for the sake of her family.

*Us before all*—just as the Atlas family had promised each other.

A promise Brae had manipulated Jericho into breaking.

The girl she was would have made excuses for him. Would have believed the ones he made for himself.

She was not that little girl anymore—not someone to be coddled and commanded.

She was the Goddess of Life. She was through with being used—and through with using others.

She would make this right. Whatever it took. Whatever it cost.

"I," she said softly, "will *never* help you again."

In less time than it took to blink, Tenebrae's countenance shifted from loving to lupine—a snarl claiming his face so thoroughly it wrung out her stomach. She'd never seen a person look so bestial—not even Soren at her worst.

"Then you're a fool," he said, voice calm despite the twisted rage on his face. "And I can't have a fool getting in my way."

Two things happened at once:

Tenebrae's hand tore away a chunk of the armor she'd formed for herself, his hand plunging into her pocket, closing around the hidden music box as if he'd sensed it there all along.

And something sank its teeth into Anima's armored shoulder, dragging her away from her brother with a vicious jerk.

"No!" she shrieked, calling forth a vine from the ground, grasping thin air in her fist—the vine mimicked her gesture, twining itself around Tenebrae's wrist, trying to halt his retreat. But the moment it touched his skin, it coiled back like a dying spider, quivering and withering in on itself until nothing but dust remained.

Whatever had her shoulder chomped down harder, this time breaking through to flesh—dozens of tiny blades sank into her skin, wrenching a scream out of her as she twisted around to face her attacker—

And found herself eye-to-eye with a wild-eyed, slavering wolf.

But not the natural sort, not animals she could speak to and reason with. The muscles beneath this wolf's coat shuddered and twitched unnaturally; its packmates paced in odd, jolting patterns behind it, jaws hanging open and pouring purple-black drool, the whites of their eyes entirely consumed with an ebony gleam.

Her stomach leapt to her throat, bringing a swell of bile with it.

Chaos magic.

Blight.

Mora had been right.

The corrupted animal's teeth sank deeper into her shoulder, a hound intent on keeping its kill. Loosing a growl that pitched all wrong, a tumbling combination of high-pitched snarls and low rumbles, the wolf released her only to lunge for her throat, stained teeth gleaming nightmarish green from the glow of her own magic—

There wasn't time to think. Wasn't time to call Soren, to order her to draw their sword.

She shot her hand out behind her, her magic blazing to life at the tips of her fingers before surging outward, plunging into the limbs of the tree she'd summoned from nothing.

The tree shuddered, a great tremor that began at its roots and traveled up into its branches. Those limbs stretched out wide, bending back…

Then snapping forward.

One of the branches slammed into the striking wolf, swatting it away from her. The wolf landed several feet away with an audible crack, a deranged howl piercing through the air.

Anima clapped her hands over her ears, cringing as the sound skated painfully across her skull. But she didn't have time to indulge in that kind of weakness—its packmates were lurching toward her on spasming legs, their heads twitching unnaturally, teeth bared and ready to devour.

She could run. Could go and find Elias like Soren had promised, leaving these wolves to find other chaos-corrupted prey.

But then her gaze drifted to Kriss. Heat branded the backs of her eyes, tears blurring the sight of Kriss's once-fierce, once-warm gaze, now empty and cold.

She owed her friend better than a frozen city street as her gravesite.

Ani beckoned the tree, releasing her order across the tendrils of her power: "Come to me."

The tree ripped itself free of the ground, roots writhing until they found footholds in the cobblestone, bark and needles scattering as it pulled itself forward with a creaking groan.

With the tree's first step, the city itself shook.

Nerves bundled at the bottom of her throat, but she swallowed down that knot, clenching her fists and guiding the tree forward, silently urging her racing heart to calm.

Goddess Great. It was high time she earned the title they'd wielded so casually.

When the tree offered its bough to her, she leapt onto it without fear, just barely escaping the snapping jaws of the wolves. She clung to the trunk, her nails digging into the grooves of the bark and her boots jammed into seams in the branches as it lifted her away from the street. She leaned into the trunk, squeezing her eyes shut, whispering into the wood: "Put them out of their misery."

Her arboreal warrior obeyed without hesitation, its trunk creaking as its roots undulated unnaturally, a slow turning that put it between Kriss's body and the four remaining wolves. Splinters and pine needles showered down on them, tiny nips of pain drawing beads of blood from her skin, but the wounds healed almost as soon as they were dealt.

A howl burst out into the night, and Ani's head whipped around just in time to catch the impact of flesh against brick. One of the tree's branches now dangled from its trunk like a broken limb, but the reward for its sacrifice spoke for itself: a second wolf now lay crumpled on the ground several feet away. Not quite dead— its tail flicked in odd directions, its front limbs spasming while its back limbs dragged behind it, eyes maddened with pain and hunger and…

*Magic.* It seeped from the creature's every orifice, its nose and mouth and eyes bleeding black, its teeth bearing ink-like stains. There were no whites to its eyes—only an endless void with no stars, a darkness that could only devour.

All at once, pity overcame terror.

She put her hand out. Closed her eyes. Dove down, down, down into herself, digging until she reached the roots of her own power, the part of her that so many of her worshippers had forgotten or ignored.

This wolf was close already…so close to setting foot in her sister's realm and removing itself from her. But it wasn't there yet.

Deep inside the animal's essence, past the writhing pain and the screaming chaos, something quieter met her magic with a soft nudge…something that pled with no voice, no language left in this creature so corrupted with her brother's corrosive magic.

*Please*, it asked without words.

And with a clench of her fist, she put the creature out of its misery.

Still infused with what little life it had left, its bones obeyed her commands. When she told them to break…they broke.

With a crack that sheared through the hunting howls and the sounds of battle just beyond this alley, the dying wolf's spine sundered. Its entire body slackened, easing into the gentler embrace of Death.

*Be kind, Mora. It didn't die easy.*

She knew how Soren felt about that particular piece of magic, how often Elias's breaking spine made an appearance in their nightmares—she braced herself for trauma to rear its ugly head, for her stomach to twist and turn, for her cobweb to start up her usual racket of protests.

But nothing came.

In fact, she hadn't heard one word from Soren since Kriss had died...nothing since she'd said her name like a warning, a caution the goddess had been in no place to heed.

"Soren?" she choked as the tree continued to obey her commands, putting down wolf after wolf with relative ease. Even magically corrupted, they were just animals—their bodies broke as easily as any other. "Soren, what now?"

Silence.

"Soren." Alarm rose like bile, burning Ani's throat, and she tucked herself against the trunk of the tree, squeezing her eyes shut and prodding around for her friend.

Instead, she found the remains of the wall between their souls.

It had been weakening over time—they'd managed to fashion it into something more like a door than a wall, something they could pass through when the other willed it. But what Ani found wasn't a door—it wasn't *anything*. Whatever had hung between them, it now lay in shreds. And beyond it...

Nothing. Hollow space.

Dread thrust its fist into her chest, dropping her heart straight down to her soles. The cold winter air seemed to turn away from her, refusing to enter her lungs until she found something.

*Soren!* Screaming now, she clawed her way past those shreds, seeking out any lingering trace of the Princess, desperate for some hint of sarcasm or teasing, even a taunt—*anything. Soren, where are you, where are you, what did I do—*

*What did I do?*

*What did I do?*

Unable to breathe, she started to turn toward the temple, to go find Elias and beg for his help...then paused.

She glanced back at Kriss.

The magic fizzing through her...it was unrestrained, unlimited by another's consciousness now. If she tried, if she poured all of it out, maybe...

Maybe she could bring Kriss back.

Maybe.

But if she did…by the time she finished the long process of bringing life back into Kriss's broken body…

It might be too late for Soren, if it wasn't too late already.

Ani hovered in a whirl of indecision, frozen in place, grief tearing her in half.

She couldn't save both.

She might not be able to save either.

And she only had seconds to choose.

# CHAPTER 54

# ELIAS

Elias had never really feared wolves.

They so rarely wandered into Andromeda—he'd only seen it happen three times in his entire life, and all three times he had walked out into their kitchen to find his mother sitting beside their open glass door, chatting softly with the massive brindle-furred creature sitting politely on their patio, its head cocked to one side as Sera tossed scraps of dried meat at its feet.

He had heard whispers on the battlefields, too—whispers from Atlas mouths that granted him a nickname of his own. *Princess Soren's war-wolf. Guards her flank like a rabid beast, follows her like a lovestruck pup.*

But these wolves were different. These wolves were…broken.

*Blighted*, Anima had called it.

And they weren't alone—Tenebrae worshippers were in this fight, too. Some faces he recognized from Artem; others from Atlas; others not at all, which frightened him more than he cared to admit.

He struck down one of them with a swift cut of his scythe, fire skittering across the blade and burning off the blood that remained. He pressed his back to the closed temple doors to take a breath in the gap between assailants, wiping sweat from his brow and taking in the temple.

The courtyard was littered with bodies, an even mix of lupine and human. Blood and fire had melted the snow to nothing, leaving behind churned-up dirt and bloodied mud. He didn't defend the doors alone—the rare handful of Mortem-blessed students had come to help, all wielding fire of their own, only one or two handy enough with a blade to bother wielding one. Those, he guessed, had come from military families.

The battle seemed to be winding down now, this the longest gasp of breath he'd managed to draw in since arriving here.

So when a beam of green light drove itself into the sky elsewhere in the city, punching a gap into the gathered clouds, Elias saw it.

And when that magic boiled over, washing across the city with a pulsing torrent of power, leaving his senses assaulted with the scent of growing things and the taste of fresh herbs, he knew something had gone very, very wrong.

But he couldn't leave the temple undefended.

Panic thrust its fist into his chest, gripping his heart and squeezing until it stopped, watching for another pulse, another wave—desperate for any sign that his battlemate and her goddess had resolved whatever was happening out there.

It had been a mistake to leave her. He'd known better.

He'd only just started to go down the temple steps when a new sight stopped him in his tracks.

A tree was walking toward the temple.

A tree. *Walking*.

And braced in its branches, armored in what appeared to be layers of bark, skin bristling with thorns and golden eyes ablaze, was Anima.

Not Soren; there was no trace of his fiancée in the girl—the *goddess*—in the towering tree's embrace. Her skin seemed even paler than usual, and her eyes were blown wide, hysteria clear even this far away.

"Elias!" Heedless of the battle still being waged in the courtyard, heedless of the fact that she was trespassing on another goddess's ground, Anima clambered down the trunk and *sprinted* for him, mouth open and panting, blood pouring from her nose and ears and eyes like something had utterly sundered inside of her.

He gripped her by the shoulders the second she barreled into him, her breath catching on hysterical sobs. "Anima! Stop, stop, you're bleeding—"

"Soren's gone!" she wailed, clinging to his shirt so hard that the thorns tore right through it, dragging scratches down his flesh that immediately seared shut.

The entire world became very, very small—only her eyes remained, flooded with broken blood vessels and tears…and entirely gold.

"What?" His voice sounded so far away.

"She's gone!" A messy, hacking sob—Ani bent into it, spitting blood on the floor before looking back up at him. She shook him by the shirt, eyes so wide he half-feared they would pop right out of her skull. "I didn't mean to, I didn't, I don't know what happened but she won't talk to me, she won't talk and I can't feel her anywhere—"

He didn't waste another second, didn't bother with another thought. He gripped her by the arm and shoved the temple door open with a strike of his shoulder, brushing the inches-thick iron away like it was nothing. He dragged her in before pushing the door closed behind them, turning and clinging on to her by her curls, gazing into her eyes and trying his damnedest to breathe.

"Soren," he said, as calmly as he possibly could, "are you with me, smartass?"

Nothing. Only Anima stared back at him, lungs rattling with every heaving breath she took, her tears ceaseless and scarlet.

"*Hey.*" Voice rising in pitch, he shoved both hands into her curls now, clutching her with all his might as he growled, "*That's not funny,* smartass. Speak up. Right now, or I'm taking that ring and throwing it in the nearest lake, and you can swim your ass to the bottom to get it back, do you hear me?"

Nothing—no flutter of an eyelash, no flicker of green, no *jackass.*

No air to breathe. No sound to hear. Nothing but a torrid heat beginning to boil in his blood, liquid iron forging a wall against his fear, denial so absolute it wouldn't even make room for the possibility that…for the understanding that Soren could be…

There was no thought in his head but *no*. No, he would not let this happen. No, this would not be the way their story ended.

No, he would not sleep even one more night without her by his side.

"Anima—" he began.

"Do it," she rambled, tears glittering on her lower lashes, her chest jerking with hysterical gasps. "Anything, anything, just get her back, get her back—"

He released her head to cradle her neck with one hand, her waist with the other. He backed her against the wall, never releasing her for a moment, pinning her in place and shoving his forehead to hers, the smoke on his breath mingling with the iron and salt on hers.

"Soren Marina Atlas," he rasped against her mouth, "don't you dare leave me."

Anima squeezed her eyes shut. A sob began to build in her—he could feel it swelling beneath her chest, an admittance that it was too late, a grieving cry that would be the final nail in Soren's coffin.

"No, no, no," he chanted, stealing that breath as his own, pressing his lips to hers and kissing her—kissing her like he had always longed to, with nothing holding him back, with nothing stopping him from pouring every ounce of love and passion and irritation into each caress of his lips, each stroke of his thumbs against her skin, each breath he shared with her. "No, no, no. You come back to me, smartass. You *come back*."

He kissed her on the forehead. Right over that little misshapen freckle he'd always said was shaped like a heart; she'd always said it was something far less appropriate, all part of her never-ending game to make him blush as much as possible. Right on the spot where he'd kissed her so long ago, when she lay dying on that Ursa battlefield, the first time he'd truly had to consider facing life without his brash, bossy, *beautiful* battlemate always at his side.

"For once in your damned life," he rasped, voice cracking, "just *do as you're told*."

And though there were no words…no flutter of an eyelash, no flicker of green, no *jackass*…there was a catch in her breath.

That was enough. That was enough for him to kiss her again, harder, not caring that she tasted of blood and magic. Not caring that her hands lay splayed at her sides instead of drawing him closer.

"You remember what we do when we're fading?" he said against her lips, terrified to move away any further, terrified he might lose what little hold he had. "We find our anchor. I have mine right here—" He gave her a shake, sharp and demanding, praying that he wouldn't leave burns behind this time. "Now you find yours. Do you have it?"

Her eyelids sank shut. Her brows furrowed.

"C'mon, smartass," he pleaded, brow to brow with her, unwilling to give up ground. "Tell me when you have it."

A slow, drowsy breath, as if waking from a dream—as if waking from something deeper.

"My…" Another dazed, dull blink.

A flash of green.

"My brothers," she whispered. "Saltwater Festival. Kallias and Finn— they're playing hide and seek with me."

Every morsel of remaining strength drained out of his body, and he sagged into her, burying his face in her hair. "Good," he managed, desperately trying to hold back the onslaught of sobs. "Good. Keep going."

"My fiancé." Her voice warmed, a note of teasing in it despite the lingering daze, the weakness that kept her words to a mumble. "He's flushed so red you could paint a barn with that color. He's about to have a conniption because I called him *lover*—"

He couldn't help it—he interrupted her with another kiss, not sure if he was laughing or crying, not sure if it really mattered.

"Gods damn you," he choked, "don't you do that. Don't you *ever do that again.*"

Soren smiled faintly beneath his lips, her eyes still closed, blood-clumped lashes leaving tiny scarlet tallies on her cheeks. "Don't boss me around, jackass." A pause, then she groaned. "Gods, Ani, stop blubbering. I'm all right. It's—Elias, will you tell her I'm all right."

"In a minute," he managed, carding his fingers through her curls with one hand as he tugged her closer with the other, not quite finished holding her. "I need a minute."

"I'm afraid we can't spare it," said a grave voice from behind him. He looked over his shoulder to see Priestess Kenna approaching, expression grim—though her wrinkles lifted in turn to make room for her cocked eyebrow as she took him in, still pinning his breathless fiancée to the wall, one hand gripping her by the hip. Cheeks heating, he quickly adjusted—not letting go of Soren, not yet, but at least *trying* to appear a tad more respectable. "You need to flee—all of you. We've managed to gain the upper hand here, but the city is overrun. Chaos spreads quickly, and it seems the Chaos God managed to get his hands on his relic after all."

Elias glanced to Soren, whose eyes unfocused for a moment—with a snarl, she said, "He took it from Ani." Before Elias could curse, she quickly added, "She didn't *give* it to him, jackass, relax. But he got away."

His heart sank. "We lost?"

"The battle, boy—not the war." Kenna shuffled forward, giving him a sharp pat on the shoulder. "Your plan still holds—better to have Anima's relic in your hands than his, whether she cares to assist him or not." A concerned look at Soren. "In any case, you best get those two separated. Sharing or not, death hovers over you, dear—you won't last much longer with the goddess sharing space in your body."

"So I've been told," Soren croaked, wiping at the scarlet streams painted down her cheeks. "Is Ravenna—?"

"I'm here." The Queen appeared as if summoned by her name alone; her velvet outfit was torn and bloodied in several places, one eye swollen shut and weeping blood, but her gaze belonged to only Soren as she pushed forward, wiping more blood from Soren's face with her sleeve. "Are you hurt, sweetheart?"

"I've had plenty worse." Soren clung to her mother for a moment before pushing back from her, lips pressing into a thin, pale line. "We all need to get out of here. Andromeda is lost."

Something fell over Ravenna's face…some emotion Elias wasn't sure he liked. But she gave a single bob of her head, kissing Soren's brow. "Captain Petrov and his battlemate made it out—I believe Officer Arcta did as well, with some palacefolk and Ember. I haven't seen Officer Lupin—"

"Kriss is gone," Soren interrupted—her chin quivered just a bit before she steeled herself, sliding her arm into Elias's and leaning against him. "Tenebrae killed her."

Pain cinched Elias's lungs tight. He hadn't gotten along that well with Kriss, but she was still part of his company—still a sister-in-arms. Her loss was another tally on a list of debts owed by Tenebrae; debts Elias was determined to see paid.

"Before we go, we need to get back to the palace, if we can," Ravenna croaked. "There's something there you two—sorry, Anima, you *three*—may need."

"That's impossible," Elias protested. "The streets are *packed* with wolves—"

"No pun intended," Soren offered.

"They know that, smartass." He looked to Ravenna as he tugged his fiancée closer. "We won't make it ten feet."

Ravenna's eyes gleamed. "Who said anything about taking the streets?"

# CHAPTER 55

# SOREN

Soren hadn't jumped roofs since that night she'd spent with Finn in Atlas, drinking hot chocolate from wine glasses and hopping above the Saltwater Festival crowds and doing decidedly ridiculous things that, somehow, she was incredibly grateful she'd taken the time to do now.

Gods knew when she'd get the chance to do something that silly, that *fun*, again.

Imagining such a time ever coming was difficult, but not just because of the situation they found themselves in—Anima had yet to stop apologizing, and the constant litany of sobbing *sorrys* drowned out pretty much any thought she tried to form.

Finally, as Ravenna hopped down from the final roof before they reached the palace gates, Soren came to a sharp halt and covered her ears with her hands, squeezing her eyes shut as she snapped, *Anima! That is* enough, *honey, seriously. It's fine. It was an accident.*

A spectral sniffle. She hadn't known someone could sniffle with their thoughts. *I could've killed you. I thought I killed you.*

*And I am so very touched that the idea of that has driven you into such a state. However, seeing as I'm not dead and would like to remain that way, do you think we can save the blubbering for forgiveness until* after *we get out of the city?*

Another miserable sniffle. *I'll try.*

*Thank you.* She paused. *Ani, I'm so sorry about Kriss.*

Now guilt heated into rage, which was better—Soren would rather carry anger than the sickly feeling of blame. *He's going to pay for it.*

*Yes, he is.*

Elias's hand brushed against her back, and he leaned in to whisper, "You all right?"

"Fine." She spared a moment to kiss his cheek before climbing down after Ravenna, hurrying to the palace gates—well, not quite the gates. The grate just to the left of them.

Escape tunnels—a wartime precaution. Ravenna's father had wanted a way to be able to escape if some war-fueled onslaught ever came right to their door, and Ravenna had kept them in order to be able to bring the citizens of Andromeda into the more-defensible castle if Atlas had ever mounted an attack on the capital directly.

Once inside, Ravenna led them up to the third floor—to her study. At the door, she paused, glancing over her shoulder at Elias. "If you don't mind, Elias," she said softly, "I'd like a moment alone with my daughter."

Oh, he minded—Soren could see it as easily as if he'd screamed it, the desperate wish to say *no* written all over his face. But she gave him a look, and he silently relented, his shoulders slumping slightly as he ran a hand over her cheek.

"Hurry," he whispered as she walked past.

"When have I ever taken my time with something?" she asked, flashing him her best wink before slipping into Ravenna's study, shutting the door behind her.

Ravenna slid behind her desk, but she didn't sit; instead, she stood with her hands braced on the wooden lip, string down unseeingly at her piles of papers.

Unease rising in her throat—and still trying to shake off the fact that she'd just nearly died for the fifth time in as many months—Soren approached the opposite side of the desk, leaning against it as well.

Blood dripped from her face to land on some of the papers, reminding her she had yet to clean herself off.

"Oops." She leaned back, putting a safe amount of space between her and the stationary. "Sorry."

Ravenna waved a hand in dismissal. "It's not going to matter, is it?"

That unease sharpened into something closer to fear. "I mean, you could take them with us…it's just Andromeda, Mama, not Nyx. We can regroup, we can…"

"*We* can't. Your path leads elsewhere." With a long, slow breath, Ravenna lifted a mug that had sat on her desk for as long as Soren could remember—so long a considerable ring of dust stayed behind when she lifted it. Beneath the mug was a key.

"I should have given these to you years ago. But better late than never, right?" Ravenna's laugh hit at all the wrong pitches—in fact, it carried more of the cadence of a sob.

Soren's heart climbed into her throat and refused to crawl back down. "Mama—"

"Here." After unlocking one of the drawers in her desk, Ravenna tugged it open, rifled around, then presented a neatly tied stack of letters—some aged and yellow, others newer, one looking as if it had only just been sealed.

"What are these?" Soren didn't take them—not yet.

Ravenna smiled sadly. "They are every attempt I ever made at telling you where you truly came from. Even when I was brave enough to consider it, I wasn't brave enough to say it out loud." She ducked beneath the desk after that—rifled around until she retrieved a flat garment box. She held it out alongside the letters, waiting. "And this…this is something you've more than earned."

Soren's heart started to pound in her throat. She took both tentatively, staring at them for a long moment before looking back up to Ravenna.

The Queen gazed at her with such sorrow. Such regret. Such love.

"Mama, why are you giving these to me?" she whispered.

Ravenna rounded the desk, reaching out to cradle Soren's face in her hands. "Because I'm staying, sweetheart."

She heard the crunch before she realized where it had come from—her fingers had curled into fists without her bidding, crumpling the edges of the letters inward, flecks of aged paper raining down on her soiled boots.

"No you aren't," she said. No emotion in her voice—no emotion left to *feel.*

She had lost half her company today. Had lost yet another battle. Had nearly lost *herself.*

She had nothing left to give. *Nothing.*

"You aren't," she said again, because it was the only thing to say.

Ravenna's thumb brushed just beneath Soren's bottom lashes, ignoring the tears streaming down her own face, staining her cheeks with silvery remnants of the star-like kohl she'd lined her eyes with that morning. Like the tails of shooting stars.

"There may yet be survivors in the palace," she said softly. "And in the city. A queen does not abandon her people."

"Mama, you can't." Tenebrae's words came back in a flash: *Who's left, really? Mortem's boy? The Queen?...Which shall I start with, Ani?* "He'll come for you. He'll…"

The words wouldn't force their way out of her throat, but they hung between them anyway, unspoken and obvious: *He'll kill you.*

Ravenna smiled through her tears, steady and sure. "Yes. But if my city falls today, if my *people* fall today, then I will fall defending them."

Her thoughts raced, rifling through a pile of reasons she should not, *could not* stay, seeking the needle in the haystack that could pick the lock on Ravenna's resolve. "Sierra—"

"—Is waiting for me downstairs," Ravenna interrupted. "I told her to go, but you know how it is with battlemates." A cracked laugh. "Nobody takes those vows lightly."

Her lip started to quiver, and she bit down so hard on it that she tasted new blood. "Yvonne. You have to come with us because Yvonne…"

Ravenna's gaze held steady. Her smile held true.

Soren's heart fractured. "Yvonne already knows."

"I sent her off with everything she needs." Ravenna stroked her hand over Soren's blood-clotted curls once more—a tender gesture, and it made her *furious,* it made her knuckles ache with the need to punch and claw and scream until something *worked.* "Oh, my darling girl." Now it was Ravenna's turn to fracture, her voice failing her at the end, a silent sob stealing it away. "Please—"

"Don't." Please, please, please. No more. No more—"Don't say it."

"I won't ask you to forgive me, because what I did…it's unforgiveable." Ravenna cradled Soren's face between her hands, reclaiming some of her composure with a sharp breath in, a sharp breath out. Her eyes glimmered with tears, a mirror to the night sky shimmering through the glass above them. "But I ask you to forgive yourself—for not finding your way back to them sooner. For wanting something other than the crown you were born to." A shaky breath. "For leaving me here, so you can finally go *home*."

"Mama," she tried, but her voice betrayed her—nothing but breath escaped, some rasping imitation of a sob.

"Shh." Ravenna held her close, shaking her head. Both of them were trembling, holding each other like they might never let go. "It's all right, sweetheart. This is what it means to be queen."

"Then don't be a queen," Soren begged, when she meant for it to be an order. "Be my mother. A mother doesn't abandon her children."

Ravenna nodded, taking in one last deep breath. She released Soren, stepping back toward her desk. "No. She doesn't. And yours never did." The Queen looked out the window at her city—at her bloodstained, burning city. "She would have found her way here someday, you know—Adriata. I don't think she knew it, but she never stopped looking for you. No matter what she told herself, I don't think she ever stopped hoping for…well. Exactly this."

Soren walked forward, planting her palms on the desk, facing Ravenna down with all the fury she could muster. "I am not leaving you here."

*That* was the order she'd wanted—the staunch, unyielding order of one who carried queenhood in her blood. It should have been enough.

It should have been enough.

But Soren was not a queen. And when Ravenna looked over her shoulder and called, "Elias, get her out of here," she knew in her heart that she would never be.

Because a queen's orders were never overridden. A queen's orders were not *ignored*.

And a queen didn't get picked up and dragged away from the fight she had not yet won, hysteria claiming all reason as she fought and scratched and shouted, heedless of Elias's pained, sorrowful apologies in her ear.

She didn't remember exactly what she screamed as Elias followed his queen's final order—didn't know if she'd pled or raged or begged.

She thought she might have said only one thing, over and over and over until she had no voice left to speak with: *Mama, please. Mama, please, please, please—*

But she would never forget that last picture of Queen Ravenna of Nyx: seated at her desk, head held high, starlight tears gleaming at the edge of her jaw as she watched Soren leave.

Mouthing one last message, over and over and over: *I love you. I love you. I love you.*

# CHAPTER 56

# ELIAS

Soren had not stopped weeping.

Silently, now—she'd at least had the presence of mind to stop screaming out her sorrow when they crossed into Andromeda proper, moving with Elias instead of against him, forsaking the fight to get back to her mother's side. Now she ran alongside him, but she had yet to say another word—her hitched breaths and shaking shoulders were all that told him she had not lost herself completely to shock.

That didn't scare him. If it had been his mother staying behind to face a fight she would certainly lose, he would have done worse; in fact, it was all he could do not to break himself, leaving his beloved queen behind.

Ravenna, who had welcomed him into the castle with as much warmth and care as if he were truly family; Ravenna, who had pulled him aside on more than one occasion over the years and asked him privately if he ever intended to tell Soren how he truly felt; Ravenna, who had housed his entire family in the castle for a month once when a horrific blizzard had collapsed part of their roof.

Ravenna, who had not even mentioned that he'd disobeyed her direct orders to go after Soren when she'd been captured by Atlas. Who had only embraced him with all her strength and quietly thanked him for protecting her daughter in heart.

But he would not disobey her final order. So he held Soren up when her strength began to fail, whispered his apologies into her ear, and no matter what he heard behind them, he never stopped moving.

It took hours…hours of wandering in strange patterns to throw off any tails, then working their way back, beginning the arduous search of the various shelters scattered throughout the vast woods for hunting parties to use when unexpected blizzards hit.

In the end, Soren started shivering so badly that she could no longer walk on her own—he had to heft her onto his back, his heart breaking all over again as she buried her face against his coat collar, still not saying a word as he butted open the door of the fifth shelter they'd checked, peering around the frame—

A blade nearly skewered him through the nose, and he barely managed to lean back in time, choking out, "It's us!"

A hushed gasp of relief came from within the shelter—barely big enough to be considered a shed, really—and a hand reached out to tug them in. Ember wrapped her arms around him—then, feeling Soren on his back, turned him around so she could pull her sister down, running her hands over her to search for injuries. "Are you hurt?"

Soren blinked at her dully, eyes red-rimmed, eyelashes glimmering with frozen tears. "Mama didn't make it."

Ember stared back at her; the only sign she'd heard her was the slight crease between her brows.

"Ember," Soren said, her voice breaking, "Mama didn't make it."

And Ember—stoic, steel-forged Ember—covered her mouth to muffle a broken wail.

As the sisters sank to the floor together, both lost in their own grief, Elias silently gave them space; though it warred against every instinct to leave Soren in the midst of her pain, this was a moment they needed to have alone. Instead, he made his way to the back of the unfurnished shelter, where Jakob was propped against the wall, seemingly deeply asleep; Varran stood up from his side with a lurch, his exhausted gaze warming a bit as he embraced Elias with a clap on his back.

No words spoken; none needed, until he noticed an absence he had not expected.

"Sam?" he croaked.

"Not with us, but we saw her get out with another group." Varran swallowed. "Rian?"

Elias merely shook his head.

"Kriss?"

Another mute shake of his head.

Varran cursed…then cursed again, though this time his voice cracked in the middle. He covered his face with one hand, hauling in a breath that trembled with emotion.

He couldn't remember a time he'd ever seen Varran so overcome. Then again, they'd never lost this much this quickly before…not even when he and Soren had both lost their battlemates in the same fight.

"How'm I going to tell him?" Varran whispered, glancing over his shoulder at his pale, injured battlemate. "He said…he told me to stay, to help you all—"

"Varran. There was nothing you could have done."

"You're right. Nothing is exactly what I could do, and I did it damn well," he muttered.

"Varran," said a different voice—fractured with grief still, but stronger. Clearer.

Elias and Varran both looked over to find Soren standing—she was still trembling, still paler than the snow outside this hut, but her jaw had steeled. Her gaze had sharpened. "I gave you an order. You followed it. If anyone's to blame, it's me."

"Soren—" Elias croaked, but she cut him off with a wave of her hand.

"We can't stay here," she said, voice utterly void of emotion—that scared him more than her hysteria had. "There could be more of those wolves wandering the woods."

"Where can we go?" Varran asked.

Ember stood up too, a stricken look claiming her normally calm features. "Havi and Safi—they're supposed to come to Andromeda. They told you they were—"

"They were meant to travel to Sanctaviv first," Elias said quickly. "They aren't due here for a few more days yet."

"But they—"

"Ember," Soren interrupted, "take Jakob and Varran and head toward the Artem border. Stop in the next nearest town, get Jakob seen to, and send word ahead to the border guard. They'll be able to intercept Havi and Safi and keep them there. You should be able to get there before they do if you hurry."

They all stared, silent, as Soren gave her orders…rattling them off with no inflection, no hesitation. As if she had no expectation other than complete and immediate compliance.

Not like a princess.

Like a queen.

"If you can find the others, find them, but don't waste your time searching," she continued. "If they were clever enough to escape Andromeda, they're clever enough to find safe places to shelter. Just get as far from Andromeda as you can, as fast as you can."

"And you?" Ember whispered. To his surprise, she wasn't bristling under the orders being given by her younger, decidedly lower-ranked sister—she merely watched her, listening, waiting for the answer to her question.

His stomach dropped, a realization settling there, weighing his gut down to his toes.

Soren *wasn't* lower-ranked—not according to her blood. Not according to her birthright.

And it was with the power of that birthright she spoke now—not as a princess, but as an Heir to another kingdom's throne.

Soren glanced to Elias, swallowing thickly. "We've wasted too much time already. We need to get to Sirena. My brothers have waited long enough."

With that, she turned aside, settling herself in one of the corners, facing away from them all—a clear indication that the conversation was over.

Elias and Ember exchanged looks; the pain in her eyes, the dread, mirrored his own. But she simply nodded, turning away and quietly conversing with Varran.

He went and sat beside Soren—when she didn't turn, he pressed his back to hers. She shivered against him, her back frigid against his ever-heated skin, but she didn't speak.

He slid his hand across the floor until he found hers. Gave it a squeeze.

Her next breath shuddered, and she leaned further into him, flipping her hand to squeeze his fingers back.

"We're going to make it," she whispered…more like a question than a statement.

He twined his fingers through hers, drawing her hand up to press a kiss to her knuckles. "Together or not at all, smartass."

Finally, a quiet, broken laugh loosened her stiff shoulders. "Together or not at all, jackass."

# CHAPTER 57

# FINN

When he opened his eyes, he was back in the cage.

Or rather, he was standing *outside* of it, eyes locked on its prisoner. Her back was facing him, shoulders hunched over to help her fit in the confined space.

Not a dream, he reminded himself, forcing his mind to think past the hazy vignette at the edges of his vision, the spasmodic change in view whenever he chose to focus on something new. *A memory.*

A memory—and not his own.

He'd stood in this room before. Had seen those bars through the eyes of the girl huddled within the gilded prison, her face bent away from him.

This time, she did not speak or sing—instead, a shrill, warbling tune played from within the confines of her bent arms and knees. She'd folded her limbs around her in some kind of wall…a shield she'd formed around herself with her own flesh and bone.

Across those limbs, beams of light danced…spotlights of some kind, not unlike the kind he'd seen stages outfitted with at a handful of theaters and finer taverns in Atlas.

Light meant to direct attention to a certain subject. Light meant to cut through shadow…and shields.

So she could never hide. Not even when she wanted to.

When one of the beams swept across her brow, she flinched deeper into herself, that birdlike coo stuttering in its smooth melody.

That fear, that pain, should have thrilled him. To see his enemy brought so low…it should have gods-damned *delighted* him to watch her cringe.

Instead, his hands formed into fists within his pockets.

Now that he stood on the outside of the cage, the sheer fabric stretched over her body caught his attention…thin, so thin it showed her freckles through it. So thin it couldn't possibly protect her from the chill in this room.

A door opened somewhere deeper in the chamber, and the prisoner shifted, the stark sight of her shoulder blades and spine moving beneath her skin choking Finn with…something. Some dark emotion that he couldn't name, something that reminded him of blood on his hands and a dark, dingy alley and someone singing as they cleaned every crease in his palms.

"Oh, Songbird," called a voice—it was smooth and deep, confident…too confident. The kind of bold, brash performance that stank of insecurity beneath.

Gild over grime. The kind of mask that rust would eventually erode through, showing its true make after one too many uses.

The voiceless song came to a sudden halt. The prisoner raised her head, peering over the barrier of her arm with bloodshot golden eyes, her dark brows furrowed, her lips still pursed.

Whistling—she had been whistling that hoarse, haunting tune.

A figure appeared, circling around the other side of the cage to face her. He was a thing made out of middle grounds—middling age, middling beauty, middling fashion sense. His clothes were fine enough, but with just enough wear in places to suggest they'd been bought second-hand and tailored. He wore very few wrinkles on his face, but considerable gray in his hair. His features were not arranged with any kind of ugly bend, but none were remarkable, either.

He was, by all accounts, average. And yet, he stood before this girl—this *goddess*—and looked down his nose at her. Called her *Songbird* with such pointed, practiced condescension that it had to be an intentional jab.

Even with the goddess chained and fettered, Finn didn't think that was the smartest of choices.

"We have visitors arriving very soon to see you," said the man, leaning in and rapping on the bars with his cane. "I expect you to put on your best show."

There was a lingering pause.

That cane beat on the bars harder, a thunderous sound that even brought Finn's hands up to shield himself; but of course this dream—*memory*—hadn't seen fit to hand him a weapon.

He always kept at least one blade hidden on his person. To exclude that detail was sloppy at best. Even his own brain couldn't keep up with him.

Those golden eyes—twice as luminous as the golden paint on the cage bars—finally fixed on the man with the cane.

"Tell me what I can expect tonight," he commanded.

She didn't raise her head, but a cracked whisper emerged from the cage of her arms: "I'm going to kill you."

"Of course." His tone absolutely dripped disdainful, patronizing indulgence. "But before that."

With slow, painful movements, Occassio unfolded from her hunched-over crouch, settling herself down on scabbed-over knees. Her feet were splayed oddly—not in a way that suggested broken bones, but at an angle that suggested they'd fallen asleep.

It was then that he saw the mirror.

A mirror he recognized, framed in jewels and silver; a mirror he'd stolen with the help of a fidgety, freckled thief.

But here, in this dream-memory-vision-whatever…here, it still had a reflection.

No empty quicksilver surface. No godly power hidden between its pane and frame.

Just a very fancy, hauntingly familiar mirror.

Occassio drew in a breath, pulling his attention back to her—she'd braced her palms on her knees, forcing herself to sit straight, her neck clearly straining with the effort of holding her head up.

Again, that white-hot emotion barreled through his veins. He forced it down.

As her eyes rolled into her head, showing the whites for only a moment before they glowed pink, he took a step closer. The scene bled around him, the lurid colors and shapes smearing like syrup before dripping back into a whole, the step taking him three times as long as it ought to.

But instead of reciting a prophecy or sharing a secret or humming some off-key tune…

Occassio jerked. Twitched. Choked on her own breath.

"Oh, please," sighed the man with the cane; he propped his entire weight on it to lean in closer. "Like I'd fall for that."

Finn was inclined to agree—the theatrics did seem a little much.

At least, until Occassio collapsed on her side, still convulsing, still gagging, knocking her mirror to the floor beside her.

Until blood began to seep from her eyes and ears and nose, her mouth clamped so tightly shut that he could see the muscles in her jaw shuddering beneath her skin.

The man with the cane swore, sounding far more annoyed than alarmed. He stuck a hand in his pocket, digging deeply into it before producing a key; he kept swearing as he undid the lock on the cage, swinging it open with a rough shove.

But instead of trying to help her—instead of doing anything even a quarter-decent person would—the man threw his cane forward before catching it with a jerk of his hand, gripping it closer to the bottom, giving him length to work with.

To strike with.

Finn realized what was happening a heartbeat too late. And by then, Occassio's captor was already swinging his cane, the metal ball at the end barreling toward Occassio's ribs—

But instead, her hand flashed up. Caught the cane in a claw-like grip.

When she looked up, still weeping blood, she was grinning—a baring of bloody teeth that had Finn stumbling back a step.

"There is no *before that*," she cooed. "I'm just going to kill you."

With a sharp jerk, she tugged the man halfway into the cage by his cane, only releasing it to grip him by the neck instead. With her other hand, she scrabbled to grab the mirror, dragging it into her lap as the man choked and struggled, trying to get out of her grip…to no avail.

Occassio placed her palm in the center of the mirror, stroking its glass lovingly.

"You," she whispered to it, "are a cage."

Her gaze flickered to the man in her manacled grasp.

"He," she murmured to the mirror, "is your prisoner."

And with a swift yank, she pulled the man into the mirror itself.

He didn't even have time to scream.

The glass surface wavered…a pool with a stone thrown in.

It did not shatter. It took its captor like a dutiful cage ought to, and the second he was through…

That glass solidified. Turned to rigid quicksilver, flawless in the spread of its smooth surface.

And when Occassio hovered over it, testing it with her fingers, a mad giggle bubbling out of her throat…

No reflection lingered at its surface.

# CHAPTER 58

# RAQUEL

Sirena was a city with roots.

She couldn't walk more than two paces without encountering some new, unfamiliar plant—bushes with leaves larger than her head, trees with boughs heavy with vibrant fruits and sickly-sweet flowers, balconies wound with streamers made of twisting vines with thorns that curled like talons ready to catch prey. There were more plants than people, more trees than houses—the city square opened to a cobbled circle with a massive tree in the center, stretching higher than any building she'd seen beyond castles, its branches strung with twinkling lights and colored crepe paper, small ceramic sirens swimming through its leaves.

It might have been the most beautiful place she'd ever seen, if she hadn't been too busy ensuring she didn't lose the two Atlas princes in her care.

Kallias was able to move under his own power, at least, but he'd been acting off all morning; scratching at his arms, soaking cloth after cloth in the sweat dripping down his forehead, looking back toward the ocean every few seconds with such fervent longing that she nearly felt guilty for forcing him away from it. Especially because it broke her heart, too—her first glimpse of what a real beach looked like, and she could barely spare a moment to marvel.

Finn, on the other hand, had to be led by both of them—he'd been hallucinating so badly this morning that they'd had to tie a blindfold around his eyes just to bring him back to his senses, and even then he'd been near-unmanageable, muttering about mirrors and songbirds and riddles unsolvable. He'd passed their new test—reciting his name, Kallias's name, and where he was from—but he'd barely finished it before dissolving into rambles neither she nor Kallias could make sense of.

They were falling apart, piece by piece, body by mind. Elias needed to get here *now*.

Patch had agreed to linger in the city for a few days—after being promised the rest of their meager coin for transport to Arborius—but gods-knew when Elias would make it here, and the restless pirate wouldn't wait forever. If worse came to worst, what was the best choice? Letting Patch leave and hoping Elias had coin left to commandeer a new ship? Going on to Arborius themselves and letting Elias catch up when he could?

She hadn't asked to be given this command, and she didn't want it. Her ambitions had always leaned toward Captain, and eventually General—not keeper of princes. But a title it was, and a title she'd take. For Elias's sake, for Soren's—for her companions, as surprising as it was—she would serve the position as well as she could.

She would not let them go. Either of them.

So she held fast to their hands as they wound their way through flowery streets and laughing crowds, Atlas drawls carried by the salt-and-nectar breeze, pollen tickling mercilessly at her sinuses until even Kallias, as distracted as he was, turned an amused look toward her wheezing breaths through her nose.

"Shut up," she said through gritted teeth.

"I didn't say anything."

"Shut up anyway."

"Try to sneeze," Finn said—the first sign he'd shown that he could actually hear them since they'd departed the ship. His palm was clammy against hers, his fingers buzzing like he had a hive of bees clenched between them, but his tone was even. "It'll clear out the snot."

"You're disgusting," she grumbled, hoping he couldn't hear the all-consuming relief that swept through her. To hear even a hint of humor back in his voice…she didn't care to admit how happy it made her.

"What? Everyone has snot, Raquel. We're all grown-ups here. We can talk about it."

"Hay fever's not surprising, considering where you're from," Kallias assured her.

"I'm not *embarrassed* by it." She sniffled again, cursing softly. "Idiots."

"Awful defensive for someone who isn't embarrassed," Finn faux-whispered to Kallias, who chuckled hoarsely. Raquel scowled. Maybe she should have left them to fend for themselves. That would teach them.

"Keep an eye out for the Boozy Bluebell," Kallias added. "I know someone there who can get us lodging."

"The *Boozy Bluebell?*" She'd heard some subpar tavern names in her time, but that one seemed particularly dissonant.

Kallias smirked, though it hung a bit wrong on his face. "I know, I know. Just trust me, okay?"

Not like she had a choice. "People know you here?"

"Not many." The light in his eyes dimmed. "If they do, it's mostly through Jericho. She studied here years ago…Ivycreek Academy is over on the west side of the city. It's a school for medimancers and physicians. It's where she met our brother-in-law."

"A necromancer was training in an infirmary?"

Kallias shrugged. "Elias says they need to be around the dead or dying. I guess maybe it helped him keep his magic in check for a time."

"Not long enough," Finn muttered.

"I think what I hate the most is that I understand it now," Kallias said, without anyone asking. "The hunger. The pain. I…I didn't understand before how he couldn't control it for us. Why he couldn't fight it." A swallow. A clench of his hand around Raquel's. "I didn't realize how hard it was."

"It's not an excuse for what he did," Raquel muttered.

"I know." But he didn't *sound* like he knew, and fear dug itself deeper into her heart like one of those curled thorns. Was it truly so terrible that he would compare it to the man who'd wrought necromantic havoc on both Atlas and Artem?

One pleasant surprise greeted them in this city, at least: the *Boozy Bluebell* was a cheerful, welcoming tavern, a wooden sign hanging from it with painted bluebells woven into the spiraling calligraphy. A wreath dotted with actual bluebells hung on the door, and music floated out to them even before she twisted the door open.

Inside was just as bright and lovely as out—the tavern walls were lined with sun-filled windows, the sills overflowing with slatted boxes that boasted flourishing miniature gardens. The scents of herbs and spices and a mixture of flowers saturated the air, but delicately, without overpowering her senses. Patrons sat at colorfully painted wooden tables, laughing and eating and sipping drinks from glass jars. Every drink had some sort of fruit, flower, or herb mixed in between cubes of ice or mounted on the edge of the glass. A boy no older than twelve sat between garden boxes on one of the sills, strumming a lyre with intent focus etched into his young face. Every so often he struck a sour note, but no one seemed to mind.

Living in Nyx, Raquel rarely witnessed spring. But this felt like spring contained within four walls, and for a moment, she was almost envious of Atlas. What must it be like to bask in this sort of beauty for so much of the year?

"As I live and breathe!" boomed out a deep voice, its tone threaded with laughter even before a joke had been told. "Is that you, nephew?"

Kallias's strained smile spread into a relieved grin, and he released her hand to slip between tables, rounding the well-polished bar counter to embrace who she assumed was the tavernkeep: a stocky man a head shorter than Kallias and twice as broad, suntanned skin gleaming near-bronze, his reddish hair cropped short and severe for such a smiling face. Good humor shone out of every pore as he clapped Kallias on the back with such a harsh, loud smack that she nearly winced.

"Uncle Roran," Kallias greeted him with a slightly breathless laugh, returning his pat on the back. "It's been a long time."

"Long time, indeed. Last I saw you, you were hardly half this height." Roran crossed his arms over his pleated leather apron, gaze sliding past Kallias to land on her. He tipped his head a bit, the crown of daisies in his hair sliding toward his brow. "This beautiful woman can't possibly be in your company?"

"She'd prefer it otherwise, believe me." Kallias's smile dropped a bit. "I hate to ask, Uncle Roran, but I need a favor."

"Of course." He looked over Kallias's simple clothes with a keen eye. "I assume this is a mission of subtlety?"

"If possible."

"Titleless?"

"Preferably."

"Of course. Anything for Ramses's boy. The room upstairs is yours to use as you see fit. Anyone asks, you're my nephews from up toward the border."

"I think we may need better aliases. No one is ever going to believe our handsome selves are related to your ugly mug," Finn spoke up, grin curling up toward his blindfold.

Roran blinked at him, squinting a moment before his eyes widened. "This can't be little Finnick?"

Finn saluted in his direction. "One and the same."

"Just as crude as ever!" The tavernkeep leaned against the bartop to get a better look. "What's with the blinders, boy?"

"Necessity," Finn said smoothly. "Sun damage while sailing."

"Ach, fool. You should know better than to sail without something to shield your lookers." Roran gestured toward the staircase behind the bar, offering Raquel a gentlemanly bow, catching his daisy crown as it fell off his head with a quiet curse. "Go on, Kallias, escort your lady up. I'll send something on for Finnick's eyes in a short while."

"This lady doesn't need escorting," Raquel muttered—too quietly to be heard, she thought, but another jolly laugh burst from deep in Roran's chest as he clapped a hand against his gut.

"I like you, Miss," he said. "Keep these boys in line, I bet. Head on up, then, lead the way."

She couldn't help smiling back as she did exactly that, guiding Finn by the elbow until he found his rhythm on the creaking stairs himself. Kallias brought up the rear, murmuring directions to her until they found the correct door.

Inside was a simple enough room: two beds, a washroom, and a pitcher with water at the ready sitting on a breakfast table by the four-paned window. A small vase of daises and bluebells sat beside the pitcher.

"Your uncle?" she asked as Finn dropped to one bed, Kallias sitting at the table and pouring himself a glass of water with a rattling hand. "I thought Adriata only had a sister."

"She does. Uncle Roran is our father's brother. Jericho stayed here with him and his daughter Azalea while she studied here." He took a long draw of his water, wiping the back of his palm across his forehead before standing with an abrupt jolt, stalking to the window and twisting open the brass latch with one hand. The glass pane swung open, and he stuck his head out into open air, pouring what remained of the pitcher over his head and shaking it out like a dog fresh out of a bath.

A shout of indignation came from somewhere below, followed by a string of words so foul they singed her eardrums. Raquel grimaced. "Was that necessary?"

"It's fine. These people don't see enough rain." Kallias gave an apologetic wave below anyway before pulling himself back in. He dragged his hair into a twist on the top of his head, water raining from his soaked strands to ford paths down his collar. "Do you have a—"

She tossed him one of the hairbands from his pack before he finished speaking. "You're not fooling anyone."

He caught it lightning-quick, knuckles and jaw flexing as he stared at her. His eyes were more gray than blue now, even in the light—a foreboding purple-gray that spoke of destruction. "I'm not trying to."

Cold trickled down her throat, and she swallowed hard.

There was a rumble in his voice that was all too familiar.

"Kallias," she rasped, "what did you do?"

Shoulders slumping, he tied his hair in a messy knot before crossing the room in three wide strides, falling to his seat on the mattress beside her. Across from them, Finn was already asleep—he hadn't even bothered to take off his blindfold.

"Nothing," Kallias whispered. "Nothing yet. He just…it's…" He shook his head. "I want this to be over. All of it."

Her heart ached. "I know."

Without warning, with nothing more than a weary sigh, he suddenly bent into her, resting his head on her shoulder and closing his eyes.

"I don't know much longer I can do this, Raquel," he whispered.

The ache in her chest sharpened, and she didn't bear down on it this time. Instead, she offered him her hand; after a pause, he took it, enveloping her fingers in his and leaning more heavily into her side.

"Not forever," she promised him, reaching over with her other hand to brush stray strands of hair out of his eyes. "Just long enough. Just until it's over."

"And what if it's never over?"

She cupped her hand around his cheek. Pressed a kiss to his forehead. Felt him stop breathing as her lips brushed his skin.

"Then I will find a way to end it," she whispered. "If you stay, so will I."

His breath expelled in an unsteady laugh. "Until the end?"

"Until the end."

Gods knew where it came from, the sudden fire in her chest, the refusal to let him bow once more to those who would bring him low. But she would not see him on his knees again. She would not see one more sacrifice from Kallias Atlas, another price he had no obligation to pay.

There was no telling how long they sat like that, her fingers tracing gentle paths over his slow-drying hair, his head heavy on her shoulder like he might fall asleep there. All she knew was that she'd just started to doze off when there was a sharp, frantic series of knocks at the door.

Finn jolted so hard he almost tumbled off the bed, swearing at the top of his voice as he scrabbled to pull the blindfold off. Kallias was on his feet before even her, striding to the door and pulling it open with a severe look on his face—before his expression went utterly blank, his hands falling limp at his sides as he took in their visitor.

"I heard rumor of an Atlas bastard wandering around here," said Elias Loch—*Elias Loch,* whole and healthy and looking a good bit more human than when she'd seen him last.

He was *smiling,* for gods' sakes.

He wore plain traveling garb, a small pack slung over his shoulder and his prayer beads only just peeking out above his collar. His ragged cloak and long-sleeved blue tunic covered his tattoos, and a patch had been affixed over his right eye—a square of cloth that made him look better fit to walk the deck of Patch's ship than the streets of Sirena.

There were new scars, scalded over rather than scabbed, too many to tally—the most obvious were twin rows of four scratches dragged down his temples to the corners of his jaw, like something had tried to claw at his ears and missed. But he stood so tall, so strong, so…different from when they'd last seen him. Like he'd finally shaken off the shadow of death that had trailed him ever since his spine had snapped in Atlas.

Kallias blinked once. Twice.

Then, with a whoop so loud Raquel couldn't hold back a hiss of warning, the prince flung his arms around Elias with a sharp *thud,* his fists pounding into Elias's back as he tugged him into his fierce embrace.

"Your timing is impeccable," Finn muttered—he looked less than impressed at the state of Elias, but his eyes were darting to either side of the Nyxian warrior, a twinge of some dark emotion dragging the corners of his bruised mouth downward.

Because Elias was here—but Soren was not. Soren or Anima.

Raquel's heart sank, but she didn't have the heart to ask—not while Kallias was beaming, grinning so broadly he almost looked like his old self again.

"You look like you took a swim through Mortem's pits," Elias said, pulling back and bracing a hand against Kallias's jaw, giving him a frank once-over as his smile bent into a more familiar scowl. "What happened to you?"

"It's a long story." Kallias shook his head, laughing again, but this time it trembled. He knocked his forehead to Elias's, shaking him by the shoulder. "I could kiss you, I'm so happy you're here."

"Please don't," piped up a voice from somewhere behind Elias; a hand popped up, waving over his shoulder. A hand sporting a ring set with a Nyxian black diamond. "That's my job now."

Raquel's heart leapt. Kallias drew in such a sharp breath that she was half-sure one of his lungs would leap straight out of his throat, and Finn…

Finn's shoulders *slumped,* like a burden he'd been carrying for miles and miles had finally slid off his back.

That pale hand curled around Elias's shoulder, shoving him out of the way to reveal Soren—or, at least, a woman who greatly resembled her. Her eyes were green again, her smile much sharper than Anima's had ever been, but something was…different. Not just her hair, which had been cut from near waist-length to a cropped tangle of curls; not just her skin, which was bruised and battered and pockmarked with strange protrusions that resembled plant sprouts in some places, thorns in others; not just her muscle tone, which had diminished even further since she'd left them, leaving her looking less battle-ready and more battle-worn.

No, the true difference lay in the way she looked at these Atlas princes, her eyes welling with tears rather than the shyness of Anima or the rage of a Nyxian soldier. The difference lay in how she took a single step toward Kallias like it ached *not* to go nearer, like that distance stretched some unseen muscle near to tearing.

She didn't waste her time with greetings. Instead, she looked at Kallias, took in a deep breath, and whispered, "I remember, Kal. I'm so sorry. I'm so—"

If she kept apologizing, Raquel didn't hear it—*couldn't* hear it, because Kallias crushed her against him before she had the chance to finish. They held each other so tightly that Soren's feet lifted off the floor, her face buried in Kallias's shoulder, and both of them were weeping—something she hadn't seen Soren do since the aftermath of Jira's pyre burning.

"Soleil," he said. Then again, like he couldn't truly believe it, like a question: "Soleil?"

"Mostly," she said, letting out a laugh utterly soaked in tears. Though Kallias didn't loosen his grip on her, she leaned back to meet his gaze, her bruised hands wiping his tears away with signature Soren roughness. "Stop that. I've made you cry enough."

"*I'm* sorry," Kallias sobbed, and the sound tore at Raquel's heart. His mouth quivered, soaked in saltwater of his own making, his eyes glazed with a decade of grief…of guilt. "I tried to find you, I swear I tried, I swear I didn't leave you there—"

"I know! Kal, I know. I *know*." Soren's voice shattered, cracked through with emotion as she wiped another tear trail from his cheek. "Look at me—no, *really* look at me." She held his face in her hands, forcing him to gaze directly at her, her features set in determined focus. "I'm all right. Say it."

Kallias's throat bobbed. "You're all right."

"I'm all right." Soren didn't blink; didn't break his gaze. "You didn't lose me—you didn't leave me. You're the one that brought me home."

Kallias smiled, but not in truth—it was a sob putting on its best costume. "You stabbed me in the leg for that."

"We'll talk about *that* later." Soren didn't release his face, but she did lean in, pressing a kiss to his forehead. "Now, will you please put me down? You know Finn can't reach me all the way up here, poor, stunted thing that he is."

"You're the *same height*," Kallias laughed, at the same time Finn said, "Rude. That's what you are, *rude—*"

The rest of his scolding muffled to mumbles as Kallias lowered Soren to the ground and they both reached out, grabbing Finn by each arm and tugging him close. Kallias buried his face in Soren's hair, still crying—Finn studied her with blood-branched eyes, taking in her own divinely struck wounds.

"Did she do that?" he asked flatly, trailing his thumb over one of her thorns.

Soren grimaced. "Not exactly."

"Is she dead?"

"Not exactly," she said again. She licked her thumb before brushing at a dried-up scarlet tear beneath Finn's left eye. "Occassio?"

Finn nodded reluctantly, submitting to his sister's ministrations with a grimace of his own.

"Is *she* dead?"

"As deeply touching as your faith in me is, if I could kill a goddess, I wouldn't have left you behind in the palace."

That phrase—*left you behind*—struck Raquel at the same time it seemed to wash over Soren, who immediately gripped Finn's chin and forced him to meet her gaze, features stony and unforgiving. "You didn't leave me behind. I told you to run."

"And I listened."

"Wonder of wonders, yes, you did." Soren reached up and pulled on Kallias's hair until he let out a noise of pain and reared back. She set one hand to each of the Atlas princes' faces, eyes narrowed, shoulders squared. The look of a woman assessing a battle, building a strategy. "No more blame. Not from you or for you. We are *all* here; we *all* made it. Now, tell me why *you* look like someone poked all the veins in your eyes with a needle, and why *you*…look, Kal, I'm not going to sugarcoat it, I think someone might've made off with your tan."

As Soren drew them toward one of the beds, pestering them for more details and giving some of her own, a brand of flame brushed against Raquel's wrist.

"How is he?" Elias asked in her ear, drawing his hand back, looking more characteristically grim.

"Not good." She pulled her own arms in, crossing them tightly over her chest as she swiveled out of Kallias's eyeline. "Skyhaven didn't pan out the way we hoped."

"So Tempest—"

She dug her nails into her own sleeve. "It's not good, Elias."

He took a moment before speaking again, his eyes trained on the trio of Atlas royals. Then: "Andromeda fell. Port Atlas, too."

She whipped to face him, mouth falling open, but he plowed on.

"Tenebrae took Princess Jericho. From what Soren tells me, the King and Queen have been removed from their thrones."

Damn. *Damn.*

"You're going to tell him?" When Elias nodded, she brushed at her rumpled clothes and stood straighter. "I should be there."

"No. I want it to come from me, and…" He hesitated. "We suffered losses in Andromeda. Soren wants to talk to you about it herself."

The faces of their company flashed through her mind: Kriss, Jakob, Varran, Rian, Samhain…all of them.

Which of those faces would she never see again? Which were already burned or buried?

"All right," she rasped. "Gently, Elias. He's not well."

Elias only nodded. And as he gathered Kallias and herded him out, leaving Soren and Finn to their own devices, the gnawing sense of dread only bit down harder on Raquel's heels.

# CHAPTER 59

# KALLIAS

As Elias led him out into the empty hall outside their room, shutting the door on Soren and Finn's irritable bantering—perhaps the best sound Kallias had ever heard—it took enormous effort to ignore the urgings of his body to seek out something, *anything*, to pour down his desiccated throat. His esophagus might as well have been filled to the brim with sand; every dry swallow ground flesh against flesh, scratching painfully, begging for moisture.

How his voice still worked…that was a mystery for the ages, and one someone else could waste their time solving. "If this is you looking to steal that kiss, you could've just said so."

Elias didn't laugh; in fact, he didn't even grimace or roll his eyes, which was somehow scarier. He just gazed at Kallias with tired eyes, his arms crossed over his broad chest, sleeves rolled up to show off his now-healed tattoos…and fresh, barely closed scars.

"You need to brace yourself," said Elias. "It's not good news."

A feeling not unlike seasickness seized his stomach, a warning he wasn't on sure enough footing for this. He mimicked Elias, leaning himself back against the sturdy wall, refusing to flinch as his whip-wounds rubbed against the rough texture of the wood. Elowyn had done a fair job healing them, but they'd only had so much time on the ship. And even if they'd had longer, her magic just wasn't as strong as others…as Jericho's.

"Braced," he said shortly. "Tell me."

Elias did him the kindness of holding his gaze; it made it a bit easier to believe when he said, "We encountered Tenebrae in Nyx."

He'd lied. He hadn't braced well enough for that.

But Elias wasn't done. "Soren and Anima confronted him…he walked in Jericho's body. He claims your parents are alive, but imprisoned." Elias's throat bobbed. "I'm sorry, Kal. Port Atlas has fallen."

No. No. *No.*

His parents. His sister. His kingdom.

He was out of time.

With no warning, no choice, no goodbye…he was out of time.

"We gathered what news we could on our way here…it sounds as though he used Jericho to announce that the King and Queen are dead, victims of Nyxian assassins. He's crowned Jericho as queen—no word on Vaughn that we heard, but we didn't want to push hard enough to stick in people's memory."

"What made her give in?" Not that it mattered…it shouldn't have mattered. But he asked anyway. "What broke her?"

"He was going to kill your parents in truth, according to Soren." Elias broke it without softening it, and somehow that helped…somehow it felt easy to believe. "She made a counteroffer. Their lives in exchange for her body."

*Oh, Jer.* Grief and guilt wracked down every limb, and Kallias covered his mouth to keep the sound of his breaking heart from escaping.

He couldn't forgive her for every betrayal, big and small, that she'd committed over the last decade. Couldn't forgive the way she'd shut them out of their own vow, not even giving them the chance to prove their loyalty to *us before all.*

But when it came down to it, she'd still kept that promise. *Us before all.* Family before anything, even themselves.

Sacrifice.

Soleil, Jericho, and Elias had all taken their turns with sacrifice. For each other, for family.

Now…now it was his turn. He felt it in the deepest parts of himself.

But not just for his family—for his kingdom. For all kingdoms.

*All before us.*

His people before himself. It was the silent vow he'd always carried out; an expectation he'd placed on himself in spite of not carrying the title of Heir, in spite of being doomed to one day leave them behind.

*All before me. Family before all.*

Vows were tricky things. They weren't easily broken like promises. Vows buried themselves in the flesh of the heart, more than word, more than thought. They lived and breathed and bled along with him. They made up the core of who Kallias Atlas was.

*All before me.*

Elias's hand brushed against his shoulder, a reminder of exactly what these vows were about to cost him. "Kal?"

He stood abruptly, brushing off his hand. "I'll be right back. I…I need a moment."

"I'll come with you—"

"I need a moment *alone.*"

The corners of Elias's eyes tightened. "At least let me guard your back."

Everything in him wanted to say yes. Everything in him wanted to admit the truth of this, if only so Elias could talk him out of it. So he could hear whatever lies would give him permission to be selfish.

Or, at the very least, to have someone walk him there. So he wouldn't be alone.

But the time for empty promises and hopeful denials and selfish wishes was over.

If anyone understood grief and its need for space, it was Elias—and though it had frustrated Kallias to no end in Artem, he was grateful for it now, because when he squeezed Elias's shoulder and said, "This is my kingdom—there's nothing to guard my back from. Stay with So…with Soren. Please?"—Elias finally acquiesced, drawing him in for a brief embrace before allowing him to fumble his way blindly out of the tavern, snatching his pack from one of the hooks behind the bar as he went, not a single person following on his heels.

One thing had not changed. When Kallias Atlas was in turmoil, he sought out the sea.

The ocean was calm today, and he was glad of it, because he was not— waves of tremors crashed over him one by one, each stronger than the last, panic sweeping over him with such force that it left him lightheaded, his consciousness bobbing like a fisherman's lure. Dropping his pack in the dry sand, he barely managed to stagger to the damp edge of the shore before falling to his knees in the surf, nausea building within him until he bent forward and vomited with a violent retch.

All that came out was water and seafoam.

He vomited again. And again. And again.

Nothing but seawater. Nothing but salt and terror in his mouth.

He was going to die today.

Not by battle, not by assassination, not by accident. He was going to die, and he was going to choose it, and that should have made it easier but it didn't, it didn't, it *didn't*.

A quiet splash. Knees sinking into the sand beside him. A hand sliding over the small of his back.

"I'm sorry," Tempest said quietly. "I didn't know."

"How? How didn't you know?"

"I'm not all-seeing like my sister, Prince."

His anger sputtered out as quickly as it had flared. Anger would not make this easier.

"I don't want to be done," he whispered, throat tight, eyes brimming with tears. He dashed them away with the back of his hand, ignoring how the salt stung his eyes. "I don't want to be done."

A sob replaced his retching, a sob so deep and visceral and *painful* that it might have been wrenched out of the very pits of him. It might have been down there for years—maybe even a decade—waiting its turn to be released.

Tempest's arm wrapped around his shoulders, cold and strong and unyielding. "You can break here," he said. "If only for a minute. The sea will hold you."

There was no need for a second invitation. There, kneeling in the ocean with the arm of a god holding him up, Kallias Atlas let every shattered piece of him fall into the surf.

The keening agony that shook itself free from his throat did not sound like him. Perhaps because it wasn't—it was pure emotion, pure grief and fear and rage and *it's not fair, it's not fair.* It was the sound of a lifetime of sacrifices, a lifetime of high roads, a lifetime of laying himself down over treacherous paths so his family could get where they needed to go safely. It was a lifetime spent in service to others without acknowledgement, without appreciation, without receiving the same care in return.

Except once.

Once, when a man from an enemy kingdom had shielded him from devouring fire. Once, when that man had told him he was worth more than he gave himself credit for, worth more to his kingdom as a person than as a bargaining chip.

But Elias could not shield him from this. And Kallias would never ask him to even if he could.

It took several minutes for the mourning to run itself out. And when he finally spent all his tears, he took in a deep gust of seaside air and pretended it was Port Atlas—pretended it was home.

He would never see it again. Pretending was all he had left.

"If there was another way, I would offer it," Tempest promised. "I swear on my magic, on the sea and the sky and the sand, I would not ask this of you if I did not have to."

"I know," Kallias whispered. He had heard many stories about Tempest, both warnings and praises—though mostly warnings—and none of them had ever claimed the god to be dishonest. "Will it be like the last time?"

"No," Tempest assured him. "You've already gone through it once, and now you've wielded the relic. You'll feel nothing at all. But you must be sure, Prince. The Eye of the Storm's time to claim your life has ended. She will not bring you back this time."

Somehow, the idea of feeling nothing—of death coming in the blink of an eye—was even more terrifying. "I need a moment alone."

"You have it." And Tempest vanished from his side once more.

A moment. How could he manage all the goodbyes he needed to say in the span of a moment? How could he neatly put a period on the end of a life not fully lived, closing the book on two and a half decades within a breath's worth of time?

His eyes went to his pack, lying further up the beach, already being surrounded by curious seagulls.

There was one way to get this done as neatly as possible. One way to not destroy himself in the process…or the people waiting in the tavern for him to come back to them.

He climbed back up the shore and picked up his pack, pulling out some paper and a pen and a little pot of ink they'd taken from their borrowed cabin in Skyhaven.

And as he sat in the sand and gazed out at his beloved sea, watching the sun paint the waves in great strokes of peach and gold, persimmon and scarlet—perhaps the most beautiful sunset he'd ever had the privilege to witness—Kallias began to write.

# CHAPTER 60

# FINN

The edges of his vision pulsed with bruise-purple pain as he waited by the tavern window, watching the door for any sign of Kallias returning.

After Kallias and Elias had left, Soren and Raquel had gone down to the bar to sit and talk with Roran, and they each now had a third cocktail in their grasp, thick glass jars filled with a gradient of color that started with sky blue at the top and darkened all the way to deep navy-violet at the bottom. Still, they sat steady enough in their chairs that he didn't worry for them. Nyxians—even Atlas-born ones—were built of sterner stuff.

"Unlike you," hummed Occassio in his ear. "Just one of those drinks would have you on the floor."

He glared at her out of his periphery, where he caught just a glimpse of rhinestone curls and a drink dyed all shades of pink. "I don't have time for this."

"Yes you do." She leaned further into his eyeline, sipping noisily at her drink. A frown bent her lips, and she pulled her straw out to reveal a loose petal jammed up in it. Screwing her face up in a mock-gag, she plucked the damp petal out and tossed it at him, letting it flop onto his hand. "Why would anyone put flowers in perfectly good alcohol?"

"Why would anyone try to crack open a perfectly good skull?" he asked, teeth gritted against the hammer and chisel hard at work in his head.

"One does what they must, that's all." She wiggled silk-soft fingertips before his eyes, coaxing his gaze in her direction. He grimaced against the illusory deception; he knew full well her fingers bore the callouses and bends and razor-thin scars expected of thieving hands. "Finn. You don't have to suffer any longer. It's over, anyhow."

"It's not over until I say so."

"*Finn.*" Frustration nibbled at the illusion masking her fingertips, letting a bit of roughness peek through, ridges of sandpaper skin outlining her fingerprints. "I don't *want* you to be in pain."

"Then why don't you stop? Why don't you leave me *alone*?"

"It's too late for that. My magic has hold of you, and it's not going to let go. I can't make it stop even if I try. And you don't have to believe me, but I *have* tried. More than once."

"You're right," he muttered, shifting himself away from her. "I don't have to believe you."

A sudden breeze rattling the windowpane drew both of their attentions a heartbeat before something smacked sharply against the glass—a flash of paper and twine that thunked into the window before falling out of sight.

"What the rot was that?" Occassio asked incredulously.

So the goddess of prophecy could still be surprised. "Do you want to look, or shall I?"

"Better you do it, I think." A flare of lavender light danced through her eyes before dimming, and her lips pinched—he couldn't tell what emotion that mask was hiding. "You won't want me to see it."

Something darker than dread tunneled deep into his gut. "What are you talking about?"

Before he even finished the sentence, she'd vanished entirely. But that feeling continued to worm deeper and deeper into his core; not fear, but…foreboding. The sense that something horrible had already happened, long before he could try to stop it. Like maggots had begun to gnaw into his corpse before he'd even registered that his heart had stopped.

*Kal, where are you?*

That painful haze of color only brightened as he stood and took stumbling steps toward the door, like he *had* consumed multiple jars of alcohol. But rather than dulling his senses, this haze only sharpened them, every flicker of light and brush of air and tantalizing scent riling him to near-desperation, the urge to crawl from his skin almost unbearable.

Madness in mind and in flesh. What more could be taken from him?

He'd barely rounded the doorway and taken a step toward the window when his boot nudged against something.

At his feet was a stack of folded paper—five pieces in all, edges pressed neatly together and tied with twine that looked sand-and-salt-crusted, like it had been scavenged from the beach.

The top paper boasted his name in familiar, annoyingly fine script.

The maggots writhed. The chisel dug in. Childhood terror brought back a briefly-forgotten memory of wine and blood staining his clothes.

He swept up the stack and opened the paper with his name on it.

*Finn,*

*I have no gods-damned idea what I'm going to write, so prepare yourself for some rambling before I find the proper heading.*

*I guess I want to start with an apology. More than anyone else, I think you're owed one.*

*When Soleil died, I gave myself the excuse of guilt and grief. I told myself the distance was to protect you and Jericho…to protect myself, too. You asked me, begged me, to save Soleil that day. To get her out when no one else could. And when I failed her, I failed you too.*

*I told myself you wanted nothing to do with me because it was easier. Easier than hoping you could forgive me for that failure. Easier than looking at you and imagining I saw blame in your eyes. But in my cowardice, I didn't realize I was hurting you…hurting you and Jericho. I robbed you both of two siblings instead of one.*

*Maybe if I'd stepped up instead of stepping back, Jericho wouldn't have gone down the path she did. Maybe you wouldn't have been forced to carry so much on your shoulders. Maybe…maybe I could have stopped all of this. I think about that more than I should, whether this all comes down to me in the end. If so, then I've probably earned this.*

*Most of all, I'm sorry to break my last promise to you. But Atlas needs a defender. It needs a god to guard its heart. I cannot save it. I cannot save anyone alone.*

Finn stopped with his thumb resting over that last sentence, his heart trying to throw itself headfirst out of his chest, breath refusing to come in or out of his lungs.

"Don't," he whispered, as if Kallias could still hear him, as if he didn't already know what had been done. What he was too late to stop. "Don't say it, you bastard, don't…"

*By the time you read this, I will already be gone.*

His knees hit the dirt.

*It's all right. I'm ready to go.*

His lungs hurt. His heart, his head hurt. Everything, everything, everything.

Even in writing, Kallias was a gods-awful liar.

*Make sure these letters land where they should. I'm trusting you with them…they're the only last words I'm going to get.*

*I love you, little brother. You owe me no favors, but do me one anyway: kick that goddess's ass. Teach her what happens to those who go against an Atlas prince.*

*Always and forever proud of you.*

*Kal*

Something was ruining the paper. Something was falling on it in droplets, thinning the barely-dry ink and making it run, staining his shaking hands.

Rain. It was raining, raining in spite of the clear sky—

"Finn?" Raquel's voice rose in alarm somewhere behind him, and her hands landed on his shoulders a moment later. "Finn, what happened? Why are you crying? *Finn!*"

Not rain.

Wordlessly, he handed her the stack of letters—the next one signed with her name. "He's gone," he said.

"What?"

"He's gone," he repeated. All he could think, say, remember. *He's gone, he's gone, he's gone.*

"Who?" But the shake to her voice told him she already knew.

When he didn't answer, she cursed, coming around and dropping to one knee in front of him, snagging his shirt in her fist and tugging him close. "Damn it, Finn, *who*? *Who is gone*?"

"Kallias." Gods, he didn't recognize his own voice, all emptiness and disbelief and the writhing of maggots in a dead man's chest. "He gave himself to Tempest."

***

Raquel combed the city for hours, Elias accompanying her, and Finn…Finn could only sit in their room, staring at the empty bed across from his, his letter hanging half-crumpled from his trembling, stiff fingers.

Soren stayed with him. She had yet to lift her head from her hands after reading her own letter, though she wouldn't tell him what it said.

*He's gone, he's gone, he's gone.*

But maybe not. Soren had fought back—Soren had survived. Kallias had lived through it the first time…on a technicality, sure, but he'd done it. There was no way to be sure. No way to know how much or how little of his brother might yet linger in this world.

No. There was one way.

Only one.

But it would require him to do something he'd never done before. A game he'd never played and won. A trick he'd not yet managed to pull off.

His fingers tightened on the salt-stiff paper.

He did not let the idea take shape in his head. If it became a thought, it would become a plan; if it became a plan, it would become future, whether it failed or succeeded. And the future…the future only answered to one mistress.

The present, however, was his to claim.

So he tucked his glimmer of possibility away, letting himself forget it. It was not a thought. Not a plan. It was a wish, fleeting as a shooting star, there and then gone. There was no god that governed over wishes; wishes belonged to the heart, to the soul, not the mind.

Occassio could keep his thoughts. All he needed today were wishes.

"Soren," he said, and she finally looked up, eyes reddened and furious. "You should go help them."

"I'm not letting you out of my sight," she said. "No depths-damned way."

"Soren," he said again, sharper. "Go help them."

She opened her mouth to protest again, that fury hardening her gaze—but then she stopped. Stared at him, lips pressing together like she was biting back a secret, her eyes narrowing only a fraction.

"I think you might be the only person left in the world who still trusts me," he said softly. "So do me a favor, little sister. Trust me."

She stared at him for a minute longer, hands loosely clasped in her lap…and the longer she stared, the more that look of suspicion and fear melted into exhaustion. Into aching, long-suffered grief.

"Finn," she whispered.

"I know." He forced a smile, reaching out for her hand—she clasped it tightly, mangling his fingers with her swordswoman grip. He squeezed back, ignoring the pain. "I know, kid. I hate it too."

"I can't…" Soren's teeth sank into her trembling lip, worrying it as she chewed on her words. They churned behind her eyes like the waves they'd sailed here on. "Not you, too. Please."

His chest cramped, aching to share his wish, his hope—aching to share everything with her. Perhaps the only person he'd ever longed to tell his truth to.

But speaking it, even thinking it, would ruin everything.

So instead, he repeated himself, all he could offer to this girl who looked as though one more loss might just break her: "Trust me, kid."

She closed her eyes. Tightened her hold on his hand.

"I trust you," she said. Not a reassurance; a challenge. "Don't prove me a fool for it."

"I don't think anyone could manage that."

"A compliment from Finnick Atlas?" She released his hands to clutch at her chest, choking, affecting a swoon. "I think I'm having a heart attack. The shock…it's too much…"

He kicked her in the shin, glad for the grin she'd managed to draw out of him. Gods knew when he'd get that again. "Get out. Go find our idiot brother."

"As you command, Your Highness." She stood up and went to the door—then paused, looking back over her shoulder. "And if he's gone?"

Finn held her gaze. "Then I trust *you* to do what you deem best."

And with a grim, measured nod, Princess Soren Atlas left his fate in his own hands.

Not her best choice. But he'd asked for her trust; she'd given it.

If only he didn't have to betray it.

When he called the Occassio's name, she came to him in a rush of light and beauty, more goddess than girl, a form of jewel and dream with a halo of visions dancing around her head.

Madness and mayhem sheathed in a pretty costume.

"What can I do for you, Trickster?" she asked. Impatient, triumphant—but there was something duller underneath, something he didn't understand.

He must truly have passed on into madness, because she almost looked…guilty. Pitying, at the very least. Some emotion that glowed a bit more blue than purple.

Finnick Atlas had never played a game of sacrifice before. That had always been Kallias's bag.

But Kallias was gone. And he'd been right—Atlas needed a protector as godly as the enemy it was being protected from.

He couldn't get any further as Finnick Atlas. It was time to fold that hand.

"I'm done," he whispered, letting every inch of fatigue and forgetfulness and heartache show. That, at least, he didn't need a mask for. "Do what you're going to do. I give you my consent. I'm done."

For the first time, Occassio's face dropped in honest shock. She blinked several times, staring at him as if she hadn't understood a word out of his mouth.

"What?" she asked blankly.

"I'm *done*." Ragged, raw. Frayed down to his last thread. "You want me? Fine. Take me. I'm done."

"I…" She swallowed, a quick flutter of muscle twitching in her jaw. "I…no. This is a trick. You think you can fool me?"

"You're the all-seeing one here. Do I look like I have any cards left?" He extended his shaking arms toward her, watching as her eyes were drawn to the myriad of bruises painted up to his elbows. Places where his own veins had burst beneath the weight of his visions, his magic. *Her* magic. "Here. Search my sleeves. See what's left."

Still, she hesitated. Swallowed again, like she couldn't quite dredge up the words she needed. "Are…are you sure?"

*Am I sure?* "What, now you want to be nice about it? *Yes*, depths damn you, I'm sure. You win. Just get it over with."

She flared brighter before settling into the first form he'd met her in…the girl instead of the goddess. She dimmed and softened until Fidget stood before him, eyes clouded and strangely regretful.

"Finn," she said, and nothing more. Like she'd gotten lost on the path to the end of her thought. Her hands curled into fists, pale-knuckled and nervous.

What little remained of the fool within him ached to prod those lost thoughts until they revealed themselves—to take her hands and find the thieving fingers beneath the polished illusion. But the fool was no longer allowed any influence here.

"Make it quick," was all he said.

Quick, before he lost his ironclad grip on his own thoughts.

Quick, before his sister came back and caught him proving her the fool.

Occassio held out her hands—steady now, though her eyes had ceased their glittering, duller than he'd ever seen them. "For what it's worth, I…I really am sorry to see our game end, Finn."

And in spite of everything, he almost, almost believed her.

He set his hands in hers, his fingertips brushing over a single scar on her wrist—a bracelet of damaged skin that whispered stories of manacles and chains and cages meant for songbirds, not seers.

"I'm sorry," she whispered—so hushed that it might have been his imagination. So absurd that even if she'd said it, it was certainly a lie. Her hands were gentle like hummed lullabies, like candlelight on bloody water, like a rag drawn over trembling fingers. "But trust me—this is the better fate."

*Better than what?* What could be worse than this?

She leaned upward, lips hovering over his forehead—then paused. Waiting.

He nodded his permission, and she pressed a kiss to his forehead, tender as a lover's touch.

Pain and light seared through his mind, burning away every piece of Finnick Atlas until nothing at all remained.

He'd played his last game. Moved his last chess piece.

His last thought was of champagne kisses and firework flares.

# CHAPTER 61

# RAQUEL

Raquel Angelov stood alone before the ever-raging might of the sea.

The salt-heavy breeze lifted her hair from her shoulders and blew it off her back, as if that was the only burden she carried. As if it were doing her a favor by removing the slightest of the weights she currently bore.

Kallias's letter crunched in her palm as she balled her fist, flecks of salt scattering to the sand as they flaked from the paper.

*You are without equal, Raquel Corentine Angelov. Rage against anything that would see you to ruin. My only regret is that I won't be there to see you win.*

*You were the one thing I would have been selfish with.*

*With any scrap of me that lives on, with any piece of me that might remember, that is what I will carry with me: out of everything, you are what I grieve most to lose.*

*Keep my brother safe. No matter what happens, stay by his side. I trust you to bring him home.*

When they'd returned from their fruitless search for Kallias, Finn had been gone as well. Roran had told them the prince had descended the stairs and breezed out of the tavern, looking much better than he had only minutes before, and had ignored Roran's calls and questions.

Which way he had gone when he left, Roran couldn't recall…which was strange, since he swore up and down he'd watched Finn's exit with the intent to memorize exactly that.

Soren had left a sizeable hole in the wall. The blow had snapped off several of the thorns growing from her knuckles.

*Against all vows, against all duty, I would have stood by your side until you ordered me away.*

*I miss you. Not even gone, and I miss you? How strange is that? This letter is going nowhere. You're probably laughing at me by now.*

She might never laugh again.

*All my life, I thought the greatest love of my life would be my crown. My kingdom. My people. I was wrong. My greatest love was you.*

Those words, emblazoned on her memory for all that remained of her wretched life. This letter, which she could not bring herself to tuck away in her pocket. This bracelet, which she could not bring herself to throw into the sea, though that was exactly what she'd come here to do.

Instead, she was just…standing. Staring. Sinking into the sand inch by inch. Letting the indomitable sea kiss her toes with the same fervency one might show while begging for forgiveness.

She did not forgive it. She forgave no power that had a hand in taking Kallias Atlas away from her.

He'd been right. There was truly nothing in the world like the might of the booming, brutal, beautiful sea.

Something warm and wet kissed the apex of her cheek, a droplet of saltwater that did not come from the crashing waves. She brushed it aside with a harsh blow to her cheekbone…a blow not halfway severe enough a punishment for what she'd allowed to happen. What she'd failed to stop.

"Raquel Angelov."

Her breath pulled taut as if hooked by a fisherman's line…a reaction that had become commonplace in the presence of that voice. But it was wrong, somehow…the same timbre, the same depth, but the tone was off in all the worst ways. Confidence instead of humility. Power instead of kindness. This was a command, a call to arms, and…and this voice had only ever spoken her name like a plea or a prayer.

She turned around to find Kallias Atlas staring back at her.

But not *her* Kallias. She didn't need to see the golden eyes to know it. His stance said it all: he stood tall and proud, imperious, regarding the waves behind her as servants who owed fealty rather than a friend he'd long missed. His face might as well have been a mask for all the emotion it showed, not a dimple or laugh line in sight. His eyes *were* gold, glowing bright against the gray sky that framed him in sharp relief, and his hair…his beautiful hair had been chopped short. No longer flowing and fierce but angled and cropped, it reached toward the sky rather than the water. He did not wear the same clothes he'd left them in; now he stood before her in winter dress despite the relative warmth of the day, his muscular chest banded in tooled leather, his shoulders sheathed in a cloak of thick, genuine wolf fur.

They stood mere feet from each other, woman and god. And the god blinked first.

Tempest drew his arms to his chest, looking down at her with a placid expression that made her furious. She wanted to tear that face from his undeserving bones. She wanted…

She wanted to rip and kill and ruin until she found whatever piece of Kallias might yet be lurking beneath that skin.

"You're angry." Not an accusation, only an observation.

"You took him." Her heart twisted, trying desperately to break. "You said you wouldn't take him."

"I said I would give you the chance to claim your debt." He lifted his chin. "You did not take it."

And that had been her worst mistake yet. "Is he gone?"

The question held its place between them, hovering gently in space as Tempest watched her curiously, almost frowning, as if he didn't understand the question.

She hadn't had much hope. But even what little she'd had withered up when he said, in the distinct tone of one who did not have time for the kindness of lies, "Yes."

For what felt like an eternity, only the ocean spoke, its roars still not loud enough to drown out the ragged beating of her hollow heart.

"He did ask for one last thing from me in exchange," said Tempest, with a step forward that shot adrenaline through her muscles, tensing them to the texture of steel. She bound herself in place with a deep breath, refusing to step back as her former god approached her, his golden eyes fixed firmly on her face. How had she never realized just how tall Kallias was? "I'm not often taken off guard by mortals, but this…this did surprise me."

"I don't want to hear this." At least her voice didn't break. "Please just go."

"I made him a promise. Would you have me break it?"

*Yes*, she wanted to say…wanted to scream. But Kallias deserved that, didn't he? To have at least one promise kept? To have one dying wish granted? "Fine."

Tempest's hand wrapped around hers, colder than Kallias's had ever been. It took every bit of fortitude she'd been taught in the army to resist the urge to rip it away.

"The only thing he asked for," Tempest continued, voice so soft she *almost* could imagine it was Kallias instead, "was that I give you back what was stolen from you."

And with a heat that seared across the surface of her bones, lightning crackled from his palm into her very veins, exultant energy drawing all breath clean out of her lungs.

Thunder roared. Lightning screamed. Her vision burst with color, the greenish-purple haze left behind by the flash of storm-light. Wind sang a melody in her ear, a joy so pure that it spun her thoughts into a cyclone. A constant croon of *welcome home, welcome home, welcome home.*

*Eye of the Storm. Welcome home.*

Her knees hit the sand. Her spine arched. Her voice swelled with thunder's world-shaking power.

And with a scream that sounded almost like a song, she threw her fingers up to the sky and cast lightning into the clouds.

The roar that came after nearly deafened her, but it could not drown out the sobs wracking her lungs to shreds.

Magic. *Her magic.*

Kallias had asked that Tempest give her magic back. With his last moments, with his last breath…he'd thought of her.

He'd thought of *her.*

When she turned to look, Tempest was gone, only the faintest imprint of feet in the sand and the crackling power of storm in her veins to prove that he had not been a figment of her wildest imagination.

She looked down to the note still crumpled in her fist. Pressed a shaking, tearstained kiss to the salt-soaked paper.

And on a beach wracked with a howling tempest, Raquel Angelov wept into the sand until her tears were well and truly spent, a scrap of borrowed paper bundled in a hand that smelled of petrichor and lightning.

Eye of the Storm. Peace within chaos. Power within peace.

In the eye of her own storm, she whispered one more title, one she claimed as her own from now until the fight was done:

"Keeper of Atlas. I'll see it done, Kallias."

Raquel Angelov would give blood and sweat and storm to see the kingdom of her enemies safe. She owed that much to a prince whose last thought had been of her.

She owed that much to the man who had reminded her what it was to be loved against all vows, against all duty, against all crowns.

Not just his kingdom's keeper, but his brother's, too.

Raquel Angelov—enemy of not one, but two deities.

It was as good a battle as any.

# CHAPTER 62

## SOREN

Elias hadn't come back yet from his third round of searching, and to be honest, it was probably better that way. If she had to carry the weight of anyone else's grief—the weight of their anger and betrayal and hopeless looks—she might just lose her will to do anything but sit here in silence.

Her brothers were both gone.

Less than a day after she'd gotten them back, and they were gone.

There were too many hurts, too many griefs, too many pockmarked pieces of her heart to sort through. It might never find its way back to some semblance of a whole.

Kallias, leaving without saying goodbye.

Finn, filling her head with promises she knew were false.

Her mother, ignoring the first order she'd tried to give, her diluted loyalties too weak for queenhood to stand its ground on.

Both of her kingdoms, held in Tenebrae's uncaring, chaos-craving fist.

Her fist tightened, bones aching to throw another punch. But broken knuckles wouldn't earn her another chance at saving her beloved few.

She'd failed.

"You know," said Roran, leaning over the bar to tap on her untouched beer—Bluebell Beer, he'd announced as he set it down unsolicited, periwinkle froth overflowing down the mug's lip— "ordinarily, when one sits down at a bar to drown her sorrows, this sort of gift is appreciated. And promptly drunk."

"I'm not a beer person," she mumbled, giving it a halfhearted poke before burying her chin in her folded arms. "Especially when it's blue."

"Ah, it's just edible dye, girlie." Roran rounded the bar to prop his stout self on the stool beside hers, leaning a meaty elbow on the counter, giving her a look so reminiscent of her father's that mist began to gather in her eyes. "Your pa wears the same look when he's heartbroken, y'know."

The mist thickened to fog. "That's the first time anyone's told me I look like him." Though she didn't know if it should feel this touching, considering it was grief they wore the same.

"Well, you carry your ma's beauty, thank the seas that bore ya here," chortled Roran, tapping her under her chin, "but that puppy-eyed look, that's all your pa. Haven't seen him take it off since the day they lost you."

Soren glanced at him from beneath her lashes, leaning back a bit to keep her arms from muffling her words. "You saw him after?"

"We made the trip for the funeral, all of us. Your Aunt Blue wouldn't hear of anything else. Said she wouldn't rest easy until she hugged your ma—and your sister." Roran sighed, turning away with a hushed curse. "I told your pa—when I saw her and that beanpole boy at the funeral, I told him he oughta send her back here for a spell. Let her clear her head and heart. Get him the help he needed. Neither Zee—er, Ramses—nor your ma would hear of it. Wouldn't let Kallias go on his voyage, neither. Broke what was left of his heart, I think."

Despite the rumble of emotion in her chest, Soren couldn't help but snort. "*Zee?*"

"Nicknames. They run in the family." Roran cracked a grin. "What'd'ya call that brooding boy who walked in here with you?"

Her turn to crack a grin, inappropriate as it felt. But laughter was better than…whatever she was doing here. Grieving or moping or staring at her own reflection in a glass mug of blue beer. "Jackass, usually. Though we've recently introduced *loverrr*." She drew out the end into a rolling purr, waggling her eyebrows up and down.

Roran chortled. "Good gods, girl. You do take after your pa. Shameless flirt in his day, you know." He glanced over her shoulder. "Speaking of lovers, your boy's back. Should I get another beer? Or is he picky like you?"

"Pickier," she chuckled, turning to seek out Elias in the shadow of the Bluebell's doorway. His head was bent, his hair sheathing his eyes as he scraped the sand from his boots, but the tension riddling his shoulders told her enough about what he'd found.

She hadn't realized she was still holding out hope until her own shoulders slumped. Until some patched-up piece of her heart finally gave way, sundering vein and artery until her blood struggled to pump through her veins, trading the marrow in her bones for grief.

"Those are whiskey faces," Roran sighed, patting the counter and pushing himself onto his feet. "Give me a moment."

"Thanks, Uncle Roran."

It was nice, how easily the name freed itself from her memory—how he didn't flinch and stare and weep when he heard it. He just saluted her with two fingers to his brow, not looking up as he went to his work.

She swiveled around in her stool to face Elias, stopping herself by shoving her heel into the balance bar connecting its three legs. The bar had emptied considerably after lunchtime, but now that the sun had set, it was beginning to fill back up. Patrons filed in to sit at tables decorated in thick jars filled with water, colorful glass pebbles sunk to the bottom, disc-like candles floating at the top.

Warm, humid air floated in from the still-open windows, the wooden shutters drawn up to reveal passersby peeking enviously into the tavern or stopping to listen to the music. The lyre-player from yesterday had been back this afternoon, but had gone home closer to suppertime; now a willowy young woman perched in the corner, gossamer skirts draped over her legs, her deep tan skin glowing gold in the candlelight as she strummed at her silver harp.

It was perhaps the most beautiful scene she'd had the privilege to be part of in recent memory, and the absence of her brothers weighed too heavily on her heart for her to enjoy it.

How had the cards changed hands so quickly? How had her lot changed from sole casualty to sole survivor?

"Well?" she asked helplessly, even though she knew the answer long before he spoke.

"Nothing. Not a trace." Elias fell into the stool beside her, clawing a hand along his scalp, staring unseeingly at the bar counter. Soot blackened the ridges of his fingerprints as he splayed them helplessly before her. "I searched every damn corner of this town. Even the docks. He's gone."

"That's because he wasn't at the docks," Raquel butted in, sliding into the stool on Soren's other side, stealing her beer and lifting it to her lips.

"Raquel, *pits*," Soren seethed, heart hammering as she twisted to face her now, biting back a grunt of pain as her ankle caught on the stool's leg. She twisted back to free it before turning all the way around, bracing her elbows on the counter. "Obviously he wasn't at the docks, that's what Elias just—"

"He was at the beach," Raquel said after slamming down the empty mug— it hit the counter with such force that the inch-thick glass at the base cracked. Soren could've sworn the impact echoed…a thud that kept on going, traveling through the air until it became a rolling purr of thunder.

Traveling through *her* until every hair stood on end, every instinct warning of oncoming storms.

That was new.

"What do you mean?" Elias's voice dropped nearly to a growl, a deeper bass than even thunder could claim.

Raquel wiped away the blue froth at the corner of her mouth with the back of her hand, fury etched in every line, every angle, every scar and pockmark on her face. "He came to me on the beach. Not Kallias," she added when Soren and Elias shoved out from the counter in tandem, Elias half-turning as if about to run there himself. "Tempest."

Elias froze in place, still partway bent over the counter, still partway facing the door.

Soren's breath grew thorns, sticking painfully in her throat.

"Kallias didn't make it," Raquel said…sounding more lost than Soren had ever heard her. Even after Jira's death. Even after Lily's. "I looked him in the eye, Elias. He wasn't there."

The tavern did not quiet—the patrons kept chatting and laughing, the harp kept humming its gentle tune, the ocean kept up its constant roar beyond the city.

But Elias seemed to capture silence. It stuck to him, muffling the heaving breaths that filled his chest, silencing the flames leaping to life in his right eye.

And it cushioned the blow when he threw himself at Raquel, slamming her shoulders-first into the wall, spreading that wave of silence all throughout the tavern in one fell swoop.

# CHAPTER 63

# ELIAS

He didn't remember moving.

One second, he'd been watching Raquel speak, a low buzzing building in his ears until it drowned out all noise in the tavern.

The next, he'd thrown himself at her like an arrow screaming free of a crossbow, shoving her into the wall.

Elias Loch had been broken more than once in his relatively short life. But this wasn't breaking.

This was betrayal.

Bone cracked. Soren and Raquel shouted in tandem, Nyxian curses that burned his ears. His hand ached from the strength of his grip around Raquel's shoulders, his fingers shaking with the effort of holding back the death he so badly wanted to deal…

And it was only when he blinked that he fully comprehended the fact that he'd pinned Raquel to the wall of the inn, the tips of his fingers blackening with barely-withheld fatality.

"You promised me." The words spit sparks. "You promised me you would stop this."

"Elias—" Raquel started, and he leaned closer, fuming and furious and so far gone he could barely remember why he had to be careful. Why he needed to keep that leash on the cold and withering thing that lived in the hollow spaces between his flames.

"You *liar*," he seethed, and Raquel Angelov, Eye of the Storm, Tempest-blessed, warrior of Nyx…whatever she saw in his eyes, she flinched back from it. "Was it worth it? Do you feel *better* now that he's dead? I trusted you with him, you vengeful—"

"I did *everything* I could—"

"And it wasn't enough!" Heaving breath. Burning lungs. Why was his face wet? He couldn't breathe. He couldn't breathe. "You left him! You left him, he saved you, he saved you and you *left him*—"

And all at once, as her expression shifted from fear and grief to something more like pity, like realization, he understood two things:

Firstly, that he hadn't been talking about her at all.

Secondly, that he was weeping so hard he could no longer see her face.

"Elias," she said softly, wrapping cold hands around his wrists, "let go."

He did, immediately. "I was here. I was right *gods-damned here*—"

Raquel released his wrists to wrap her arms around him instead, burying her face against his shoulder. And he didn't think it was the heat of his magic that made her skin seem so cold…didn't think it was sweat that soaked into his shirt as she clung on tighter, trembling.

When she lifted her head at last, there were twin trails of tears drawn down her cheeks…and vengeance blackening her eyes.

"Kallias chose his path," she said, "and it's our turn to choose ours. Sit down. We need to discuss where we go from here."

# CHAPTER 64

# RAQUEL

When the sun rose the next morning, it found Raquel already on the road leading east.

The warmth of the dawn had been disconcerting, at first—even though she'd quickly gathered a layer of sweat beneath her borrowed jacket, she'd been reticent to discard it. The kiss of the breeze brought too many whispers with it, too many cravings…an itch that only the strike of lightning could truly relieve.

She'd forgotten what it felt like to carry magic in her bones.

She'd forgotten that magic liked to sing.

So when she finally gave in, peeling the jacket from her skin and shoving it in her pack, leaving her in only loose travel pants and an Atlas prince's stolen shirt, she walked with a melody buzzing through her body.

The wind nudged itself beneath her thick braid, cooling the sweat pooling beneath her heavy hair. But that breeze did nothing to ease the burden resting on her shoulders.

Not just a grudge held against a prince any longer. Not just a death-right gone sour.

A grudge held against gods.

The rescue of a kingdom she had sworn to see to its ruin.

Two notes, one far shorter than the other, nestled deep within the confines of her bag.

The longer one penned by Kallias.

The shorter unsigned, unsealed, unbearably vague: *Keeping my promise. Will you keep yours?*

She hadn't told Soren and Elias about the second note, found just after the Second Prince of Atlas had taken his leave of the tavern—she hadn't wanted to get Soren's hopes up. Hadn't wanted to get her own up, either.

To them, she had laid out her mission in two simple strokes:

Get to the King and Queen. Get them out.

Soren had returned the favor, stating their plan as a trio of near-impossibilities, her grief-hollow eyes fixed on the hole she'd left in the wall:

Travel to Arborius. Get Anima's relic. Find a way to separate the girl from the goddess.

There was no plan for meeting afterward—though none of them had been willing to say it, the reasoning was clear in the way the battlemate pair stole glances at her, tired and resigned, knowing they'd lost the fight without even bothering to fight it.

They didn't think she would make it back out of Port Atlas.

She didn't think so, either.

Her grip tightened on the strap of her bag. A spark of static popped as the metal ring holding the strap to the actual body of the bag knocked against her hip.

*I am the Eye of the Storm, the peace within chaos, the power within peace. They cannot touch any piece of me I do not offer.*

But for Kallias, for the kingdom he'd loved enough to lay his life at the feet of a merciless god, she would offer it all.

For Finn, an unexpected friend among enemies, she would follow what little heading she'd been given.

Weakness.

The girl who'd escaped her teacher turned tormenter by fleeing into the wolf-infested forest, weeping to her silent god for mercy, had cast aside the last of hers in favor of newer, better strengths. But the woman she had become—the woman who'd taken a whipping for the object of her vengeance, the woman who'd stood before that same silent god and demanded he return what was rightfully hers, had taken on something new.

A weakness for starry-sky freckles and sea-glass eyes and a promise he might have kept if she'd given him the chance.

*Say the word, and you have me.*

A weakness that would see her straight to the center of her enemy's stronghold.

Straight into the eye of the storm.

# EPILOGUE

# OCCASSIO

Cassandra Medeis had never been sorry, and she wasn't too keen on starting now.

Still, despite her near-perfected method for truth-bending and eye-tricking, she had yet to learn how to lie to herself. And the truth of the matter was that she had yet to look into a mirror since making herself at home in this body.

She was taller, which didn't help—she didn't have to crane her neck or heap all her weight onto her tiptoes in order to catch a glimpse of herself in mounted mirrors or helpful windows or even a polished metal bowl. It took effort to avoid catching sight of herself, and even that wasn't perfect—there was always a hint of reddish-brown in her periphery. A flash of a freckled, dexterous hand. A sigh that carried too much of his voice with it, startling her until she realized it was *her* voice now, that the clearing throat or occasional mutter wasn't a sign of him pulling off the same trick his sister had.

Until she realized, with a twinge she didn't quite like, that she would never hear a word from him again.

Cassi ground her teeth, forcing her spine out of its reader's slouch, batting aside the strange pinch in her chest as easily as one might swat a fly.

He had no idea what she'd spared him from. No clue what the future had promised if he'd lived.

It was a shame, that was all. A shame to see such a clever, cruel, cunning mind go to waste.

But she had no need, no room, for shame. Tenebrae would smell it on her if she gave it any ground, and she was the one member of their shattered family without a weakness for him to exploit.

She'd seen what he'd done to the others. She'd dance on Finnick Atlas's ashes long before she allowed Tenebrae's special brand of malice to find its way to her doorstep.

For most people, it would have taken weeks to travel from Sirena to Port Atlas on foot. But Cassandra Medeis wasn't *most people*.

Though she could pretend to be, when required of her.

When Finnick Atlas had demanded truth from her mouth, it had taken *work* to shape it. It had taken effort in triplicate of what she normally had to offer to a lie; after all, lies were her first language, a tongue she had ripped straight from the mouths of those who would have seen her and her family ruined and razed. She had cut her lips and bled her conscience until she took on the shape of the perfect vessel for untruth, an unfailing mirror held up to whatever someone wanted out of her.

Most wanted a goddess who could help them cheat…a goddess to give them a little glimpse into time not yet come true, a goddess to help them earn an extra coin with their paltry visions, a goddess who could whisper whether they should fold their hand or double down.

A goddess they could cage and coerce, a goddess they could chain and starve and *own*.

Finnick Atlas had been different.

Finnick Atlas had wanted a friend.

That want had been easy—it was a con she could've pulled off in her sleep, if she hadn't been conning the one mind in this whole rotting world that could have been a match to hers. No, it was what had happened after that had been hard…it was the part where lie began to bleed into truth that she'd found herself fumbling.

Mirrors, luckily, offered no such conundrum or confusion. Mirrors didn't mind if you lied to them.

So instead of taking the weeks to walk, Cassi had lied instead.

She'd pressed her lips to the wooden-framed mirror in a quiet little dress shop on the far side of Sirena, and she whispered a lie to it, avoiding her own gaze in its glass.

She told it she was made of light, and it believed her without a second thought.

The secret to mirror travel was barely a secret at all—one only needed to convince the simple pane of glass that they were an equally simple thing, a ray of light welcome in its crystalline confines.

Cassi had stepped out of the mirror in Finnick's room to find someone had done her the kindness of uncovering it—it would've been embarrassing to trip her way into Port Atlas, regardless of whether there were witnesses or not—and had settled herself in to await her brother's return. He'd be grumpy if she showed her new face here without allowing him the courtesy of pretending to listen to his plans for her.

That had been a week ago, and Brae had yet to return from his little escapade in Nyx.

Huffing, she brushed off Finn's lounging clothes, taking a moment to assess his space for the fifth or twentieth or two hundredth time. It hadn't changed since she'd visited as a different girl, a different guise—in fact, the blanket he'd offered her still lay crumpled in a pile of knit yarn on the floor, spread before the long-dormant fireplace. She hadn't bothered to tidy…well, anything. Everything was where he'd left it.

She paused.

Fidget. He'd offered *Fidget* that blanket, not her.

*Figments*, she liked to call them—the deck of characters she'd created over the many, many, many years she'd been playing her games, similar to the *Jaskier* persona he played with such smug-ass energy, his pride gleaming from every sultry grin and exaggerated wink.

Step by reluctant step, she approached the blanket, scooping it up and running her fingers over it. Fingers that were now longer, smoother, but still capable of picking a pocket as easily as one might pick a flower.

Fidget had been her first new figment in decades, crafted specially for Finnick Atlas and his particular wants…and on some foolish, fanciful whim, she'd chosen her first face to wear as her costume.

He'd taken the bait…hook, line, and sinker, he'd pounced on the perfect victim of his own selfish schemes, the perfect window into Queen Esha's retinue.

But that wasn't what had stumped her, if briefly, forcing her to change tack mid-con.

No. What had nearly ruined the game was that when Cassandra Medeis made her first appearance past the figment…when he'd let a hint of menace out past his mask, and she'd done the same in return, unable to resist the call of that threat…his eyes had lit up.

Not with fear, but with excitement.

With intrigue.

With…other dangerous things she needed to forget already, because he was dead and gone, and she'd done it, and there were new games that needed her undivided attention.

And that meant getting past this ridiculous *feeling* that kept drawing her eyes away from reflections.

Humming out her agitation, she shook out her itching bones before pirouetting to face herself in the mirror. Well, herself, sort of: it was Finnick's face that looked back at her, his eyes the exact same shade of brown they'd always been, his complexion decidedly improved now that her magic had settled in with her, his lips hooked in what, admittedly, was not a particularly pleased look.

There were secrets she kept even from herself. And the bend of those lips threatened to compromise the integrity of one of those secrets.

Though her auramancy was nigh-flawless—not one person in this damned castle would see a flicker of goddess-gold in his eyes if she didn't want them to—

she was not fooled by her own magic. A phantom reflection layered in with Finnick's visage, an echo of her true form: her wild curls, her jewel-crusted brows and lashes and nails, her ethereal purple silks and piercing gold eyes.

Those eyes, much to her chagrin, stared at her from the center of Finnick's chest.

Most of the time, she liked being short. It helped others underestimate her, usually to her benefit. But this just felt a little ridiculous.

*Glad you agree,* a voice suddenly purred…not in her ear. In her head.

Shock froze her in place, her hand still stretched toward the surface of the mirror, fingertip to fingertip with her reflection.

It was hardly the first time she'd had strange voices in her head.

But she *knew* that rotting voice.

"*How*—" she choked.

But before she could ask—before she could even think past that one word—the voice interrupted her.

Bored. Drawling.

*Amused.*

"Surprise!" he said—this time with her mouth, with her voice.

With his mouth. With his voice.

And with such speed that even the Goddess of Time could not hope to outrun him, he leaned into the first mirror she'd looked in since stealing her way inside…

And he told it an older, better lie.

"You," he told it, "are a cage."

"She," he told it, "is your prisoner."

And with a *shove* of a will made not of mortal stuff, a shove made of adamant and power and wicked, wicked cleverness, Cassi found herself shunted between panes of glass—normally a place where she held dominion, a place where she could walk freely, a path of light and fractured facets that could take her anywhere she wished.

But not this time. This time, those panes pinned her in, a cramped pocket of unreality that only had one window.

Panting, panicking, Cassi whipped around to face the front of the mirror, pounding her fist into the glass.

"Let me out!" she shouted.

Those words bounced off of a million lost reflections, mockeries buried in glass: *Let me out, let me out, let me out.*

Outside the mirror, a prince bent down to meet her at eye-level.

Finnick Atlas smiled at her, winking with eyes that now shimmered gold…gold, despite the fact that she was *here* and he was *there*, he was—

He was—

Not dead. Not gone.

He'd been *waiting.*

"Thanks for the ride," he said, idly adjusting his cuffs, giving his hair a quick tousle in the mirror. "But I think this little arrangement leans more in my favor."

"*You*," she seethed—disbelief rendering even the simplest words nearly unspeakable. "*How*—"

"You wanted to break Finnick Atlas? Congratulations, you did it," he interrupted, suddenly so cold that the glass itself shivered…his reflection trembled with it before coalescing back into a whole. He leaned in so close that his nose brushed hers, only a sliver of glass between them. "Now you have to deal with me."

Panic threatened to shatter her into a hundred more shards, a hundred more fractals. She bore down on it, reaching out, pushing at the mirror, telling it lie after lie after lie, all the ones that had never failed her before.

The glass did not believe her. It did not bend to her will.

"And who exactly are *you*?" she spat, masking that rigid terror with her favorite flavor of anger: defiance.

He smiled. No—snarled. His eyes glimmered, topazine and condescending and...

Deific.

"The *Trickster God* has a nice ring to it, don't you think?"


# THE END

# ACKNOWLEDGMENTS

YOU MADE IT! Yay!

(Also…sorry, lol)

First and foremost, I want to thank YOU: every single reader who has stuck with this series from beginning to middle…and hopefully to the end! Thank you for your Instagram love, your wonderful reviews, and your constant enthusiasm. They mean more to me than you could ever know.

Thank you to God, who continues to sustain me even through the most difficult seasons.

Thank you to my mom and dad, who continue to be stalwart supporters and constant sources of love and encouragement. You're the best.

Thank you to my siblings, who continue to inspire me to be a better person and storyteller—and sister, sometimes—every day. I never laugh harder than when I'm with you.

Thank you to Renee Dugan, without whom this book genuinely wouldn't exist. Your encouragement, tough love, and reassurance are invaluable…as are your stories! Your books remind me why I fell in love with writing to start with. (Read all Renee's books, fam.)

Thank you to Miranda and Kristin, who helped me get through my very first year living on my own—and my first year of having a license. You guys push me to be braver and better every day!

Thank you to Caitlan Honer—for nothing, because you live TOO DANG FAR AWAY and it's NOT FAIR. But actually, thank you for the screaming sessions, voice notes, memes, and constant enemies to lovers content. You feed my obsession daily and I'm so thankful. Also, you're a beautiful human who brings so much joy and laughter wherever you go, you've done and will continue to do amazing things and I'm SO PROUD OF YOU! (Read These Gilded Bones May Bloom, everyone, it's a masterpiece)

Thank you to Lina Amarego, who's always there with a piece of advice, costume inspiration, cover art ideas, and so much more. You're a brilliant woman who has taught me so much about the power of small victories and sticking to the story YOU need to tell, regardless of what others may think. You're an absolute queen. (Read the Children of Lyr series, also.)

Thank you to my beta team, Jenny, Kayla, Caitlan, Brina, Chelsea, Cayla, Katie, Lina, Heidi, and Caroline—you guys were AMAZING. You all gave amazing feedback, hilarious comments, and read through this beast of a book in no time at all. I'm forever grateful for you all!

And last but not least, thank you to Hillary Bardin, who crafted not one, not two, but THREE incredible covers. Your art takes my breath away, and you capture my characters so perfectly every time. You have so much talent and you're a joy to work with!

See you all in the next one…where our favorite Trickster God will be stepping into the spotlight. I cannot wait.

# ABOUT THE AUTHOR

Cassidy Clarke is a proud Michigander, freelance editor, and NA author who subsists on chicken tenders, ketchup, and fantasy books. She recently graduated with her BA in Creative Writing, which has allowed her to pursue her passion for storytelling and helping others make their books the absolute best they can be. *THE BLOOD AND WATER SAGA* is her debut series, a high fantasy love letter to the lost princess daydreams of her childhood and an attempt to put her experience growing up with three younger siblings to good use. She spends her days writing like she's running out of time, binging Critical Role on Youtube and GBBO on Netflix, and baking the world's best chocolate chip cookies.

www.ingramcontent.com/pod-product-compliance
Lightning Source LLC
Chambersburg PA
CBHW050947210726
48287CB00004B/1163